The
Papillion
And The
Oubliette

The Papillion And The Oubliette

P W Stephens

Published by **PWS**

© Copyright P W Stephens 2020

THE PAPILLION

AND THE OUBLIETTE

All rights reserved.

ISBN 978-1-703-98588-7

Book formatted by autumnalmusingformating

Table of contents

- Chapter 01: The Pebble and the Boy
- Chapter 02: Growing Pains
- Chapter 03: The Viking King
- Chapter 04: Birth of a Monster
- Chapter 05: York Avenue
- Chapter 06: Into the Fire
- Chapter 07: Sunshine and Stick Insects
- Chapter 08: Changes
- Chapter 09: Alice and the Looking Glass
- Chapter 10: Father of the Bride
- Chapter 11: Living by the Sword
- Chapter 12: Triggered
- Chapter 13: Changing of the Guard
- Chapter 14: It Follows
- Chapter 15: The Summer Breeze
- Chapter 16: The End
- Chapter 17: Wires
- Chapter 18: News from Home
- Chapter 19: Sepia Tone
- Chapter 20: The Crow and the Girls
- Chapter 21: Fragmenting
- Chapter 22: The Drugs Don't Work
- Chapter 23: The Nightmare Sleeps
- Chapter 24: In Dreams

Table of contents continued

- Chapter 25: The Curtain Call
- Chapter 26: The Harlequin
- Chapter 27: The Light and the Lighthouse
- Chapter 28: Scar Tissue
- Chapter 29: Ruby Slippers
- Chapter 30: Infants and the Abyss
- Chapter 31: The Tell-Tale Heart
- Chapter 32: Sliding Doors
- Chapter 33: Johnno was a Local Boy
- Chapter 34: Nurse Bonnie
- Chapter 35: Freudian Slip
- Chapter 36: The Hand that Rocks
- Chapter 37: Brand New Start
- Chapter 38: The Last Day
- Chapter 39: I Do
- Chapter 40: I Move the Stars for No One
- Chapter 41: Godfather Death
- Chapter 42: To Whom It May Concern
- Chapter 43: Glad Rags
- Chapter 44: The Kraken and Her
- Chapter 45: The Light Between Us
- Chapter 46: Parlay and the Mourning Son
- Chapter 47: My Dorian Gray
- Epilogue

Authors Note

'I remember a time, a time before you, before the doubt and before the pain. I remember a time when my skin wasn't laced with scars and when the creature at the bottom of my bed had no voice. It was a time when I was too young to realise why I felt so constantly numb, why I felt so alone, and then you changed that, you changed me. But I know now, I know that I had an illness, I know that it became stronger when I found something in my life that I was reluctant to lose. But I must admit it was your arrival in my world that gave the creature its voice. I had nothing before you entered my life so it's just a shame that it followed you through the open door to my heart.' I am Jacob Brooking but I am no less Alice Petalow.

Acknowledgements

Thank you to my family and friends for your unwavering support.

To the whole of team Stephens... Especially Grace Natasha.

To the crows that call my name as I walk home in the dark.

To the Kraken that haunted the shadows of my youth.

To the boys that bullied Jacob so badly that he had to write a novel about it.

To Poe, Lovecraft and King for inspiring me.

And lastly, to Whitstable, Canterbury and Rye Harbour. You built my dreams with a reality of ocean waves and cobbled stone.

To Jacob
You got this

Chapter 1: The Pebble and the Boy
Song of the day
"Stanley Road" by Paul Weller

Autumn 1994
Tankerton, Kent UK

In late Autumn, one might assume it was too cold to be sitting on the cold wet stones of Tankerton seafront, but Jacob never conformed to normality and it seemed like he wasn't the only one. Who was this girl with hair of October leaves and November embers? She who has watched him vividly for an hour or so as she sat opposite him on the far side of the heavy wooden groynes that separated the same stretch of beach that they shared. He had been out all morning taking photographs of different coloured stones with an old German Franka 25 that his grandad had given him at the beginning of the year. A gift that sadly came before his passing not a few weeks later. It was certainly a robust piece of kit that had surely seen some amazing stories unfold in its twenty-year life. Jacob loved it though and found its dents and scratches endearing, whilst the grainy washed look 35mm film gave each picture more character than he knew any flashy Nikon would provide.

'You know, if rocks are what you are after, there are plenty more on my side of the fence,' said the flame haired young girl that had somehow used Jacobs daydream to sneak up on him unseen. He couldn't remember ever having met such a beautiful girl, not that he had witnessed many during his short tenure on earth; but those he had met certainly held nothing on her, *so why is she talking to me?* Jacob asked himself within his thoughts.

'You know you don't say much' the girl was clearly mocking him but held a playful giggle in her tone which brought a smile to Jacob's lips non the less.

'Sorry,' he said adjusting himself to a more masculine pose. 'I'm Jacob, Jacob Brooking,' he stuttered his name like he had a stammer, much to the amusement of his new shadow who was trying and failing to catch his gaze, probably due to the fact he couldn't stop looking at his feet.

'I know who you are you big wally, you just joined the Howard George, right? I'm Alice.'

'Alice ...' Jacob repeated her name softly back to her as if letting it sink in. 'That's a beautiful name and one I would surely remember, but I'm not sure I recall seeing you around school because, well ... you know, it's a boy's school,' Jacob knew that what he was saying was factually accurate, Alice though, seemed to giggle at him even more.

'Doesn't mean I 've not noticed you at the fence everyday, I notice lots of things, you don't play well with the other boys, do you?' Jacob finally mustered the strength to look up into her eyes, *my god,* eyes so beautiful and blue that they could easily be cut from the very things that dreams are made of.

'Have you been stalking me?' Jacob asked.
Alice smiled, her perfectly straight bright pearls gleaming back at him, 'let's say admiring instead of stalking shall we?'

She took a seat next to him on the old worn blanket and watched intently as he balanced different shaped pebbles one on top of the other.

'You're an interesting boy aren't you Jacob, and you seem so different to the other idiots on the boy side of that big fence that separates our schools.'

'How do you mean?' Jacob inquired with a quizzical look upon his face.

'Well for a start you are taking pictures of rocks on a wet beach at the weekend, whilst all your class mates are probably playing football.'

Jacob laughed loudly 'I guess that does make me a little different.'

He reached over and picked up an azure coloured rock that had been worn down into a perfect oval by an aggressive and violent ocean.

'They are not rocks though Alice, they are pebbles and do you know what I love about them?' Alice didn't answer but motioned for him to continue.

'I've always loved how there are no two pebbles the same, the same colour, the same shape or weight; each one unique, each one special.'

'That's beautiful,' said Alice 'But what about these two?' She held back a curious grin and held up two clearly matching pebbles.

'See, you think you have caught me out, but you're not looking at the big picture, well, the little picture really,' Jacob smiled as he took both pebbles from her and turned them over and over repeatedly in his hand whilst running his thumbs across them as if he was trying to summon a Genie.

'Look at this one ... its flawless right?' Jacob held out his left hand and Alice ran her index finger over the top of the exposed pebble whilst not fully understanding his point. 'Now this one,' he said opening his right palm, which led Alice to mimic the same procedure of gently following the lines of the pebble under her fingertips' soft caress.

'Ok, so there's a tiny crack in it, I get it, but they are nearly the same and I think you know I'm at least a little bit right,' Alice nudged her shoulder into his with a smile.

'The crack represents a journey, an incident and I guess a history, something has happened to this rock, that didn't happen to the other, and that thought process gets my mind excited.'

'Because its broken?' Alice quipped.

'No Alice, because it's unique,' Jacob smiled.

That night, as Jacob reached under his pillow for the battered old Sony Walkman that sung him to sleep each night, his thoughts turned to Alice, he thought of her curly red hair, of her bottomless blue eyes and of her beautiful laugh, the laugh that seemed to pull him ever closer to the frightening Abyss that was undoubtably his Oubliette. Never had a word been more fitting to a soul, she had made his forget, if only for a moment, if only for a heartbeat and for that brief dreamlike passage of time, he had felt real.

I hate you!

Jacob span around quickly, pulling off his headphones as he searched for the source of the voice. His bedroom was a mess, a pig sty his mum would say for sure, but it wasn't a large room in any way shape or form and it took but a moment to confirm his suspicions that no one was there. He slowly replaced his headphones and the sound of Paul Weller filled his ears once more. As he lay back on his pillow and closed his weary eyes to think again on his day with Alice, he couldn't help but wonder, what a girl like her could ever see in him. The perennial loser, whom no family or friend had ever believed in, could never be of interest to a girl like Alice. What had compelled her to talk to him? He would never understand it and right now he just wanted to enjoy the moments as they came, with a date in the park organised for tomorrow and phone numbers swapped, he could certainly feel warmth in his heart as he started to fall into a comfortable slumber. 'No monsters under the bed tonight,' he whispered as the waking world left him for the embrace of sleep.

I HATE YOU! Said the voice once more.

Jacob sat bolt upright as he felt a wet and viscous tentacle wrap around his ankle, teeth and barbs punctured flesh as, despite his futile struggle, he found himself dragged under the bed by the strength of a Kraken, a Kraken born from the mind of a thousand terrified sailors.

Spring 1995 Canterbury, Kent UK

Jacob hobbled down the stairs gingerly as his legs failed to respond to the instructions his young brain was giving them.

'Mum, I can't feel my legs again.'

'Well, rub them, honey. I'm not sure what you do in your sleep, as this is happening every day now.'

Jacob's mum, Marie Brooking, was an amazing mother and a fantastic woman. But she rarely minced her words, and today she seemed genuinely concerned with her eldest son's inability to walk properly. Jacob was ashamed that at 15 years old he still slept with his legs crossed, just to make sure there was no chance of one stray foot falling out from under the duvet, as everyone knew what a dangerous place outside of the quilt was for any leg to be. And it was this and this alone that gave him dead legs in the morning.

He sat at the table and was greeted quickly by a bowl of Coco Pops and a cup of milky tea. His baby brother sat opposite him, trying to get all his Weetabix under the surface of his milk without spilling it from his bowl, so as to avoid the crunchy breakfast that no young boy wanted. He was failing miserably.

'Mum, I don't feel too good,' Jacob said for the third time that week.

She sighed curtly without taking her eyes off the task at hand. 'What's wrong now?'

'It's my stomach again. I feel sick.'

'Well, you can't have any more time off, Jacob. The school are already on my back with concerns about all your time off.'

'BUT MUM!' he protested, in a whine so high pitched that the dog's ears pricked up. 'Oh Christ,' Jacob cried. 'The dog!'

'Muuuuuum, the dog's on fire,' Samuel bellowed.

Jacob's younger brother, five years his junior, always liked to overreact, but this time Jacob had to admit that Samuel was right to raise the alarm so noisily.

Peepo always point-blank refused to move from her spot right in front of the fireplace, and today was no different, even though her jet-black fur was starting to smoulder. It must be nice to be that lazy, Jacob mused. I bet she has no dramas in her life. Well, apart from her heavy smoking habit, he giggled to himself. Jacob jumped down from the table and patted her down before forcibly sliding the overweight beast a couple of feet across the carpet. She had always been a pot-bellied dog, and moving her was never easy.

'Mum, I really don't feel right,' said Jacob, his words turning into a plea for help.

'He only doesn't want to go to school because they call him Gummy Bear,' Samuel mocked.

'SHUT UP,' was the immediate response to his brother.

'Just say to them that sticks and stones will break my bones, but names will never hurt me,' Mum preached as always.

Little did she know that they did use sticks and stones to beat the life out of his bones most days, and usually they would call him names while they did it.

Gummy Bear.

Gummy Bear.

Gummy Bear.

Jacob heard the voice in his head. But it didn't sound like the kids at school. Its repeatedly aggressive cackle almost overshadowed the words. Jacob hated the voice in his head but had come to accept its presence in his life. He just assumed everyone had one. He hoped other people's inner voices were nicer than his, and he honestly suspected they would have to be. He had once tried to describe it to his dad, but he felt silly talking to him about inner turmoil. Stern-faced in the presence of emotional weakness, his parents would say, 'Just smile and be happy. What is the point in talking negative, son?' So, Jacob had decided this was something that was best dealt with alone. He had always felt ashamed talking of such things with his hard- and endlessly working dad. Paul Brooking worked three jobs, often far from home, just to keep his family fed. He didn't deserve to hear on a daily basis how pathetic his son was.

'I suggest you stop daydreaming and finish your breakfast. And for god's sake sort your tie out,' said his mum, breaking the hazed look on his face.

'Yes, Mum,' he replied with an acceptance that left him feeling hollow.

I hate you, Gummy Bear, the voice said.

I know, he thought clearly and with absolutely no fight. *You tell me every day.*

The Howard George School for Boys had never been a nice place to be, and Jacob didn't have one fond memory or many friends to make the experience worthwhile. Well, he had Alice, who was in the neighbouring girls' school and would meet him at the fence every day for lunch, just so they could talk music that she clearly only pretended to like to impress him. He loved that she did that and would show her due respect by always giving her his Marathon bar, which more than likely she would break in half for him to enjoy with her. But to get to her, he would of course have to get through to lunch, and right now he wasn't sure how promising that seemed.

'Your coat looks shit, Gummy Bear,' they laughed.

'Your parents are clearly poor.' Simeon Bennett mocked him while at the same time punching him in the shoulder repeatedly. 'No wonder no one likes you.'

He's got you there.

That was a mistruth, of course, as Jacob was sure lots of people liked him in his small unique circle that he kept. It was just his ability to attract the attention of this wolf pack of baying idiots that meant he was often avoided by everyone, lest they might stray too close and attract the attention of the bullies themselves.

'You're scum,' shouted David Taylor, the brute of the group and the axe handle to Simeon's sharp wit. He looked down at the pinned Jacob and spat on his coat.

Jacob tried to recoil in disgust but was being held in place by a third goon, who was unidentifiable due to his position behind Jacob's back.

Simeon started to do his usual party trick of emptying Jacob's bag all over the classroom floor before spitting inside it. Jacob's dad had once told Jacob to fight back and earn the respect that, in his opinion, was the only thing that would stop kids like this. But the one day Jacob had caught David with a low blow hard enough to do some real damage, it had resulted in a beating far worse than he had ever received previously, and they had dragged him by his throat behind the sports block after classes had ended and punched him repeatedly while screaming, 'DON'T YOU EVER HIT ME BACK EVER AGAIN.' It just wasn't worth it.

Simeon looked down at him, sneering like a demonic version of the Cheshire cat from *Alice in Wonderland*. Slick, jet-black hair and matching thick brows framed his dark, rat-like eyes, which seemed far too small for his elongated face. He was always smiling, yet Jacob doubted he had ever been happy. He had heard rumours that he was the way he was due to a sexually abusive father, but no one was brave enough to bring this up in conversation. He had heard of a boy, David Shelly, from the year above, who'd mentioned it in conversation the previous term and hadn't been seen at school since.

Simeon Bennett had been kicked out of his last school for violence towards a teacher and had joined the Howard George just a year before, instantly using all his wit and guile to get the stronger and more thug-like David Taylor on board. David, whose straw-like mop of hair sat on his thick, square forehead like a bird's nest, always stunk of smoke and was rarely clean to any respectable level, which left Jacob feeling saturated by his bullies' touch. Heavier and thicker set in physical appearance and mentality, David was actually the less imposing of the pair due to the clear absence of a brain, but he was always the one who left Jacob bruised. And today was a bad day for Jacob.

With a sharp yank, his third oppressor pulled him backwards off his chair. Jacob hit the floor with a sickening crack that drew all the air from his ribs in one giant expressive breath.

'See you later, Gummy Bear,' whispered Simeon, as he smiled maliciously like the Grim Reaper, all teeth and no lips and his mouth almost too wide for his face.

As they walked past his winded frame, David gave him a solid boot to the side of the face, drawing a shriek of pain from Jacob. This final act appeared to have been carried out to reiterate that they thought of him as scum.

Jacob sat up. His cheeks were flushed and his face was stained with tears. He hadn't realised he was crying. He started to collect his belongings and put them back into his satchel, using his gym top to wipe the spit off everything first. It was only then that he looked up to see the other members of his class staring at him from the safety of their desks. Unsure whether the looks on their faces were pity or ridicule, he decided he had best get out as quickly as he could. He shoved the rest of his things away before pulling himself up to his feet, his face throbbing and his ribs feeling like a knife was wedged in the cage that held his breathless lungs. He scrambled out of the classroom without even closing the door behind him. The further he got from the door, the louder the whispering from the other students became as they talked once again of how lucky they were not to be him.

'Baby, what happened?' asked Alice as she reached through the wire fence to brush his bruised cheek with her fingers.

He recoiled slightly. His face was still sensitive, and the area she caressed was flooded with a burning sensation. 'It's fine, Pebble. It's just boys doing boy stuff, I guess.'

'You don't truly believe that, do you, Jay? That this is normal behaviour for boys? Or even animals, for that matter?'

[17]

'It doesn't matter what I believe. I'm sure I deserved it regardless. And no, before you ask – I really don't want to talk about it.'

'OK, grumpy bum,' Alice retorted with an air of mischief. 'Why don't you kiss me instead?' Her head tilted to the ground as she spoke, but she looked up at Jacob through her auburn bangs.

He smiled the kind of smile that came deep from inside, with no falsity to it whatsoever, as he realised he could never resist her when she did that. No matter his mood, she would always bring him round, without even trying too hard. Her hair just failed to hide her piercing blue eyes, and her glossed red lips wore a smile that transformed her from cute to something else entirely as she took her bottom lip between her teeth.

Oh god, he thought as instinct took over. He pressed his face up against the fence as tightly as he could and pursed his lips together as far forward as the wire would allow. And there she was, the warmth of her lips seeming to defrost the pain in his cheek almost immediately. As they reached for each other and linked fingers through the mesh, she started to withdraw, and he gently took her lip between his teeth.

When she was finally released, she looked at him open-mouthed. 'Jacob Brooking, what would my father say?' She giggled. She turned her back to him before starting to walk away with a skip in her step and the slightest of wiggles in her bum. Well aware of what she was doing and fully aware Jacob was watching, she headed back to class.

'I love you, Jay,' she called over her shoulder.

'I love you, Alice Marie Petalow,' he whispered as she disappeared through a door.

All of a sudden, his world felt darker.

Shame you don't deserve her, isn't it, Gummy Bear? said the voice as Jacob drew in a deep breath.

It would be a long walk back to class. Maybe Simeon and his minions would ignore him if he just shut his mouth and sat at the front of each class where the teacher could always reach him. Or maybe the barbs would turn to punches once more and would do him a favour and finally silence the voice in his head. Maybe then he would have peace. Ending it had often seemed like the only option to him, but like the voice said, he was too much of a coward.

Do it, the voice said. *I dare you.*

The dark was his protection. He couldn't see a thing, and that meant nothing could see him. But it was also his enemy, for the shadows were where the creature slept, where it plotted and where it watched. Hiding from monsters under his quilt was becoming a far-too-regular occurrence. For a boy of 14 years, Jacob had to admit that he felt a little childish. He had told his mother a few days before, but her attention always seemed elsewhere as she dealt with the demons of her own past.

'Just be brave, Jacob. You're a big boy now. You don't hear Samuel complaining of monsters hiding in the shadows, do you?'

'No, Mum, he doesn't.'

Marie Brooking lit another cigarette and ruffled his hair. She loved him, Jacob knew that, and he certainly had no right to complain about his upbringing, but he had always felt like he was the wrong piece in his mother's picture puzzle. Like she was disappointed he wasn't quite the child she had wanted him to be.

He had told his brother too, but Samuel had started to freak out at the thought of a creature in the room next door, leaving Jacob no choice but to pass the whole thing off as a joke.

So, he was here alone, as per usual. His exhalations were trapped inside the confines of his safe house, and his breathing was becoming difficult. The quilt was tucked under his body so tightly that no limbs could reach for a hold on him. Jacob had pictured himself as a caterpillar getting ready for its transformation, a chrysalis of anxiety and panic. It had started when his father had turned the hall light off and closed his own bedroom door with a heavy thud. Jacob felt alone; in fact, today he had felt more alone than ever.

That Morning

Jacob climbed into his dad's car and excitedly turned on the cassette player. His father's taste in music was, at least in Jacob's young eyes, second to none. A lover of soul and country rock, Paul Brooking inspired his son in more ways than he would ever know, but the first way he was to influence Jacob was with music.

The Electric Light Orchestra came on, much to the delight of Jacob, who quickly pulled on his seat belt as his father got in the car. The nearly new Peugeot 505 GTI was an amazing car to sit in, and he would admit to anyone who would listen that sitting by his father's side was his favourite place to be. The blue velour seats were warm and welcoming, and the sporty nature of the car seemed to hug him as his father went round corners with youthful abandon. His father had offered to drop him off at his friend's house. It wasn't a long walk there, but the rain that showered down on the cold December day would certainly have made it an unpleasant one.

'Did you read that article I left you out, son?'

'The West Ham United one? It doesn't make for great reading, but I think Harry is the right guy for us. I know you disagree, though.'

'It's not that I disagree, as I'm not sure there is anyone better out there right now in terms of leading us forward. There's just something about his car-salesman nature that rubs me the wrong way. Still, we should beat Charlton at home this weekend.'

The rest of the journey played out in silence. That wasn't uncommon for time spent with Paul Brooking, a man who didn't believe in conversation for the sake of it. When Paul said something, it always paid to listen.

The grey Peugeot rode the kerb gently as they arrived at Dinger's house. He wasn't a friend that Jacob's father particularly liked. Paul had accused him on more than one occasion of only hanging out at the Brooking house because Jacob had the better computer. No comment had been made today, though, with the play having been organised at Dinger's house for a change.

'Thanks, Pop,' said Jacob as he unbuckled his seat belt and leaned over to kiss his father on the cheek.

Much to his surprise, his dad pulled away and instead just tapped him on the leg with his open hand.

'Getting a little old for a kiss goodbye, son. You just go and have a good day.'

He doesn't love you anymore.

'Oh, OK, Dad, sure, I'll see you at home later,' Jacob said in shock as he climbed out of the car and gently pressed the door closed.

He still kisses Samuel goodbye.

Yeah, but Sam's younger, thought Jacob, trying his best to convince himself that this wasn't a personal thing. But it wasn't something that he was ever going to forget. Jacob had always wanted to be treated like a young man and not a kid. But now that time was here, he was frightened. He just couldn't shake the feeling that it was the first sign of his father giving up on him.

Paul Brooking, though, never gave that moment another thought, for Paul loved his son.

I can see you, said the creature, as Jacob felt the weight of its mass press down on his mattress.

I can smell you, said the creature, as it wrapped its long viscous tentacles around Jacob's cocoon.

I can taste you, said the creature, as it enveloped him in such a grip that Jacob thought he would surely be crushed.

They are right to bully you at school, the creature spat.

They are right to love you less than your brother, you are pathetic and I taste only the weakness that drenches your

skin as you cower from me, like a beaten dog, under the very
cover of darkness that you know gives me strength.

Jacob wasn't sure if the voice – or the creature that
projected it, for that matter – was real, but he knew that the
pain was real. He knew that he couldn't breathe and that he
was starting to black out. Why it hated him Jacob didn't
understand, and his hope that the other kids at school were
tormented by monsters of their own had been misplaced – the
few students who had been willing to talk to him about it had
found no middle ground with him at all. It seemed he was
alone in his relationship with the shadow leviathan, and as the
weight of its mass started to crush him, and his ribs started to
splinter and crack, he realised that actually he had very little in
his life other than the creature's hate. His parents seemed to
not even recognise his place in the family anymore. His
brother had started calling him Gummy Bear, just like the kids
at school, and what chance did he possibly have with that
beautiful girl from the school next door? The last of his air
escaped his lungs and his body started to convulse.
        'Son, I'm here, little buddy,' said his dad, pulling the
quilt from around Jacob's constricted body and holding him
in place as he thrashed around like he was afflicted by some
kind of demonic possession.
        'Dad!' called Jacob. He reached forward with tear-
stained cheeks and rasping lungs.
        'I'm here, son, just breathe.' Paul pulled his son into
his chest and kissed his brow. 'Where has all this come from?
For weeks now I've seen you at war with yourself, and I can't
for the life of me understand where all this angst is coming
from.'
        Jacob couldn't find the words to explain what he was
going through. He felt broken, alone and like no one else
would understand his pain. What could he say to his father
now that would help him rationalise his conflict?
        'It was just a bad dream,' said Jacob, trying to regain
some composure. 'I couldn't even tell you what it was about.'

'OK, son. Just know that I'm only next door, OK?'

'Yeah, alright, Dad, thanks.'

Jacob's father left the room and left the door ajar, just enough for the hall light to shine on his son's face. Leaving the landing light on may have seemed like a small gesture to others, but to Jacob it meant the world.

Chapter 2: Growing Pains
Song of the day
"Dreams" by the Cranberries

Spring 1995
Canterbury, Kent UK

Even though she was a slight girl, Alice was still finding it hard to balance on the toilet seat. She had been hiding in the cubicle for ten minutes, as the three girls who had come into the bathroom shortly after her were not friends of hers, not in any way whatsoever. Graffiti marked the inside of the door: 'Katlyn Baily is a slut'. The girl in question was on the other side.

'I just don't get what Alice likes about that retard Jay Brooking,' Katlyn said while the three of them applied too much make-up to faces that at such a young age needed little.

'She's a whore, Katlyn, you know this,' said Chloe with a cruel bite in her voice. Chloe Durby was the sinister one in the trio of vultures, as Alice called them. While Katlyn was the poor little rich kid who lied and complained about anything and everything despite its irrelevance to her own life, it was Chloe who, Alice imagined, tortured cats in her garden each day.

The last member of the group, Emily, was quieter, and Alice had always thought that she was in the clique because it was safer than being out of it, rather than because she had an innate desire to be mean to others. But she would still agree with everything the girls said in public.

'Well, she's not a whore, is she, girls?' said Katlyn with bold assurance.

'And why's that?' asked the two mocking birds by her side in unison.

'Because she doesn't get paid,' Katlyn laughed. 'I'd fuck Jay for money. But I wouldn't touch him for free.'

'Not that the ginger tramp is anything to look at either, so maybe they're made for each other,' Chloe snorted.

Alice was seething at what she was hearing but knew that getting her head flushed down the toilet by three bigger girls was not going to solve anything at all. Instead, she focused on her footing and controlling her breathing so she would hopefully go unnoticed until they left.

'I have a friend in his class, they say he talks to himself,' Emily joined in. 'They say he refuses to talk to many of his classmates except a very select few and that Alice is his only true friend.'

'Alice Petalow doesn't have any friends,' said Chloe. 'That's why I never understood why she's always so undeservedly fucking happy.'

'It annoys the shit out of me,' said Katlyn, who seemed genuine with every statement.

Alice felt her heart break as she racked her mind to try and figure out what she had done to any of these girls to deserve the words she was hearing. She heard the door to the bathroom open.

Over her shoulder, Chloe shouted, 'See you later, Ginge. Don't stay in there all day.'

The three girls started singing as they skipped down the hall in search of another victim to tear down. And they would find someone, they always did. People like Alice were the carcasses that these vultures would feed off. Alice knew her place in the school social structure. And she felt a wave of pride wash over her for escaping a bathroom beating at the vultures' hands, even though they had known she was in there all along. She climbed down from the porcelain pedestal and opened the cubicle door. The mirror stared back at her. The dirty mirror had a large crack running diagonally through it, which seemed to cut her image in half. Her hair was tied in a tight French plait and her eyes were glazed over as she looked at her reflection and tried to laugh off the girls' comments, but it wasn't coming easily.

The left side of the crack was warped and reminded her of a circus mirror in some house of horrors or freak-show parlour. Her forehead was elongated and her jaw misshapen. Yet to the right of the break was a crystal-clear reflection of a confused 16-year-old girl who couldn't figure out why anyone would be as mean to her as the three vultures had been. Alice knew in her heart she couldn't have lived with herself if she had ever made anyone feel as low as they constantly made her and her friends feel. The warped reflection seemed to be smiling at her as she adjusted the collar of her blouse.

'And what are you smiling at?' Alice quipped.

Failure, the reflection answered.

Before Alice could figure out how to respond to a completely inanimate object talking to her, the door to the bathroom burst open. Chloe led the charge like a raging bull, and Katlyn followed her with an air of graceful authority. Emily was last. She pulled the door closed behind her and guarded it while looking squarely at the floor.

'I've changed my mind,' said Katlyn. 'I'm sick of you, Petalow, and I think you need to learn a lesson for listening in on our conversation.' She drew a pair of scissors from her waistband. 'Chloe, grab a little of that beautiful hair, would you?'

Alice wanted to scream for help, but what would have been the point? She collapsed into the corner of the room, cowering from what was about to happen. The mirror just kept smiling at her as long locks of her beautiful red hair fell to the floor around her.

Chapter 3: The Viking King
Song of the day
"Nightshift" by The Commodores

1995
Mile End, London Docklands UK

The commodores, rang through the tinny speakers of the paint-splattered radio hanging from a makeshift hook rammed into the back wall of the dockyard fish market in Mile End, east London. Jay had always loved the band and today was a great day to hear them play. It took him back to car journeys with his dad. Riding in the back seat of that old grey Peugeot while his baby brother poked and prodded him to antagonise the life out of him. His dad always had some Motown cassette on, or something full of soul. It had been the catalyst for Paul Brooking's oldest son to become the romantic and unique young man he had become, one who truly believed in the task in front of him today, although it was too many years of listening to Motown that had led him here on this suicide mission, and his belief that love could somehow always find a way would be the reason he died.

Jacob was sitting in what could only have been a 1920s Catholic-school chair, built with the sole purpose of causing pain and discomfort to all that sat in its tight embrace. His adversary in this game of awkwardness was a lot more 'the man' in this power play. Twice the size of Jacob in size and stature. His office in the very rear of the stinking hangar was covered in photographs commemorating his achievements in life. First was a black-and-white sepia piece of this grey-haired behemoth with his brothers in arms, possibly in the Falklands, standing on some ridge in the pouring rain. The war appeared to have taken its toll. From their hollow expressions, it was clear that each man had lost something. He was too well spoken to be a paratrooper, so Jacob suspected he'd been a Royal Marine. Then he was dressed in a shirt and tie at the rugby club, possibly five years later, with his team mates from Canterbury RFU around him, and he was holding no fewer than six trophies at an end-of-season awards presentation of some kind. These were interlaced with a plethora of fishing-trip pictures. In each one, he was holding a hooked fish that was easily as big as Jacob himself. Not a great sign for what was to come, Jacob mused, as he sympathised with one large pike in particular. But one final picture took his eye more than the others. This one didn't hang from the wall. It stood to proud attention on the man's desk. It held within its frame the most beautiful woman Jacob had ever seen. Possibly in her 40s, she had red hair like that of an autumnal dream. Her eyes were a piercing blue, the likes of which he had never seen nor believed could exist. By her side was her daughter – his Alice. A perfect reflection in all but age. Jay had loved Alice since the day he first saw her. More than anyone he had ever seen. And he could make that statement knowing he had seen more of the world than most 16-year-old boys. He doubted another creature could stop his heart and yet keep him alive like she did all at once. Like in the Star Wars film he had loved growing up, he would go to the dark side for her, without hesitation, and no mystical wizard with a laser sword would tell him otherwise. His concentration was halted swiftly as Mr Petalow senior, noticing Jacob's gaze, put the frame down on its front with enough force to make his simple gesture an exclamation point.

'What do you want, Brooking?' he barked.

This wasn't a good start, Jay thought, as his heart rate kicked up a notch.

John Petalow was six foot four with cropped silver hair and a beard to match. He had the same piercing eyes as the two ladies in his life, but his seemed to send a different message. Where theirs were welcoming, warm and mischievous, his were full of calculating intellect. His pupils were a little too dilated, like those of a hungry great white shark. Menace radiated from the very air that was released from his lungs. He sat in a huge leather chair, with oak legs that looked to have been carved from a tree so giant only the man upon this throne could have done it.

'Well, boy? Do I look like I built this business up from nothing by sitting in this office waiting for children to reach puberty?'

'Sir – John. Sir John,' Jacob stuttered in hilarious fashion. In his head he wanted to argue that he had already reached puberty, but he decided it would take him down a discussion he didn't want to start. In fact, the further he stayed away from that subject, the better.

'Mr Petalow will do, boy,' he declared. 'Now, please,' he went on, his tone softening at seeing Jacob's unease. 'What is it you need here?'

'Alice, Mr Petalow – I need Alice. Or, rather, I would at least like Alice to come out with me on Saturday evening. Maybe to the cinema or theatre. Could I at least ...'

Jacob was cut short by John's hand shooting up. Mr Petalow looked like he was stopping traffic, but Jacob knew he could just as easily have been stopping a rampaging herd of buffalo.

'What makes you think Alice's mother or I would allow this during her studies? Tell me, what do you offer her?'

'I'm a good man.'

The voice laughed at the same time as the Viking king. Jacob felt that the voice was laughing at him pretending to be good, while Alice's father was laughing at his belief he was a man.

'And I've loved Alice since the day I met her. I would do her no harm and I would keep her safe.'

'It's my job to keep her safe,' John Petalow boomed, his words now coming from deep inside a hollow void where Jacob was sure his heart should be. 'Tell me, boy, are you even working since you left school? And left school with nothing, I hear, or am I misinformed?'

[29]

'No, sir, I am not working as such, but I want to be a chef. It's all I've ever wanted to do. I've applied everywhere but to no avail.' He could feel his palms leaking at such a profound rate that he panicked they would all drown and even the fish on ice would have the means to swim back to the Thames.

HE'S NOT BUYING YOUR LIES, said the voice with a cackle.

Mr Petalow just looked at him. Maybe looking through him would have been a better way to describe it. Jacob had no idea if he should return the gaze or if he should avoid it, like the Medusa from that Harryhausen film he had loved as a child, the hero of which had always been an idol to him. But instead of finding his inner Perseus, he settled for looking into his lap, where his hands were shaking.

'Listen, son. Jacob, isn't it?'

HE KNOWS YOUR NAME.

HE'S TOYING WITH YOU.

Mr Petalow reached into a secure drawer under his desk. Jacob's chest tightened at the thought of what he was hiding in that drawer. Maybe the severed fingers of all the previous prepubescent boys who had dared to date his teenage daughter. Or, worse still, it could be the instrument that removed those fingers.

Mr Petalow pulled out a pen and tore a piece of paper from a notepad on his desk. He scribbled for a second and then with one ridiculously muscular hand pushed the note across the desk.

'You're nothing. I don't believe you will ever be more than nothing, and Alice deserves something. I want her to have something with someone more,' Mr Petalow said with weight.

'Sir,' Jacob blurted.

'DON'T interrupt me, son. If you're talking, you're not listening, and right now I really need you to listen. This is the number of Pierre DuPont, head chef and patron of the Travelling Trout. He needs a junior chef right now, and I hold favour with him. It's a prestigious establishment. You will be bullied and overworked for little pay, but it will give you an opportunity.'

'What for?' Jacob asked meekly.

'To prove me wrong, Jacob. Come back to me in six months, and if you have nailed that position down, you can take my daughter out, as at least then she would have finished her exams.'

Jacob's mouth opened to protest, but he found himself too weak to argue. Six months was a long time. And he had set his heart on taking Alice out this Saturday.

YOU'RE NOT GOOD ENOUGH.

Jacob rose from the confines of his torture chair and offered his hand. 'Thank you, Mr Petalow.'

Jonathon Petalow stood, and it suddenly hit Jacob just how huge his adversary was. It was like he was cut from a single monolith of granite.

He shook Jacob's tiny hand and whispered in his most subtle voice yet. 'This isn't all about Alice. You do know that, right? Don't let yourself down, and don't let me down.'

HAHAHAHAHAHAHAHA

Shut up, Jacob thought.

NO, YOU'RE A FOOL.

SHUT UP, he repeated in his head.

NO NO NO NO NO NO NO NO

Chapter 4: Birth of a Monster
Song of the day
"Scars" by Michael Malarkey

Spring 1996
Canterbury, Kent, UK

Alice had been battered during what had been the most intense 60 minutes of lacrosse she had ever played – a 13-9 loss to a Maidstone side that, on a different day, couldn't have held a candle to the league leaders at Canterbury WLC. Alice was only playing in the colts, as she was still short of 18, but the side she had faced today had been full of adults each a little quicker and more educated on tactics. The freeze pack on her knee was starting to become useless as the afternoon sun, on a particularly warm May afternoon, melted the ice quicker than she could replace it. Another graze on her forearm would need cleaning when she got back to the locker room; Alice had picked most of the gravel out, but she could feel throbbing as though a foreign object was lodged deep inside her skin. Alice was normally the motivational coach for the locker room. She was the club's top scorer, at least in the colts, and found it easy to give the pre-match pep talk, but today she was struggling to find a good reason why she wasted her Saturday afternoons getting beaten up with hard balls and harder sticks.

'You looked good today, Pebble. Just wasn't your day, I guess,' said Jacob as he joined Alice on the sidelines and took her hand into his own.

'Our bloody defence let us down again, but can you blame them when the opposition is fielding a team of semi-professional players? Thank you for coming to watch me though, bubba. It means a lot, even if we lost. I know you don't get much time off.'

'Don't be silly. I only took that job to shut your father up, so getting to watch his daughter run around in these little shorts for an hour is kind of bliss, to be honest.' Jacob tugged at the waistband of a figure-hugging pair of white shorts.

'Baby, please come back home and find something in Canterbury,' pleaded Alice as she discarded the ice pack. 'I know you are doing well, but I can't see why you have to be stuck out there on the outskirts of London.'

'I promised your father a year, and I want to prove the old fool wrong. And things are going bloody well. Who would have guessed? Jacob Brooking, young chef of the year.'

'I am proud of you, Jay; I just miss you. It's unfair that I must be alone whilst all those waitresses get to flirt with you every day.'

'Even if that were true, do you honestly think that I could ever have eyes for anyone but you? Never could I find such beauty in another, my love.'

Jacob went down on one knee in a mock proposal, and Alice reacted by pushing him over for trying to be funny.

'You'd better get cleaned up if you want us to spend some time together before the Viking king takes you away from me,' said Jacob from his new position on the Astroturf.

'Yes, boss,' replied Alice, bending over to kiss Jacob firmly on the lips. 'I'll be quick.'

'Great game, losers! Reminded me of when we were kids playing junior league,' taunted a spiteful blonde who could only be a year or two older than Alice. 'Hey, ginge, good job missing that open goal at the end. Real classy bit of play to spoon it into the crowd.'

'If you call the group of boys getting far too excited about your bust a crowd, then, yeah, I guess you are right, blondie,' retorted Alice with a smile.

'The fuck you say to me? You snotty bitch, I will wipe the smile off your face before I go out there and fuck that cute little thing that was watching you.'

The blonde girl rounded on Alice but got no rise from her, as Alice refused to take her head out of her locker.

Coward, the voice whispered.

'I didn't say anything,' said Alice. 'Anything at all actually. You must have misheard me.'

'That's right, you misheard her, blondie. So why don't you climb back onto your coach and fuck right off,' said Holly, Alice's best friend and the club's vice captain.

'Or what?' snapped the blonde. 'You gonna eat me, tubs?'

Holly stepped forward, towering over her much slighter opponent. 'Oh, you fucking wait and see what I do.'

'Come on, Laurie, let's leave the kids to play with each other, yeah,' said one of the older girls. She pulled the blonde round and shuffled her out the door.

'Take care, ladies,' said the Maidstone captain, who was the last of the opposition to leave the locker room.

'See you later, bitches.' Holly waved as she bounced her curvaceous hip off of Alice, almost knocking her into her locker.

'Yeah, see you in the play-offs, ladies,' said Alice. She pulled off her kit and dumped it in a pile on the floor. 'Why does everyone we ever speak to have to treat us like we're a bunch of weak-willed fairies?'

Holly laughed. 'You speak for yourself, ginge. I don't get much trouble.'

'That's because you look like a hungry, hungry hippo when you're pissed off, Holl.'

'You little ...'

Holly was cut off by sounds of laughter from outside and went to see what the commotion was, while Alice struggled to get a towel around her.

Jacob was sitting next to, and talking to, the blonde. She laughed and touched his arm before bouncing up and heading over to the coach.

Alice tripped over herself as she tried to get her jogging bottoms on. 'What's going on out there, Holl?'

'Nothing. Just Jacob talking to himself and the Maidstone bitches all trying to squeeze those big heads onto the coach.'

'He does that a lot,' said Alice, wondering how much of her boyfriend's craziness she should divulge in public.

'Babe, you knew Jay was crazy when he met you. Don't pretend this is a new thing.'

Alice's inner voice started to laugh with a dry rasping cackle. She looked at herself in the locker-room mirror as she threw some perfume on and tied her hair back. *That will have to do*, she thought.

The mirror's reflection of her was moving a fraction slower than she was – a vision that didn't change as she rubbed her eyes and tried to regain her focus.

He's not the crazy one ... is he?

Autumn 1997 Canterbury, Kent UK

The seaside town of Whitstable was home. It was where they both lived. But they had grown up to be the young adults they were now on very different sides of the county.

Alice had been born and raised just ten miles up the road in the historic city of Canterbury. She had enjoyed a much more privileged childhood on the cobbled streets of the heritage site. Culture poured from every narrow alley, each containing a unique shop or store selling handmade crafts or jewellery. Students from schools across Europe visited each day to see the cathedral lit up at night. A magnificent sight at any age. But for a child it was the best place in the world for letting your imagination run wild. And Alice had come back to her city of origin to pick up supplies for a big art project the college had entrusted her to run wild with. The picture she had in mind was beautiful, and this city would be her inspiration, as it had been so many times before.

This particular Saturday wasn't a beautiful day by any stretch of the imagination, though. Rain lashed down on the stone streets and ran in rivers through the cracks, with little estuaries forming into puddles at the soles of Alice's pumps as she pressed her body tight against the wall to avoid the biblical downpour. She had found a haven under a tiny shop awning angled over the doorway to a vintage fudge confectioner. The awning was doing its best to deflect all but the worst of the storm, although Alice had resigned herself to getting soaked to the bone due to the sheer volume of rain coming down. She had run blindly down this alley for shelter, but now that she was trapped here, she saw it was filled with tiny and unique shops selling anything you could desire. It had an almost magical feel to it, and even in this horrid weather she couldn't help but marvel at the unique beauty of the city. Canterbury was old and it showed here, as the cobbles met the uneven brickwork and gave everything an almost drunk appearance. All off-kilter and crooked. And it was that which made it so attractive to Alice. Sweet seventeen and full of confidence, Alice took a hairband from her wrist and tied her hair into a tight bun. Pulling a dark blue woolly bobble hat from her shoulder satchel, she covered as much of her hair as she could and buttoned her coat up as far as it would go, readying herself for the dash to the bus stop, because, she whispered to herself, 'It's just a bit of rain.'

She sprinted out of the alley to her right and into the open high street. The rain still thundered down aggressively and was stinging her head and back, even through her clothing, with its sheer force. Hitting the ground hard and at pace, with every step sending up an explosion of rainwater, she sped towards the cover of the bus shelter, which was just a few hundred feet ahead of her. Being vice captain of the college lacrosse team meant stamina was not an issue, but traction was proving a problem, as her feet kept slipping on the wet cobbles. She rode her luck a few times, until the inevitable happened. As she took a sharp left around the edge of a parked taxi, her right foot went from underneath her, and in one rapid motion she crashed down to the wet stone and found herself on her back, staring up at the sky. In a heartbeat, all the air was forced out of her lungs, and her hot breath bellowed from her like she was a mythical dragon in a legendary tale of valour and heroism. As flashes of light danced around her vision like some pyrotechnic display, she was suddenly hit with a sharp lancing pain through her shoulder blades, which prevented her from moving. Every attempt to raise herself up felt like something was stabbing deeper into her body and was soon to pierce her heart. Alice gasped as her lungs allowed her to breathe again. All of a sudden, a hand reached down and clasped her arm in a muscular grip.

'Alice,' the boy asked, 'are you OK?'

Her answer was a tear-filled croak, but the boy smiled as if he understood.

'I'll take that as a yes, shall I? Here, try and sit up. Did you hit your head?'

'No,' Alice slurred. 'Just my back and my bum.'

Visibly in pain, she was pulled upright by the stranger.

'OH MY GOD – I know you,' Alice said, embarrassed.

'We go to the same college, so I should hope you at least know me a little,' Thomas Levit joked.

Alice breathed deeply as Thomas took her hands and smiled.

'One, two and three,' he said, pulling her to her feet.

Alice stumbled a little at first, and Thomas wrapped an arm around her waist to support her. He was a broad man. Muscular with little body fat and hands like shovels. Pulling Alice to her feet was akin to lifting a child for him.

'So, no Jacob today?' he asked, holding her steady as he guided her to the bus shelter.

'He's working as always. He decided against college. He was never the academic type, I guess. How do you know my Jacob? I wasn't aware you had gone to the Howard George.'

'Nooooooo.' Thomas laughed. 'I'm a King's boy, but we have mutual friends through rugby.'

'That's right – you're first team captain at Canterbury. I'm sure I watched you play in the cup final last year with Dad,' Alice recalled.

'Your dad is a legend at our club. John the Viking Petalow has a photo on every wall of the clubhouse, and in each one he's lifting a trophy.' Thomas seemed starstruck as he spoke.

Alice couldn't believe what she was about to say to possibly the coolest guy in her year, if not on the whole campus. 'Well, if you have a few hours spare you're more than welcome to come and meet him. He's only at home doing chores for Mum. I promise he's not always the superhero you guys make him out to be.'

'I'd love to, but does that sound a little bit like a date?' Thomas sounded hopeful. 'Will Jacob mind?'

'Of course it's not a date.' Alice laughed. 'I couldn't do that to Jay, but I do think Dad would enjoy having a man about for an hour or two. He gets bullied by Mum and me constantly.'

'Well, I would be honoured to be the man who saves him from such turmoil. Shall we go, my lady?' Thomas extended his arm out and Alice looped her own into it, neither of them noticing the rain had stopped.

'So, this is the famous Petalow ranch?' said Thomas, closing the wrought-iron gate behind him. 'It's smaller than I thought.'

The sun was out and steam was rising gently from the grass on the front lawn.

'What did you expect? A castle, maybe?' Alice slipped her key out of her back pocket and put it in the door, but to her surprise it opened before she could turn it and her father filled the open frame.

'Bloody hell, Alice, I'm used to you bringing home strays, not the captain of the under-23s.' John kissed his daughter on the head. 'Great game last Saturday, Thomas. You really have those backs working as a unit at last.'

Thomas met the compliment with a strong handshake and a wry smile. 'We have a long way to go, but at least we are reading from the same play book now.'

'Good lad, Tom. I have every faith in you to sort them out. I didn't know you and my Alice were friends?'

'We kinda just happened, Dad,' Alice giggled. 'He rescued me from a fall and drove me home.'

'Well, Tom, I owe you a debt of thanks for that.' John finally let go of his hand and turned to his daughter, scanning her from head to toe. 'Are you hurt?'

'No, Dad, just wet from the landing.'

'Well, I'm glad, and I suggest you go and get the kettle on for this fine young man while I pick your mother up from her mission to bankrupt us.'

As he said his goodbyes and approached his oversized Range Rover, which seemed all too appropriate for the Viking king, he turned and gave Alice one last look, mouthing *I approve* at his bemused daughter, who just shook her head in response.

Thomas closed the door behind him and was instantly aware of the fact that he enjoyed being in this position. John Petalow was a legend at the rugby club, and there was no doubt in his mind that legendary status would be his too if he ended up banging the Viking's daughter.

'I'm just changing out of these wet clothes,' Alice said while bouncing up the stairs, stripping as she went. 'Get the kettle on, Tom.'

'Yes, my queen,' said Thomas, whose search for the kitchen took him down a hallway filled with pictures of Alice's mum, whom he was amazed to discover was a prettier and bustier version of Alice herself.

'What I wouldn't do to get my hands on that,' he whispered, knowing full well that even the great Thomas Levit

[39]

would be pushing his luck to try and hit on John Petalow's wife of 30 years.

In the kitchen, he picked up a framed picture that had mother and daughter in red bikinis on some ridiculously clean beach with white sand pooling around their feet. Just as he was about to put the picture back to rest, Alice grabbed him from behind and shrieked, 'Stop eyeing up my mother, she's happily married, don't you know.'

Without conscious thought, Tom grabbed Alice and pulled her into a kiss she didn't see coming.

Alice pulled away from his grip immediately. 'What are you doing!'

'Surely it's clear to you?' Thomas proclaimed calmly. 'Or are the rumours of Jacob neglecting you for work exaggerated?'

Alice didn't know how to attack this situation without upsetting Tom or his ego, as in fairness he had been nothing but a gentleman all day to this point.

Thomas once again placed his right hand on her wrist and leaned in to kiss her. Still in complete shock, Alice didn't pull away but clenched her lips tightly into the kind of face you make when you suck on a post-tequila lemon wedge.

'Thomas, whatever you think is happening today isn't going to happen like this,' Alice affirmed as he pulled back.

Thomas remained calm but increased his grip on her wrist to a point where she was aware of his strength.

'So, what has today been about then, Alice? Come to meet my parents, come in my house – was this all a game to you, or did you just want the lift home?'

'No, of course not, Tom. Don't ever say that. I never even thought you would look at me like that. I mean, look at you, for god's sake!'

'Well, I do look at you like that. And now you know how I feel, surely it changes things between us.' An air of arrogance not noted before had slipped into his voice, and without warning he forced himself forward again, pushing his tongue straight through her lips in a motion that nearly caused

Alice to bite it clean off. Instead, her free hand shot up in an aggressive half arc that ended up with her watch catching the side of his ear. Thomas recoiled, bringing his hand up to the wound. A small gash on his inner lobe was bleeding.

'You fucking bitch. Who the hell do you think you are? No wonder Jacob works away. I bet he's fucking every waitress at that crappy restaurant.'

'Get out of my house now, Tom,' Alice shouted. Her eyes were beginning to well up, but anger drove her, not fear.

'Fine. I don't need this shit from the likes of you anyway.'

With that he turned to head towards the front door. But as he reached the hall next to the kitchen entrance, he stopped in his tracks. His broad shoulders filled the frame of the door. 'You know what, Alice? Why should I leave with nothing when I feel you owe me? Or should I have just left you to lie in the pissing rain, looking like trash?'

'Thomas, just go.'

'No. I think I'll stay if it's all the same with you.'

He moved back towards where she stood, looking straight through her.

Alice had backed herself into the corner of the kitchen without realising and was suddenly aware she had no idea how far he was willing to take this.

'Stop it right now, Tom,' she barked sharply. 'You know this isn't going to happen. I'd never cheat on Jacob, so why not just leave?'

Thomas had stopped responding to her directly and instead seemed to be conversing with himself. He took her this time tightly by both arms and squeezed her together like a human accordion.

'Tom, please – you're hurting me.'

'I'm not hurting you. This is what you wanted, remember? To come over, to be with you. Didn't even hesitate when your dad said he was leaving us alone, and then what? You ran upstairs to get changed and came back down in this little summer dress.'

'I was soaking and filthy and it was the first thing I found, so don't you dare try and justify this. GET OFF OF ME!'

Tom came in again and started planting wet kisses and small bites on her exposed neck and shoulders, while Alice tried without success to fight him off. Her anger now turned to fear and she screeched at him again and again, until he pulled his face level with hers to spit more venom. Not yet broken by his animalistic behaviour, she brought her head forward into his with all the might she could muster. Every fibre of her body wanted to be free of his disgusting grasp, but as her brow connected with the forehead of a man used to being hit hard, Alice realised she had made a massive mistake. She collapsed to the floor, and for the second time that day the world around her went dark, with the only light coming in aggressive, flashing white spots. She could still feel herself fighting him, although it felt like one of those dreams where you are trying to run yet feel weighed down by some phantom apparition.

Flashes of Thomas's broken face hit her at intervals every few seconds between lances of pain from behind her eyes.

'See, I knew you wanted it. Why else would you stop fighting me? You're not that hurt if you want me this bad.'

Alice was unsure if her head was completely smashed to pieces, because she felt like she was fighting for her life and screaming at the top of her lungs. Yet some conscious part of her mind was telling her the truth. She was completely and silently still.

'Get off me,' she cried in her head.

Without warning she felt her underwear tear under pressure and almost instantly the warmth of something running down her leg. She screamed again inside her prisoned mind at the thought of wetting herself, but it suddenly occurred to her it might be something else. Something worse. The sharp pain in her head left her for a moment as her

[42]

insides turned to fire and she was violated beyond her threshold for pain.

'You dirty bitch,' he laughed, 'but I'm still game, as you clearly are.'

Alice was crying inside at the realisation that he genuinely thought she wanted this.

'Get off ... GET OFF!'

As she felt him enter her over and over again, her body started to convulse at the damage being caused inside of her. The screaming in her head wouldn't stop and was now overwhelming her senses like a perverse choir of murdered girls begging for release. But it took over everything. She heard nothing but screams. She felt nothing but pain. And she broke, with everything she held within her turning to blackness.

She woke up unsure of how long she had been out for but realised quickly that she was alone. Her head throbbed violently as she tried to stand unaided, but rather predictably she fell against the kitchen worktop. She felt and then saw the trickle of blood and semen running down her thigh to her calf, and she just about made it to the sink, where her stomach emptied itself of everything it held, including its own lining.

They won't believe you.

Alice looked around for the source of the voice, but no one was there.

Why would they? Silly little Alice.

Alice looked over to the kitchen table, where a note stood proudly folded into a tent shape.

She staggered over to it, and her heart sank once more at the words written within.

Alice, I had an amazing time. Dinner? Tom xxx

Finally, her body allowed her to cry, and she sank back down to what had become her most common position today. As she lay in the mess that had been created, she brought her knees up to her chest and sobbed uncontrollably.

'Jacob,' she whispered.

He won't believe you either.

Chapter 5: York Avenue

Song of the day
"Undenied" by Portishead

Autumn 1997
Canterbury, Kent UK

Alice had been sitting in the cold bath for three hours straight while the tap kept running and what was now freezing-cold water poured into the overflow. She hugged her knees tightly into her chest and kept the last of the heat from leaving her body, although her hands were shaking enough to start a small fire had they been wrapped in kindling. She had stared blankly at the same spot without moving since she had dragged herself upstairs. She was still fully dressed, and the blood had tainted the water, which had become a murky brown. She knew no one would believe her. She felt plagued by the events of the last six hours; she felt like she could never be cleansed of the thoughts that were eating away at her soul. She had scratched away most of the skin from the inside of her legs and crotch, and yet she felt as dirty as she had the second that Thomas had touched her. Tears were still rolling down her cheeks, and her eyes felt too wide to ever truly close again. The hurt in her womb hadn't subsided as such, but the lancing pain that had previously torn her asunder was now a deep and thunderous ache, the likes of which one could only experience after the nightmarish violence of the past 24 hours.

A loud knock at the door shook Alice to her very foundations and caused a wave of water to be thrown across the floor of the bathroom.

'Alice, are you OK, petal? You've been in there for hours. Is everything OK?'

Alice struggled to get her words together in a way that would mask her emotion, but she knew that silence would be worse. 'I'm OK, Mum, just really bad period pains. And I'm missing Jacob, I guess. I'll be out soon, you don't need to worry.'

Alice didn't believe her own lies, so she doubted her mother would either.

'OK, sweetie. We're here if you need us. Your father was going to cook some dinner, but I'll tell him you're a little off colour. I'll bring you up a glass of wine and a water bottle.'

Alice reached forward and turned off the tap while pulling on the plug chain until she felt the little pressured pop of air from beneath. She pulled herself slowly up to a half slump, and, for just a second, she caught herself in the antique mirror hanging on the back of the door. Her heart froze. The reflection looking back at her wasn't hers; rather, it was a version of her reimagined by fear. Her eyes were as black as the depths of the ocean and her bones almost sick with malnutrition, but it was still her, and for that moment the reflection looked back at Alice almost quizzically, weighing her up like a warrior scouting its enemy before a battle.

She stepped out of the bath and placed one foot on the bath mat, expecting resistance to meet her wet flesh, but instead she sank straight into a void where the floor should be. She tumbled into darkness until her world went black, and she fell until she hit the surface of a dark world she never saw coming.

She awoke dazed and confused from the journey, with no idea where she had come from or how long she had been unconscious. She put one hand down to raise herself up from the thin, hard-wearing carpet.

'Where am I?' she murmured to herself as she tried to stand, realising something was really out of place. She was at least three feet shorter than she should have been, and, looking at herself in the reflection of her mirrored wardrobe door, she had a strange sense of coming home. She felt as though she was in the bedroom in which she had grown up, in a small property on York Avenue, just outside the city. She hadn't lived here since she was six years old, and as she looked at herself in the mirror and saw an innocent young Alice, with a tight French plait and white knee-high socks, looking back at her, a sudden and unparalleled sense of dread washed over her. She had very few memories of this house, but there was one thing that she had never forgotten, something that had left her crying in her parents' bed each and every night, and she knew it was coming for her.

Alice had to hide, and, as always, this place had no intention of helping her. The walls had always seemed so tall, the ceiling so high and the windows so large that with bright sunlight washing over the plain white paint, the room felt a thousand times larger than it actually was. And yet, as had always been the case, Alice could see no place to hide, and hiding was imperative, because she knew what was coming. She could hear its footsteps already, close together and moving at pace, while a childish giggle was carried on the air in the distance. Alice dropped to her knees and kitten-crawled under her bed so as to be hidden by the thin, overhanging quilt, which she prayed was enough protection. She wrapped her hands in a seal around her mouth. The giggling increased when it entered the room, and as it paced around, searching for her, its tiny shadow was the only thing Alice could spy through the small slit that separated the quilt from the floor. Alice knew the drill: it would leave her bedroom and search elsewhere, and she would have to make a run for the staircase; it didn't ever follow her outside, and if she could get to the front door, then she would be safe, although the more she thought about it, the less she seemed convinced that she had ever made it outside, and it became apparent that the safety of the "outside" might just be something she had made up as a child to give her hope.

The giggling continued and followed Alice's stalker down the hall and into her parents' bedroom. This was her opportunity, but she had to move quick, and she could feel the fear pulling her back. For just a second, the tormenter's laughter stopped, and Alice took only a second to turn a belly shuffle into a sprint as she darted for the staircase, which, she realised all too late, seemed a thousand steps deep. Alice must have been halfway down when the giggling started up again. It sounded close, and her heart was racing. She bounded off the bottom step and headed towards the 20-foot-high front door. Chancing a look over her shoulder, she saw *It* standing there, watching her from the top of the stairs, causing her to scream in fear. She turned back to her escape plan and realised with a sinking heart that she couldn't even get close to reaching the knob to what was now a thousand-foot slab of gloss white wood so giant in stature that she was unsure she had seen a mightier door. Alice knew what was next, but as she heard the rapid pitter-patter of feet closing in on her, she also knew that this was playing out exactly as it always did. Running straight into the light of the kitchen, she dived for the safety of the round kitchen table, whose dinner cloth would provide her with some cover, if only for a moment; she knew, as she pressed her hand hard over her mouth to stop her heavy breathing giving her location away, that her relief would only be temporary. It was only ever a matter of time.

The laughter stopped, as did the sound of tiny footsteps, and Alice knew it was time. She leant forward, holding her breath, and went to lift the dinner cloth up from where it touched the floor, but before Alice even touched it she started screaming with the shrill pitch of a girl being murdered, as the nightmare in front of her yanked the sheet up and lurched forward.

Alice woke up crying on her bathroom floor. Her dress was still sodden and her hair was drenched and matted, and a six-year-old demon version of herself was giggling at her from the mirror.

You're it, the creature called as it ran into the shadows, leaving Alice to pull herself over to the toilet, where she threw up until only blood was leaving her body.

Chapter 6: Into the Fire
Song of the day
"Electric Man" by Rival Sons

Winter 2000
Biggin Hill, London UK

The Travelling Trout was a beautiful gastropub nestled in the Kent countryside. Not far from London, the area was affluent to a high degree, and all the chimney stacks you could see belonged to big detached houses with far too much land to share. The pub itself was an Edwardian property surrounded by the beautiful Biggin Hill woodland, which gave the pub a haunted look. Cast-iron street lamps cast a warm glow over the stone walls and the thatched roof, which housed a family of barn owls that were now protected by the RSPCA and so were unlikely to be evicted anytime soon. Jacob had never understood why anyone would want to evict the little beauties in any case, as they ate all the bugs. A line of expensive cars filled the car park, and another big Audi pulled into the gated entrance and drove up the gravel track. This was an old English pub. But it was really high end.

Matt entered the rear of the building to searing heat and the noise of industrial fans. He passed Jacob some fresh herbs he had taken from the garden. Jacob was barking orders at the waiting team as Sam hurriedly dropped hot pans into his sink of soapy water, creating an aggressive sizzle. The kitchen was roasting hot, even at this time of year, so Matt always tried to hide in the preparation section at the rear of the kitchen, far away from the flames. He started unloading the dehydrator, knowing Chef was about to collar him on it, while Sam the kitchen porter and general dish pig looked on, oblivious to the world around him.

7.10pm

'Where is my carving knife? Sam,' demanded Jacob, 'where is my carving knife?'

'Erm, it's out the back, Chef.' Sam looked at the ground as he spoke.

'Why is it out the back, Sam?'

Jacob stopped what he was doing and looked Sam square in the face, while Matt slid quietly into the background so as not to get caught as collateral damage.

'I was opening a ... well, a jar,' said Sam unapologetically. 'I was opening a jar.'

'With my carving knife?'

'Yes, Chef.'

'My knife?'

'Yes, Chef.'

'Sam. Find my knife. Put it on the pass. Then I suggest you get out of my sight.'

'Yes, Chef.'

'Matt?'

'Yes, Chef.'

'If you see Sam touch my knife again, I give you permission to beat his ass blue.'

'Oui, Chef.'

7.15pm

'SERVICE!' shouted Jacob while patting the little bronze bell incessantly for attention.

The two wild venison fillets that Jacob was presenting under the heat lamps were glistening in their own buttery juices. One at a time, he took them onto his little wooden chopping board, which was weathered with cuts and scars from years of abuse, and sliced them into four disks, fanning the meat out. The perfectly seared exterior was offset by the scarlet centre. They had been rested to perfection, retaining all of their juices.

He took each fan of meat, lay it atop the celeriac and potato boulangère in the centre of the plate, and gave it a gentle squeeze to form a flower-like shape. Turning the plates to make sure everything was symmetrical, he took a tablespoon from a little steel tankard of hot water that he held by the pass and gave his chocolate and juniper jus a stir before drizzling a little over the centre of the meat and spiralling out to dress an inner circle on the plate.

7.16pm

'SERVICE!' he shouted again. 'Matthew, parsnip flutes – where are they?'

'Here, Chef.' The scrawny young chef de partie scurried from the back with a tub of what looked like shards of golden glass.

Jacob placed one atop each plate, cresting the meat like a crown before once again rotating each plate to be sure of continuity.

7.17pm

'BLOODY SERVICE!' Jacob shouted, slamming his hand down on the bell one last time. A young waitress rushed through the double door to the side of the pass and straightened herself out before looking at the check in front of her.

'Table seven, Molly.'

'Yes, Chef.'

'And Molly, they reach the table the same way they leave here, OK?'

'Yes, Chef.'

The petrified young girl scurried away with a plate in each hand.

7.18pm

'Matthew, I need two sea trout on my board and a venison garnish up in three minutes.'

'Yes, skipper,' he responded without hesitation.

Jacob put a stainless-steel pan on the heat and sprinkled it with sea salt and a little lemon-tainted rapeseed oil. The young chef returned to Jacob with two large trout fillets, and as soon as he placed them on his blue chopping board Jacob was seasoning both sides and scoring the skin, which he then pressed down into the hot pan before sliding it into the oven to dress his venison plate as he placed the latest fillet onto his resting rack.

7.19pm
'Do you have a minute, Chef?'

Jacob looked up to see Robert standing there. Well dressed as usual, in a rural fashion. His tweed jacket and flat cap made him look like he had returned from a shoot with only his shotgun and springer spaniel missing. Robert Richardson was the owner of the Travelling Trout. As well as being a very well-respected restaurant owner, he was a fair man, and he had looked after a very inexperienced Jacob five years before.

'Of course, boss. As long as you don't mind talking while I work, I'm all yours.'

Jacob didn't take his eyes off the plates he was preparing, but Robert knew he had his full attention.

'Pierre has officially quit his position as head chef. I know it's been a turbulent few years, but I'm hopeful that he taught you something in that time about running this kitchen.' Robert was looking for a reaction, and he appeared to get one as Jacob paused while taking his trout out of the oven. 'You are one of the best chefs I know, but can you do the orders? The logistics? Manage the team?'

'Rob, Pierre was a great chef – maybe too good. But he won't be missed,' said Jacob, flipping his trout over with a little pallet knife to reveal the crispy, salt-mottled skin he had hoped for, before placing it next to the venison on the rack.

'I'm glad you feel that way, Jacob. You know I don't do formal, so what do you want?'

Jacob stopped, looked up and gazed into his boss's predatory eyes.

'Thirty-six thousand to start. We promote Matty to sous chef and get a new chef de partie. He has buckets of potential and won't cost us much more.'

'Deal.' Robert leaned in and offered his hand through the hot lights on the pass.

Jacob gripped his hand firmly and shook it vigorously.

'Matthew,' he called out.

'Yes, Chef?'

'You're promoted to sous chef.'

'Thank you, Chef,' Matt replied without stopping what he was doing.

'And Matthew.'

'Yes, Chef?'

'Where's my bloody samphire?'

'Coming, Chef.'

'Thank you, Rob.' Jacob smiled and released his boss's hand. 'We won't let you down.'

'Good show, Jacob. Enjoy your service, boys. Oh, and Alice has just arrived with her mum. I've put her on table one.'

'Thank you, boss. I'll be out in five.'

7.22pm

Tossing the fresh samphire into the hot pan the trout had previously occupied, Jacob started to construct the plates.

'Matt, come here, mate.'

'What's wrong, Chef?' said Matt, whose chef whites were splattered with sauce.

Jacob offered his hand and placed the other on his young apprentice's shoulder. 'In the week since Pierre left, you have been a rock for me, and, honestly, I need you more than ever now in the coming months.'

'I'll do my best, Jay.'

'I know you will, and that's all I ask. Now, help me get this last check out so I can go see my beautiful girlfriend.'

7.25pm

'SERVICE!'

The trout sat on its bed of samphire, a smear of hollandaise sitting beside it, dressed in fresh dill leaves. While Matthew applied the finishing touches, Jacob was meticulously inspecting the plates. One more rotation of the dishes and Matt got a pat on the back before Jacob rang the bell a final time.

Molly came through the door, but to Jacob's surprise she was followed by a giggling Alice. She truly was the best thing he had seen all day, and she was dressed so quintessentially Alice that a brief moment of nostalgia and love overwhelmed him. She wore a green floral dress, white neck scarf and bangles galore. Her hair was straightened, and the extra length brought it down to near her breast line.

'Pebble, you look amazing. I was trying to get out to you, but I had this to get out first. Table nine please, Molly.'

'Baby, it's fine.' Alice leaned in and kissed him. 'I know you're busy, but what's this good news Robert just told me you have?'

'Well, it turns out I'm the new head chef.'

Alice screeched. 'That's amazing! So he met all your demands?'

'Without any hesitation.'

'I guess that means congratulations to you too then, Matthew.'

Matt couldn't look at Alice without blushing, so he ran to the back of the kitchen while trying to look busy, murmuring his thanks as he went.

'Let's just hope I'm good enough,' Jacob joked.

Alice pulled Jacob by the arm so he was out of the busiest part of the kitchen and placed her hand on his cheek. 'Baby, I believe one thing more than anything I've ever believed.'

'What's that?' replied a hopeful Jacob.

'That you got this, baby. You got this.'

Spring

[54]

It was three years since Jacob had accepted the position of head chef at the Trout. Three years of graft, three years of missed sleep, combined with convincing Alice every six months that she didn't need a holiday just yet.

'But Jay,' she would complain, to no avail.

She understood, but the desire for a little time with her boyfriend was of course something he could understand.

Years of hot pans and stupid waiters and here he was, frozen in anticipation, with the letter from the *Good Food Guide* on his desk in front of him, and he was too scared to open it. He had never felt good enough for anything or anyone, and to avoid the obvious failure that any journey would bring, he had always avoided starting any journey at all. That was until he was challenged to 'be enough for Alice' – he said the words out loud, throwing his thoughts out into the public domain, although no one was there to hear him. No one would disturb him today; no one had even offered him a coffee this morning.

He finally gathered the courage to move to the right side of his desk, and with a deep breath, he allowed himself to collapse into his chair. *You can do this, Brooking*, he told himself, taking the letter into his hand. It felt important. It had weight to it, and as he opened the corners of the envelope, he noticed the off-white quality of the paper, thick and textured like it meant something.

Jacob held the letter out in front of him and started to read.

To all those concerned at the Travelling Trout ...'

Jacob opened the door to the restaurant, and two things awaited him: complete and utter silence, and his entire team standing and looking at him – even those that weren't on the rota to work today had come in.

At the front of the ensemble was his beloved Alice, who, just like the rest, was trying to gauge his reaction for any subtle giveaways. Jacob walked gingerly into the restaurant and propped himself up against the bar opposite his team, refusing to give anything away just yet. Alice – who was in a very formal-looking black skirt and white blouse, her hair pulled back into a tight ponytail, and with a touch of black eyeshadow, which brought out the exceptional brightness and beauty of her blue eyes – looked like she was ready to explode. Her hands were clenched tightly and she couldn't stop fidgeting. She had been helping Jacob run the floor since finishing her art degree in June and felt truly invested in what was about to happen.

'I didn't know you were eagerly waiting out here, guys. Had I known, I may just have taken another hour to build the suspense a little more.'

Raising no laughter from his terrified crew, he decided to put them out of their misery.

'Firstly, I would like to thank you for all the hard work you've put in this past year. Everything you do gets noticed by myself and Robert, despite his usual absence, so whatever the outcome, I need you all to understand one thing. I value you all as a team and as a family, and if one day I have my own restaurant, I will take every one of you with me.'

'Thank you, Chef,' said everyone in the crowd, until Alice took a step forward.

'Jacob.' Alice motioned with her hands.

'Yes, of course.' Jacob stepped forward, a few feet from where Alice stood, holding the letter out in front of him. 'With everyone here in front of me, I'd like to show you this.'

He held out the letter from the *Good Food Guide* and then lowered it in one motion to reveal a large sapphire and platinum engagement ring, which the restaurant lights made twinkle like a candle. In one continued fluid move, he lowered himself down onto his right knee.

'Alice, without you I wouldn't have even started this journey, and without you I wouldn't have made it this far, and, yes, without you we wouldn't now be a three-rosette restaurant.'

The crowd cheered – all except Alice, who was shaking and looking at her Jacob, tears of joy chasing her mascara down her face.

'It would be an honour to be your everything, if you would do me the honour of being my wife,' said Jacob.

Alice collapsed into his arms, putting her forehead against his. 'Yes, baby,' she whispered. 'A thousand times yes.'

They kissed over and over, with Alice peppering Jacob's face with little pecks as he placed the ring on her finger.

'I'm so proud of you, baby,' Alice said.

'You deserve as much credit as me, Pebble.'

'I'm going to marry you, baby,' she said with tears still flowing down her face.

'Yeah, you are,' Jacob laughed, pulling her up to her feet so that everyone could gather round her to offer congratulations.

'Matthew, get over here,' Jacob demanded.

'Yes, Chef,' said Jacob's most loyal team member.

'Don't congratulate me, son – we did this together. And with that in mind, I'm promoting you to head chef with immediate effect. But keep it on the low low for now.'

'But Chef, I'm confused. You're the head chef.'

'I have different plans, mate, but let's talk later.'

'Thank you, Chef,' said Matthew, offering his hand. But instead, Jacob embraced him in a bear hug and said quietly to his young protégé, 'You got this, son.'

Chapter 7: Sunshine and Stick Insects
Song of the day
"Heavy California" by Jungle

Summer 2002
The South East Coast UK

She could hear the honking outside, but she was sure he could wait a little longer. The dress she had settled on was a perfect vision of summer class. A burnt orange colour, light and floral, low cut and shorter on the thigh than her dad would allow if he was here to see her bound out the door. And bound she did as she shut her bedroom door on a plethora of dresses, all tried on and thrown about her bed with gay abandon. After kissing her mum quickly at the bottom of the stairs and pressing a finger to her lips to hush a dress-related protest that was surely coming, she was free.

The sun was shining down harder than she could imagine was possible in the UK even at this time of year, and not a cloud touched the canvas of blue above her. She ran straight to Jacob's car and jumped in. The air conditioning hit her like an ice-cold slap across her brow, and she licked her lips before leaning in for a kiss. Jacob was there, ready to receive. His lips, far too perfect to be wasted on a man, were warm to her touch, and he pushed her mouth apart to gently probe her with his wanting tongue. He always liked to remind her of the power he had over her. She felt a tremor of excitement run up her thigh. And then, as always, he sharply pulled away and started talking about his day. She listened intently as he enthused about the latest Lenny Kravitz song he had heard just an hour before. Not understanding a thing he was saying, she still loved hearing him talk so passionately about music. He had always claimed it was a dying industry.

That writing music that meant something important just never happened in this day and age. Alice sat and watched him as he negotiated the roads ahead. She loved him. For all that he was and all that he was yet to be.

As they made their way down the Kent coastal trail, it was hard not to fall into a blissful daydream. To the left was a drop of 200 feet; at the bottom, the ocean reared up against the cliff face, like some ancient war was taking place on an elemental level. They drove south towards Dover, before stopping for an iced coffee in the little town of Sandgate, which overlooked the ocean from the top of the cliffs. The warm breeze from the sea washed over them like a light blanket. A few speckled clouds appeared, blocking just enough of the afternoon sun to stop their already tanned skin burning. To the right of them was the most fantastic array of homes – so expensive that they would forever be out of reach to all but the richest folk in town. But it was nice to dream, as Alice always did when they made this journey. Not that they didn't do OK. Alice had been running her father's company for two years – at least, the financial part of it. Her dad called her his PA, but she knew this was a little in jest. He hated the office work, and she had taken that off his hands, to her mum's delight, although the promise of more free time had turned quickly into more time for fishing. Jay had become the Travelling Trout's youngest head chef and been instrumental in winning the restaurant's third rosette just last year. Things were certainly on the rise. Alice knew she would swap it all for a little more time with Jacob, and, deep down, she knew he would swap it all for another rosette. But she loved him all the same. Because how could you not, she thought, as he ran his fingers once more up the inside of her thigh.

'Jacob Brooking, I suggest you behave, unless you are planning on following through with your actions right here in front of Doris and her husband.' Alice motioned to an elderly couple holding hands over a pot of tea by the fence, before looking back into Jacob's gaze and biting her bottom lip with playful intent.

'In that case, my beautiful Alice –' Jacob leaned in to kiss her, but at the last second he changed direction and stood up, offering his hand. '– we had best be off.'

'You bastard,' she laughed. She teased him, telling him that he would pay for that later.

Back on the road, Alice looked down to see a text from her father flash up on her phone.

'I hope your dress is not as short as your mother has described to me, young lady? You're not married yet,' read the message.

She sighed and slipped her phone into her clutch bag. Dad still hadn't accepted the relationship, but after six years of permanent rejection, he at least gave an occasional nod of acknowledgement when he saw Jacob now. Having them in the same room was tough, but it was possible.

The Mercedes purred as they took the winding descent to the coastline. The scorching red leather stuck to her leg and refused to let go as she adjusted her frame slightly. Jay pressed down a little more on the throttle. She loved being driven around by him, and the close line he walked between gentleman and bad boy was never more visible than when he was behind the wheel of his car. She watched him as he focused intently on the road. He wore a tight V-neck T-shirt in the same gunmetal grey as his Mercedes. The T-shirt was cut in half by a low-hanging rope necklace, with just a metal loop attached to the end in a knot. In his beige chino shorts and with bangles everywhere, he was like a walking catalogue model. His mirrored sunglasses hid his constant moody glare. Actually, moody was the wrong word. Maybe troubled was more accurate. She loved how deep he was as a person and as a man. It was certainly a rarity with men her age, but it always seemed like he was at war with himself. Always giving the impression that he was mid-argument with an invisible enemy. But she understood that more than most. At least her demons only spoke back to her in the reflection of the mirror. *I'm sure he's fine*, she continued to muse. The pressure of work was constantly pushing the boundaries of control, and she was forever proud of him for all that he had achieved, especially knowing full well that this journey had started for the sole purpose of winning over her father.

They reached sea level and continued to push further south towards Dungeness. Houses along the route became less clustered as a wilder and more rustic beach line started to dominate the view. He loved it here. This was Jacob's safe place. When things had been hard, before they were allowed to see each other, this had been where he had escaped the world. And now it was a place they both shared. They would follow this road down past Camber Sands and head into Rye for a walk down by the harbour. Down along the estuary past the nature reserve, where the grass was allowed to grow unhindered. Where long-legged birds played in the marshland and spiders made webs in reeds without fear of them being broken by passing traffic. Eventually, it would meet a shoreline of pebbles, all multicoloured and broken, like a shattered stained-glass window. That's where Jay had given her the name Pebble.

'You're unique,' he had said. 'No two pebbles are alike, and that's what you are – unique.'

It had hurt to walk on them without shoes on. But Jay had rightly proclaimed this to be the reason no screaming kids could be seen whenever they came. And he was right. It was their beach. Only the occasional dog walker would pass them as they sat on a blanket, nibbling on an exotic picnic he had prepared. You could almost see France on a clear day. Jacob would sit quietly staring out to sea, almost hypnotised by its beauty. She loved it. Loved that they shared something so very 'Jacob'. He had let her into his world. A world where he let no other. A world he held so precious was now their world. The whole area was just an amplification of Jacob's own character. Untamed and unmanageable to any great degree. To walk here was to walk through Jacob's heart. But, strangely, it seemed to be the only place to calm his soul.

'Baby?' Alice chirped. 'You've missed the turning.'

'Have I indeed?' he scoffed. 'Maybe you're confused as to our destination.' His lips creased into a playful smile.

'I thought we were going to Rye as normal, bear?'

'We are, Pebble, but first we need to make a detour, as there's something I need to show you.'

'OK, bear, but don't forget, the last time we did that in public, the farmer got a fright.'

Alice restrained her laughter until Jacob erupted, and they giggled until he pulled into a restaurant car park just off the main stretch, only a short walk from the beach.

She knew this place despite never having been. In his youth, Jacob had never shut up about it. The Gallantry was a fabulous restaurant with an amazing reputation. Renowned for its local produce, it wasn't as prestigious as where Jay worked, but it was charming and rustic in ways the Travelling Trout could never be, with a loyal following to boot.

Jacob unbuckled himself and gave Alice a quick look. She opened her mouth to ask the obvious questions that were lining up, but he shot forward and planted a long kiss on her lips. He took her bottom lip between his teeth as he pulled away. She found herself speechless as he started to get out the car.

'Come on, Pebble,' he said.

As she opened her mouth to respond, another voice got there first.

'Good afternoon, Mr Brooking, and welcome back,' said the far-too-attractive stick insect in front of them.

'What's going on, baby?' she asked, with a little more demand in her voice this time.

'Well, it was supposed to be a surprise for later in the year, but amazingly the pen-pushers were quicker than we thought. This, my beautiful Alice, is my new place of work.'

'Don't be silly, Jay,' Alice laughed. 'I know you speak highly of this place, but they will never be able to match your wages at the Trout.'

'I know, I know, and I thought you would say that, so I took my plea to the owner.'

'And what exactly was his response? Because I'm fairly sure he didn't offer you the £50K a year you're currently making.'

'You're right,' Jacob grinned. 'He said that if I wanted that kind of money, I'd best buy the place.'

Alice could clearly be seen putting together the jigsaw in her mind.

'Baby ... You haven't bought this place, have you?'

'Would you be mad at me if I had?'

'YES, I BLOODY WOULD BE MAD,' Alice screeched, while somehow retaining an idiotic smile. 'How? Why? When?' she asked.

Jacob walked around the car and gripped her waist. His eyes locked on hers.

'Pebble, it's OK. It's ours. I've done this for us. We can run it together. You always said the next step was to buy a restaurant, and you must have known this place was on the dream list.'

Alice slowed her breathing. A deep sigh came from the back of her throat.

'Jay, it's not that I think it's the wrong decision. God, it's probably the right decision. But it should have been OUR decision.'

'Well, I think it's a fantastic move, Jacob,' the stick insect interjected, laying her hand atop his forearm. 'This can only be positive for us.'

'Us?' Alice snapped.

'Yes, us here at the Gallantry. What else would I mean, Mrs Brooking?'

'It's MISS Petalow,' Alice snapped.

The stick insect smiled. 'Of course it is. My mistake.'

Alice looked down, and in the reflection of the car mirror a familiar face looked back.

SHE WILL TAKE HIM AWAY, YOU'RE PATHETIC, the reflection bleated.

[63]

'Baby,' said Jacob, 'I have a little paperwork I need to grab from Evan, and then we can drive down to Rye and talk it all over.' He opened the car door for her to get back in.

Alice looked him straight in the eye and let out a heavy sigh before climbing back into the passenger seat. Jacob closed the door behind her and walked over to whoever this tart Evan was. Alice watched him put an all-too-familiar hand on the small of her back as he guided her into the restaurant. She felt herself falling.

The car journey to Rye had felt strained at best. Jacob started talking work, and she all but phased out most of what was being said, giving stock replies to all his questions. She was happy for him but couldn't help but feel that no consideration had been given to her feelings on this matter. Didn't he trust her or value her opinion? Or was she just less of a part of his big plan than she had believed?

It was a little cooler now that the sun had dipped and the fine hairs across her arm were picking up goosebumps. 'Jay, can we just go home? I'm not feeling great.'

He decelerated sharply and threw the car onto a grass verge.

'You're mad at me, aren't you?' There was an air of superiority in his voice. 'This is the thanks I get for trying to do something for us?'

'But it wasn't for us, was it, Jay? It looks more like it was for you and your new best friend.'

'Evan? She's just the restaurant manager. Why do your insecurities always get in our way?'

'Maybe if I hadn't been made to feel like the third wheel in yours and Evan's decision, I'd have more faith in what was going on here,' Alice barked, with absolute faith that she was right. 'I mean, you are expecting me to run it with you. What happened to me going to do my master's after university? What about my dreams, Jay?'

Jacob knew he didn't win these situations often and started to panic.

'Alice, you're the most beautiful woman I know and have ever met. I tell you every day I love you without fail, and this is all for ...'

'DON'T YOU DARE SAY IT'S ALL FOR US! THAT'S ALL YOU EVER SAY!' Tears started to fall from her face. 'When have I ever asked you for anything other than YOU?'

'You're right,' he said in a resigned tone, 'but you don't know what it's like. I've never felt good enough for you, and certainly not the world you come from. I just wanted to make you proud.'

Alice tried to calm herself, but spoke with enough authority that she hoped her point would still hit home. 'Since we've been together, I've tried not to keep secrets and I've made no secret of the fact I am nothing but proud of you, so I need to know if WE will ever be enough for you? Or will you always be trying to prove something to someone?'

YOU WILL NEVER BE ENOUGH, the voice in his head barked.

'You're all that I want, Alice,' Jacob said through a trembling voice.

Alice noticed his clenched fists shaking against his legs and regretted taking him to this place of self-hatred that she knew she would struggle to pull him out from.

'Baby, it's OK. We have said our piece. Let's just head home.'

But Jacob was gone, and Alice knew he wouldn't be back tonight. It would be a long journey home. And she knew nothing she said now would make a difference.

'I hate myself. HATE HATE HATE,' he shouted, punching himself repeatedly in the thigh with his fist.

WE HATE YOU TOO, the voice gargled like it was laughing. Laughing with water filling its poisonous mouth.

Alice reached over and put her hand over his fist. 'I could never hate you. And I know that means nothing to you when you're upset, but it's true.'

SHE LIES.

[65]

SHE ALWAYS LIES.
NOT LIKE EVAN.

Chapter 8: Changes

Song of the day
"Underwater Love" by Smoke City

Summer 2004
Camber, East Sussex UK

'Let me get this straight,' Evan mused. 'Her father still hates you.'

'Oh yes,' Jacob grinned. 'He hates me alright.'

'Despite the fact you have done all he ever asked of you and more.'

'Yep.'

'You supported his daughter through her degree.'

'I did.'

'And he wouldn't pay for her tuition because he wanted her to go to university further away from you.'

'Yep.'

'So you paid for Alice.'

'I did.'

'And saved for this restaurant at the same time.'

Jacob nodded.

'And when you asked his permission to marry her?'

'He said I needed to prove I was ready.'

'So you proposed anyway, you rebel.' Evan was grinning, marvelling at Jacob's audacity.

'I did.'

'But now he wants to come to the wedding.'

Jacob sighed. 'Of course he does.'

'And Alice of course wants her dad there.'

'Of course,' Jacob said with a distance in his voice.

Evan reached over the bar to put her hand on top of his. Her long, painted nails wrapped around his fingers with a

[67]

gentle squeeze. 'You're a better person than I am, boss, as honestly I wouldn't deal with that amount of disrespect, especially when you're as successful as you are.'

'Don't call me boss, Evan,' said Jacob, bringing her hand to his lips to thank her for the kindness before releasing her to take a sip of his drink. 'I don't look at you as one of our minions.'

Evan was behind the bar, polishing the wine glasses that she had just removed from the wash, while Jacob was emptying the last of his expensive Japanese whisky into his tumbler. End-of-week paperwork was spread out in front of him as he tried to find out why his turbot had increased in price so dramatically over two invoices.

'You have been a massive help to us during the transitional period,' said Jacob. 'I couldn't have had such a problem-free takeover without your hard work.'

'Don't be silly, Jacob. You and Matt have that kitchen nailed down, running better than ever, and bookings are already up on last year.' Evan placed her hand gently under his chin and raised his eyeline up to hers. 'That's down to you, and there's a buzz around Camber because of what you are doing here.'

'That's down to *us*,' Jacob said while raising his glass, which Evan happily toasted with the expensive French white Jacob had poured her.

Evan came round Jacob's side of the bar and sat beside him. She straightened out his collar as she perched and patted down his crisp white shirt.

'I do love it when you help us out front, Jacob Brooking, but if you could look a little less fabulous, you might find the waitresses get more work done.' She smirked while giving his biceps a gentle squeeze.

'Don't talk to me about distracting the staff while sitting there in that bloody dress.'

Evan jumped to her feet and twirled around. Her black dress rode up as she spun, revealing her toned thighs, while her thinly strapped top fought an epic battle to contain her more than ample cleavage. 'You approve, kind sir?' She giggled.

'I certainly do, my most treasured employee.' He jumped to his feet and took her hands, and they both danced to the New Orleans blues playing over the restaurant speakers. 'But I can't afford for our male staff to keep dropping plates every time you bend down to get a glass.' They both fell into laughter and collapsed into their seats.

'So, tell me – any doubts?' Evan asked. 'About Alice?'

Evan looked at him with complete devotion, hanging on his every word.

'Sometimes the situation with her family gets me down, and between you and me, she's not been the most sexual person the past ten years or so.' Jacob paused for a second after this and almost had to force himself to say a little more. 'But no, of course not. Anyway, what about you and that dumbass bodybuilder? Please tell me you've ditched him.'

'Of course I ditched him. Right after he bought me this marvellous dress, of course.'

Once again they found themselves in a fit of laughter.

'That's my girl. He was never good enough for you, Evan. Punch higher, as few men should be lucky enough to get the opportunity with you.'

She smiled and looked at the ground, blushing. Her long blonde hair fell from behind her ears and covered her face. She pulled it back into a loose ponytail and exposed her neckline to Jacob.

'She didn't think I could do this, you know. Alice, I mean.' Jacob seemed to speak with genuine sadness. 'She looks at me the same way her father does at times, with doubt and very little faith.'

'I see that,' said Evan. 'She hated me from day one, and I think it's because she knew we would make this place work and prove her wrong.'

'You may just be right on the money there,' Jacob agreed. 'And you're right. She does hate you,' Jacob said with good humour.

'She must see the way you look at me,' Evan joked with gusto.

Jacob got up and put his coat on to leave. As he walked past Evan, he leaned in behind her and left a lingering kiss on her cheek. 'Once again, my beautiful Evan, I think you might be right on the money. Let me know you're home safe, angel.'

Jacob pulled a mustard yellow scarf around his neck and slid out the door, singing to the music they had previously danced to.

'I will, Mr Brooking.' Evan smiled while touching her cheek gently where the kiss still tingled. That smile stayed the duration of the night. Evan rarely didn't get what she wanted from life, and Evan, of course, knew exactly what she wanted.

Winter 2003

Evan and Heather 8pm
Song of the moment:
'Make It Rain' by Foy Vance

The Voodoo Lounge was a club that seemed to have been transported from the depths of the Louisiana swamps. Candles flickered with an excited enthusiasm at every table and in every window. Old glass liquor bottles of all shapes and colours were being used to decorate every unusable flat space in the building, giving a cluttered effect that almost made it feel like an organised dumping ground. Voodoo dolls and skeleton masks hung from the walls, with random words scrawled like graffiti in and around each one. *New Orleans*, *Cajun*, *Gumbo* and *Big Easy* were written almost haphazardly, while *Mardi Gras* adorned the bridge of the bar proudly. The dancefloor was heaving. So many people were crammed into such a small space that it gave the impression that the whole dancefloor was a living, moving and breathing organism, swaying as one to the modern R&B music, which didn't suit the theme at all. Evan Laurie sat opposite her equally blonde doppelgänger in a corner booth lit largely by the four candles surrounding them, with only the empty wine glasses making the scene one of a bar and not some witches' coven.

'What is wrong with you, Ev? I have never seen you turn down attention from a guy that looks that good.'

Heather Hollis had been Evan's best friend for longer than either of them cared to admit and never held her tongue on a night out. The Heva and Eva show didn't hit the town as often lately, so it surprised her that her best friend was a little off-colour.

'Well, I've never seen you turn down anything from any man, regardless of how many bags he needs to wear over his head,' replied a tipsy Evan with a little grin. Her face was masked in immaculate make-up, and her swollen lips, which had recently been botoxed, were thick with ruby-red gloss.

'How bloody dare you?' snapped Heather. 'I'll tell you now that I rarely drop below a seven.'

Evan laughed out loud, taking Heather's hand firmly. 'But that's seven out of a hundred, my beautiful friend.'

Heather couldn't help but laugh too. 'You cheeky bitch.'

'BITCH? Do you kiss Mumma Hollis with that mouth?' Evan giggled.

Heather put a finger against her bottom lip. 'Nope, the only one I kiss with this mouth is Daddy Laurie.'

Evan slapped her friend's bare leg, causing a little squeal of excitement as Heather started to see the old Evan reappear.

'So, what's going on Ev? You seem a little quiet for the usual Saturday night at club Heva. It's not a boy, is it?'

As soon as the words left her lips, she noticed the smallest flutter in Evan's long lashes.

'Oh my lord, it's a bloody boy, isn't it? And judging by the fact you haven't told me anything about him, and this is me we are talking about, I'm guessing it's someone you shouldn't be thinking about. Tell me I'm wrong, Evan?'

The smile disappeared from Evan's lips, replaced with the smallest of sighs and a bite of her bottom lip. 'No, Hev, it's not someone I should be thinking about, but I am, quite a lot, really.'

Heather stared like a bird of prey into her squirming eyes, even though she was doing her best to avoid the gaze. 'It's your bloody boss, isn't it? That guy Jay you keep going on about.'

Evan bit her tongue, but the look in her eyes betrayed her.

'I don't suppose I need to warn you of the consequences of pursuing the owner of 55% of the restaurant you work at – the guy who's marrying the girl who owns the other 45%?'

Heather knew that the chances of stopping Evan were slim to none. Once Evan had set her heart on something, she rarely let anything get in her way.

'I think,' said Evan with an air of mischief, 'that we need another round of tequila.'

She bounced out of the booth, with all the eyes in the place drawn to her curves, and danced over to the bar, ignoring the queue as she always did, because Evan Laurie didn't stand in line for anyone.

Alice and Holly 8.30pm
Song of the moment:
'Colour Me In' by Damien Rice

'Holly, that can't be right,' Alice choked.

'Two lines again means pregnant, bubba, and this is the third test in 30 minutes. You're as pregnant as they come, so am I happy for you or disappointed on your behalf?' said Holly with a hint of apprehension.

'Oh shit,' said Alice. She fell against the wall and slid down to the floor. 'Shit! Shit! Shit!'

Holly realised that the time for humour had ended, while also realising that she held something in her grasp that her little cousin had just peed on. She dropped the test into the empty sink and then sat down next to Alice. Her mother was a Petalow, the sister of Alice's father, but although they were related by blood, Holly and Alice had always considered themselves friends first and foremost. With just six months separating them, they had been in the same academic year and had been inseparable since pre-school. Holly was far shapelier than Alice, and her faux red hair was a more aggressive shade than Alice's autumnal tones.

She wrapped an arm around Alice as she saw tears escaping the hands that shielded Alice's face. 'This is a good thing, right? You wanted kids at some point?'

Alice pulled her hands away, exposing a mascara massacre right out of a gothic horror story. 'Of course we wanted kids, but now? With everything that's going on, with the wedding and Jacob? What is he going to say?'

Holly squeezed Alice closer to her. 'What about Jacob?'

Alice was trembling as she struggled to find a reply. 'He's just ploughed everything we have into the restaurant, and he's so stressed, like he never stops.'

Holly guided Alice's face around with a gentle touch. 'When is Jacob not stressed, and when is he not under pressure? Why don't we forget about everything that revolves around money and Jay Brooking and think about the one question that matters right now?'

Alice looked up as Holly asked the one thing she hadn't often had to answer.

'What do you want, Alice?'

Alice and Jacob 9.45pm
Song of the moment:
'Dance Me to the End of Love' by The Civil Wars

Tick tock

Jacob was stuck in the tiny box room that had become his office these past few months. His large mahogany desk – a piece of antique furniture that he had loved at first sight during a rare trip north to the Derbyshire town of Buxton – barely fit in the space. Once, when he'd been filing invoices for his accountant, he'd stretched out to yawn, the type of yawn a bear might make after awakening from its winter hibernation, and in doing so he had realised he was touching three of the four walls: his feet were against the skirting underneath his desk, and his palms were flat against the oppressive walls. It was a prison of isolation and paperwork, and Jacob had been trying to fight the urge to drive to the restaurant to pick up the missing invoices he had left on his work desk. His obsession with getting all his paperwork done on his one night off had become a compulsion that he was finding hard to shift. The paperwork didn't need to be done, it could wait until tomorrow, but it would bother Jacob – that wasn't how he worked at all. He would wait until Alice got home from her night out dancing and then enjoy a late-night coastal drive to grab the paperwork. 'Yep, that's what I'll do,' Jacob whispered to himself. Maybe Alice would come with him. He hadn't spent enough time with her since buying the Gallantry, and he was aware that it was bothering her. Her demeanour had been distant and a little shut off this past week. *Must try harder* was his mantra for dealing with Alice, yet time had constantly seemed to slip away from him lately.

Tick tock

He heard the slow rotation of the front door's brass lock and the clicking of pins sliding out of place, before the slight pressure change pulled up the hairs on the back of his neck. The cold sea air, pungent with the scent of the ocean, flooded the corridor. Jacob heard Alice hanging up her coat.

Tick tock

'I'm in the office, Pebble,' he called out, while staring blankly at the paperwork in front of him, as he had done for hours. The constant ticking of the wall clock had been mocking him. Its relentless noise was like nails dragging down a blackboard.

Tick tock

Alice wrapped her arms around Jacob's shoulders after she approached him silently from behind. He smiled at her poor attempts at being a second-rate ninja but played along anyway.

'Oh my god, baby, you scared the life out of me, my dear heart is racing,' Jacob said dryly while hiding a playful smile. 'Are you OK, my angel?'

Although she was windswept and full of freckles after a weekend of early summer sunshine, Alice was the absolute picture of grace.

Am I OK? Alice thought about this for a few seconds before dropping herself onto his lap with an exhausted sigh. She leaned into his oncoming kiss and held it for longer than Jacob had accounted for, causing a little gasp as she finally pulled away.

'We need to talk, Jay.'

Tick tock

'You're pregnant?' Jacob choked on the words as they left his mouth almost unwillingly.

Alice stood in the middle of the kitchen, her hands linked gently in front of her waist, almost protecting the asset she had known nothing about just a few hours earlier.

'Yes, Jay. I know it's hard to believe with all the romantic and passion-filled time we haven't been spending together,' said Alice. His unwillingness to look at her gave Alice a strength she never had when his emerald eyes were gazing on her. 'Jacob, you need to talk to me, please.'

You can't do this. You are not your father. You are not half the man he was, the cackle was loud in his mind but for once easily ignored.

Jacob spun around and jumped towards Alice, picking her up in an embrace that took her clean off her feet. He spun her around in a circle that caused her red hair to fan out like a phoenix. 'Alice, this is wonderful news. How you could think that I would react differently is beyond me. I love you, Miss Petalow, with a warmth my heart feels with only you by my side. No being or object comes close to the unbridled joy that you, my heart, have brought me with this news.' Jacob spoke poetically as he dropped her back down to the floor. Her feet skidded on the hardwood flooring.

You are not your father, the voice grew in volume but still struggled to break through Jacob's walls.

'I need to go into work for an hour to pick up these bloody invoices, but I promise I'll be back so we can celebrate. This is a celebration, right?'

Jacob held his Alice tightly, while she struggled to find her voice through what had become a beaming smile.

'Yes, of course, my love,' she said. 'Of course it is.'

With that he picked up his car keys and headed for the front door, with only a brief moment of pause as he took Alice by the hand and kissed her gently on her forehead.

'I love you,' they said in unison, before Alice was left alone to ground herself from the whirlwind that her Jacob had just become.

Jacob and Matt 11pm
Song of the moment:
'Low' by Lenny Kravitz

'I get what you are saying, mate, but brioche burger buns are not getting on that menu just because your latest celebrity chef man crush has convinced all the lonely housewives that it adds a touch of class to a simple dish, and I don't give a flying fuck how good your bastard burger patty is.' Jacob had been talking with his prodigy at the Travelling Trout for the whole journey to the Gallantry, during which time he'd realised that Matt needed the occasional reminder that *Menu by Jacob Brooking* was still emblazoned at the top of the Trout's menu and he was still executive chef there. 'Matt, if you feel the Trout needs a burger to bring a dish to "the people", then you serve it open on some bloody good home-made sourdough or something. Put a bit of theatre, OK, son?' He could hear Matt sigh down the phone, followed by what sounded like an empty mop bucket being kicked.

[77]

'Yes, Chef, I hear you.'

Jacob smiled, as he'd been exactly the same when he was Matt's age, but with experience he'd come to see that Matt needed his reins pulling at times. 'I know it's frustrating, but until your name is above the door – and I promise you it will be one day – you have to toe the line a little.' Jacob slumped into the pitted-green leather armchair and took a deep breath. 'Look how far you've come these past few years – youngest head chef of a three-rosette restaurant in the country, when it seems like yesterday your spotty little arse was turning mushrooms for me in the prep room. I will back you all the way if you come to me with your own ideas and not something you have stolen off a TV chef, and you know I'm bloody right.'

Matt finally conceded and let his defences relax. 'Yes, Chef, I know you're right. I get it. How's Alice getting on since the move?'

Jacob couldn't help but smile, thinking of his conversation with Alice just an hour before, but he knew it was too soon to say anything. He swapped the mobile over to his left hand, freeing up his right to pour a little Tennessee bourbon into his favourite tumbler. The cube of ice he had taken from the bar had lost its structural integrity ten minutes before, but it would do for now. 'She's OK, mate. Her father is still a royal pain in my arse, and I'm not sure how long I'm going to put up with her not backing me when it comes to his relentless difference of opinion. I have a list of people I wouldn't mind dragging through the mire and his name is at the top and underlined in bloody red pen.'

Matt boomed with laughter at Jacob not mincing his words. 'You know Alice, Chef – she doesn't stand up to the big man. Does he at least give you cheap fish still?'

Now it was Jacob's turn to laugh. 'Does he fuck, but you know what, none of it will matter when I get that ring on

Alice's finger, because I'll be damned if I let him keep treating me with such emotionless disdain.'

'Still carrying that chip on your shoulder, I see, Chef,' Matt said playfully.

'Well, I guess you can kiss my arse too, you little turd. Now get back to masturbating over whatever celebrity chef is currently giving you a semi-on, and I'll see you Monday for the summer menu brief, OK?'

Matt chuckled. 'Yes, skipper, see you Monday.'

John Petalow will always hate you, the voice was calm and collected. *You know this, don't you?*

'I do, and I will always hate him,' Jacob whispered.

Jacob and Evan 11.30pm
Song of the moment:
'An Honest Man' by Fantastic Negrito

Jacob threw his phone onto the table and sank the last of his bourbon before standing and straightening himself out in the mirror. 'You got this, Brooking; you need no justification from that bloated old Viking.' He pulled his jacket over his broad shoulders and went to open his office door, only to find it spring open, with the slender figure of Evan standing there to greet him. She looked ridiculously stunning. Like Monroe only better, her hair half up, with ringlets rolling down her shoulders and over her heaving chest, her make-up pristine, and her eyes focused on Jacob. She was dressed all in black, with a skirt that barely contained her dignity and a top that could barely contain her bust.

'Hi, you,' said Evan quietly, but before Jacob could ask why she was here on her night off and especially this late at night, she hushed him by placing a finger on his lips. She pulled her knees together, dragging one foot to the side as if trying to figure out her next move. She reached out for Jacob's hand as she noticed him taking her in. Evan stood tall in stiletto heels that finished in an ankle boot, her legs toned and muscular for a woman so slim, and infinitely longer than they needed to be for the height of the girl. Her black skirt and thin-strapped summer top could have looked whorish on anyone else, but a short-line leather jacket and a low-slung belt that served no purpose other than an aesthetic one brought the whole thing together with style.

'Evan,' said Jacob, 'are you a bit drunk or a lot drunk?'

He could not take his eyes off Evan's lips, which looked ready to explode at the mere mention of imminent pressure.

'Just a little bit, boss,' she said. Their hands played delicately with each other. 'But I have to say, I'm drunk enough.' She pulled him into her, sinking her hot wet tongue into his wanting mouth.

Tick tock

'Evan, what are you doing?'

Jacob recoiled in shock, falling into his armchair like a ball into a catcher's mitt, pulling his fingers to his lips as if poisoned by a venomous snake.

'Don't play coy with me, Mr Brooking. That wasn't the kiss of a man that didn't want to be kissed, and I've not missed the signals you've been throwing my way.' Evan followed him to his chair and mounted him, not unlike a lady side-saddling a stallion. 'I know what you want,' she said with both a hiccup and a smile.

Jacob jumped to his feet, spinning her around in the process of trying to maintain her equilibrium. He pinned her by the waist so that she was half sitting on his desk.

'Oh, Jay.' Evan bit her lip before pushing all the paperwork on the desk to the floor. 'Right here, is this where you want me?'

Take her.

'Evan, I have neither the vocabulary nor the time to tell you how very beautiful you are to me, or to tell you how much brighter my days are with you by my side.' Jacob took her opposite hand in his. His worn and calloused fingers interlinked with her slender digits, which were tipped with deep scarlet pointed nails. 'But we can never be more than we are right now.'

Evan looked at him quizzically but with a wanton desire. 'What we are right now? What exactly is that, Jay?' Her free hand rose up to stroke Jacob's stubbled jaw. She leaned in to kiss him, this time with a gentle certainty that told Jacob this wasn't just the drink talking. As Evan's full lips touched his own, he felt no desire, none whatsoever, to pull away.

She's beautiful, the voice soothed.

She's much more … us.

Jacob raised his own free hand and ran it through her golden locks until he was cradling her head in a kiss that grew increasingly into something that might overcome them.

Tick tock

The clock snapped Jacob back to the real world – one where he was staring into the abyss of the situation he was falling into.

'Evan, you need to go.' Jacob spoke softly but with purpose, yet he was still to move his hand from her neck and their foreheads still touched.

[81]

'OK, Jay,' Evan said, kissing him a few times more for effect. 'But we do need to talk about this tomorrow, so dinner at mine after work, please. Don't let me down.'

You need to do this.

'OK, Evan, I'll be there.'

She leaned in and kissed his lips one last time, while her hands spun him around so that he was pushed tightly against the desk. Her hands dropped down between his thighs and rose to squeeze the growing bulge that had appeared unknowingly in his jeans.

'Until tomorrow, my love,' she called while power-walking out of the office door.

Tick tock

Jacob slumped back into his armchair to try and figure out where the ticking clock was sounding from, as there was no such device in his work office.

Chapter 9: Alice and the Looking Glass
Song of the day
"Night Blindness" by David Gray

Spring 2004
Knightsbridge, London UK

Jacob couldn't take his eyes off her. But he couldn't breathe. Her face had never looked more radiant, and her eyes shone with supernatural power, the blue almost seducing him to drop to his knees. Still he couldn't breathe. Her hair seemed longer and fuller than ever before. Like November fire, it lit up the darkness that surrounded them. Yet he still couldn't breathe. Her voice was gentle and kind, yet she was crying, and as he stood opposite her on that dark plateau outside of Medway Hospital, he couldn't draw breath, as she repeated over and over, 'This is what you wanted, right, baby?' She was holding a stillborn child in her arms, in front of her blood-soaked white gown.

Jacob woke up screaming. Tears flooded his face as he searched for Alice in the dark. His fingers wrapped around her and he pulled her closer than ever before while he tried to control his breathing.

'Baby, what's wrong?' asked Alice, as she struggled to open her eyes and wipe the dribble from her lips.

'Nothing's wrong, baby. Nothing at all. Just a dream.'

THE WRONG LIFE WAS TAKEN AND YOU KNOW IT.
SHE WILL NEVER FORGIVE YOU.
MURDERER...

Dr Vivian Phillips sat next to Alice on a long green chesterfield sofa that wouldn't have looked out of place in the Nome King's palace from her favourite film. Alice had always felt a kinship with Dorothy, and right now she wished a flying monkey would grab her and take her back to Oz and the Emerald Palace. Indeed, Alice looked on in complete awe as the doctor perched on the edge of her sofa, appearing to be the spitting image of Judy Garland herself. The same age as Alice's mother, she carried herself like a movie star from the 1940s. In fact, there was a photograph on her desk that Alice could have sworn was Veronica Lake, but in actuality it was the good doctor on her wedding day many years before. She was the sexiest woman Alice had ever seen, and yet not one inch of flesh was on show. But the respect Alice held for the doctor was not because of her stunning good looks, but due to her absolute command of everything in the room. When Alice had first entered her domain, she had felt trust and respect for everything Doctor Phillips was offering. Her office was filled with books and memorabilia from her travels. There were golden artefacts from Egypt and South America and silks from India and Thailand. Vivian Phillips hadn't graduated and opened a practice here in London. She had lived. And she had knowledge that couldn't be taught, but could only be found through exploration. Alice had been waved over to sit on the green couch while the doctor had finished a phone conversation in what Alice thought was fluent Italian. After hanging up, she had joined Alice holding an expensive leather-bound notepad and fountain pen and had offered her a drink in a soft, well-spoken Hertfordshire accent. Alice doubted Dr Phillips had ever said a single word without intent. Procrastination did not seem her forte.

Alice felt at ease. But she knew in her heart that no lie she told would be bought by her adversary, so she wasn't even going to try. She pulled the cushion from behind her back and held it across her stomach. Failing at first to find the words she needed and had hoped to find the strength for, she looked at Dr Phillips for help.

'Alice, it's OK. Don't feel rushed because I'm here. Let it come naturally. Tell me about the baby.'

'The baby?' Alice had a tremble in her voice. 'Jacob wasn't happy when he found out I was pregnant. In fact, quite the opposite.' She adjusted herself on the chair. 'I was afraid to tell him, especially with the restaurant doing so well and the wedding planning taking so much of our spare time.'

Dr Phillips leaned in towards her. 'How was Jacob's involvement in the wedding?'

'Minimal to say the least. He would always find a reason to work his day off. It feels like he is changing his mind.'

This came out more like a question she was trying to answer rather than the statement she had intended to make.

'I know it's not easy for him,' she continued. 'He gets a hard time from my family, especially my father, who has never welcomed his presence in my life.'

Alice spoke from the heart, and it was plain to see for Dr Phillips that because of the love she held for Jacob, it hurt her to see him struggle so.

'He's never been allowed to feel like he's enough for me,' Alice went on. 'He puts his heart and soul into improving himself and the business so someone will cut him some slack and remove that chip from his shoulder.' Alice exhaled slowly. 'I just wish he could see the truth.'

'What truth is that, Alice?'

'That he was always enough to me. That this idea that he has to lock horns with my father means nothing to me, and actually I think that battle ended without him realising many years ago. He is what he is and my father's the same. There is no judgement there, so, honestly, I think he is fighting himself.'

Alice stood up and walked over to the window, which had a beautiful view over Notting Hill Park.

'He gets so angry when he's challenged,' she said, 'yet I feel the argument he ends up having is completely internal. Like all his thoughts and ideas contradict each other.'

'So, no joy for your big news then.' The doctor's tone was still calm and gentle.

'He was happy for a minute, before he seemed to confuse himself with how this might play out. Then anger kicked in, like I'd ruined a plan I knew nothing about.' Alice paused and looked to the floor. 'Then he asked me to have the abortion.'

'Just like that?' the doctor asked.

'No, not quite. He said we should consider our priorities – that the business needed us and that the wedding needed to come first, before we properly planned our family life together.'

'He said all the right things to convince you?'

'I guess so. But as conflicted as he seemed, I do believe he meant what he was saying.'

'Did he go with you? You were 18 weeks – that's not an easy process.' The doctor patted the couch next to her. 'Was there any support?'

Alice moved and sat back down beside the doctor. 'He dropped me off and picked me up the following day – if you can call that support.'

'Did you tell him that they found the baby still on your arrival?'

'Honestly, I didn't see the point. I guess the outcome was the same regardless, so why complicate things?'

'And how do you feel now, Alice?'

'About Jay?' Alice asked.

'About the baby, Alice.'

'Hollow. I thought I was making the wrong choice but for the right person. And, yes, before you say anything, I know that's wrong and stupid beyond measure, but I guess now I know that whatever choice I had made would have been irrelevant. It's made me question if I even deserve to be a mother.'

'I'm not here to judge your choices, Alice. I'm here to guide you to your own answers. How do you feel about Jacob now?'

'I constantly hear myself in the mirror. It tells me I'm not good enough for him, that I hold him back and that I'm not pretty enough for him and that he deserves more than I offer. And sometimes I think it's right.'

'Yet all the other people in your life say the opposite. Why do you think that is?'

'Because they don't know my Jacob,' Alice snapped back, all of a sudden feeling less like Dorothy and more like Alice tumbling down a rabbit hole.

Chapter 10: Father of the Bride
Song of the day
"A Beautiful Mine" by RJD2

Autumn 2005
Camber, East Sussex, UK

There was a thunderous knock at the door.

'Come in,' Jacob shouted with gay abandon. He didn't have much time, and his blasted tie wasn't falling right at all, but he was doing his best to look presentable on his wedding day. Of all days, surely this was the one on which his tie must hang impeccably. Jacob looked over his shoulder to see the hulking figure of Alice's father squeezing into the small room, much like a rhino trying to turn around in an elevator. His father-in-law was an intimidating man to everyone. Even the muscular frame of Jacob seemed quite pathetic compared to the behemoth that was John Petalow, and it wasn't even muscle that made the man so big; he was just huge, his arms like tree trunks and his barrelled body like a samurai's suit of armour. It was Jacob's hotel, but even he would have been hard-pressed to take the much larger bridal suite off his fiancée, so they would have to dance around each other here.

'What can I do for you, John? I must confess, I'm a little pressed for time,' Jacob said as he turned back to the mirror.

Don't turn your back on him, you fool, said the voice in a shrill and almost surprised voice.

In the next few minutes, Jacob would realise two things: firstly, that his years of training at the gym and playing rugby for Canterbury meant absolutely nothing when it came down to life and death; and, secondly, that the monster in his head didn't always lie to get him into trouble.

John Petalow's hands were like shovels, and as he gripped Jacob's neck from behind, much like an adult lion might carry a new-born cub, there was nothing Jacob could do to escape. His face was smashed up against the mirror in front of him, causing a crack that ran from top to bottom. Jacob tried to speak out in protest at the violence being forced on him, but his oppressor's massive hand was restraining his airway to the point that nothing but a whimper was escaping his throat.

'Son, of all the things I am known for, after breaking necks, the thing I am known for most is never forgetting, and I remember saying to you many years ago, when you sat in front of me, begging, like a dog, to take my Alice from me, I said, "If you're talking, then you are not listening, and right now I need you to listen." I remember those words clearly.' John Petalow leaned in close to Jacob's ear and, in a low growl, said, 'Jacob, do you remember those words? Nod once if you do, OK?'

Jacob felt his head nod once as John's hand shook him like a rag doll.

'Good. Now the same rules apply. So when I let go, you are not going to speak, because I need you to listen. Nod again if you comprehend what I'm saying.'

Jacob once again felt the involuntary shake of his neck result in the most basic of nods, and then he felt himself released. He crashed down to one knee and drew breath like never before, although he showed enough resolve to stand and face John, knowing better than to say anything. He gritted his teeth and prepared for the bullshit "if you ever hurt my daughter" speech that he was certain was coming.

He was wrong. And the next few words out of John's mouth knocked the colour out of Jacob's tanned skin and the broadness out of his shoulders.

'I know about you and Evan Laurie. You were seen by my delivery driver, at the crack of dawn the other day. He had ten kilos of Scottish salmon for you that he couldn't get a signature for. Why? Well, I'm glad you asked. It was because when he went to find you, you had that restaurant manager of yours bent over your desk. Tell me, Jacob, am I missing anything so far? Nope? Then I shall carry on.'

As he spoke, John never took his eyes off Jacob's, and Jacob felt smaller with every second that the gaze fell over him.

'You had the fucking cheek to ring me a few hours later, to tell me, ME, just how disappointed you were that my delivery drivers have stopped bothering to ask for a signature when they leave their invoice. "It's just bloody lazy" were your words. The thing is, that delivery driver wouldn't have said a word to me had I not called him into the office to reprimand him on your behalf. Does that taste good, Jacob? Because I hope you choke on that fucking irony.'

John finally turned his back on Jacob.

'This is what we are going to do,' he said, in a quieter tone, knowing that he didn't have to shout anymore to be heard. 'I will not have Alice hurt. As much as I detest your very existence in her life, it would destroy her to know what you are, so you cannot tell her, and no one else can know, so you need to manage that slut you are keeping.'

Jacob raised himself up to his true height. 'She's not a slut, John.'

The Viking king responded in kind and instantly towered over Jacob's false bravado. 'You have some fucking cheek, son, fucking fronting up to me. I will tear your cunting face off. Sit down, SIT FUCKING DOWN.'

Jacob did as he was told in an instant so that his lecture could continue.

'You have 12 months. That's time to build the business and sort out your double life. In 12 months we are going to talk about this, and if your affairs are not in order and Evan is not long gone, then I will take Alice from you, and bury you in a travellers' field.'

He reached down and grabbed Jacob's shoulder with such force that Jacob almost buckled in half like an accordion.

'Jacob, I can't emphasise this enough, do you understand me?'

Jacob nodded.

'Then I will say no more, and I will go and tend to my daughter before her big day begins. I'll see you out there, son. Don't let me down.'

What will you do now?

Jacob took a pocket square to the trickle of blood running down his forehead. *As we are told,* thought Jacob.

We do not answer to him and I fear no physical power that he possesses, said the creature with venom.

Then what do you fear? Creature in my thoughts, voice that watches me trip up at every hurdle while apparently giving me advice to survive. What do you fear? WHAT? Asked Jacob without parting his lips.

WE FEAR EVAN!

And you have no idea what you are doing, do you, child?

'Did I ever really know what I was doing?' Jacob voiced in reply.

YOU LOOK DISGUSTING.

No, I don't. Not today I don't. I'm not listening to you.

Alice in truth looked more divine than ever before. It was a virtually impossible task to dress her up in anything that would increase her desirability as a woman. But today was no ordinary day. Her classic dovetailed ivory wedding dress hugged her delicate size-eight frame, which only a woman as humble as her couldn't have appreciated having. The clean and uncluttered dress fell strapless from her petite bustline, hanging on as though by invisible wizardry all the way down her body until the most delicate curve of her hip broke the angle just a touch, before the dress fell once again into a simple fantail spread out behind her. The thinnest of splits running from the ground to just past her knee revealed the most exquisite of strapped heels, with ribbon running from the shoe and looping three times around her ankle and lower calf. The tall, slender heel would have been a nightmare to walk in for anyone without the lightness of movement this angel had always possessed. Her hair was tied back for the first time in what seemed like forever, not counting the simple plait she threw in each night before bed. A tight bun crowned her head, with diamonds, studs and slivers of silver hairclips catching the light every time she moved. These were matched by a diamond bracelet that her mother had given her that morning as a wedding gift. A necklace she had picked out herself as an engagement present fell between her cleavage, where a slender V cut out of the dress line revealed more of her inner and lower breast than her father would have approved of had he been part of the buying process. The tiny stone that hung from the white gold pendant sitting just below the centre of her breasts highlighted their ample shape all the more. Only the sapphire on her engagement ring broke the colour code. 'You're too unconventional for a diamond engagement ring,' Jacob had said, reminding her that she was unique. 'You shouldn't wear the same ring as all the other brides.' But at least it had matched her eyes.

She looked to die for. And no voice, real or otherwise, would make her believe a different viewpoint. Not today.

They were to be married on the beach just down from their restaurant in Camber. It was a beautiful day with crystal-clear skies and a gentle breeze, which stopped the guests, in shirts and ties and stunning summer frocks with matching hats, from overheating. Alice hadn't seen it herself yet, but her bridesmaid had reported a scene like Ladies' Day at Royal Ascot, as they waited for the most beautiful of them all to arrive.

The Gallantry had made a wonderful effort for its owners. The bridal suite was dressed in white and orange rose petals, and more than a hundred little gift boxes from the staff were arranged in the corner, all wearing burnt-tan ribbons. Alice felt like the princess she hoped she looked like. If only just for a day, she thought.

Alice took one more deep breath and took herself in for the last time top to bottom. The beech mirror stood seven feet from floor to ceiling and for once her reflection was her own. It seemed like the doubting voice in her was silenced completely. The witch that haunted her days was nowhere to be seen, and Alice prayed it would stay that way. A noise startled her from her blind side, and she adjusted her view in the mirror ever so slightly to see her father standing there proudly.

'You look wonderful, monkey,' he said adoringly while placing a reassuring hand on her shoulder.

She knew she would always be monkey to him, just as he would always be Pappa Bear. The only thing she had never doubted was the love she received from her mum and dad.

The only thing you have never doubted?

Really?

WHAT DOES THAT TELL YOU ABOUT YOUR PRECIOUS FIANCÉ?

She shook her head clear and sat on the edge of the mattress, trying her best not to crease the masterpiece she was wrapped in.

Her father joined her on the queen-sized bed and took her tiny hand in his shovel-like palms. 'You look just like your mother on our wedding day, and it never ceases to amaze me just how alike you both are in beauty and in soul.'

'Don't be silly, Dad. Mum is much more beautiful than I am.'

'And she would say the same thing about you, Alice Marie, and that is why you are both so beautiful to me.'

He looked down, as though composing himself.

'Listen,' he said. 'I've never liked Jacob.'

'NOOOOOOOO! Really? I have never picked up on that,' Alice giggled.

'Just listen, you little diva. I'm trying to impart some knowledge here. He works hard, he's ambitious, he provides for you, and I guess some really distant people might squint and find him an attractive man. So have you ever thought to ask me why I don't like him?'

'I just always assumed it was because he was so bloody flaky at times. So inconsistent.'

John Petalow laughed with a deep bellow. 'Yes, inconsistent for sure – and full of himself. But no – it's because he reminds me of me in one very specific way.'

Alice chose not to comment and instead let her father move the story forward at his own pace. It was rare to hear him open up like this, and she felt honoured to be part of the conversation.

'When I met your mum, well, I wasn't a good man. The war had taken its toll on me and I had blood on my hands.'

Alice was surprised to hear him mention the Falklands, as it was a subject everyone avoided with him. 'But I thought you knew Mum from school?'

'I did know her, but she never knew me. I was a big ungainly rugby oaf, and she was the prom queen. She was all class, and I'm not sure she noticed me until the day I returned home. She was working the bar at the welcome home party. It was at the Ship and Winkle Inn, just down from your grandad's house. She grafted all night, while a load of us battered young veterans sat quietly, not talking about what we had seen and done on that shitty little island.

'I got talking to her after more than a few pints of Guinness had restored some of the courage I seemed to be missing.'

Alice was engrossed in this story – a story she had only ever heard in snippets from her mother.

'That night, as we said goodnight, she placed a hand on my cheek and said, "John, I am going to fix you."

'And as I looked into her eyes – the mirror of yours – I knew that as long as she was with me, she would never have to fix me, as it's her very presence that fixes and completes me.

'And that's what scares me.'

Alice was both concerned and confused. 'What, Pappa?'

'I know you look at him the way your mum looks at me. I know he needs you to fix him the way your mum fixes me.

'But I know what I did. I know where I have been to be broken, what I have done to others to be broken, and I know what I am always capable of, with only your mum being the difference between the man I am and the wreck that I could have been.

'But I look at Jacob and I honestly don't know what he has done or what he is capable of to be so broken that you look at him the way your very tolerant mother looks at me.

'But I'm being silly.' He smiled. 'You clearly both love each other, and despite what you all think, that has always been enough for me.'

Her father rose to his feet and offered his arm. 'Shall we? It's time, my beautiful girl.'

Alice rose and looped her arm into his. She smiled and kissed her dad gently on the cheek before turning to exit for the short walk down to the beach. Catching herself briefly in the mirror and noticing her skin looked a little grey, she heard her reflection whisper to her.

But you know what he's capable of.
YOU KNOW.

'Yeah, I know,' she whispered, as she held her stomach ever so tenderly.

Chapter 11: Living by the Sword

Song of the day
"You Know I'm No Good" by Amy Winehouse

Winter 2005
Old Romney, Kent UK

'Look what you made me do,' Evan spat, as Jacob ground his jaw to take the sting out of the slap that had woken his bones from a long day in the kitchen. Evan couldn't really hurt Jacob in a physical way. Despite being a more imposing figure than Alice by virtue of her dancer's body, she still gave up seven stone to his very broad frame, and he sometimes wondered if not really hurting him was the exact reason she hit him; she got to release her frustration on Jacob, who was strong enough to shrug it off and would just stay quiet while taking the occasional blow on the chin. There had been one occasion when she had really wanted to make him feel pain. When he had shrugged off an open hand, with no sign even of a whimper, she had let her frustration get the better of her and scratched his face with her long, sharp, painted nails – a method she employed knowing full well that he would have to explain the injury to Alice somehow. This had left Jacob with a conundrum of sorts: he didn't want to show Evan any kind of weakness, and yet he could certainly do without Alice finding out about the affair he had unknowingly started three months prior. He decided that the easiest thing to do was to wince, clench his jaw and pretend that she had hurt him in more ways than merely stripping away his masculinity every time they got into a fight.

'Evan, you know I have to consider her role in this. She owns half of the company by default – a company you work for. Do you really want that drama?'

Jacob was trying to shrink himself down so that Evan would feel she was fully in control of all aspects of this situation. This wasn't his first dance with her.

She turned her back on Jacob and shook her giant blonde mane like she was trying to regain some form of composure, but Jacob knew this was only the beginning of this evening's games. 'I don't remember you being too worried about Alice and her role in the company when you wanted your dick sucked, Jay, so don't give me that shit. GOD, YOU ARE SO FRUSTRATING.'

Jacob had been trying to work his way out of this relationship since the minute it had started, but when Evan wanted something, she got it, and Jacob had found it easier to nod and agree to everything she wanted rather than start a fight, and that had included sex. He had to admit that the sex was amazing – not that it wasn't with Alice, but it was aggressive and lascivious in an almost primitive and carnal way. It was the only time he felt in charge of the situation with her. So, it happened a lot and often after a blazing row like this.

'I need to head home tonight, Ev. You know this. I can't just not go home.'

He knew instantly he had said something wrong. Evan turned back around to face him, with hate filling her eyes.

'HOME, JAY?' She threw her hands towards the ground in childish frustration, and angry tears glossed her eyes. 'You know, there was a time when you wanted to be "home" with me, Jay. When did that change?'

Jacob was acting slow but thinking fast about how to get out of this situation. 'Baby, you know what I meant. You know how I feel about you, about us.'

Evan stepped dangerously close to Jacob's space and was shaking with an adrenaline-fuelled rage. 'No, Jacob, I don't know how you feel about me, because I'm this big fucking secret, am I not? Do we go out with my friends or my family? No, we don't, because of how you feel for your precious Alice and her love for you.'

Evan swung for Jacob once more and was surprised to see him catch her wrist just before her open hand connected with his cheek. For a second, they paused, looking each other up and down, waiting for an opening to appear.

Hahahahahahaha!

The creature's laugh threw Jacob, giving Evan the avenue of attack that she needed. She brought her left hand up and caught him with a glancing blow to the temple. Jacob snapped and pushed her forcefully away, his muscular frame sending his athletic but slender opponent tumbling onto and across the huge bed behind her, leaving her crumpled on the floor on the other side of it.

Fool! She will definitely tell Alice now, the creature mocked and warned all at the same time.

'Baby, I'm sorry.' Jacob rushed over to Evan's prone body. He helped her sit upright, realising with relief that she wasn't physically hurt. He witnessed the first real tears he had ever seen her cry. He put his hands on her cheeks and kissed her on the lips – a kiss that was unreturned.

'Baby, I'll sort it, I promise,' he said, kissing her once more, getting a little more return than the first time.

'Promise me we can do something with my friends at the weekend, Jay. I don't want to be a secret forever.'

Jacob kissed her again before he whispered exactly what she needed to hear. 'I promise, Ev.'

Liar! the voice shouted.

'I'm sorry I hurt you,' Jacob said, pulling her forehead against his own.

LIAR! the voice screamed.

'I'm sorry, too, baby,' Evan said, pressing her lips passionately against his.

I want Alice to find out, the voice snorted. Because then I can get to her as well. I wonder if her broken-hearted disappointment will taste as good as your constantly sweet fear of conflict. Let's see, shall we?

Jacob could hear every word the voice was saying but chose to push it to the back of his mind. One battle at a time was all he had to win to survive. *Just get through the next few hours*, he kept thinking, over and over. *Just get home to Alice, and tomorrow can take care of itself.*

Coward, screamed the voice, *you're a coward and a fraud.*

I know, Jacob replied in his mind, before pulling Evan up onto the bed. His lips lightly fluttered against her belly as he pulled down her black silk shorts, which were already wet with excitement. *When have I ever denied those monikers, my old friend?*

I'm not your friend, Jacob, the creature snapped.

'Then why the hell do you KEEP TALKING TO ME!!!!!!!!' Screamed Jacob, drawing a confused look from Evan.

Chapter 12: Triggered
Song of the day
"How Can You Mend a Broken Heart" by Al Green

Winter 2006
Camber, Kent UK

Jacob Brooking had been sitting on the tiny gardening stool opposite his father's memorial stone for two hours. A fine rain had turned to mist in the warm air and left him feeling like he had got dressed after a shower without drying himself properly. Yet he had found it impossible to leave his father's side. He felt comfort here and a peace that often eluded him. The day was drawing to a close and the sun was slowly meeting the world's end as the light began to fade. The temperature was going to drop soon enough, and Alice would be upset if she got home to an empty house once again. Jacob knew he should go home, to save his own hide, if nothing else. But something had stopped him leaving. Not something he could understand, not something physical. Just something subtle that he couldn't quite comprehend the origin of. There was a voice, soft but full of malice and sharp intellect. A voice that sounded familiar yet alien and not of this earth. A voice that resonated from his own head and seemed to follow him everywhere, except, for some reason, this particular spot.

The creature had no master and yet could not leave this place. It hated the man. The man who had imprisoned it here in this hollow of darkness, surrounded by webs of vanity and self-indulgence. Jacob, it had suspected he was called, although over the years the other man things had called him many different names. But it was irrelevant to the creature. Its hate was real and justified, so the man's moniker mattered little.

The creature hated the fact that without the poor excuse for a human, it couldn't exist. It hated that more than anything. That the prison holding it here would let it see the open world through the eyes of the man but would not let it escape. Well, not for long periods of time, at least. The dripping-wet leathery skin of the creature trembled as it began to move. Like a monster straight from the darkness of the Mariana Trench, it writhed on a bed of long tentacles, each covered with an array of suckers and barbs. Its oversized head was too heavy for its body to support easily. It slunk slowly from its exposed space, its long black tentacles pulling it forward one after another, each making a slapping sound as it whipped down on the moist ground. The creature was so black that it seemed light was scared to touch it, although amazingly its eyes still shone like lifeless ebony beacons. As empty as the voids above, the eyes seemed so reflective that a person might see their own soul looking back at them, if they were unlucky enough to be in the presence of such a creature.

The creature pulled itself into a dark corner of the man's mind, its octopus-like body able to fit into places its mass shouldn't have allowed. It wrapped its wet, slime-ridden tentacles around the frame of the nest it had found and backed into it as far as the nest would accommodate, looking somewhat like one of the shiny black spiders that live in tunnelled holes in your garden wall, its dripping maw grinding against itself in constant frustration. It had a three-pronged version of a beak, like that of a bird of prey, in place of a mouth. Its words were not spoken; instead, they resonated within the air. The man didn't deserve the happiness he felt, didn't deserve anything of the sort, and the creature wouldn't let him be happy. Couldn't let him be happy. He would get only the pain the creature would reflect on him from its own tortured existence. But the creature couldn't kill him. It knew this, knew it needed him to survive. But it would make him suffer. It would make him hurt and it would enjoy the feeling.

The creature's massive eyes blinked as it thought of all the times it had ventured outside of the man's mind. It took a tremendous amount of effort to leave the prison, and even then it was only possible when the man was weak and his guard was down. But it was always worth it. To see him scared, to see him hurt and to see him fall. Each time, the creature would push a little further, a little harder and for a little longer. But the creature would always retreat when the man's blood flowed. The creature, with no concept of an afterlife, was unsure what would happen to it if the man never woke. But it was sure their paths were linked in such a way that they could never travel alone. So it would always retreat when the man hurt himself, although it would savour every drop of blood that drained from him. And for a time it would be content.

It closed its soulless eyes one last time to rest. It had toyed with him today, had whispered terrible things in his ear. Just enough to create a little doubt. Just enough to make him hate himself the way the creature hated him. It hadn't even had to be specific. Single words often enough.

Ugly.

Useless.

Pathetic.

He was easy to throw off his confident stride. For all his muscles, he was weak of will. He was still the child that had spawned the creature all those years before. But even toying with the man was exhausting for the beast. It needed to rest, and it would leave him be for a few days while it regained its strength. Its mind slowed as it fell into a grave slumber. But the hatred was still there. It was always there. Its maw still gritted. The prison that the man kept the creature in would be its playground. But it was still a prison regardless. One of flesh and of bone. The creature opened its mouth to yawn one last time before it fell deeply into the abyss, and at that moment Jacob breathed out, and for the first time on that rainy Saturday, he felt a little better as he raised himself up. He folded up his little stool that had been his perch and headed back towards the car.

'Goodbye, Pops,' he whispered, as the creature turned in the sleep of the wicked, thoughtless and content with the work it had done.

'To what do I owe the pleasure of your company?' Jacob asked with a tremor in his voice akin to a young boy asking for an answer he didn't want.

He couldn't be doing this, could he? Could he really be hiding under the cover of darkness from a malevolent evil he thought was long gone? He was sandwiched tightly between the wall and the sports mattress he'd had made specially to try and ease the constant ache in his shoulder. The ache had been with him since he had attempted to swan-dive into a crystal-clear lake in Connecticut one summer's evening while on holiday with his parents. The water had been so clear he could see the bottom like it was a high-definition photograph, but he had misjudged the depth on a giant level and had crunched fairly conclusively into a heap in barely six feet of water. Almost unwilling to climb out of the water due to his embarrassment, Jacob eventually broke the surface and did an amazing job of hiding the dislocated limb's searing pain. The pain from that incident had never healed. He had vowed that day that he would never again do anything stupid to impress a girl. He wished that he had kept this promise, as 'You shouldn't have done that' seemed to be the sentence he used most in his life.

He had come into the room to look for an old photo of his dad when the radio, which was playing Absolute Soul throughout the house, had stopped him in his tracks. 'How Can You Mend a Broken Heart' started to play – the classic Al Green version, not the original Bee Gees one or the poorly constructed Pendergrass version. His dad's favourite song. At first it warmed his soul to hear it, especially while he was looking for something related to his old man. But the longer the song played, the wider his eyes dilated, and the faster his heart raced.

WHY DIDN'T YOU MOURN? The voice screeched.
DO YOU THINK I'D FORGOTTEN, CHILD?
And suddenly he was 12 years old again.

1991

The Medway towns were not an amazing place to grow up. This commuter area just outside London was apparently coastal, but Jacob, like everyone else, refused to believe that being attached to the Thames river's filthy largest estuary made it coastal. But it was home. And it was all he had ever known.

It was a Sunday morning in late September, and that same song he could hear playing in the recess of his mind was playing on the old radio that Dad had used whenever a garden choir had beckoned. Mum was in the kitchen, as she always was on a Sunday. One of her fantastic roast dinners was en route – god, he could taste it. It was beef, no doubt about it. Overcooked and dry as a desert summer, but somehow it would still be delicious. Not one for following British protocol, Mrs Brooking would make sure there would be mint sauce and stuffing to go with the Yorkshire pudding. It may not have been traditional, but it was their tradition. The Brooking way.

Dad was mowing the lawn and Peepo was chasing him round the garden. The young Labrador puppy was as scared of the lawnmower as she was the Hoover, but would always chase and bark rather than flee, a flight animal she was not. Paul Brooking pushed the old green mower around the garden with a strength Jacob knew he would never have. His dad was a great man. A man some would say he idolised too much, making the task of filling his shoes in the future impossible. But it was because of him that Jacob Brooking of London Road in Rainham, Kent, had led a safe and happy childhood. He owed his mother and father an unpayable debt. And it was that debt that would forever overshadow his own achievements.

Suddenly, without noticing the day go, it was dark and no one was with him. He could hear his mother asking him to go to bed, but he couldn't see her. It was school tomorrow, and he struggled to get up in the morning. He looked through the rear patio door to where his dad had been in the garden just seconds before, but no one was there. The light was fading fast and not in a way that looked natural to him. It was more like some giant mythical god had poured a pot of black paint over the end of the garden, and the void-like mass was moving slowly towards the house, trying to envelop his home. He ran upstairs to his bedroom, busting in the door with as much force as a 12-year-old boy could muster, and leapt onto his top bunk. The bottom bed was empty since his baby brother had demanded his own room. Jacob quickly hid his toes from whatever might be lurking outside of the quilt's protection and pulled his Sony Walkman out from under his pillow. Seeking the protection of his music, he checked the tape. *American Anthems*. A collection of songs that a friend had given to his dad, which had now been passed down to Jacob in the hope it might grow his knowledge of great music. Peter Cetera came on and he was safe. All was good again.

Jacob knew this was a dream. He knew full well he wasn't 12 years old anymore. But he was home. So how could he be down? Well, unless this wasn't a dream. Unless it was school tomorrow. Where the bullies were. Where Simeon Bennett would terrorise him. Where he would spend every lesson trying to hide in plain sight so as not to get noticed. Jacob would of course pretend to be sick in the morning, as he did every day. It worked at least once a week. It amazed him that not one person ever commented on this. How had no one noticed? He'd had one day off sick every single week for five years in a row. Maybe they did notice. Maybe no one cared.

With the quilt pulled up to his nose and 'Glory of Love' playing loudly in his ear, he looked into the dark opposite corner of the room. Waiting for it to appear. As it always did. But nothing yet rose from the shadows. Maybe

tonight would be different. Maybe it had left him. Maybe …
His Walkman slowed a little, as though the batteries were
dying, and then with a sharp whine it stopped. The curtains
swayed in the draft from the window that his mum would
never close, and the moonlight broke through like a laser just
for a moment. And it was there. The light caught it for a
second. Pure blackness like obsidian liquid. It writhed and
grew quickly. Leaking darkness, it slunk across the ground like
one of the jelly octopuses he had thrown against the wall as a
child to watch climb down as if alive. It moved unnaturally in
a way only a creature with no bones could move. Jacob's
breathing was now so intense that he swore his heart would
burst as the black kraken reached the foot of his bed. As it did
every night, it pulled itself up onto his bunk one wet black limb
at a time, reaching under his blanket to wrap itself tightly like
a python around his ankle. Jacob felt the powerful pinch of its
barbed suckers attach to his flesh. It pulled with the force of a
thousand horses, and he disappeared into the darkness
he knew and feared so much.

2006

His eyes opened bloodshot and filled with tears. He was back
in his marital bedroom. And he was back staring at the
writhing black shadow in the corner. He couldn't yet see it –
rather, he could see where it wasn't. Once again, the light
seemed to avoid its very touch. But like his childhood, this
kraken struck fear into him with a different weapon. He wasn't
a kid anymore. He was 17 stone of muscle and sinew. He had
been afraid of nothing in a physical sense for years. So the
beast didn't reach for him. In fact, it backed away. Expanding
its shadow against the wall, it increased in size and stature, like
a midnight-coloured peacock.

ALICE WON'T TOUCH YOU BECAUSE YOU'RE
DISGUSTING. YOUR BODY, YOU CLOTHING AND YOUR
WHOLE DEMEANOUR REEKS OF FAILURE.

The sound came from his own mind, despite the creature in front of him clearly being the source.

SHE MOCKS YOU. YOU HEAR HER FAMILY SAY YOU'RE NOT ENOUGH. GIVE UP!

I can't, Jacob whimpered. *I love her. I know I don't deserve her, but I love her.*

NO, YOU DON'T, YOU LOVE YOU.

Why are you back? I haven't seen you in years.

YOU'RE AS DISAPPOINTING AS A HUSBAND AS YOU WERE A SON, HOW WAS YOUR FATHER'S FUNERAL, BY THE WAY? I NOTICED YOU DIDN'T CRY, YOUR MUM MUST HAVE BEEN SICKENED BY YOU.

He had wanted to cry. His heart was broken. He just couldn't. He had felt hollow and couldn't feel the emotions he had wanted to feel on the outside that dark day. But he had felt them a thousand times over every day since.

YOU WERE NOT THE SON HE DESERVED AND YOUR TEARS MEAN NOTHING NOW.

Jacob reached up to his stung eye sockets and noticed he was crying his eyes out. He was also shaking like an untethered washing machine. But worst of all, he felt like he was sinking into the carpet. He was definitely slipping into the floor around him. No, he wasn't sinking; he was shrinking. He was already half the size of his adult self. Now he was smaller and lighter than he ever remembered being, his clothes draped over him like loose robes. His heart raced as he felt powerless once more. Before he could react to what was happening, the shadow tentacle reached forward, sensing his childlike fear, and gripped him tightly around his legs with so much force he felt like his bones were shattering. Then, with a thundercloud-like clap of noise, he was yanked into the shadows and awoke underwater.

The kraken was wrapped around his lower torso now, and he was being dragged deeper with each second. As he thrashed around for air, he could see the moon as a pinprick of light above the surface. He couldn't escape. He could barely move at all. He could feel a beak biting at his ankles, and the water around him warmed as it filled with his own blood, heating him and somehow choking him at the same time. Water was filling his lungs, and the more he tried to scream, the more water got in. Through the sheer panic, he didn't notice what was saving him. The more he bled, the less the kraken gripped him. The blade-like maw of the creature was sharper than a surgeon's scalpel, and he could feel pieces of him being quickly dissected, until, finally, with an almost disappointing groan, it released him. But it was too late. His body fell into a death roll, like a puppet having its strings cut one at a time, and he started to jerk and spasm in an almost chaotic dance. His eyes filled with blood as the pressure of the deep finally took him into a sleep he craved.

'WHAT ARE YOU DOING?' Alice screamed at him, her face one of pure terror as she saw her husband slumped in the corner, tearing the flesh from his arm with his fingernails.

Jacob looked back at her, taking a second to figure out where he was before erupting into floods of tears.

Alice ran over and wrapped herself around him, pulling him closer than even the kraken had managed and kissing him repeatedly on his forehead. 'Baby, why are you doing this again? Talk to me. I'm here. I'm always here, and I'll always help you if I can, but you have to let me in.'

See, you don't deserve her, it whispered, as if Alice would somehow hear its shallow, shrill voice within his mind. You never did.

'I know I don't,' Jacob whispered in reply.

'Don't listen to her,' Alice responded without looking up at the creature.

Chapter 13: Changing of the Guard
Song of the day
"Time Is The Enemy" by Quantic

Summer 2006
Knightsbridge, London UK

Jacob had been sitting opposite the doctor for what felt like an hour. She was just looking at him, observing his every move. Testing him somehow. Judging his reactions to every point she had put to him. But it had been so long since she last spoke, he was losing track of the conversation.

'I don't quite understand.' Jacob rose to his feet. 'You're saying I have more than one personality?'

The doctor watched him stand and then gave a gentle sigh as he stomped around like a scolded child.

'Sit down, Mr Brooking, please. You need to listen to what I'm saying in its entirety. Don't just take the negatives from every sentence and disregard the rest. I'm here to help you, so please sit down.'

'You sound like my wife,' quipped Jacob.

'I'll take that as a compliment, having spoken to your beautiful Alice.'

Vivian Phillips was the best psych doctor money could buy and she knew it, so she never pussy-footed around anyone or anything. Alice had put Jacob onto her after going to her to cure that silly body-hatred thing Alice always talked about. He never understood it. She was the most beautiful woman he knew. Surely she saw that same reflection in the mirror.

Dr Phillips moved from the desk where she had been leaning and sat on the green chesterfield next to Jacob. A beautiful woman who must have been in her mid-50s, she carried herself in body and form in a manner that any girl half her age would have been envious of. Jacob struggled to understand his emotions towards her. Was he petrified of her or besotted with her? He wasn't sure. But he was pretty sure it was a decent amount of both. Tall and curvaceous, her body seemed to be on a mission to free itself of the white blouse that was tucked tightly into her high-waisted black trousers. Her dark hair was pulled back into a neat bun, and she wore thick-rimmed black glasses. She waited for him to speak, opening her hands in a gesture of calmness.

'OK, what's the script, Doc? Explain it to me like the idiot I clearly am.'

'You're far from an idiot, Mr Brooking, and I am not your enemy, so please be less curt in your tone, if you don't mind.

'You have a condition where your impulsive behaviour will often dominate your emotional behaviour and certainly your rational behaviour.

'You will often see things differently to everyone else, take conversations completely the wrong way, and you have abandonment issues, which may leave you acting irrationally.'

She paused after each sentence to gauge his reaction and to make sure it was sinking in.

'It can be treated with both psychological and medical treatment,' she continued, 'and, given time, you might live a life with zero side effects.

'But the possibility that you have either bipolar or, more likely, personality disorder isn't what worries me. I'm more concerned that you're showing signs of schizophrenia to a level where your psychosis is blurring your version of reality on a massive level. I'm unsure of your ability to distinguish clearly between what is real and what is fabricated by your sense of escapism.

'Tell me about the squid that haunts your dreams.' Dr Phillips noticed the reaction the word 'squid' had received. 'Does it ever appear in your reality?'

'I'm not a psycho, doctor.'

'No one is calling you anything of the sort, and this is a condition more common than you would believe. Now tell me. Do you ever see this squid in ....?'

'IT'S AN OCTOPUS.'

'Sorry, Jacob – do you ever see the octopus in your waking world?'

'Sometimes, but more often I hear it.' Jacob seemed to sink in stature as he slumped in his seat. The colour drained from his face. 'I hear its voice throughout the day, mostly when I'm under duress. If I'm having a bad day or I've fought with Alice, it tells me things I don't want to hear.'

'Always negative, I assume? Telling you that you're not good enough, that you're unable to perform whatever task has been put before you?'

'The voice isn't my friend, doctor. It hates me.'

'"It", Mr Brooking? "It" is you. You're hearing your own voice throw self-hatred at you, and we have to find a way to silence that mindset. You can't allow it to be given form or voice. Does the creature use your own voice?'

'I guess so. But it always sounds like it has half a mouthful of water. Like it's drowning in its own hatred of me. Doctor, I want to be better, but I'm not crazy, and I can't go on some stupid mind-numbing medication. My working day is non-stop. The restaurant has Michelin inspectors due any day now, and we are a sous chef short for the next few weeks.'

Dr Phillips took a measured and deep breath. 'Mr Brooking, I need you to understand the seriousness of your condition. Alice found you harming yourself while screaming at this black monster to leave you alone. I'm amazed you have got this far into a fully functional life without ending up in hospital or worse.'

Jacob looked down at his left arm, which was heavily bandaged from last Monday's incident. Tears of frustration started to well behind his eyes.

'I'm not crazy,' he whimpered.

'Mr Brooking. Jacob. JACOB BROOKING.'

The doctor's last words found their mark as she raised her authority to a level he wasn't used to people using against him.

'I'm going to advise we have an assessment done at Nightingale's Hospital, Royal London,' she said. 'I'll be with you the whole journey. We will come out of it with a much clearer view of where you are and how we move forward.'

'I don't want anyone to know about this. I want complete confidentiality. Even Alice.'

'You might find her support invaluable during the coming months. I implore you to reconsider not telling your wife, but it has to be your call. Mr Brooking, are you taking this all in? Mr Brooking?'

'OK, OK. I need to go. Just let me know about this hospital thing, and I guess I'll be there.'

Jacob shook the doctor's hand and left the room without another word. He moved swiftly out of the building and halted at the edge of the drive, searching for his car. His heart rate rose as anxiety took over and he started to panic.

This couldn't be real. What would Dad have said? What would his mum say? And where was his car? His eyes darted left and right and he could feel the frustration building in his heart. His lungs started to close up and restrict his breathing.

I just want to go home, he cried to himself as he slumped down on the kerb.

SHE DOESN'T KNOW YOU, UNDERSTAND US OR THE RELATIONSHIP WE HAVE. YOU KNOW YOU CAN'T LIVE WITHOUT ME. YOU HONESTLY THINK YOU COULD HAVE ACHIEVED ALL YOU HAVE IN THIS WORLD WITHOUT ME?

With a sudden, cold realisation, Jacob looked up and saw the Mercedes parked in front of him not five feet away. He pulled himself up to his weary feet, feeling like the weight of the world was trying to drag him back to the ground.

Managing to unlock the door, he fell into the low-profile seats with a thud and pulled the seatbelt over his already restricted chest. It felt like he was being cut in two as it snapped closed around him.

He pressed his thumb down on the bright red starter button and the large AMG-tuned engine purred into life like a mechanical monster emerging from hibernation. Taking hold of the steering wheel to move off, he found himself frozen still, unable to release his hands from the death grip they had on the wheel. Sweat started to pour from him, running off his brow, making his eyes sting with venomous spite. He realised quickly that it was not just his hands that were frozen, but his whole body. He started to wet himself as he lost all measure of self-control. Floods of tears now mixed with the sweat dripping from his chin. His clothes were sodden. His paralysis had held him in a fierce embrace for what felt like hours, but was more likely minutes.

A loud knock on the window woke him from the nightmare dream state that was holding him prisoner. His vice-like grip released instantly as he looked to the right to see a concerned Doctor Phillips.

With all his might, he pulled his hand over to the window control and opened the gateway to the telling off he knew was coming.

'Mr Brooking,' the doctor whispered in the most gentle voice. 'Tell your wife. Tell Alice. And I'm going to be blunt here: tell her tonight.'

'OK. Tell Alice. Right, I can do that.'

He raised the window back up and pulled away with a little squeeze of the accelerator.

Tell Alice, he thought. *I can do that. She thinks I'm crazy anyway.*

SHE THINKS YOU'RE PATHETIC.
NOT LIKE EVAN.
LET'S NOT TELL EVAN.

'I think we should go away for a bit,' Jacob suggested. 'I think the break will do us good.'

'No way are you suggesting a holiday!' Alice couldn't believe what she was hearing. 'Not a chance.'

'It's a little more than a holiday, Pebble. I've organised a year-long excursion to the West Coast of the United States.' He took Alice's hand and sat next to her. 'Dockside accommodation in San Diego, and we get a boat.'

'Are you fricking kidding me? A bloody year? How could we ever afford that?'

'We can't, but we will. I'm just waiting for you to give me the go-ahead, and we can leave in two days.'

'But what about the restaurant?'

'I'm going to employ Charlie, the manager at the Mermaid, to work with Evan.'

Alice scrunched her brow. 'But what about the Mermaid?'

'The brewery is pulling the plug soon due to a buyout, so we are effectively doing Charlie a favour. He's well up for it.'

'OK, but what will we do for money?'

'I thought you could sell art from the dock and I could do some consulting while we're there. But relax – we have savings, and we're entitled to take some money out of the business as well. We didn't build this empire for nothing, you know.'

Jacob laughed. 'Oh my god, are you crying?'

'Baby, it's been 12 years since we first kissed, and we haven't been away for more than a day or two at any point during that time. We couldn't even have a honeymoon due to your bloody choice of career, so, yes, I'm fricking crying.'

Jacob pulled her into an embrace and kissed her head. 'I know it's been hard and I know I've not been easy to deal with at times, but I've always tried to be the best man I can for you.'

'I know, baby, I know.' Alice looked up cheekily. 'Is San Diego a hot place to relax?'

'Yes, you can go bikini shopping.'

Jacob looked down and saw his phone flash up with Evan's name on it, like a warning sign. He reached down and flipped it over, knowing it was something he would have to deal with sooner rather than later.

You're in trouble now.

'I'm going away for a bit,' said a very coy Jacob as he hurtled along the coastal roads.

'You need to come see me, Jay. Don't do this over the phone, please. Or should I be having this conversation with Alice instead?'

'Evan, don't be stupid. She's a joint partner of the business that employs you. What would that achieve?'

'I'm telling you now, Jacob, if you don't change your plans, all hell is going to break loose.'

She hates you.

'If you want to remain with us at the Gallantry, I need you to give me this,' Jacob told her.

'Who do you think you are, Jay?'

Who do you think you are?

'You don't tell me how to act,' Evan shouted. 'Fuck you, Jacob!'

She's going to tell Alice everything.

Jacob put the phone down. Within seconds, his phone rang again. He pulled over and blocked Evan's number. His phone rang again, this time with the number withheld. He ignored the call until it rang out.

Within a minute, the glove box to his Mercedes sprang to life as Alice's phone started to vibrate. Jacob had taken it without consent after telling her a bullshit story about needing to change her number for the States; as yet, it hadn't gone through the process, and he hadn't wanted to take the risk of leaving it with her. He had blocked Evan on all her social media until this died down, hoping that she wasn't tech savvy enough to notice. After the news he had got from the consultation, he couldn't stay here right now, as he was unsure which choices over the last few years had been his and which had been his apparent psychosis. All he knew was Alice had always been the right choice and being with her was always the choice he would make. A break and then a new start was all it would take to make this right. His phone rang again. He answered knowing what was coming, but also knowing it was something he had to deal with.

She will end you.

'Don't you ever put the phone down on me again, you piece of shit!' screamed Evan.

'I can't take this, Evan. I need you to stop.'

But she won't stop.

'I'll stop when I'm fucking ready, Jacob.'

'How is this going to make anything better, Evan? It can't!'

'I'll do what I need to do, Jacob, to make sure I'm not made a fool of, do you understand me?'

SHE WILL END YOU.

'What can I do, Evan?' Jacob begged. 'What can I do to stop this?'

The phone went silent. Jacob's hands-free system emitted a burst of static that hurt his inner ear, as though it was trying to convey Evan's hatred.

'£5,000 in my account by 3pm and I won't say another word on the matter.'

'Five grand and I have your word?'

'Don't you dare fucking talk to me like that!' Evan screeched. 'I don't have to give you my word, Jacob, when your word means shit to me.'

'OK, I'm sorry. Before 3pm. I'll do it now.'

He put the phone down and immediately pulled away from the side of the road. His body trembled with fear. He tried to find the strength to control his breathing. Anxiety was taking over, but he was free, and his world could start again. He knew that this was a close call, though, and his heart was letting him know how lucky he was.

You can't escape me, though.

AND YOU CAN'T BUY ME OFF, the voice said with pure hatred.

Free of doubt and with a clear direction in front of him, Jacob had found the strength to push forward. The bank was an ancient stone building reminiscent of a cathedral wing. In the centre of Canterbury, this was no surprise. It fitted in perfectly with the flow of the medieval city's style.

As he pushed through the heavy security doors, however, he was greeted by an air-conditioned modern room that was a hive of activity. Old gents were out collecting their pensions, just happy to be out of the house, while young families tried to pay bills with screaming kids in tow and well-dressed bank workers fluttered around them like bumble bees trying to pollinate as many flowers as possible.

Jacob walked up to the bank teller and introduced himself. The teller told him that the regional accounts manager would see him in a few minutes. Jacob was led down a long corridor where the murky green carpet was heavily worn down the middle from years of endless trudging by demotivated employees, who must've been dragging their feet as they struggled to deal with handling so much money while having so little themselves.

The bank clerk sat him down in a large office with a very formal feel to it. The furniture was incredibly efficient and cost-effective but was warmed slightly by two small potted cacti and a large coffee mug that had World's Best Dad written across it. Right next to the desk was a picture on the wall of the bank manager in question, sitting with his picture-perfect family on what looked like a Butlins holiday, one girl on his shoulders and a slightly older one holding his hand, while his beautiful, pregnant-looking wife was on the other arm. Jacob couldn't help but feel safe here.

'Mr Bennett will be here in just a second, Mr Brooking,' said his handsome but ever-so-camp new friend. 'Can I just ask, Mr Brooking – are you OK?'

'I think so, thank you.' Jacob smiled as his ego told him that his new friend clearly had a crush on him.

So, Mr Bennett was his man. Jacob sat quite contently back in his cheap plastic and foam chair. But before he got too settled, he had to rise back to his feet as the door behind him opened.

'Hello, sir,' the bank manager said, shaking Jacob's hand enthusiastically. 'I apologise for keeping you.'

He placed his other hand on Jacob's shoulder and guided him back to the chair. The manager seemed to look him in the eye with friendly scrutiny, as if taking him all in for just a moment.

'Before we start, is there anything you need? Coffee? Tea? Or maybe just a glass of water?'

Jacob sat down. 'No, I'm fine, thank you.'

The bank manager was a tall man with tidy black hair that was receding slightly across his angled brow. He was clearly a smart man, whose slim frame boasted a little pot belly that told Jacob that here was a man who enjoyed more than the occasional pizza night with his family.

'So, what can I do for you, sir? And please forgive me – I don't have the paperwork in front of me, so I don't have your name.'

'Brooking,' Jacob replied.

The bank manager smiled. 'Well, what can I do for you, Mr Brooking?'

'I need to transfer £5,000 from my personal account to a partner of mine at work, but it needs to be done within the hour, and as I don't have my bank cards with me, they told me to come and speak to the main man.' He coolly pointed at the bank manager.

'That's not a problem, Mr Brooking. But before we proceed, are you sure you're OK?'

'I'm fine, really,' Jacob said in a paranoid tone, wondering why people kept asking him the same question.

[118]

'I only asked, Mr Brooking, because apart from being as pale as the paper I'm about to write on, you are visibly shaking, and you have clearly been crying, sir.'

Jacob looked down and saw that the bank manager was right. His sweaty, nervous hands were moving outside of his control.

'I don't know what to tell you,' he said. 'I thought it was OK. I've been going through some stuff today and these past few days. I've had a few hard choices that needed a few tough resolutions, so I guess I've been struggling more than I thought, obviously.'

'Mr Brooking, it's OK. We've all had weeks where the tough call was the right one.'

'Please, call me Jacob. Mr Brooking is a much wider man than his son, I promise you,' Jacob joked.

'Hang on, Jacob Brooking? From the Howard George School?'

'That's me, unfortunately,' Jacob replied.

'Jacob, we went to school together. Simeon Bennett. Surely you remember, mate?'

Simeon got back to his feet and once again offered his hand.

'Sim?' Jacob stood uneasily, unsure of the reality in front of him.

Simeon rolled his eyes, and then smiled. 'I always hated that you lot called me Sim.'

He thinks you were friends.

'Look at you, though, man. I'm so proud of you, getting out of that godawful school and making a name for yourself.' Simeon seemed a little starstruck. 'In fact, I took my wife to your restaurant for our anniversary, but I wouldn't have put this man in front of me as the name I saw above that restaurant door.'

'What do you mean?' Jacob asked.

'What do I mean? Are you kidding me? I look like a taller and fatter version of the rat-faced kid that used to chase you round school. You, on the other hand, look like a *GQ* magazine just shat you out.'

'You're too kind, Simeon. I must confess, I never thought you liked me at school. You were not the nicest kid to have chase me round the playground.'

'I had a rough childhood, Jay.' Simeon glanced at the picture on the wall. 'If I was ever out of line, it was only down to my own unhappiness, a pain I've promised to never put my own kids through.'

With that said, Jacob took Simeon's hand and shook it well.

'You seem like a great dad, Nathan, and I hope one day I can be that man.' Jacob spoke honestly and somehow felt lighter for doing so.

'Right, let's stop reminiscing about the bloody Howard George and sort your money out. Five thousand pounds, you said?'

Chapter 14: It Follows
Song of the day
"King for a Day" by Jamiroquai

Spring 2007
San Diego, California USA

As the day drew to a close on the San Diego coastline, it almost looked like the sun was falling into a warm bathtub. The sky, a fading viridian green, melted slowly into a sea of deep teal, while the sun itself, a pale, burnt-terracotta version of its normal vibrancy, started to rest peacefully on a bed of oceanic mist, which took the edge off its impetuous glare. Flocks of gulls chased a large and battered-looking trawler that was returning to dock. The ship had the words *Sarah Grace* written upon its bow in a deep claret that contrasted beautifully with the fresh white paint job, which did little to hide the age of the vessel. Jacob realised that this ship had been under maintenance at the Marina Cortez, and its belly was clearly empty of anything the gulls might desire for dinner. Yet they chattered loudly among themselves and fought for the right to take the first bite of a meal they were yet to discover was a fabrication of their dreams. They would all be disappointed and hungry tonight.

Jacob lay at rest on a jade leather chaise longue, his hands on his chest and his fingers interlaced in stoic contemplation. His head was propped gently against the arm of the chair, just enough for him to take in the beautiful sunset, which danced gently like an autumnal kaleidoscope as the light began to fail. He reached over and took his crystal tumbler off the small slate coffee table that Alice had picked up at the goodwill market the weekend before last. They were not a poor couple, by any means – in fact, quite the opposite could be said about the Brooking empire, as he had often called it – but that had never stopped Alice looking for a bargain. She claimed that something used, worn and even damaged would always carry more character than anything new and shiny. *Maybe that's why she loves me so much,* Jacob had thought to himself, giggling, before sighing at the reality of how damaged and worn he was.

Jacob could have sworn that he could hear some light jazz that was being carried on the wind from a nearby Parisian hipster café, but he had to wonder if it was just his imagination playing tricks on him once more, as it seemed far too perfect a backing track to the scene being played out in front of him. It was almost impossible at times to know what was real and what was his mind's psychosis, as he knew how much the internal voice loved to trick him with alternative versions of his own reality, and yet he had felt far more settled here in the States. The move had been relatively stress free. Alice had taken an instant shine to all the locals, who had already given her a backlog of commissions for paintings and sketches of their coastal homes. She'd found a rhythm here that he had rarely seen from her previously, and seeing her happy had warmed his soul beyond words. As well as his own mental health seeming to settle, he had also noticed that Alice was taking compliments with a more natural vigour. This would often lead to her bouncing over to him for a passionate embrace. Maybe this trip had been good for them both. Jacob sipped his Tennessee bourbon and pondered what he would have to do to make this move permanent. What was really left for them in the UK? Just bad memories and two families who had shown nothing but disappointment in Jacob and all he had ever brought to their lives. He snarled as he thought about his godawful father-in-law, who looked down on Jacob as he held his wife and daughter up on that perfect pedestal, while Jacob's own parents had noticed nothing about his life positive or otherwise, as they had only ever existed within their own bubble of team Samuel, who had carved out quite a successful career as a semi-professional golfer and then a golfing coach.

They had been to every championship he had ever competed in, no matter how small. Yet had they ever eaten or even stepped foot in one of his restaurants? He couldn't remember if they had, but it couldn't have been a long visit, that was for certain. Nope. There was nothing for him there, especially since his dad had passed. His mum was now more withdrawn than ever.

You're as selfish as you always were, the voice whispered.

It didn't have the energy to fight with real conviction, which made it all the easier for Jacob to ignore.

He finished his bourbon, the ice now melted in the Californian evening air. *I was never good enough for their perfect little girl, so I'll just take her away*, he thought, as he lay his head back down.

Where was Alice, anyway? She had disappeared over an hour ago with the promise of a cold meat platter once she had Skyped her mother. He loved it when she cooked dinner, even if it was just leftovers of things he had cooked over previous days. Despite his obvious skill in the kitchen, he had always hated his own cooking, and the joy of anyone else bringing him food was unparalleled. Jacob still carried his muscular rugby-playing frame from his youth and had maintained it in the gym most days, but it was this constant need to be fit that caused him to be almost permanently hungry. She would hopefully throw on some of the apricot white Stilton that he'd had sent all the way from the Sussex coast, and at quite the cost. The Yanks were great at many things, but the subtle nuance of fine cheese was not their strong point. Alice had named him the dairy pirate, smuggling culture into the relaxed West Coast vibe for three months straight. Jacob had pointed out that the lack of a parrot meant he couldn't be a pirate of any real worth, so Alice had instead suggested a wooden leg. When he'd looked at her in bemusement, she'd kicked him in the shin hard enough that he'd collapsed. He'd proceeded to chase her round their large yacht, which came as part of the rental agreement on the dock house they rented.

He picked up his empty glass and sat up, stretching his arms out wide and arching his back until it cracked into place. The warm air was dying around him, and the sun was only a sliver on the horizon as it put itself to bed for the night among the flock of miserable seagulls now floating on the water. The chill from the air made his skin feel like a gentle current was running through it and told him it was time to head into a warm embrace and a platter full of food. He rose to his feet, fully taking in the beautiful view one last time before turning to open the porch door.

'Honey, I'm home!'

Jacob closed the door behind him. A crystal tumbler like the one he was carrying smashed in an explosion of noise against the frame of the door. Shards of glass and splinters of wood showered his face, luckily avoiding his eyes, as the thickest part of the tumbler's base fell to the ground. He looked around to see Alice slumped on the floor. Wet from the tears she had been crying, her hair was stuck to her face, and her mascara had run all the way to her neckline. Her bloodshot eyes were a dark royal blue, instead of the electric azure that normally pulled his soul into hers.

'Why, Jacob?' Alice growled quietly.

'Baby, you're scaring me,' Jacob replied. 'Why what?'

'Why did we move here, Jay? Honestly. Tell me honestly.' Her voice was deep and broken. 'Why are we here?'

'Because we deserve the break, baby. You kno ...'

A shoe hit him in the gut, and Jacob winced, feeling the venom with which it had been thrown.

'What on earth have your parents said to you this time, Pebble?'

'DON'T CALL ME THAT! I AM NOT YOUR FUCKING PEBBLE. AND DON'T YOU DARE PIN THIS ON MY PARENTS.'

Alice staggered to her feet. 'Why don't we talk about the email I just received from Evan instead?'

She knows, whispered the voice.

'Well, Jacob? Shall we?' Alice was growing in stature with every step forward. 'Shall we talk openly and honestly as husband and wife about how we swore to always be together in everything we did?'

You deserve this.

'Shall we talk about you fucking Evan Laurie for a month before our wedding and then paying her to keep quiet?'

You can't win this.

'Or how about how you had me murder our baby so that you could get away with it a little longer? No?'

Alice was only a few feet away from Jacob now.

'SAY SOMETHING TO ME YOU FUCKING PIG!'

That seemed to come from Alice and the voice in his head at the same time. Jacob couldn't differentiate between them.

Alice reached forward and gripped him around the throat. Her nails pinched his flesh and broke the skin.

Jacob couldn't respond. He had convinced himself not only that Alice would never find out about the affair but that it hadn't actually happened at all. He honestly believed at times that his psychosis had made it all up. That it had just been a friendship out of hand. That it was nothing.

'You told Evan you loved her.'

'But I didn't,' Jacob muttered.

'I suggest you find somewhere else to sleep right now, Jay, because I can't look at you one second longer, and you clearly have nothing to say and no explanation worth hearing.' Alice grabbed a set of keys from the glass bowl next to the door and shoved them into his chest. 'Why don't you go and sleep on that precious boat, since you love it so very much.' Tears were rolling down her face as she turned away in disgust.

Jacob took the keys and went out onto the front decking. The cold night air caught him off guard. He walked down towards his Audi, which was parked at the bottom of the yard. He took one last look over his shoulder at the devastation he had caused.

Alice was curled up against the door. 'You may as well keep on running, Jacob. It's all you have ever known how to do.'

Jacob heard her words but just looked at the ground instead.

LOOK AT HER, YOU COWARD.

'I did nothing wrong,' Jacob muttered once more.

YOU DID EVERYTHING WRONG.

YOU NEVER DESERVED HER.

Chapter 15: The Summer Breeze

Song of the day
"All That I Want" by Rival Sons

Spring 2007
Somewhere in the Pacific Ocean

The ship was being thrown aggressively back and forth on the waves of the Pacific Ocean as if it were a paper vessel trying to navigate a hurricane. The witching hour had brought more lashing rain and a thunderous grumble born from a war between the gods – a war that was being waged ever closer, with each angry boom from within the clouds sounding louder and more violent. Jacob's mum had always said that a storm was just furniture being moved in heaven, but he doubted that was the case here. That good Christian belief seemed weak compared to what was clearly a very Greek and very angry Zeus throwing down the law to a very disobedient Poseidon, as each bolt of lightning was matched by another crashing wave of titanic proportions. It would have been nearly impossible for another vessel to make out the ship's lines against the maelstrom. Her form was all but invisible, except for the sheet lightning that illuminated her hull every few minutes. For a second or two, white light reigned, before the waves once again dropped her out of sight underneath the massive swell of an angry sea. One tiny speck of light remained throughout, though, almost like a firefly dancing in a Louisiana swamp. The tiny candlelight came from the ship's living quarters and lit up the small aft window like a beacon of hope in a place of endless sorrow. It had become the only constant in what was a violent dance that the ship was enduring very much against her will.

'

Jacob sat in the small cabin on the lower deck of the yacht – a vessel he had got as part of the deal to take on the boathouse for a year – and mulled over his first lines. The diary in front of him was leather-bound and heavy like some book of ancient lore. The weapon in his grasp, a fountain pen of a delicate design, had a craftsmanship that radiated expense. A gift from his father many years before, it was something Jacob held dear. It was more than just a pen to him. He saw the gift as a symbol of his father's final wish: that Jacob would open up at last, with the pen serving as the means to aid that unusual practice of telling the truth – unusual for Jacob Brooking, at least, a man who had got used to telling the truth only when things were good. As of now, things were far from good. As the violent motion of his surroundings did their best to throw his stomach off course, he found comfort as he pressed the nib of the pen down on the first page. In the light of a pair of large candles, Jacob started to talk honestly, for the very first time, to Alice.

To my heart

The apology you are owed cannot be voiced with mere words. In fact, my meagre existence here in this life is really an affront to the true remorse I feel, for I have left my life forfeit with my actions towards you these past few years. I'm sorry, Alice – not for my past catching me up, but for taking far too long to tell you exactly what drives my every action throughout the days when you are not by my side, for it seems that when my hand is entwined with yours, I fear nothing and fall rarely. Your love it seems is the anchor that holds me through storms and your patience the rudder that guides me, and now you are lost to me, and I have not one person to blame but myself. So, I am sorry – sorry for being too proud to tell you how far I have so often fallen from the pedestal you put me on. I am a man falling from grace, at a rate I cannot control, and a man who knows that redemption is further from reach than it has ever been before.

Day 5

I have been at sea now for a few days. I had started writing this letter to you in the hope of seeing you that same day I first put pen to paper, yet fear consumes me – fear of confrontation with you. Truth be told, confrontation with anyone scares me more than anything rational should scare a man, yet here I am, still writing instead of turning this ship around. What has become of me? When did I become so weak? The shrink has told me I need to write everything down, because I panic when I get myself into heated procrastination, and who am I to argue with Dr Phillips? "Write it down, Jacob, then read it back to them later when emotion has left the room." And so I guess that's what I'm doing – writing down what I should have been able to say to your face so many times before, and for that I am once again sorry. Maybe when I dock I'll find you waiting, and I can read this to you in the hope it will adjust your view on the choices I have made, yet I feel my heart will be broken to find you gone, and maybe that is the fear that stops me from turning the wheel right now. I've done all I can to push you away at times, and yet the idea of a life without you scares me more than the nightmare creature that fills my waking dreams. Its hate has haunted me all of my life. The constant fear of the darkness only exists because of the ominous threat It poses my sanity from the shadows, yet the pain and suffering it has brought constantly to my life pales in comparison to the void that your absence has left within my ever-diminishing soul.

Day 10

I'm sorry for Evan, I'm sorry for what I did in its entirety, but I know it hurts you more that it was her. I never loved her, but I enjoyed feeling like I was good enough for someone, like I was enough. I'm a bad man and my heart has always been filled with a darkness born out of hatred, a hatred that in turn was born from the chip on my shoulder. I never felt good enough for you, I never felt good enough for your father, who constantly expected more from me. But with Evan, I felt a kinship with her own self-loathing, and that made me feel enough for her, and just for a moment then I felt enough for someone. But I was wrong, and by the time I'd realised my mistake, it was too late. You know what she can be like, you know the violence of both her words and her actions, and it was the fear of what was surely to come which stopped me from walking away the second it happened, and for that Alice I am so truly sorry. It has only reiterated what I already knew: I have never been the man you needed me to be. But I do see now that you loved me even when I hated myself, and had I realised that at the time, then maybe I would have acted differently.

Day 36

I've shut the engines down for a day while I try to find my bearings. I've realised that the few classes in open-sea navigation that I took after getting this boat have quickly been forgotten. Once again, my ego has blinded my ability to learn lessons that might actually benefit my life. I wonder how many times I have ignored your advice because I thought honestly that the great Jacob "fucking" Brooking knew better. I always said that my only dream in life was to be like my father, to be a good husband and eventually a good dad, but the apple has fallen pretty far from the tree with me. I'm a disgrace to my family and to yours, and I can't help but feel that this is karma rounding up on me for the final kill. The voice in my head has screamed at me from dawn until dusk today. It hates me, tells me I'm stupid for writing this, as you will be long gone by the time I have summoned the courage to return to you. But it's wrong. It must be. Because I love you, and I know you still love me, you must still love me. Even as I write, its shrieking and bitter voice is cutting through my resolve to survive this ordeal. I need you here to guide me. It wants me to hurt myself, wants me to end my apparent sad existence, and there is a part of me that thinks it might be right.

Day 42

I have no words to explain the loss I feel knowing I will never see your face again. I want to make things right. I want to explain the choices I have made, and maybe, just maybe, you will look upon me as you once did.

I've held off writing too much lately in the hope I might get to explain my feelings face to face, but it seems that even with all the will in the world, fate is still against me this time. At 2.37pm yesterday I finally ran out of diesel, and no soul seems to be answering any distress call I have sent. I guess I have run for so long, I never considered I might eventually run out of road. With my biggest fear always the idea of being caught by my demons, it's come as quite the revelation to find the only thing I'm running from is my own heart. Indeed, it's quite the surprise to me that no matter how far or fast I run, I can't escape my own true self. So now I am here, with my only companion the cold presence of death. He hangs over me once more. I feel his skeletal hand clamping metaphorically down on my soul with focused desire. He wants me, and I feel this time he will take me. I will write more soon, my Alice, in the hope that even when I'm gone, you might find this book and know that I am truly sorry.

KNOCK KNOCK KNOCK

Jacob was woken with abject horror by the sound of a visitor's warning. He turned about in earnest to locate the source of his wake-up call but found nothing – nothing but the shadows dancing to the one lamp that still had a candle burning brightly.

KNOCK KNOCK KNOCK

'The window,' Jacob whispered.
Rising with the stiffness of a man who had slept in an armchair at his desk and the apprehension of a man searching

for a body where there should of course be none, he moved across the bedroom to peer through the circular window, which was lined and latched with polished brass. He could see nothing except the setting sun and an assault upon the glass, one of salt water from both above and below. The dying light lit up the sky like a rescue flare, with the burning sun sinking into the ocean as if melting into the sea. But he could see no reason for the knocking. Maybe his guest was just a seagull pecking his reflection in an act of territorial masculinity, or maybe Jacob was still dream–

KNOCK KNOCK KNOCK

Jacob spun around in panic as the same noise that had shaken him from his slumber moved from the window to the large wooden door that led to the upper deck. He moved down the hall towards it, readying himself for both the rescue he knew he wanted, and the disappointment he knew he deserved. The dancing candlelight threw shadows against the walls in unnatural shapes that played out a story, and the closer he got to the door, the more real the stories became to him. He saw a ship bobbing on rough seas, and a beast from beneath the waves rising up and pulling it deep below the surface. Jacob's hand gripped the doorknob, and the fear of the moment seized him. His sweat-filled palms made the brass feel wet in his grasp.

'No – this can't be ...'

Jacob realised that it wasn't sweat on his hands, but blood. Darkness all but consumed him as panic sought to control his actions.

KNOCK KNOCK KNOCK

The noise was now behind him. Jacob turned, expecting to see a monster or a demon. Instead, he saw Alice. She was laced in the white of her wedding dress. Her womb was dripping with scarlet, and her hands were outstretched.

'GIVE HIM BACK TO ME, JACOB,' she cried in a howl of pain.

Jacob looked down to find himself holding the unborn son he had made her give up. The child's body was drenched in blood. His eyes were shut tightly, as if they had never opened, and his tiny hand was tightly gripped around Jacob's thumb.

Jacob woke up at his desk, screaming, his face drenched with sweat and his eyes filled with tears. He swallowed hard as the dream faded and he took in the quiet all around him – no Alice in sight, no voice, no creature, just empty, dead silence.

Silence, that is, except for the slow drip, drip, drip of the blood running off his forearm. The nib of his fountain pen poked out of the top of his arm, embedded in the deep wound he had made in his flesh.

Jacob hadn't moved in hours. The water was deadly still. Not a ripple crossed the perfectly mirror-like sheen of what was possibly the calmest ocean that could exist on this earth. He had sailed in the Pacific before, but he couldn't recall ever hearing of this place, a shallow where he could just about see the bottom beneath almost waveless tides, although he couldn't recall much of anything lately. No current of real strength was pulling the boat, and there was no tide of relevant power in response because of this. The place was home to a thousand wrecked pre-combustion-engine ships that had simply stopped without the air to move them forward. And this was where the last of his diesel had burnt up.

The carcasses of skeletal 16th-century ships were littered around him. No signs of life except for the boys. The boys had been with him since he had pulled to a standstill. The first was a rather large and menacing barracuda, which lived among the wrecks in the shallow waters beneath him. Even within the confines and safety of his ship, Jacob felt sure that this fish had a plan, that this fish of ungodly length had developed a scheme to get him sooner rather than later. The second of his two new friends was of course the large obsidian octopus that dominated a rock formation aggressively breaking the surface of the water. It appeared each dusk to soak in the last of the sun's rays, but it bore such a resemblance to the kraken in his dreams that he was unsure if it was real or just his aching eyes playing tricks like some perverse mirage. It was close to midday, now, so a more pressing issue was at hand. Could and more importantly would a seagull eat a dead body rotting on the deck of a boat? Or, even worse, a dying body not yet devoid of sensory feeling? Jacob had been toying with this riddle for days and had promised himself that whatever happened, he would decide today and accept the verdict regardless. He thought over and over on this as he lay motionless on a worn, thick shag rug. The rug had previously been happily at rest in the living quarters of the *Summer Breeze*, the 40-foot sun chaser that had been his home for two long months; but Jacob, with great effort, had dragged it to the top deck, as he refused to die in what he considered to be a readymade crypt. If he was to go, it would be with the sun or the moon on his back.

His parched and broken lips, which were cracked from a combination of dehydration, the roasting midday sun and the spiteful evening chill, had sent a shot of pain through his mouth as he swallowed, and it hurt him more than physically, as his demeanour was that of a proud man, and now he couldn't even swallow without wanting to cry. He felt pathetic. Unchanged since the day he had left San Diego, his sullen look now broke into the smallest of smiles as he realised he hadn't even seen a seagull for two weeks, so it was a moot point. Could he really have travelled that far from land? By his watch, it was the 28th of June and he had run out of fuel a month ago. Where the tide had taken him up until the boat had settled on this motionless mirrored plane of glass he couldn't work out, and the more he thought about it, the more it occurred to him that it had said the 28th on his watch for at least two days. The 28th. Alice's birthday was a month away. What were the chances? It had been two months since he had walked out on her. Since he had left her sobbing and heartbroken on their patio deck. Again, he was suddenly aware of the pointlessness of all these numbers, as like it or not he was here with no propulsion, no food and no water – which was, of course, an irony not lost on a man surrounded by nothing but water. With the last of his strength slipping away from him, he was fully resigned to what was inevitable. He was going to die.

His wildly cut hair, once a beautiful chestnut brown, was sun-bleached and reminded him of the autumns he used to witness on his breaks to New England during his youth. A time that seemed so simple to him now. And a time that seemed a lot further away than the 25 years it had actually been since his last family holiday to the East Coast with his folks. His bearded face was narrow and gaunt, and his eyes, which were once bright crystals of emerald that were always considered too green to be his natural eye colour, were now glazed with a white sheen, as blinking had apparently become too much and was beyond him. A man so obsessed with his body and so driven by people's opinion of him now lay dying on the top deck of the majestic ship. His muscles were wasting away and his skin was broken and thin. He would die surrounded by regret. And one in particular would follow him to the boatman's call. He wished she was there. If only to hold him as he slipped away.

Out of nowhere, there was a noise, faint and delicate over the deafening silence. It was distant, but it was definitely there. What was it? His thoughts rushed at him all at once. A ship or a plane maybe? Help? Could it be help? He turned his neck up to the sky as much as his broken body would allow and looked through the deep blue of the open air above him. And his brow creased in sadness as he realised that the two large gulls circling above him might just answer his question after all.

Two more hours passed as Jay lay dying on the mahogany deck of his yacht. The two seagulls that he had once thought his enemies were now sitting on the plush cushions lining the bench next to where he had made his final home. Jokingly, he had named them Tommy and Gina, because they looked like a very loving couple as they nestled up together. Tommy had a long curved yellow beak and was the larger, while Gina was more speckled in colour, her face more eloquent and her grey beak small and pointed. He smiled at his new friends and realised he hadn't felt any kind of depression in weeks. And somehow, without the constant voices of others to cloud his thoughts, his own voice had finally prevailed. How much of the last year was real? How much of the last ten? Or was it all psychosis? Had he ruined his relationship with Alice over nothing but confusion over what had been his own voice? Certainly, he had done nothing but love her since he had met her, so why would he push her away? He had done nothing but miss her since the day he had walked out on her. A world of regret had heaped itself on him since the day his engine had choked and died. He had spent his twenties overcompensating for the work his bullies had done with him. He had gone on to believe the world owed him everything for what he had been through. That chip had never left his shoulder. And now he would pay.

His girl was amazing. He had never deserved Alice. At his best he was punching well above his weight. Yet his swollen ego had led him here to die. Well, he was truly humbled now. And he would die here humble and alone, and all because when his doctor had diagnosed his bipolar and all the other self-destructive conditions he had, his ego had made him walk out the room, never to mention it again. Having these mental conditions wouldn't kill him. Denying his conditions, the honest conversation with his wife, would be what did it.

He would die here. And for the first time in his life, Jacob Brooking admitted he probably didn't deserve it.

Summer 2007 San Diego, California USA

'Hi, my name's Jacob and I have bipolar disorder with traits of personality disorder and extreme psychotic delusions,' Jacob said to the group before taking a seat nervously among a mixture of people all either looking through him like he was glass, or looking at the ground around him with an unwillingness to accept his presence. He had heard them whispering in the corridor as he had arrived at the conference centre for the first of his group therapy sessions. 'There's nothing wrong with him,' they had said. 'Look at his expensive watch,' one had murmured with nasty intent. 'I heard he pulled up in an Audi R8, so what could be wrong with him?' Jacob had ignored them and just shuffled into the circle of truth.

He had barely spoken since the Hawaiian naval vessel had come across him stranded at sea. He remembered little from the rescue event other than the giant Marine medics who had carried him off the *Summer Breeze* and below the surface of the *USS Boston*'s main deck. He remembered his sunburn being treated with freezing-cold creams and lotions. He remembered eating for the first time in weeks and then throwing it all up before having to eat once again. And then he remembered the doctor who looked like his father.

'Talk to someone, Jacob, before it's too late,' he had said with concern.

Now, three weeks later, he was here. He assumed someone had told Alice he was alive, and he hoped that this would be the first step to proving he was serious about fighting this demon inside him, but as of yet he hadn't found the strength or the courage to speak to her or even message her.

'Hi Jacob,' said the group in a drone-like unison.

'Hello, Jacob,' said the group leader. Duncan Stewart was a small man with round features and a receding hairline whose thin gold-framed glasses made him look like the brains behind an evil genius in an old Russian spy film. In fact, he was clearly a god-bothering scout-leader type. He was pleasant enough, if a little tactile for Jacob's taste.

'Or do we call you Jay?'

'Either is fine,' said Jacob without looking at him.

'I've read your file, Jacob, and, let's be fair, there's some heavy stuff in there, so only communicate what you feel comfortable with, and maybe let's just spend this week listening to the rest of the group.'

Duncan brought his eye level down to try and catch any sign of agreement from Jacob but caught nothing.

'Who wants to go first?' asked Duncan.

'I'll go first. I want to talk about my useless son.'

Jacob looked up to see his mother sitting there knitting right in front of him.

One year earlier

'What do you mean, you're ill? There's nothing wrong with you.' Marie Brooking didn't even look up from her newspaper.

'Well, I think it's obvious that I've always struggled, Mum. I'm unsure how you and Dad never noticed.'

'Noticed what, Jacob? You've been a popular guy all your life.'

'Mum, even if that was relevant to what I'm saying, which I can assure you it isn't, I'm not sure how you can say that. Name one of my friends without saying Alice.'

'All I'm saying is I've never noticed anything that you might say makes you disabled.' Marie pronounced the word disabled as though there were quotes around it. But still she didn't take her eyes off the paper on the table in front of her. 'Ultimately, Jacob, you just have to be positive, as really what does all this negativity bring you?'

This would be different if it was your brother.

They actually like him.

[138]

'Mum, I'm not sure you are getting this at all. I'm struggling with a mental illness. I'm not disabled as such, but it certainly doesn't go away with just positive thought.'

She must be so disappointed in you.

'Are you telling me you never noticed signs?' Jacob was starting to get irate at his mother's inability to see anything wrong with his childhood behaviour. 'What about school?'

'You were fine at school, Jakey.'

'No, Mum – I hated school, every day. I honestly don't remember having one good day at school. How do you of all people not know that?'

She thinks you're lying.

Shut up, Jacob thought.

I think you're lying.

'SHUT UP.'

Just making excuses for years of cowardice.

'SHUT UP SHUT UP SHUT UP.'

'I hope you're not talking to me, Jacob Brooking,' his mum snapped.

'No, Mum, of course not. I'm just talking to myself.'

Marie looked up and tilted her head. 'Is that a sign of your disability?'

'Mum, it really would mean a lot if you could take this seriously. Maybe come to a meeting with me or something.'

'Jacob, you know I love you. Isn't that enough? Have you spoken to your brother lately?'

Oh, here it goes.

'He's working so hard right now,' his mum went on. 'I do worry about him.'

Jacob sighed. 'I know, Mum. I worry too.'

Doesn't worry about you, does she?

Jacob got up to leave, as the situation was quickly getting away from him. He kissed his mum on the head and thanked her for the coffee. 'Thanks for the help, Mum.'

What help?

[139]

'Just remember to keep positive, Jacob, my boy.'

She returned to her paper without another thought.

2007

Jacob shook his head clear as the girl in front of him, who was clearly not his 62-year-old mother, finished her story.

'That's great, Annabelle. Thank you for sharing.' Duncan looked around. 'Who's next?'

A man who now looked like Alice's father stood up to speak. Jacob, realising what the monster inside him was doing, quickly intervened.

'I'll go next,' said Jacob, 'because otherwise this will be a long day for me. Let me tell you about the voice in my head.'

Chapter 16: The End
Song of the day
"I Can't Go on Without You" by Kaelo

Summer 2007
San Diego, California USA

Three months had passed since he had left home. No one had heard from him, and now he was back on the lawn of the dock house, trying to find the strength to turn that door handle. But he was scared, he was frozen, and his heart was pounding. The medication has stopped the voice in his head to a certain extent, but he knew Alice would never forgive him regardless, and he didn't need a monster in his head to tell him that. But he was here and that had to be a start.

Three months had passed since Jacob had left home. No one had heard from him, and he had pissed so many people off that very few questions were asked regarding his whereabouts anymore. But she was alright.

'I'm alright,' she whispered while straightening herself in the mirror for the fiftieth time.

Screw him. Screw Jay and his narcissistic face. Despite her best efforts, her long curly auburn hair kept falling over the earrings her mum had sent her all the way from England for her birthday. Uncontrolled mane or otherwise, it was only the second first date she had ever been on, so if he didn't like the way her hair fell, then she could afford to be picky, and she was sure there were men out there who would love how untamed her hair could be at times. How untamed she could be full-stop. Her freckles had come out today with the sun, and her button nose was covered all over. Her piercing blue eyes cut through everything, though. With her whole look screaming subtle class and her demeanour carrying a deserved swagger of classic beauty, it was left to eyes of crystalline aquamarine to stop time where it stood. To be caught in that gaze was to get lost in a place of oceanic wonder.

A strapped summer dress fell over the curves of her slender athletic frame and danced around her knees. Her exposed shoulders revealed more freckles, which went all the way down her arms. Her fingernails were painted in a clear and clean gloss. The dress, a summer-sale buy from a trip into San Diego, was white lace flecked with tiny turquoise flowers that matched her eyes. The only accessory was the necklace. Bright and gleaming in the sunlight, it matched her sparkly azure five-inch heels. It was the necklace that Jacob had bought her for their anniversary. What a disaster that sunny June day had been. An embarrassed flush of colour washed over her once more as she remembered everyone looking at them as Jacob screamed at her less than an hour after giving her the gift. For that reason, she had toyed with selling it, but she loved it like no sane person should love an inanimate object.

What had she seen in him? All he had ever cared for was his job and his money. Ambition to be more and to have more than he had was all he dreamed of. She had never been part of that plan, she saw that now. And he had never been the man she had hoped he would be. The man she deserved. *And look at you now*, she thought. *Look at what you have become.* 'You're everything he wouldn't have allowed you to become,' she proudly voiced.

She grabbed her door keys and smiled one last time in the hall mirror, her pearl-white teeth lighting up her face.

Her reflection looked back at her and snarled.

WHO THE HELL DO YOU THINK YOU ARE?

I HATE YOU.

'I know you do,' said Alice.

HATE, the mirror proclaimed back, with all that I am. I'm disgusted we share the same form. You were never good

[142]

enough for him. You were never good enough for anyone of any calibre. WHERE IS HE NOW, PIG?

The mirror screamed at Alice, but it wasn't Alice looking back at her. It could have been. The same basic shape was there, the same clothes, the same eyes. But that was where the similarities ended. Her skin appeared bloated and cracked. Her hair was greasy. No, this wasn't Alice at all. But Alice thought it was. She believed it was her true reflection. But she still couldn't figure out why or how it was talking to her. She had always heard the voice berating her in the back of her mind. But this was different. This wasn't a quiet echo within the silence of her thoughts. It was confrontation. She was watching her reflection in a full-blown argument with herself, yet her real lips hadn't moved once. The new two-dimensional version of herself, though, didn't seem to care about the laws of physics.

The only man to ever love you has left you for a common tart. He was pathetic, half a man, and still too good for you. DO YOU MAKE ANYONE HAPPY? the demon reflection screeched.

'No, I don't, I guess I never have.'

Alice wept. Her eyes filled slowly with the kind of salt water that only comes when you're ready to give up. It had been a month since she had cried, and three months since Jay had left her. She thought she was coping. Yet here she was losing an argument with herself. She missed her mum and dad. She missed Canterbury. And she missed her husband.

'I FUCKING HATE YOU,' Alice screamed.

Her hands, previously frozen, snatched at her phone, fumbling in frustration at her inability to turn it on. She found his number. She had to talk to Jay.

Go on, ring him. I BET HE DOESN'T ANSWER.

She held the phone to her ear and, despite herself, let hope slip into her heart that his familiar east London accent would answer.

Yet nothing but three loud beeps greeted her. Her eyes glazed over with a final realisation that Jacob wasn't coming back. The weight of the situation washed over her like a lead blanket, and she began to crumble from within.

Alice looked up from her phone. As she stared at the nightmare creature, leering back at her from the mirror, she noticed the reflection wasn't crying at all. She reached up to her face and caressed the wet trail driving a path down her face. Why was she crying when the creature wasn't? That's what broke her finally.

Alice snapped from the very deepest part of her soul. Her entire mind turned into anger, and she launched her phone at the mirror with a force she didn't know she had. Like a supernova, the mirror exploded into a million shards, each shining like a swarm of fireflies as the hall light caught them in its warm embrace.

She slumped to her knees with the pieces settled around her. The last of her strength faded away as she realised her hope of silencing the demon voice was gone, because the one creature was now replaced by a thousand laughing Alice demons. Each shard had an image of Alice within it, and each one mocked her. All laughing at her, mocking her and grinning. Each one more grotesque than the last. But all with an unnaturally large smile filled with broken and filthy teeth.

Hours passed. The laughing continued. The mocking, like a murder of crows fighting over roadkill, just didn't stop. Alice sat there, broken into as many pieces as the mirror. She had only ever loved one man since her father, and she had pushed Jacob away because she knew she wasn't enough. How could she be?

And yet just as she believed the last of her strength had left her, she summoned something from inside her very core. A resilience not to let the demon Alice win. She reached down and picked up the largest shard of glass she could find and brought it to her throat.

'DO IT,' Alice said.

This time it wasn't the reflection talking. Those words came from her own lips as the demon looked on in horror and fear.

Don't do it! We need you.

Blood started to trickle down the shard of mirror.

Jacob stood in the doorway, looking down at the kraken-like creature climbing out of the remains of a shattered mirror frame, its barbed tentacles pulling at Alice's wrists, trying to stop her cutting her own throat.

'Get away from her. GET AWAY FROM HER.'

Chapter 17: Wires
Song of the day
"Headphones" by Bjork

Summer 2007
Psychiatric Hospital of San Diego county California USA

Alice had been lying deadly still on the hospital bed for what seemed like days. The room was clinical and open, with nothing inside it that didn't have a purpose. She lay on her side, crunched into a foetal position, with just one white pillow folded beneath her plaited auburn hair. Her gown was a horrible green hue that left her lower back exposed for no reason that she could understand, especially as the only reason she was here was the damage done underneath the white compress bandage around her throat, yet she didn't have the strength to question the doctors. And what would have been the point? The antipsychotic drugs they had filled her with had left her almost paralysed with exhaustion. The sun radiated through the open blinds, highlighting the fact that everything in the room was bright, sterile white. The hairs on her skin were raised slightly and surrounded by her summer freckles as she lay motionless, staring at the card on the bedside table next to her.

It contained a simple message of get well soon and had a rather sad-looking picture of a navy-blue heart emblazoned on the front, an irony not lost on her own very lonesome real heart.

Just past the card was the glass door to the en suite, and within its reflection was the main reason Alice had been lying there mesmerised for hours. She had never believed in antidepressants, or in medication in any form, really. But for so long she had been unable to see anything in the mirror that wasn't tainted by the nightmare creature that was her demonic reflective image. If she just glanced at herself quickly, she would see a perfect reflection. But if a choice had to be made – hair up or hair down? A dress or something more comfortable? – the creature would take over, always announcing its presence first. Its gargling voice was like a tremor through her head, telling her nothing but spiteful and hate-filled mistruths. Then, as her reflection would fade to grey, her skin would peel and crack and her teeth, rotting and broken, would start to fall out. She would see only the creature's image. Only that version of herself would remain. And the broken Alice would take over.

But not now. Now her reflection was real. What she saw was still far from perfect. The image seemed blurred a little. Fuzzy where it came to the finer details. Like it was still not her, just a lot more her than normal. And she could still hear the creature trying to scream at her. Yet somehow it seemed further away and trapped in such a way that Alice struggled to make out what it was saying. For the first time in a long time, her exhaustion overcame her fear and all she had the strength to do was look at this imperfect reflection of herself while she waited for tomorrow to come and Jacob to pick her up.

'Jacob,' she whispered to herself.

Alice hadn't seen him in months, except when he had walked in and saved her from taking her own life during what had been the worst psychosis she had ever had. Actually, the more she thought about it, that was the first psychotic episode she could remember since he had walked out on her all those months ago. She mused for just a moment that maybe the siren creature she saw was connected to Jacob in some obscure way, but she quickly discounted the notion. She was just broken, numb and unable to move in any substantial way. She was still feeling too much right now. The stitches in her neck were small, but they felt like an alien body nesting in her skin, and a gentle throbbing pain reminded her of what she had done to her body that dark and painful day. Her mouth was dry, so she tried to move to reach the plastic safety cup beside her, but her strength had left her as the medication did its best to calm her, to stop her doing anything other than just breathe. Instead, she just lay there, on her side and on her own. Looking straight at her reflection in the glass door. Awaiting the return of the siren, which, somewhere in the distance, she could hear calling her name.

The door to her room opened slowly and with care, and a doctor walked in carrying a small leather-bound file filled to bursting point with paper, all bearing Alice's name. Doctor Luke Fisher was a handsome man, who looked far too young to be in the lofty position of psychiatric consultant, but he had been polite to Alice every time he had stopped in over the past few days, so she gave him a pass each time. His thick-rimmed spectacles made him appear very geek chic, and his naturally curly and messy hair was unashamedly unkempt. Alice thought he would look more at home busking on the high street back home in Canterbury. More Ed Sheeran than Doogie Howser MD.

'Good morning, Alice,' he said with a warm West Coast accent. 'How are you feeling today?'

Alice opened her pastel-pink lips to reply, but no real sound came out.

'Well, that's better than the last time I asked,' the doctor said kindly. 'But at some point, you need to take a step forward with us in beating this.'

Alice averted her gaze in an act of defiance.

'OK, Alice, I'm not here to stress you out, and for that matter neither are any of my staff, but I do need to discuss a few things with you regarding the scars on your thighs and the reason you tried to take your own life.'

Realising this conversation was going to happen at some point whether she liked it or not, Alice took the offer of the doctor's hand and tried to sit upright. He passed her some water and took a seat beside her.

'The scars on my leg are old and from an angst-filled version of myself that I don't really recognise anymore, doctor,' she said while patting her leg almost sarcastically. Her throat hurt at the first full sentence she had uttered since the surgery. 'I don't think that's the problem here.'

'With all due respect, Miss Petalow, I have spoken to your doctor in the UK, and I have your case history here.' He patted the leather binder. 'These scars on your right thigh are completely fresh.'

Alice laughed like it was a lie. 'How fresh?'

'Miss Petalow, you didn't have them when you came here four days ago.'

Alice took her gaze away from the doctor and looked down to where she had just patted her thigh to see small patches of claret forming on the crisp white sheet that covered her lower half. Confused and scared tears started to form and roll down her cheeks.

The doctor relocated to the far side of the room and beckoned over the two nurses who had entered the room behind him. 'How did she hurt herself in a bloody safe room?' he asked them angrily, before realising that Alice could hear him. At that point, the trio lowered their voices so that they were almost inaudible.

They are talking about you, said the distant voice.

They think you're crazy.

'Jacob,' Alice whispered in hope.

Have you learnt nothing, the voice intoned quietly in response.

Autumn 2007 San Diego, California USA

'Well the term "Shared psychosis" is the common definition of what is actually a very rare occurrence, and one of you is going to find this really hard to deal with, I'm afraid,' said Vivian Phillips. 'You need to understand the journey that each of you is about to go through, and preferably without turning on one another. Normally, I'd suggest you go your separate ways whilst you undertake the various therapies we have on offer, but that's not an option, is it, Mr and Mrs Brooking?'

Jacob and Alice looked at one another.

'No,' said Alice. 'Whatever it is, we face it together.'

'Why will this be harder for one of us?' asked Jacob.

'The honest answer will not be easy to hear, Mr Brooking,' said Vivian, 'but I think one of you is to blame, as a shared psychosis usually forms in one and then transmits to the other. If you take away the primary, the secondary will eventually get better, if that makes sense.'

Alice leaned forward with nervous anticipation. 'So, I could be making Jacob ill with my body dysmorphia?'

'Actually, Mrs Brooking, I think it's Jacob who is unknowingly projecting the effects of his personality disorder onto you as his closest companion. Your condition has come much later on in life, whereas Mr Brooking has been affected by his psychosis since his teens.' There was a sadness in Vivian's voice as she shared the one thing she'd been reluctant to say since she'd landed at San Diego International. 'I think you will both struggle to get better while you are together.'

Alice immediately started to well up.

'Doctor,' said Jacob, 'I went through hell and back trying to get myself right for Alice. I nearly died on the godforsaken boat trying to figure myself out. Surely that's a good thing?'

You went to three group therapy classes. Is that trying?

The creature was subdued, but its voice still rang through Jacob like a church bell, causing him to grip Alice's hand all the harder, a motion that she noticed and reciprocated, whispering, 'It's OK, baby.'

'A few group sessions doesn't fix what you're going through,' said Vivian. 'You are suffering, Jacob. This will be a long, slow process. Are you really willing to risk Alice for that period of time?'

'That's my choice to make, not yours,' snapped Alice in defiance, as she raised her husband's hand, their fingers tightly entwined.

'Mrs Brooking, I couldn't make you leave your husband even if I had the power to do it, and neither would I want to, but you have to understand that folie à deux can be temporary, and you could live a life free of its effects, given time. But Jacob's condition is forever. Things may get better and easier to manage, but he will always be a risk to himself and others with this level of psychosis.' Vivian leaned towards them. 'I just have to advise you to talk about this and communicate about the options in front of you.'

Alice was about to rebuff Doctor Phillips, but before she could do so, Jacob stood up and offered his hand.

'Thank you, Doctor,' he said. 'As always, I'm not hearing what I want from you, but certainly I'm glad I know where I stand moving forward.'

So, you're leaving her, you pathetic excuse for a man.

Jacob reached down and took Alice by the hand. Still weak from the surgery to her neck and the medication flowing through her veins, she struggled to get up without assistance, and despite her fiery demeanour, she was truly struggling right now.

You think leaving her will help? it laughed.

I OWN BOTH OF YOUR SOULS.

Chapter 18: News From Home
Song of the day
"Everybody Knows" by Sigrid

Winter 2009
San Diego, California USA

The San Diego sun was sinking into its final throes as a low-lying sea mist fought to conceal its light early. This was Jacob's favourite part of the day. He'd done two consultancies for the little dockside restaurants just down the strip, and he was about to meet his beautiful Alice for a late lunch that she wholeheartedly deserved after a morning of selling her pictures to a local art gallery. The Alice Petalow range was actually outselling some much more prestigious names in both the shops she sold from, and Jacob was more than a little proud of what she was achieving. Things had been better for them recently, but winter had crept up on them, and Jacob hoped that the magic of the West Coast wouldn't be lost with the change of season. It rarely snowed this far south, but there was certainly much more bite in the air, and when the sun dropped below sea level, it paid to be dressed a little warmer. Jacob sat once again on the decking in front of the boathouse. Marshmallows for his s'mores caramelised on long steel skewers over a roaring firepit, next to a carafe of mulled wine that Alice had lovingly made. Jacob had to be honest, she had done a beautiful job, and he doubted any of his chefs back home could do any better.

Back home – Jacob laughed. Had it ever felt like home? Thinking about the UK, now, reminded him of being kicked from pillar to post by every bully at the Howard George. It reminded him of his family, who never seemed proud of anything he did, and his in-laws, who constantly looked down their noses at him. It reminded him of Evan, who scared him more than any man ever had, and of a litany of mistakes he had made. Alice was his home, and he hoped beyond hope she decided to make the move here permanent. After all, things had been better, for a little while at least. They attended therapy together every Monday and Friday and never left each other's side during the day unless work called.

Jacob's train of thought was pulled quickly from the moment as the breeze picked up a little, causing the firepit to spit aggressively at him while he cautiously rotated his marshmallows in a tight formation.

'Alice, it's nearly ready,' Jacob called. 'It's just a few minutes away, so get your sexy little butt out here.'

Jacob was full of spirit, with Christmas joy abundant in his voice. No reply greeted him, so he gave her another minute before he called once more. Again, his words went unanswered. He started stacking his chocolate and marshmallow sandwiches in soft sugar crackers he had made earlier in the day. It wasn't at all sophisticated, but it was decadent in all the right ways and had become his favourite indulgence that he'd picked up from the natives.

Pulling his tired body up off the bench, he went in search of his wife and found her slumped in the kitchen doorway, tears streaming down her face, a smashed telephone in her grasp.

WHAT have you done?

Ignoring the voice, Jacob ran towards her. 'Baby, what's wrong?'

'It's Mum. Mum's died.' Alice wept into her hands. 'What will I do without my mum?'

[153]

Jacob collapsed next to her on the floor and embraced her, wrapping his arms around her as if protecting her from the cold outside. 'I'm here, Pebble, I'm here.'

For a moment, Jacob was all there and nowhere else. She lay cradled in his arms, sobbing as he stroked her back and gently kissed her forehead. He knew nothing he said would help her, so he did all he could to show her that he loved her, to show her that he had her safe in his embrace.

'I've got you,' he whispered. And he meant it.

I have always hated flying. It's not who I am; it's not who I will ever be. And I know that's why you are here, why you are watching me. I can feel you here. Your presence is cold on my skin, and your glare constantly tells me that you know I'm afraid. You always appear when I fly. But I must confess, I've not seen you in so long that your presence surprises me. Even after all these years, you still feel new to me. I know you can't hurt me, that your words are just empty threats. That, actually, you are just a process of my mind playing the hate game once again. It's a song I've heard a thousand times. And, yet, as I look at you now, down the aisle of this bloated jet, lying in the open doorway of the cockpit like a coiled spider, too much mass squashed into too small a space, I am once again afraid. Yet I know it's unreasonable, because you are not real. You are not the monster I see in front of me, all teeth and tentacles. You are me. And I will not let this fear choke me. Not now, not when Alice needs me. We don't need you.

BUT YOU DO NEED US, JACOB.

AND WE THINK YOU KNOW THIS.

4pm UK time Wednesday

Alice had said very little during the flight. She had very little to say anyway, but she'd appreciated Jacob holding her hand throughout the journey, even if she knew it was more of a comfort to him than to her. He'd always hated flying but had never let it stop him, and she couldn't help but admire him for that. He'd gripped both her hand and the armrest tightly all the way from Washington, only letting go as the wheels touched down at Gatwick.

As they rode in the taxi on the two-hour drive back to Whitstable, he tried to reassure her a few times, but he knew her heart was broken, and he wasn't going to gloss over her pain with positive reinforcement. Still, she was glad he was there. She didn't want to sleep alone right now, not that she had slept since getting the news three days ago.

6pm Wednesday

Alice opened her arms into a wide embrace and bounded into her father, who gripped her like she was a child once again.

'It's a shame it took something like this to get you back home, monkey.'

Alice knew he had a point, so she gripped him tighter to avoid the combative response she would normally give him.

'Jacob, how are you?' asked the Viking king, not caring what the answer was.

'I'm fine, John. If there's anything I can do, then please don't hesitate to ask.'

John Petalow looked through Jacob with his piercing blue eyes, almost cutting him in two. 'There's nothing you can do, Jacob. There's nothing either of you can do.'

9pm Wednesday

'All these years together, and this is the first time I've been in your bedroom,' said Jacob, trying to lift the gloom a little as they got ready for bed.

Alice slipped a navy silk nightie over her head. It got caught on her ponytail, and she spun around, like a dog chasing its tail, as she tried to twist out of the tangle.

Jacob reached over and unravelled his half-naked wife, pausing to kiss her gently on her forehead.

Alice looked up into Jacob's deep emerald eyes. 'Thank you, baby, for everything.'

'I haven't done anything,' Jacob replied softly.

'You have, baby. You really have. Do you think I don't know you after all these years? The last few months have been wonderful, and I've really seen you try to be the Jacob I know you can be.' Alice paused for a second, before adding a touch of weight to her next sentence. 'I know how much you hated the thought of coming back to Kent. I know this isn't home to you.'

Jacob sat on the edge of the bed and took Alice by the hand. 'My beautiful Pebble, I've never felt at home. I feel constantly lost, like a ship at sea being thrown about by storms and ungodly forces, yet by your side I find comfort, I find warmth and I find nutrition of my body and soul.' Jacob pulled her face round to his own. 'So you never have to thank me for anything that requires me to stand by your side.'

11am Thursday

Alice stood cold and alone, looking down at her mother's recently filled grave. Earlier, the coffin had been lightly covered with a few handfuls of soft dirt that were thrown down onto it by the people who had been close enough to Angela Petalow to be allowed the honour. Alice had been standing there for an hour, while Jacob sat guarding her from a distance of a few hundred feet. He knew not to bother her. This was her time to grieve. He would pick her up if she fell, but for now he waited quietly and patiently. Alice looked up as it started to rain, the cold wind biting and snapping at her exposed neck. A rumble of distant thunder rolled overhead. As she brought her eyes back down to sea level, Alice was surprised to find another woman standing opposite her. The newcomer looked directly into the tear-filled eyes of a heartbroken daughter.

Alice looked at the woman and knew straightaway she wasn't real. She had black eyes and rotting skin and wore a black dress that draped around her, pooling five feet in every direction, like Batman's cape, giving the impression of shadow falling all around her.

I can't remember the last time I saw you without a frame around you. Alice looked at the apparition of the witch in front of her and showed no change of emotion, completely unfazed by the fact that her antagonist had chosen to appear on this sacred day. *Do you really think you can scare me today of all days? I've lost and buried my best friend. So, say what you want, bitch, as it really changes nothing in my empty and desolate heart.*

The creature looked at Alice silently and with utter contempt, tilting its head to the side, almost confused by the audacity of her words.

What makes you think I'm here for you?

The creature's mouth didn't move, and yet Alice heard every word. The rain lashed down harder. Alice dropped to her knees. Her frozen limbs left her watching what unfolded in front of her with little choice. The creature's arms extended down into the grave. Limbs stretched to unnatural lengths as bones broke and skin tore and, finally, the monster tore her mother's body straight through the lid of the coffin.

DO YOU THINK EVERYTHING IS ABOUT YOU, ALICE DEAR?

It was the monster's voice, but the creature spoke through her mother's pale and broken corpse, the lips moving like that of a ventriloquist's puppet. The creature held Angela's body out to Alice almost as an offering, before it rammed its clawed hand straight through Angela's back, tearing the very heart out of her and holding it out for Alice to see, black blood oozing through its fingers. Alice couldn't speak. The creature's jaw cracked open like a boa constrictor, far wider than was physically possible, with the snapping of bones becoming the only sound Alice could hear. Angela looked helplessly at her daughter as the monster put the heart straight into its gaping mouth and, like a seagull trying to eat an overly large fish, swallowed it down whole. The monster clamped its razor-sharp teeth closed with a wicked smile, before its long forked tongue started licking the rotten black blood from its jaws. Alice finally screamed, her throat almost torn open by the magnitude of her release, and in a heartbeat the rain stopped, as if her very voice had commanded it. The creature was gone too, taking Angela's corpse with it and leaving the stench of death lingering in the air.

'Baby, it's time to leave,' said Jacob. 'Your father will be waiting.' He placed his jacket over Alice's freezing shoulders. 'And I'm not sure a scream, no matter how loud, will wake the dead in the way that you want.'

Alice turned around and put her head against Jacob's firm chest.

'I saw it,' she sobbed. 'The creature from the mirror.'

'And did you stand up to it, like the therapist told you to do?'

'I did, baby. I mean, I tried. I really tried.'

Stand up to me?

Is that what was happening as I took your mother's soul to hell? Your mother's heart tasted only of disappointment.

'All you can do is try, Pebble. Your mum would be proud of you. I'm proud of you.' Jacob pulled her in close and kissed the top of her head. 'Never stop being you because of that thing I've inadvertently created.'

'This isn't your fault, Jay.' Alice looked up at him and put a hand on his cheek. 'We both have our demons.'

With no more to say, they started walking back to the car, not letting go of each other for the whole journey back across the sodden grass. If they had nothing else, they at least had each other.

Chapter 19: Sepia Tone
Song of the day
"Blackbird" by Rumer

Winter 2009
Canterbury, Kent UK

John Petalow sat stoically in his favourite chair, a beaten old throne of cracked leather and worn brass. It was an impressive size, and it had to be for the measure of the man. The deep burgundy of the chair fought to dominate a white living room that had only last year been given a fresh and modern look at the behest of his beautiful wife. But John would not consign his chair to a slow death in a second-hand shop. It was his thinking chair, his planning chair and apparently now his melancholy chair, where he would think of Angela and the day she had saved him. He had been fixed from that first kiss 42 years ago. So, what was he now? The old John was seeping back in every day, as proven by the argument he'd had that morning with a fish supplier. A fight that could easily have been avoided for the sake of a lost order of sardines, but he had almost relished the opportunity to put someone in their place and would have throttled the guy on the phone had he been within striking distance. Angela would have told him off, told him to apologise to the poor man, and he would have done it too. He would never let his queen down. But she was dead. And he had no one to answer to anymore – well, except Alice. His angelic daughter had fallen asleep in her mother's jumper while they looked at old photographs of Angela, in which she'd never looked more lovely. He'd covered Alice up with an old throw to keep her warm and pulled her hair from her dribbling lips. She was the very picture of her mother in her thirties and had the pure-of-heart attitude to match that same fire-filled spirit. By all accounts, she hadn't slept since the day her mum had passed, so he sat quite happily, listening to her snore like an overtired puppy; occasionally, she would kick her leg and let out a murmur of discontent at whatever she was chasing in her dream. It was probably a husband that didn't abandon her at the first sign of trouble. Jacob was upstairs, already packing their bags for a flight tomorrow that John knew his daughter didn't want to take. It was too soon. She needed to be home, and this had always been her home – not halfway across the globe, playing fairy tales with that idiot. He could hear Jacob clattering around up there. Maybe he would cave Jacob's skull in and then dump the body in the river that ran behind the house before Alice awoke. Or maybe go and drop him off the coast somewhere in his fishing boat, let a few hungry sea bass nibble at him. John found himself smiling a little too honestly at that thought process and decided a murdered husband probably wasn't what his daughter needed right now. She needed her mum, just like he needed his wife, but right now all she had was him and Jacob.

1984

John waded through a rock pool, trying to find the little fishing net Alice had dropped while trying to catch a small crab running through a shallow.

'You know,' said Angela, 'we really did create something beautiful, didn't we?'

Alice was sitting in her swimming costume, trying to grab the ocean every time the tide washed up to her feet, a tiny giggle bursting from her when the water reached her toes.

'We did, lover, we really did,' said John, bending down to pick up the rescued net from under his foot.

Long before Alice had been born, they had come to Broadstairs beach every August as a summer date. This was the first time they'd brought their little monkey, and it warmed their souls to hear her laugh so freely, her curly red hair thrusting out from under the little white sun hat that Alice would take off as soon as they turned their back. Not that John ever turned his back for long – he was overly protective of them both. He walked over and sat next to his wife, who offered him an overdue kiss. Her bathing suit made her look almost Audrey Hepburn-like, with oversized sunglasses to match. As he pulled his lips away from her, he had to gaze in wonder at just how lucky he was.

'What are you looking at me like that for, baby?' Angela asked playfully.

'Just telling myself not to wake up, because you make me think I'm dreaming at times.'

Angela took her glasses off.

'My darling,' she replied, with nothing but regret in her voice as she brought her other hand up to his cheek. 'You are dreaming.'

John awoke in his armchair with a shudder as the painful realisation of the dream seized him. That would be the only way he would see her now, in dreams and in photographs. And it broke his heart.

'Dad.' Alice was awake and upright, the throw wrapped around her like a cowl.

'What is it, poppet?' he replied, rubbing his eyes.

'I want to stay, Dad. I want to come home.'

SHE DOESN'T WANT YOU.

SHE NEVER WANTED YOU.

'But I love you, Alice,' Jacob pleaded.

[162]

Alice took his hands in hers and softened her expression to an understanding smile. 'Baby, your love for me has never been in doubt, even in your most despicable moments, and I promise that I love you more than you will ever know. But I need to come home, and I want you to come with me.'

Jacob released her grip with a broken-hearted sigh that resonated from deep inside his blackened soul. 'I can't stay here, Pebble. I hate it more than you know. I've found peace away from this place that I've not found anywhere else.'

Alice took a deep breath before saying the thing she had dreaded more than anything. 'And that's why I have to let you go, baby.'

THIS WAS HER FATHER'S IDEA.

Jacob's demeanour changed in an instant. 'Was this your dad's idea?'

'No, Jay, it wasn't anyone's idea, but thank you for once again blaming every choice you don't agree with on my father. You are aware I have a mind of my own, right?'

SHE'S WALKING AWAY.

'Don't walk away from what we have, Pebble, please.'

Alice looked her husband in the eye one last time before she turned for the door. 'I'm not walking away from anything, Jay. Don't you see? I'm tired of running from things, so it's time to come home. Where you see your place in all that is completely up to you.'

Alice pulled the protective wrap off the brand-new sign above her new studio. Papillon Noir. Written in a gloss ebony on a white backdrop, the sign was exactly what she had wanted, and the local company she had used had captured her vision with gusto. She had found the store by accident while shopping for her father's birthday present one sunny afternoon. She had tripped almost acrobatically over the front step while dancing down the little cobbled street with her headphones playing far too loud and had ended up almost falling through the 'For sale' sign. It was an old building with stone walls and exposed brickwork. She had fallen in love instantly and had pressed her face tightly against the glass door as she tried to figure out how best to turn this beautiful room into a business. And now, just three months later, it was nearly ready. She had used up most of her inheritance in advance to make it happen, but she knew that this was her true calling in life. She pulled back the smaller sign underneath like it was the unveiling of her life plan.

'Papillon Noir by Alice Petalow,' she read out loud with glee, completely content with her choice of font and colour. Her name was written in a rich jade green, giving it an air of class that prompted her to whisper to herself, 'That'll do nicely, Pebble.'

Alice hung the last of her watercolours up on the brick wall behind the small seating area she had designed for her more prestigious customers and took a step back to check it was level with the others. The shop was now filled with her own work, a lot of which Jacob had sent over to her from the US, and it left a feeling of pride resonating within her. Photos she had taken at various beaches across the world were available to buy for a small fee, with the larger paintings fetching upwards of £1,000 each. Whitstable was an affluent town, and she could really make this work if she played up to the right people, so she kept a couple of overpriced French wines in the back for those who needed a little help loosening up. In fact, a glass of Château Cheval was exactly what she needed now to celebrate. She poured herself a glass and slumped onto the forest-green chesterfield to admire her handiwork.

'I wish you were here to see this, Mum,' she said to herself.

Not for the first time, she felt a surge of loneliness wash over her as she realised the creature's voice was not the only one that had left her recently; she could no longer hear her mum's reassurance, and it scared her that she was doing this alone. But she was going to make this work. She had to make this work. This was her opportunity to shine.

Chapter 20: The Crow and The Girls

Song of the day
"No Ordinary Love" by You + Me

Summer 2011
San Diego California USA

The girl was a perfect representation of a teenage boy's dream. With the curves of her body making her look like a Coke bottle, she could have been a centrefold. Curls of brown hair rolled in cascades down the length of her spine, pooling into the small of her back with an almost chaotic beauty. She was angelic – or at least she would have been had she not been passed out and drenched in sweat. Jacob watched her lying face down on the Egyptian cotton sheets that he had purchased the day before at an obscene cost and nearly spat his wine out in disgust at what he had just done to a girl half his age upon them. He would cut her loose in a few days, of that he had no doubt, and yet an hour ago he could have told her he loved her. In truth, he couldn't love anyone but Alice. He would give the girl some excuse about work or maybe going back to the UK. But she wouldn't be the last to fall for his charms. In fact, she probably wouldn't be the last this week, and it sickened him that he didn't need a creature in his head to tell him how sad and pathetic he had become. But whether he needed that negative voice or not wasn't relevant, as it hadn't said anything lately that had caused him too much bother. On his bad days, he heard whispers and hisses of spite, but even these were few and far between, with the meditation and group therapy pulling him through what the doctor's elixirs could not. The creature that had spoken to Jacob all his adult life had retreated into the recesses of his mind, causing a calm to wash over him that he had never felt before. He felt that he could describe his bipolar best through colours, and that there was very little middle ground. If he was manic, he was red; low would be blue; and the rigmarole of day-to-day life left him vanilla, with no shades in between. And yet since he had started his treatment, he had only felt grey. Somehow, the monster, although retreated, seemed more dangerous than ever as it whispered rather than screamed its intentions to him.

The bedroom at the boathouse had full-length windows running along the west wall, and the setting sun was reflecting off the latest conquest's skin in a kind of holy radiance. Jacob poured himself another glass of Harlan Estate Cabernet Sauvignon and continued to hate on himself for the man he had become and the situation he once again found himself in. He wanted her gone but couldn't quite figure out how to remove her without having to talk to her first, and talking to her was not something he wanted to do.

As he took another sip of his wine, his eyes were drawn quickly to the large carrion crow watching him from the patio railings on the other side of the open French doors. The bird was easily the size of a seagull, and Jacob could hear its beak clashing against the railing as it tried desperately to rid itself of an itch. Jacob admired the beauty of the beast for a moment more before turning his attention back to the wine glass in his hand. 'How have you ended up here again?' Jacob whispered to himself, wondering how much Californian poison was left in his cellar. The crow answered his question with a loud *kraa*, which echoed through the bedroom, and opened its wings into a flutter that gave the impression that it was flexing its dominance over the scene. This impression hardened as the flutter turned to flight and the giant creature glided through the open door and perched on the thigh of the unconscious wench. Jacob didn't even react; he had seen too much these past ten years to be scared by such things, and he knew full well this could easily and most likely be part of an oncoming psychosis.

You know you can't stop, said the voice calmly and quietly.

And do you even want to stop without Alice here to pull you up on your behaviour?

Its voice, now almost constantly persuasive rather than the spiteful aggression Jacob had known for so many years, seemed to be coming from the direction of the crow rather than the space at the back of his mind where only the dark things were kept.

The bird started to walk up and down the bare skin of the girl. Its long, sharp talons, as ebony as anything Jacob had ever seen, were piercing her soft flesh with each little hop the bird took, leaving a trail of thin blood lines running the length of her leg. The natural reaction to this would have been to help the poor girl, who didn't even stir at the pain. But Jacob couldn't find the compassion to help a person he held absolutely no feeling for.

You really are broken, the creature called out as the crow tilted its head at Jacob with a knowing glare.

Jacob grinned, hearing the voice whisper in his mind. The creature's barbs had very little power over him since his doctor had found a balance of antipsychotics that worked; the medication helped Jacob safely across most hurdles and gave him the strength to argue back. Jacob could even find the creature's comments amusing at times.

'You know I don't have to listen to your shit anymore. I can shut you out at any time,' Jacob scoffed arrogantly.

Then why don't you, Jacob? the creature cackled. *Why don't you just wish me away? And maybe, while you're doing that, you can click the heels of your ruby slippers and take yourself home too? Oh, but you can't, can you? Because there is no one there for you anymore. Tell me, Jacob, do you keep me here sedated in the back of your mind just because you are lonely?*

[168]

Jacob let out a deep sigh as he listened to the voice echo simultaneously from behind his eyes and from the beak of the bird. He knew the creature was right, but he had to admit that he took just a little pleasure taunting *It* all the same. It was what *It* had done to him for 30-odd years.

The crow turned its attention back to the girl and started to take little bites out of her skin. Strips of fair flesh were consumed with each dip of the crow's fat neck, and yet Jacob still couldn't intervene.

Downing the rest of the glass, he pulled himself up while letting his bath towel fall to the floor around his feet. He felt no shame in front of the large bay window and didn't even blink at the baying murder of crows watching him from the patio. He counted six at first, with two more joining the flock a minute or so later. With both caws and kraas as his orchestra, he presented himself brazenly in front of his audience while he emptied the last of his wine bottle into his glass – a glass that was swiftly downed, before a loud snore brought his attention back to where it needed to be. He glanced over his shoulder to find the lead crow staring through his very soul.

Your humanity has left you, Jacob. You think you have me controlled, but look at what you have become.

The crow snapped its beak at him before driving it deep into the meat of the girl's leg.

'SHUT UP,' Jacob shouted with authority but absolutely no anger as he threw the empty bottle, which smashed into the bedside unit, destroying a lamp and a picture frame in the process.

The drunk waitress from the dockside bar down at the beach sat bolt upright, her complexion whitewashed with fear, panic and intoxication. 'Oh my god, what just happened?'

The bird disappeared, as Jacob had imagined it would. There was no sign of the horror it had inflicted on her leg. He turned back to his view and watched the seemingly real crows leave one by one.

'Sorry, love, did I wake you?' Jacob smirked without even turning to face her.

'God, my head's killing me.' The girl struggled to wake herself and rubbed her eyes frantically. 'Honey, can you take me out for something to soak some of this wine up?' She stretched her arms wide above her head.

'Sorry, Clare, I have work to do. In fact, I'm going to be a little snowed under for a few weeks now.'

'It's Clara! And you didn't seem that busy with work when you were trying to get my clothes off in the bar last night?'

She's called you out quicker than most, maybe we have misjudged her.

'You need to go, love,' said Jacob. 'I can't help being busy. I'll call you in a day or two.'

'You know what, jerk, don't bother.'

Clara started grabbing pieces of clothing from around the room and virtually fell out of the front door, still putting her boots on. Her mood mattered little to Jacob, who doubted he would ever see her again. And, honestly, he didn't care.

What have you become? the creature laughed.

I don't know, Jacob thought. *But I know it's better than hurting Alice*

Spring 2012 Canterbury, Kent UK

The chime of the little copper bell rang once more as a man opened the door for his partner. Taking her hand, he helped her up the front step before guiding her through the open door into Papillon Noir and its bustling interior. Alice greeted them with a wave and a nod but was mid conversation with another couple, who were about to blow a filthy amount of money on two of her oil paintings of the Reculver coastline, just a few miles down the road. For now, the newcomers would have to wait, and in fairness they seemed content to browse the work on the wall.

Business was good and the money was growing daily; Alice was already starting work on a second studio just a few miles outside of Canterbury city centre.

'OK, you have a deal,' said the stern-faced old husband, who had clearly been dragged here kicking and screaming by his much younger and more attractive trophy wife.

Alice was fairly sure this woman wasn't spending her own money, and thinking of what such a pretty young lady would have to do in order to get what she wanted from this fat old aristocrat made her skin crawl, although in fairness they probably both got what they wanted from the relationship.

'Thank you, Mr Whittingham,' said Alice. 'I'll organise our courier to deliver both pictures framed to your door on Friday, if that works for you both?'

Alice offered her hand to close the deal and the old pervert kissed it like she was one of his handmaidens. She shared a short look with his wife and realised quickly that the woman didn't give a damn. *You would be doing me a favour* was the message that the woman seemed to be conveying to Alice, who felt her skin crawl again. Still, five grand for three pictures was a good deal, and it made her realise that maybe she was a better artist than she gave herself credit for.

As soon as the transaction was concluded, Alice bounded over to the new couple. 'I am ever so sorry about the wait. Is there anything I can get you to drink while you have a look at what we have to offer?'

'No, my dear. We know what we are here for.'

The man pointed to a large oil painting above the entrance. The painting was of the Camber beachfront in East Sussex: golden sand and a deep blue ocean contrasted by a morning sunrise that almost looked like a photograph.

'The Camber piece. Well, I have a funny story about that if you would care to listen?' Alice offered the seating to the couple with a wave of her hand.

The couple sat down, and Alice continued with a sparkle in her eye but an almost regretful tone in her voice.

'Me and my husband – well, ex-husband – own a restaurant in Camber, and for the time that I lived there, I would walk down to the beach each morning and try to draw the ocean. Nothing would ever look right. It was as if the paper was rejecting the magic I saw in front of me.'

The wife, who was gripping her husband's hand, motioned to Alice to continue.

'And then, years later, I was sitting at home one night and I saw it, and even though I was thousands of miles away, I finished it in one sitting.'

The husband stood up and took Alice's hand. 'We'll take it. We loved it anyway. The story just adds another layer to it.'

'Great. Would you like it gift-wrapped or delivered?' Alice asked, before being interrupted by a man at the door.

'Or I could help you take it to the car,' said Jacob, taking off his sunglasses and looking his wife directly in the eye.

Alice closed the door behind the couple before wrapping her arms around Jacob. 'What are you doing here? I haven't heard from you in months.'

She went to release him, but he held on tight and kissed the top of her head continuously.

'I've just missed you,' he said, 'and missing you has slowly turned to needing you.'

Jacob finally let her go and placed a hand on her cheek.

Alice pulled away from him slowly. 'I get that, baby. But why now?'

'I've finished my therapy. I'm happy with my medication. I guess I finally felt ready to come home.' Jacob pulled up her chin with his index finger. 'Baby, I've moved home.'

Jacob finished the sentence by kissing her powerfully on the lips.

In reply, Alice slapped him hard across the face. 'How dare you think you can just waltz back into my world, into my gallery, and after nearly two years just slide back into my life?'

Jacob brought his hand up to his stinging face. He didn't dare reply until Alice had finished speaking.

'I've not heard a voice in my head for nearly 12 months, baby. I wanted to be right before I spoke to you. I couldn't risk making you ill.' Jacob placed his hands gently around hers. 'I love you, Alice.'

'Don't,' Alice snapped.

This prompted Jacob to bring himself down to Alice's eye level and interlock his fingers through hers.

'I LOVE YOU!' he said, one last time, before Alice jumped forward and pushed her tongue straight into his mouth.

Dumbstruck by the sudden move, Jacob staggered back a little, but failed to shake Alice's grip. Like a strong tide throwing a child to shore, she pulled him and guided them both into the back room. Jacob first took in the smell of paint and new canvas, noticing how messy the studio was in contrast to the pristine gallery. Before he had time to dwell on it, Alice pushed him up against a workbench and started to unbutton his jeans, her tongue not leaving his mouth. She made light work of his belt and dropped to her knees. Jacob, still not knowing what had hit him, let out a deep moan as she pulled his growing cock from the confines of the tight hipsters he always wore.

'Baby, I ...'

Jacob's words were cut off as Alice took him deep into her wanting mouth. Gladly accepting his fate, he ran his fingers through her hair and fell into a world of bliss that lasted only as long as Alice allowed, because as soon as he was hard enough, she pushed him aside with commanding authority and pulled herself up onto the workbench. Alice hoisted her light blue summer dress up around her thighs, and in one fluid and almost perfectly practised motion, she lost her underwear, gripped a fistful of Jacob's hair and forced his head between her thighs. She knew what she wanted, and she was getting it from the only man she had ever wanted it from. She bit down on her lip so hard that the metallic taste of her own blood filled her mouth.

'Baby, I want you,' Alice begged.

He rose up to kiss her lips, pulling her legs around him. He easily entered her wanting body and drove himself into her until they were a writhing body of orgasmic pleasure. They didn't stop to take breath, as is the way with two people in love when they have been kept apart for so long. Jacob's strokes were slow and measured but deep and powerful nevertheless.

'Cum for me, baby. I want to feel you inside of me, I've missed you so much.'

Jacob didn't need telling twice, and as his hips ground against hers, faster and deeper than ever before, he kissed her and filled her with everything he had to give.

'Pebble, I love you,' he said in a gentle voice, broken only by his need for oxygen. They soon lay in an embrace, trying to regain their breath, with Jacob stroking Alice's back gently. She clung to him like a koala, and no words were needed to explain the feelings of fear and excitement they both felt.

Alice waited to hear the voice reappear, but she heard nothing. She hoped that Jacob had the same luck, but the creature had other ideas as to what he deserved.

Chapter 21: Fragmenting
Song of the day
"Old Habits Die Hard" by Mick Jagger

Summer 2013
Whitstable Bay, Kent UK

A year had passed and finally Whitstable felt like home once more. The sound of the ocean lashing against the coastline felt like an old friend, while the smell of fresh fish coming off the harbour took him back to his youth every time he opened the car window.

Jacob was waiting in his Mercedes outside of Papillon Noir for Alice to finish getting ready. Why she hadn't chosen to get changed at home he couldn't figure out, but he admired her drive in pushing the business forward, as she had no doubt worked right up until the very second he had pulled up outside and beeped his horn. He had found a different Alice on his return to England. She was strong and independent. She was still 'his Alice', of course, but she was also something more now, and he couldn't stop telling her how very proud of her he was.

His daydream shattered as the car door popped open and his flame-haired soulmate looked back at him from the passenger door.

'Hey, handsome.'

She giggled like a schoolgirl, like she always did when she saw him, and he wouldn't have changed it for the world.

Jacob patted the passenger seat. 'Baby, we'll miss our table if you don't get that cute little ass in this car.'

Alice, who was wearing a beautiful summer dress in a dandelion-yellow shade, slid in next to him. Light caught the glitter on her pristine white heels, which matched a bangle on her left wrist. Her style was always simple, yet she accessorised with such elegance that she never had to wear designer clothes. Jacob was fairly sure that since the day he had met her gaze across the playground all those years before, she had never once looked bad. In fact, it was a constant sense of wonder to him how he had ever got such a beautiful creature to look at him in the same way he looked at her.

They pulled into the car park of the beautiful seaside pub. The Sportsman at Seasalter was the best restaurant in the area, and they had made it with ten minutes to spare. Jacob jumped out of his Mercedes and rushed over to the passenger side to open the door for his beautiful wife. He was ever the gentleman; it was a character trait he had got from his father and one that Alice had always found highly attractive in her man.

The sunlight was starting to fade as they were shown to their table. Jacob was pleased to see his favourite dish on the specials board as they passed it.

'You see that, Pebble?' Jacob nudged Alice as he pulled the chair out from under the table for her.

'Your slip-sole special? I did, my love. I might have it too today to see what all the fuss is about.'

An attractive young waitress was immediately on hand with a wine menu, but Jacob interjected quickly with a smile.

'I can't drink tonight,' he said, 'so just a mineral water for me, but my beautiful wife will have the most ridiculously priced glass of champagne you have to offer.'

The waitress smiled at Alice and tilted her head, pulling the wine menu to her heart. 'A special occasion, Mrs Brooking?'

'I don't think so,' said Alice. 'Oh, Jesus – it's our anniversary.'

She mouthed an apology to her smiling husband as he reached for her hand across the table.

'Pebble, you are working so hard that I didn't want you stressing over tonight. I love you.'

Two courses in, the conversation was flowing as easily as ever, with Alice giggling herself into tears on more than one occasion. Things had really seemed different these past few months, and Jacob's return had never felt like a mistake. But as she topped up her glass with the last of the wine, she realised her anniversary was about to fall apart. Alice went pale with shock at the sight of the man being seated behind Jacob.

'Pebble, are you OK?' Jacob asked, concerned for his wife, who looked like she'd seen a ghost.

Her silence did nothing to put his concerns to rest, so he turned to see what had paralysed his wife with fear.

'Is that Tom from the rugby club?' he said. 'I've not seen him in years, the pretentious prick. I never liked him. Looks like he's put on some timber, though.'

Jacob smiled to himself as he turned back to his meal, content that nothing serious had startled Alice. But as he looked at her again, he realised something was still wrong. 'Baby, what is it?'

Jacob took her hand, and Alice jumped as if she had left the room for a second and not realised she had returned to the table.

'Baby,' said Jacob, 'what on earth has got into you?'

Alice shook her head clear and tried her hardest to remain calm. 'I'll tell you on the way home, baby. Let's not ruin our dinner.'

WHAT THE FUCK WAS THAT?

SHE'S HIDING SOMETHING!

Jacob stood behind Alice as he wrapped her large Moroccan silk scarf over her shoulders, kissing the back of her neck as he did so. He was unsure what had been wrong for the last hour, but it hadn't taken away from how much he wanted to ravish her. Nothing would stop that happening tonight. Noticing Thomas looking at her, Alice dropped her gaze and turned to leave. Jacob got the door for her as they said their goodbyes to the waiting team, before making their way over to the car.

'So, tell me, what's been up?' Jacob asked politely, but making it known that his curiosity as to what had nearly ruined their night had been piqued.

'Can we talk about it when we get home, baby?'

Alice didn't want to say any more than she had, which only drove Jacob harder.

He pulled her round by her arm. 'Pebble, what the hell happened?'

Alice knew by his tone that she couldn't escape this situation any longer, and she let out a sigh of immense proportions. 'OK, but I need you to stay calm.'

But she knew that wouldn't happen.

Alice had been sitting alone in the car for 20 minutes. Jacob hadn't said a word during the whole conversation they'd had; however, his facial expression had said enough to put the fear of god into Alice. To his credit, he had held her hand tight while she explained her history with that pig Thomas, and he had brought her hand to his lips gently before he got out the car, whispering that he loved her as he walked back to the restaurant front door without breaking stride. She hoped he was OK, but more than that, she hoped he didn't kill Thomas. She wanted Thomas dead of course, and she had done for years, but she wasn't prepared to lose Jacob for 15 years in the process.

The car door opened, and Jacob jumped in without a mention of what had happened.

'Shall we go, my beautiful Alice?'

He pressed the ignition and pulled away before he had even put his seatbelt on. His knuckles were red and bruised and there were flecks of blood on the sleeve of his shirt. It was clear what had happened, but Alice didn't care; she just needed to know he was OK.

She placed her hand on his thigh. 'I love you, baby.' A stream of tears trickled down her cheek.

WHORE, the reflection in the window whispered to Alice.

Ten minutes before

Thomas lay bleeding on the floor of the restaurant bathroom. His mouth and nose were busted open in a mess of claret and broken bone, while one of his eyes had swollen so badly it would be a month before he saw clearly out of it again, and yet as he tried to draw breath into his cracked ribcage, he knew he couldn't go to the police. He knew he had more to lose than Jacob did. Jacob's blood-stained Timberland boot crunched down on Thomas's hand, and through the ringing in his ears, Thomas heard the last warning he would ever get in relation to Alice Petalow.

'If you EVER so much as look at her again, I'll kill you. If we walk into a restaurant, you walk out, do you understand?'

Thomas nodded as best he could. He started to black out as he watched his attacker walk away. His last sensation before his body shut down was a complex mix of guilt and hatred, but underneath it all was a question. *Who had Jacob Brooking been talking to while he was hitting me?*

Monday

Why was Thomas in her house, anyway? Can you answer that?

'She is allowed friends,' Jacob bit back.

Sounds like they were more than friends, don't you think?

'I know what you're doing.' Jacob clenched his fist at the unseen adversary. 'It won't work, I'm telling you straight.'

What I'm doing, all I'm doing, is telling you the truth.

'I won't let you get to me.'

A resilience in Jacob's voice made the creature grin within his mind.

Do you think I'm stupid, Jacob?

'Sick, evil and twisted, maybe, but no, I don't think you're stupid, although maybe I am for having this conversation with myself.'

Then ask yourself where I'm getting my thought process from. For if I am you and you are me, then surely you know the truth, the same as I do?

'What truth?' Jacob snapped.

She wanted it while you were winning her father's favour, laughed the creature.

'Shut up.'

Tuesday

You must have noticed.

'I noticed nothing, and I had an amazing time,' Jacob said while making the bed that he had just shared with his wife.

Well, sure you did, but did she? the creature mocked.

'Of course she did. She always does.'

She felt distant to me, like she was somewhere else or with someone else.

'Don't be stupid.' Jacob laughed. 'It's hardly an area I struggle with, is it?'

Your ego means nothing here. She wanted you to take her from behind an awful lot last night. Does that not strike you as strange?

'Not really, why should it?'

She normally likes to kiss you while you make love, doesn't she? Seems strange that has changed since you sorted

[182]

Thomas out. The creature gurgled its deep and broken laugh as it spoke.

'I know what you're doing.'

I'm just letting you know what I saw last night, and you had better believe that I see everything.

'Just shut up.'

But ...

'NO! SHUT UP!'

Wednesday

You never were a good chef.

'Because she didn't finish her lunch? Give me a break. She wasn't hungry.'

Jacob wasn't about to be pulled up on his cooking; it was the one thing he was sure he was good at.

She didn't look interested, in lunch or in you.

Jacob had no time for the creature's games today. 'SHUT UP!'

What exactly are you going to do if I don't, you disgusting and pathetic excuse for a man? YOU HAVE NOTHING THAT SCARES ME.

'I preferred you when I was haunted by you at the bottom of my bed. This medication just makes you talk more.'

Jacob's voice trembled, but he believed in every word that he threw at the creature. Lately, the creature had just spoken to him. It never appeared to him physically, like it used to. The antipsychotics he was taking day and night seemed to keep the worst of its voice at bay, but he still heard it speaking to him, and it had been worse since Sunday's incident. Jacob looked down at his still-swollen knuckles. Why had Thomas even been at her father's house, a place that Jacob had rarely been welcome? It was a question he didn't need the creature to ask; he had asked it a thousand times himself. Why had he been working 16-hour days just to show John Fucking Petalow he was worthy of being on Alice's arm, while she was making friends with the captain of the rugby team? Jacob waited for the voice, but nothing came, and he had a sickening feeling that wasn't a good sign.

Thursday

Jacob had been looking in the shed for at least a quarter of an hour, and yet the gloss paint that Alice swore was buried in here was still missing. He was getting frustrated and didn't want to be in this nightmare haven for arachnids, some of which were bigger than the desert recluse he would sometimes see run across the deck in San Diego. Jacob pulled out a drawer from under his workbench and saw the missing paint hiding under the old picnic blanket they used to take to Camber with them each summer, but as he pulled the blanket away, he disturbed the queen of all spiders, which had apparently made its home, with its sac of a thousand children, underneath. It ran at him as if startled by the light, and Jacob, in a hurry to avoid the raging beast, fell backwards, smashing his head against the lawnmower, which was hanging against the wall.

'I fucking give up today,' he swore, as he brought his hand to the back of his scalp to find the extent of the damage.

The spider, startled by the sudden noise and movement, darted under Jacob's old toolbox for safety.

'Yeah, you'd better hide, you little bastard.'

Jacob brushed himself down as he stood up. Through the shed's cheap plastic window and the patio doors to the cottage, he could see that Alice was on the phone to someone. The conversation looked heated. Was that why she'd sent him out to look for something she knew was hidden away? Was it another man?

YOU KNOW WHO IT IS!

The screaming went through Jacob, and he looked for the source of the voice, as for once he didn't feel it originate from within his own head. The origin was somewhere within the confines of the shed. As the noise spun him around, he felt drawn to the rear. The back of the shed was pitch black and looked longer than Jacob remembered it. He took a few tentative steps forward, noticing that the more he tried to look into the dark corners, the narrower and more nightmarish they became. Eventually, something took his eye, something glistening white and grid-like just in front of him. Carefully, he reached forward to take it, his eyes drawn to it because it was the only thing in the recess of the shed that wasn't ebony black. Before Jacob realised his mistake, the white grid opened into what was actually a mouth containing a thousand tiny white fangs. The giant spider, which was easily eight feet in height, lurched forward as its shiny jet-black body was caught by the light pouring in through the window. It clamped its massive jaws onto Jacob's upper arm and shrieked with joy as it tasted the man's blood exploding in its mouth. Jacob cried out in pain, but he fell silent again as the spider's arms wrapped around him. Its eight limbs were all chitinous, like those of a crab, but with coarse black hairs protruding from every crack in its armour. Still trapped in its bloodied jaws, Jacob found himself face to face with the creature. Its many eyes, all like obsidian stone, were polished to such a degree that he could see his image in every one, yet in every eye the reflection was different. All were versions of Jacob, some laughing hysterically, others crying and heartbroken, all of them alone, but one of the faux Jacobs lay on the ground, his arm torn open and bloodied. The creature bit down again, and Jacob felt his arm bone shatter into pieces as the spider tore it clean off, as easily as pulling chicken from the bone. Jacob pulled away and thrashed around the shed while the missing limb was replaced by a pressured fountain of crimson. Unable to take the pain, Jacob blacked out, leaving the giant creature smiling, with blood rolling off its hard carapacelike rain off a windshield.

Friday

'So, you woke up in the shed with your arm torn to shreds by the gardening shears and no giant spider in sight?'

'No spider and no sign there ever was one.' Jacob spoke quietly; he was completely defeated.

Dr Phillips looked over her glasses at Jacob. 'How long has it been since you last self-harmed, Mr Brooking?'

'Two years, give or take,' Jacob replied, with a little pride still intact.

'And you feel the medication is working?'

Jacob sat upright before he answered, looking Vivian Phillips square in the eye. 'I think I could certainly up my dose.'

NO!

NO!

NO!

Chapter 22: The Drugs Don't Work
Song of the day
"Skinny Love" by Birdy

Summer 2014
Whitstable Bay, Kent UK

Alice stomped her feet theatrically in a show of frustration. 'I wanna go out, Jay!'

'Then go out, baby,' Jacob responded calmly, without looking up from his book. 'I'm not stopping you.'

'I want to go out *with you*, douchebag,' said Alice, in full tantrum mode, almost jumping up and down while she protested.

'Why do we need to go out today? It's Sunday. That's my day of rest.'

Jacob gave a little grin at his joke, but he knew it was about to backfire.

'Well, I'm sorry, my lord, but the flaw in your statement is that we don't do anything any day anymore!' Alice took a seat next to him. 'I'm sorry, baby. I know the medication is hitting you hard, but the sun's shining and our cameras have sat idle for months now. Just come for a walk with me, maybe?'

Jacob looked up from his book and got trapped in her eyes like a deer caught in headlights. 'Of course, let me get dressed.' His response was half-hearted, like everything he did lately.

She's bored of you.

'I know,' Jacob whispered to himself as he put on a clean shirt.

Better off without you.

'She would be, I have no doubt.'

It was hot down on the seafront, the kind of hot he imagined would set vampires on fire even if they were in the shade. Jacob had stripped down to the skin, with only his jean shorts and olive-green Adidas on, to try to cool off a little. His skin, which always held a light, was burning under the intense heat of the sun's rays, and he felt good for absorbing some of the sun's power; he felt almost fixed and recharged by its light. He had hoped to get some nice pictures of Alice, but it had become impossible to keep up with her as she bounced excitedly from rare flower to exotic butterfly. She was a feather from the wing of an angel, and she was forever caught in the gust of a whirlwind. She was infectious with her positivity, though, and after being shut in the house for two weeks trying to deal with the effects of his change in medication, it was a blessing for Jacob to be soaking in more than the effects of the sun. Alice darted over to the fence of the nature reserve, which ran parallel to the harbour bay, and stood watching the herons fish for dinner, their long legs wading in and out of the marshland as smaller birds played around them. Jacob pulled his camera up to his eye and adjusted his lens to bring Alice into focus. She looked radiant as always, and her hair seemed all the more electric in the light of the summer sun. Jacob was hesitating to take the shot due to a figure lurking in the background who was clearly intent on draining the colour from his picture, as she wore nothing but grey and black while doing a fantastic impression of the word dishevelled. Her hair was as long as Alice's but almost black with filth. She hovered behind Alice as if she was about to pick her pocket, and it gave Jacob a sense of unease that felt strangely familiar. He pulled the camera away and rubbed his eyes before bringing the camera back up to refocus. His dark guest had left the shot. Actually, she had more than left the shot; she was gone. Jacob couldn't see her anywhere. He quickly snapped three shots while Alice pretended not to pose, and he smiled at his luck as she turned to face him, bit her lip and then ran off giggling. He walked slowly behind his excited girl as she flitted from side to side, skipping to a beat she could clearly only hear in her own thoughts. He knew he didn't deserve her. He knew she deserved more than he offered her. He hadn't wanted to come today; he wished he was home now. He had promised everyone that he would stick to his medication, and no matter the cost, he wouldn't break that vow. But it had hit him hard. He hadn't adapted well to the lithium. He was sleeping most of the day, while Alice ran two studios, and he was hardly being proactive when he was awake. He was getting to the gym at least, but even then he was a hood-up, music-on kind of guy. No one dared talk to him, and he was glad of that. He hadn't shaved in weeks, and he had never had a full-enough beard to pull off the fuzz that adorned his face. The constant tiredness wasn't just physical, though, as he actually felt numb inside too and imagined that he was coming across completely uninterested in everything Alice was bringing to the table each night. That was of course far from the truth, and he had never loved her more. But Jacob was finding it hard to get excited about anything of late, and Alice was noticing more each day.

'Come on, misery guts,' she called over her shoulder.

'I'm here, baby,' Jacob called out, not wanting to spoil her day.

He caught up with her staring out to sea, her beautiful red hair fluttering in the breeze, and was instantly in love with her all over again.

'Baby, you still love me, right?' said Alice.

'What? Of course I bloody love you. Where has this come from?'

Alice slipped her fingers through his and returned her eyes to the ocean. 'You never want to do anything with me anymore, baby. I feel like getting you to spend time with me is an effort you would never consider unless I was nagging you to do it.'

Jacob knew she was right, but it wasn't because he didn't love her. If he knew anything in this life, he knew that. 'I'll try harder. I promise I will.'

Jacob could hear a voice in his head saying something, but it was too distant to understand, and so, assuming the medication was doing its job, he allowed himself to be a little more positive for a second.

'How about a paddle?' he suggested.

'Mr Brooking, you do know the way to my heart after all.' Alice giggled as she skipped and stumbled down the pebble bank into the sea.

'I love you,' Jacob whispered to himself. 'I'd do anything for you.'

Winter 2014 Whitstable Bay, Kent UK

In the floor-length mirror was something Alice had only seen once before: fear and panic in the black soulless eyes of the creature. Its hands, withered and claw-like, were pressed against the glass portal, and it was pleading for help. It was still Alice in demon form, and yet the creature seemed to be making more of an effort to look like its counterpart as it tried to find a middle ground to meet Alice on.

SAVE HIM, it begged, for it knew without him there was no existence.

WE LOVE HIM.

The creature dropped to its knees as it gazed at the real world from its prison and saw the only thing that could possibly scare it. Jacob was lying in Alice's lap. He gripped her hand tightly with one of his own, while his left arm fell limp to the side, cut from elbow to hand. The creature watched tears roll down Alice's face as she grieved for the man she loved. And then, in Jacob's last heartbeat, it ceased to exist. And it was free of its prison. Dissipating into the nothingness of the void, it failed to hold its form, and then there was silence.

One hour before

You won't do it.

Jacob sat in the freezing bath, horrified at the task in front of him. He was sure of what he had to do, but that made it no less painful. He was tired of his existence and his sad little life. He had been unhappy for so long that he couldn't remember a time when he had felt consistently content in his world. And yet his own misery wasn't the reason he was here in the endgame; it was the misery he had put onto Alice and the realisation it wasn't getting any better after 20 long years together. For a long time, he had infected her with a negative mindset that was down to him not accepting the chip on his shoulder, which had developed solely from years of being bullied. When he'd refused to believe that someone as fantastic as Jacob Brooking could have any kind of mental illness, he'd started to transfer his condition onto her. And now, heavily medicated and too tired to respond to the voices in his head, he realised she was bored of him. She hadn't said as much, but he knew she deserved more. He didn't want to go out anymore; his drive was gone, his passion was waning and his ability to surprise her had been lost so that he could safely live a mundane life. And his beautiful Alice – so creative, so full of life – well, she deserved more. He could just leave, of course, but he knew he would always be drawn back to her. Jacob had watched her flourish when he was in

San Diego. Watched her start her own company and watched that company grow. Her painting had improved beyond recognition, and her work now fetched obscene amounts of money on a regular basis. His Alice deserved someone of equal stature, someone who would help her smile and could excite her with every touch. She deserved to be free, and as he picked up the short-bladed lock knife that he had taken rock climbing with him years before, when he had a life outside of his cage of misery, he knew that she would be.

DON'T DO IT.

The pain was overwhelming and frightened him into believing he had made a grave mistake. He clambered out of the bath and stumbled at every hurdle, smashing his body against every piece of furniture en route to his phone, which was downstairs on the kitchen table. He realised he wouldn't make it that far when he fell down the last six steps and collapsed in the hall. The bathroom towel wrapped round his forearm was soaked red and dripping with blood. He was starting to feel the life slip away from him, when the front door opened and his wife, in shock, froze in the entrance.

Save him, the voice said to Alice, sounding as scared as she looked.

'JAY, WHAT HAVE YOU DONE?'

She rushed over to pick him up, but Jacob was too heavy for her to lift. He collapsed down again, falling into her lap; his wound bled freely onto her white dress and a puddle started to form around where they lay. Alice fumbled for her mobile phone, but before she could enter any numbers, Jacob used the last of his strength to push it out of her hand; the phone clattered to the floor, swimming in the red fluid that was pooling around them both.

'Baby, what have you done?' Alice repeated. 'I need to call the ambulance.'

Jacob looked up at her and used his right hand to hold her tightly. 'You deserve to be free, baby. I can't do this anymore.'

Alice felt her heart implode. Erupting in rage at what was happening in front of her, she screamed at Jacob, for she knew that she couldn't lose him. 'FUCK YOU, Jacob. You're a coward. Don't you dare do this to me.'

She looked at the cut flesh under the drenched towel and felt her stomach rise to the back of her throat.

'Don't let it win.'

Alice kept whispering that same sentence over and over.

She looked up and saw her demon self in the full-length mirror, begging for help.

YOU HAVE TO SAVE HIM.

WE NEED HIM.

'Don't let her win,' she said.

Her head dropped as she cradled Jacob in her arms.

'Baby, don't do this to me,' she begged.

'I love you, Pebble.'

Jacob closed his eyes and rolled into her lap as if preparing to fall asleep. His arm dropped limp to the side as the last of his blood pumped onto the floor. Tears overwhelmed her, and she let out a guttural pain-filled scream.

SAVE HIM, it begged. WE LOVE HIM.

Alice looked up at the mirror and realised that the creature was gone, replaced by a more horrific picture – that of her dead husband cradled in her lap as she wept uncontrollably.

Chapter 23: The Nightmare Sleeps
Song of the day
"Wings of Speed" by Paul Weller

Winter 2014
Rainham, Kent UK

'I can't believe no one showed up, Sam,' said Alice softly. She was sitting with her brother-in-law in the front row of Rainham Church – the same church Jacob's and Sam's parents had been married in.

'Jacob made his own choices a long time ago, Alice, and you know that making and keeping friends was never his forte.' Sam took her by the hand. 'This isn't on you, sis. You do know that, don't you?'

Sam spoke with kindness in his heart. He wasn't muscular like Jacob had been, but he was taller and just as broad – a real man's man, who had never seen a hair product in his life. For him to talk so tenderly was a surprise, but one Alice was truly grateful for.

'He loved you, Alice, and if I'm completely honest, I've been unsure at times that Jacob could love anything in his life other than you.' Samuel put his hand on her shoulder. 'Jacob hated himself, even at his most arrogant. But you, Alice – you were the only thing he never doubted and the only thing he ever let in that later on in life he didn't regret. I hope as time passes you see that, and it helps you through the tough nights ahead.'

2004

Alice stood at the front of the church as Jacob, Sam and two of their uncles carried Paul Brooking to the front of the ceremony. A deep mahogany and trimmed with brass handles, the coffin was simple but clearly heavy and sturdy, exactly as her father-in-law-to-be would have wanted. They walked him down the aisle while an old ELO song played over the old church speakers. All of them were at least six feet tall, and yet the burden upon them took its toll. Paul had been a much-loved man within the Brooking family, and his loss would be felt in many circles. Jacob turned and walked towards Alice as his younger brother, who had always seemed like the older of the two, wrapped an arm around him. Jacob hadn't said anything all day. He was yet to show any emotion at all, and Alice worried that he had fallen in on himself, as she had seen him do so many times before. She had watched as his beloved grandparents had died, and as his Labrador had been taken to the vets to be put down, and she had witnessed not one tear being shed. Just silence, before months of emptiness and self-harm, both mental and physical. He took every loss as something personal to him, as if he was feeling guilt for any hurt he might have caused. He couldn't mourn his loss because of the anger he felt at himself for letting that person down. Jacob sat with her and she placed her hand on his, his stoic glare not showing a trace of emotion. She could see it happening once more. Maybe he would be OK. But she knew that was unlikely. Alice would be by his side, as it was all she could do, and she would love him as she always had, but she knew that the next few months would be hard, and she just hoped that he came out the other side.

Present day

Alice walked out to Jacob's freshly filled grave without realising that she had even left the church. A light rain fell around her; the cold bite of winter was starting to creep into every day.

'I love you,' Alice whispered to her lost love, before the last of her tears dried up on her flushed cheeks.

I love you too.

Alice shot around, not knowing where the words had come from, but certain it had been Jacob's voice that spoke them. She had to be dreaming; there was no other way to explain it. She couldn't calm her heart rate as she spun around in circles, looking for the source of the voice.

Find me, Pebble. Jacob's words were more powerful than before. *I'm here, find me.*

There was nothing around Alice other than gravestones, a few trees and an old path flanked by tall, expensive mausoleums, which she imagined rich families buried their loved ones in. She ran as quickly as her short heels would allow across the wet grass and skidded to a halt as she hit the gravel path.

I'm here, Jacob whispered.

Out of the corner of her eye, she saw a shadow of her love move between the stone buildings. She chased him to that spot, but as she turned the corner, she was met with a dead end.

Don't give up, I'm here.

This time, the voice came from behind her. She turned around so quickly her footing nearly went as her world spun in circles. Once again, Jacob flashed quickly between two buildings, almost mocking her as he called out.

I love you, Alice, he said one last time, as she rounded the corner behind him and found him there waiting.

An ancient stone water fountain built into the wall of the mausoleum towered over her. Rainwater poured through the open mouth of a gargoyle in a waterfall of crystal light and was pooling in the stone basin beneath. Within the water, she could see her Jacob.

'Baby, what's going on?' said Alice.

Apprehensively, she reached forward and broke the fall of the water with her outstretched hand. She watched, bemused, as Jacob's image danced and shimmered with the movement of the water.

I'm here, I'll always be here, and whenever you can see yourself, know that it will be me looking back at you.

Jacob reached forward and looked like he was going to take her hand but stopped just short of the water's end.

'I can't believe you're gone, baby. Oh god, I feel sick at the thought of living life without you.'

Alice wept once more, as Jacob smiled back at her through the streaming oasis.

'What do I do without you?' Alice begged, pressing her hand into the waterfall.

Pebble, you've got this, you always had this, so just carry on being you.

As he spoke these words, she swore she felt his touch.

'But I don't even know who I am without you by my side,' Alice said, with utter defeat in her voice.

Jacob smiled and whispered as he began to dissipate into nothingness. *You will always be you to me, whomever you now choose to be.*

Alice woke from her daydream with a jolt as the vicar rested his hand on her shoulder.

'It's not often I find people out here on dark, wet days, Mrs Brooking. Shall we get you home before you catch a cold? I'm sure your day has been long enough.'

Alice responded with a nod and let the vicar guide her back towards the car park, where she was saddened once again by the fact that the only car there was hers.

Chapter 24: In Dreams
Song of the day
"She's a Rainbow" by Lola Marsh

Summer 2015
Whitstable Bay, Kent UK

The sun was pouring through the window like a flood and filled the bedroom with the colours of heaven. Alice didn't have to stir, because as had been routine since Jacob had passed, she had woken up long before the sun had even thought to rise. She lay on her side of the bed, looking at the empty space, as she did every morning. The smell of his aftershave still lingered on his pillow, no doubt down to the bottle of 212 she kept in his bedside table. It had become a habit to spray his pillow once a week, and it genuinely helped her sleep, but she knew it wasn't good for her in the long run; she knew it would have to stop.

The radio came to life as her alarm went off; Aretha Franklin was the order of the day.

Who's zoomin' who indeed, Alice thought, as she sat upright with a stretch that caused several of her bones to pop. She jumped out of bed with the verve and inner gusto of someone half her age and looked out the window at the glorious sunshine, leaning on the windowsill for just a second to soak in the rich nutrients from her favourite star while taking in the glorious blue sky that surrounded it. She gathered her thoughts into something productive and decided to get dressed, with a rush of excitement filling her at the prospect.

'Morning, baby,' Alice said to her bathroom mirror while popping her toothbrush into her mouth. 'I have an entire diary of appointments to keep today, and honestly I'm not sure how I'm going to do it all without dying in that ridiculously hot studio of mine.'

Alice's words were mumbled at best, as she spoke while brushing her teeth. But since the recipient was her bathroom mirror, she doubted the clarity of her words made much of a difference. A mouthful of Colgate shut her up for a minute while she tied her hair back into the kind of loose ponytail that most models would spend hours perfecting.

'So, how do I look, my love?'

You look like my Alice, like the most beautiful woman I've ever met.

Jacob looked back at her from behind the mirror and smiled. Alice knew it wasn't real; Jacob hated his smile, and the reflection only smiled at her because she loved it. But real or not, these reflections were all she had, and she couldn't give them up.

Alice kissed the mirror, leaving her print on Jacob's reflection. 'Have a good day, baby.'

Well, I'm not going anywhere, am I? Jacob replied.

Alice placed her hand on the mirror, suddenly a little heartbroken. 'You have made that promise to me before. Please try and keep it this time.'

The day did not go to plan. Four meetings and only a few small sales of photographs. It was ridiculously hot in the shop, and Alice was impatiently waiting for her last client so she could run across the road and get herself an ice cream from Sundae Sundae. 'Pistachio and mint,' she whispered to herself, gazing longingly at the store through the window. Sweat dripped down her neck as her little air-conditioning unit struggled with its heavy workload. She would not be denied that ice cream. 'I have worked hard for that bloody ice cream,' she said to herself.

All of a sudden, the doorbell rang and snapped her attention back to the room.

'You must be Mr Jones. Welcome to Noir Papillon – to – to Papillon Noir,' stuttered the off-guard Alice to possibly the most beautiful man she had ever seen.

'Please, call me William,' he said, offering his hand.

Alice gladly accepted, noticing that both his arms were covered in tattoos from wrist to shoulder. His right arm had a nautical theme, full of anchors and old ships, whereas his left was more mythical, with a strong emphasis on what looked like Japanese cultural history. Alice, still a little out of sorts, looked up into his eyes, which were even more blue than her father's. William had white hair with a short but full beard of matching colour. His ears were pierced with two small black rings, and he had a delicate handlebar moustache that was curled to precision, which left Alice thinking he looked more like one of those new-age hipster barbers than a man who might spend thousands of pounds on her work.

'Miss Petalow, you seem a little lost in something. I can come back if you prefer?'

'No, I'm being rude, Mr Jones. Please, come and take a seat while I fetch you a coffee.'

Alice dropped down next to William on the leather seat as if her legs had forgotten how to keep her standing. 'So, what you are saying is you want to buy everything I have in the studio? I don't want to scare you off, but what on earth would you want with so many paintings?'

'My parents are hosting their annual ball in a few months, and all of the parasites of the Kent Art Society will be

[202]

there. Unbelievably, I've managed to convince them to let me hold an auction there, with the profits going to my foundation.' William did not break eye contact as he took Alice by the hand. 'We could really use your help on this. In return, I'll make you the star of the event. You have a wonderful reputation within this community, and this could increase your exposure tenfold.'

William, realising how passionate he got at times, let go of Alice's hand and apologised.

'No, it's fine,' she responded. 'I'm truly flattered, and of course I would love to help. What is it your foundation does?'

'We are a conservation group for animal and wildlife habitats. My parents, of course, hate me for it. They always assumed I'd use their millions to grow the family empire, and I'm not sure they know what to do with an eco-warrior son.' William looked at the floor. 'My parents are good people but more selfish than I am when it comes to the world we live in. But enough about me. Do we have a deal?'

'We most certainly do, Mr Jones. I will just have to work out the value, which may take a few hours. If you're in a rush, I can call you with a figure later?'

Alice stood ready to shake on the deal of a lifetime, but William instead rose to give her the hug he had been eager to give from the second he had entered her world.

'I'm in no rush, my Papillon. Why don't I go and grab us an ice cream while you get started?'

Alice giggled for the first time in a long time, and then blushed. 'An ice cream sounds wonderful.'

Autumn 2015 Whitstable Bay, Kent UK

The night was wonderful. Alice's pictures were auctioned for three times the amount she had sold them to William for. It boosted her confidence immensely to see her work so sought after, and it made her feel truly special to speak with so many important people within the art community, people whom she had never been lucky enough to mix with before. It filled her mind with ideas for future projects, and a few high-end commissions were booked off the back of the evening.

But when the rush of the night died down, she was in a position that left her conflicted in so many ways. She was walking home along the seafront, a journey she had made a thousand times before, a journey she had loved making with Jacob, and yet as she made it tonight, she was struggling with the fact that it wasn't Jacob holding her hand; it was William. Of course, she fancied him. How could she not? William Jones was in all probability the product of a Norse god who had mated with a playwright equal to Shakespeare in talent. But he wasn't Jacob. How could he be? Then again, she kept asking herself, was that a bad thing? Jacob, in all fairness, had been a very inconsistent part of her life. And yet when things had been good, they had been amazing, and Alice felt like she was betraying that memory even by contemplating the fact that she most desperately wanted to kiss her new partner in crime. Jacob had died less than two years ago. Surely it was too soon. What would everyone say, and more importantly what would Jacob say?

'I can't do this,' Alice said, pulling her hand from his.

'I'm sorry. I never meant to break any kind of boundary with us.' William seemed distraught that he might have compromised his blossoming friendship with Alice. 'Please don't think ill of me for overstepping myself.'

'No, William, I'm being silly. It's just ... I don't know, I'm a little lost, and I ...'

William placed a warm hand on her chill-bitten cheek. 'Alice, I ask nothing from you but your company and your beautiful smile.' His demeanour was open and kind. 'And if anything I have done or will do should jeopardise that, then I fall at my own mercy for ruining such a beautiful thing that I have found.'

Alice looked into his crystal eyes and swore even in the darkness of the witching hour on a cold November night that she could see her reflection in his soul.

'It would be a crime I could not forgive myself for,' he said.

He turned and carried on walking along the seafront, this time with his hands secured in the pockets of his tweed trousers. But, to his surprise, Alice caught up with him, looped her arm through his and pulled herself closer to him. They continued in matching stride, both content with what had been said.

Alice turned to face her protector as they reached the door to the ocean-view cottage that Alice had called home for the past year. Bought with the money from the sale of her and Jacob's shares of the Gallantry, the cottage was a fresh start for Alice, and she'd made it her own in every respect. It was as Alice as any building or inanimate object could be.

'Would you come in for a tea before you head home, Mr Jones?' she asked nervously, looking at his chest so that she avoided the bewitching effects that his eyes seemed to have.

'I think you deserve the rest your mind surely craves after such a wonderfully successful night. You should be proud of what you have done today. I know I am proud of you.' William took both of her hands into his own and kissed her gently on the cheek. 'Rest well, my Papillon.'

His words fell away as he turned and walked into the night, leaving Alice clutching her heart for a moment.

'Goodnight, Mr Jones,' she whispered to herself as she closed her front door, resting her head against it as she bolted the lock into place, a sigh escaping her in sadness at once again being at home alone.

She hadn't seen Jacob's reflection much of late. He seemed distant and fleeting at every visit. Did he know how conflicted she was? She walked to the end of the dark hall, where a large, ornate mirror leaned casually against the wall, and placed her hand against it.

'Help me, baby,' she said in a choked voice. The guilt she was experiencing as a result of having feelings for William outweighed her pride in the night's work and the money that had been raised for his charity. 'Where are you, Jacob?' she pleaded.

I'm here, I'm always here, he whispered back.

Alice fell to a slump next to the mirror. 'Baby, I'm sorry. I'm so sorry. I've been weak.'

Don't be sorry. You have done nothing but be the woman I fell in love with, my beautiful little Pebble. Or was it Papillon?

Chapter 25: The Curtain Call

Song of the day
"I See You, You See Me" by The Magic Numbers

Winter 2016
Whitstable Bay, Kent UK

'I can't let you go,' said Alice as she fell to her knees in front of the small bookcase that carried the last memories of her marriage.

A black-and-white portrait shot of Jacob stood proudly in a silver skeleton-edged frame next to their wedding rings on the top shelf. Below that was a montage of Polaroids taken with a vintage camera her father had bought her 20 years before. The pictures were of moments they'd shared over the years and were all very natural, full of smiles and laughter. Underneath that was her first Canon SLR: a dusty old bit of kit that was considered cutting edge when Jacob had bought it for her. It still contained a full reel of unprocessed pictures of wild flowers and rare birds at Rye Harbour. Undoubtedly, it would have a few shots of Jacob she had squeezed in stealthily while he wasn't paying attention – although she had a feeling he always knew what she was up to, since he always looked like he was flexing in every single picture, a fact he denied with vigour. Every time, Jacob would smile and say, 'I'm not flexing.' She could hear him now, and, honestly, right now she needed to hear him.

Alice grabbed both wedding rings off the shelf, putting hers on its rightful finger and Jacob's on her thumb, and walked over to his old chair in front of the fire, collecting a heavy wool blanket from the back of the sofa as she walked past. She wrapped herself up in the blanket like a silkworm ready to transform and sat watching the open flames dance and spit in a display of exotic colours, doing their utmost to light and warm the cold, stone-clad room. As if Alice had found her final resting place, she drifted off into a comfortable sleep, in which she almost instantly felt Jacob take her hand.

'This is a dream, isn't it?' asked Alice, already knowing the answer, as she and Jacob walked hand in hand along the beachfront.

'Your whole life is a dream, my beautiful Pebble. Tell me, have you ever stopped dancing through life?' Jacob said playfully, which caused Alice to grip his hand all the tighter, as she knew this was a moment worth savouring.

'What do I do, baby?' said Alice with a heavy heart. 'It's getting harder each and every day to sit alone looking at your picture. I need you. I need you to help me.'

'Pebble, I couldn't tell you what to do when I was alive. What on earth makes you think I have that kind of power now?'

Jacob leaned in and kissed her, his lips warm to the touch and softer than velvet. Alice closed her eyes as Jacob's hand released hers, only to fall around her waist and pull her closer. His free hand began exploring her hair as he gently probed her mouth with the tip of his tongue. As she felt him pull away, she opened her eyes and, with a sickening blow, realised he was gone. Not even a goodbye this time. She pulled her dress from under her and sat down on the beach, looking out to sea.

'What do I do, baby?' she asked Jacob, knowing no answer would come.

She slipped off her sandals and spread her toes out in the soft sand. The warm air from the sun washed over her as she remembered why she had loved coming here so much.

Closing her eyes, she thought of William and of his determination to win her heart. She smiled at his overly polite nature and his willingness to help everyone he met. Could she ever really love another man? Could anyone ever really love her, once they knew where she had been? He seemed to, despite her unwillingness to let him in. And Dad seemed to like him. That was certainly new. Maybe he was going soft in his old age. Or maybe he had fed off her pain all these years, the way she had fed off Jacob's.

'I hope you have found peace, my forever,' Alice said painfully as she sat up and looked out over the calm blue ocean. She pulled herself up and, carrying her sandals in her right hand, started walking towards the sunset. In her left hand, she played with her wedding ring. Slipping it off and holding it in the palm of her hand, she decided that when she woke up, she would come up with a plan for the two rings, as, surely, holding onto something that meant so much was never going to help her move forward.

Wake up.

Alice opened her eyes in a panic and checked her surroundings. She was still wrapped up in the armchair. The fire kicked up amber fireflies into the dark room.

Find me.

Recognising Jacob's voice, Alice stood up, confused and scared. The cold stone floor bit her toes.

Find me, Pebble. I'm here.

Alice moved through the living room to the door where the voice had originated.

I love you.

'Baby, where are you?'

I'm here, Jacob whispered.

Alice walked past the kitchen to the base of the stairs.

I'll always be here in your heart.

Alice rushed up the stairs two at a time and dashed into her bedroom, her heart pounding. And there he was. Jacob stood where her reflection should have been, in the full-length mirror leaning against the wall. There in his prime. His hair was that slightly longer length, which she loved more than she would admit. A clean and crisp white T-shirt hugged his muscular frame, and jeans and sand-coloured Timberland boots finished his look. His wrist, however, which would normally be covered by bangles, had a scar that ran from there to his elbow, and it was a sight that caused her heart to sink.

Alice moved towards Jacob's reflection. 'Baby, what's going on?'

You know what's going on, Pebble. He put his palm up to the mirror. *It's time to go.*

Alice burst into tears. A mixture of joy and heartbreak overwhelmed her as she brought her hand up to touch his. For just a second, she swore she could feel their fingers entwine. For just a second, she felt him.

'What will I do without you?'

Alice sobbed, looking at the floor as if hoping that the world would open up and swallow her where she stood.

I love you, Pebble.

'I love you, baby,' she cried, as she looked up and realised Jacob, her Jacob, was truly gone. And she realised the reflection in front of her was a very rare sight indeed. It was her own.

And then, out of nowhere, his voice echoed once more in her mind for what she knew would be the last time.

You've got this.

For the first time in 20 years, she felt truly alone.

Spring 2017

She knew she could do it, she had complete faith in herself, and yet this last step was feeling more improbable with every passing second. It was the simplest of tasks, too, with not a thing stopping her, and yet she failed at every opportunity to take what could be the most important step of her recent existence.

'You can do this, Petalow,' she said, with more fire in her belly than the previous two or three times she had said it, although her words, which were meant for self-motivation, served only to delay what needed to be done.

In a daffodil 1950s Lindy Bop dress tied high on her waist, with a white belt, designed to look like an oversized bow, sitting just above the curve of her hip line, she certainly looked the part. Her fiery red hair curled into ringlets as it flowed from underneath a white headband and spilled over her right shoulder, giving her the look of a young Maureen O'Hara. She felt as good as she looked, and there was no doubt in her mind that she was more than capable of doing this. So, with a final push, she took the last step forward and went to knock on William's door. Hesitation held her back for one last second before her knuckles made contact with the gloss navy-blue door.

To her surprise, it opened instantly and as if by some magical force.

A smiling William Jones stood proudly in the doorway.

'I did wonder how long it would take you to knock on,' he jested loudly, but his demeanour was that of a man who was ecstatic to see the girl of his dreams.

Alice stepped straight inside his personal space and placed a finger over his mouth.

'Oh, do shut up, William,' she said. She leaned in and, this time without hesitation, pressed her ruby red lips hard against his.

Somewhere deep inside of her, the creature stirred, disgusted by the unbridled joy the woman was feeling. It grunted and spat as it turned in on itself. They had always called it the Voice, but for now there was only silence. For now, it would rest; and, for now, it would wait. The creature was human in frame yet moved unnaturally, like a marionette with its strings tied wrong. It had a feminine kind of appearance, but with its grey broken skin and jet-black eyes, it lacked any softness. The Alice creature had called Alice a witch, but it knew she couldn't fathom its true form or existence in any rational sense. For now, it was irrelevant. It was weak and it had no voice. Backed into a corner of Alice's mind, the creature closed its eyes and began to dream of the things that only the wicked might dream about, until, once again, it was given the power it needed, to feed.

Chapter 26: The Harlequin

Song of the day
"Telephone Line" by ELO

'If you continue to wear so many masks, my son, you will one day forget which one your true face is.'

Jacob read the quote out loud from the crumpled note it was written on as he sat on the beach in the thundering rain. He had given up caring about the downpour when he realised there was nowhere for him to shelter for at least a mile in any direction; instead of sprinting for cover, he had sat slumped against the sea wall, accepting he was going to get wet. As always, he was overdressed for his location, in a classic white linen shirt with the cuffs rolled back to his elbows, matched with a tweed waistcoat and a cross-hatch flat cap that made him look like a farm owner about to have his cow named "best breed" at the Kent County Show. All he had in his possession were his book, an old first edition of *The Rats* by James Herbert that he held tightly in his embrace, and a few quid to buy himself a coffee on the way home. He had left his phone at home, so as not to be distracted by the online world while he tried to clear his thoughts out here in the real world, but finding the note had preoccupied him more than any social media app could have done. It was a note from his father, hidden inside Jacob's favourite book maybe 25 years ago, just before he had gone off to start his apprenticeship in London. Paul Brooking had always had a way with words, either written or spoken, although admittedly he shared very few of either. A quiet man from a working-class family, he had loved both his sons more than anything and had prided himself on being a family man. This little nugget of advice would have been placed there with wholehearted purpose. As a boy, Jacob had always put on a front, completely dissatisfied with the young man he was, and he had often changed his friends and surroundings to avoid anyone finding out what a loser he felt like most of the time.

He had stolen and broken both hearts and material possessions to try and prove to the world that he was the man that he claimed to be. He had thrown away everything that had ever mattered to him to prove that he didn't need anyone or anything. And his father had seen through it all and never intervened, never pulled him up; instead, he'd tried to guide him with music. Jacob remembered every song his dad had ever asked him to play. There was a day, many years ago, long before Alice had lost her dear mum and long before Jacob had lost his best friend and father, when Jacob's father had given him the album *Stanley Road* by Paul Weller on cassette, passing it to him with the words, 'If you listen to every song on this album properly, I'll never have to teach you a life lesson ever again.'

Jacob would of course not be so lucky, but he understood the sentiment well enough. His father was a man of few words, but everything he said had weight and purpose. Jacob had idolised his father, and it was failing to emulate his achievements as both a husband and a son that had caused Jacob so much pain these past 20 years. 'I've only ever let you down,' he would whisper every time he thought of his relationship with the greatest man he had ever known. The voice of the creature, now muted in the back of his mind, would agree with Jacob in a heartbeat, but really there was no need. Jacob had made peace with the man he had become. He had made peace with his failings as a son, as a brother and as a husband. He was wounded and hardened with a body made up of scar tissue. And he had started to realise each day just how tired he had become. Yet today he felt lighter, almost free of the burdens that had tied him down for so long. In fact, he felt a little dreamy, as if everything was a little more beautiful. As the rain had started to fall upon his aching skin, he had felt warmed by its gentle wash. He could nearly smell

[214]

the rain today, and each breath Jacob took seemed to take him to a new high. Jacob wondered if this was something he had always been able to do and this was merely the first time he had noticed.

As the rain subsided and a break in the clouds brought a ray of light more bright and vibrant than any he had ever seen, Jacob realised he wasn't sure how he had got here. He couldn't remember leaving the house.

'Hang on,' Jacob said out loud.

He bounced up to his feet with a mixture of shock, confusion and surprisingly renewed mobility, the arthritis in his left knee, a product of lower-league rugby throughout his youth, having completely cleared up for the first time in years. He spun around, realising that he had no idea what beach this was, causing the sensation of not knowing how he had got here to become panic at the thought that he didn't even know where "here" was. As if sensing his fear, the sky cleared completely, and the warmth of the sun washed over him like a comfort blanket, bringing with it an immense calm. He couldn't remember ever feeling safe in any capacity unless ...

'Alice.'

The whisper escaped his lips like he was talking in his sleep. He had only felt safe with Alice by his side. But where was she now? His thoughts on this morning were still whitewashed, like looking too closely at the sun. The last thing he remembered clearly was waiting for her to come home from work. He had missed her terribly, and yet he'd had a feeling of fearful trepidation due to her imminent arrival. Why? Why would he fear his beloved coming home? What was he afraid of? The monster! Jacob remembered fighting with it throughout the best part of the day. It had been trying to stop him from doing something, but Jacob was unsure what, or why that would have caused him to be afraid of Alice coming home, which was always the best part of his day.

'It's going to be OK,' said a familiar voice – a voice both soft and full of the kind of wisdom one can only gather over many lifetimes.

Jacob knew it had come from behind him, and yet his body wasn't ready to turn around. He knew the voice like he knew his own – better, even – and yet it couldn't be. How could he be here?

'You're safe here, you never have to be scared again.' The man's voice moved closer as footsteps displaced the pebbles beneath.

'You left me when I needed you most.' Jacob's words were joined by the sound of his tears dropping onto the book, which was firmly clenched in his hand. 'I couldn't find you.'

'I never left you. I've watched you every day since you were born. I've been with you through it all, Jacob, and do you know what I've learnt over that time?' He placed his hand firmly on Jacob's shoulder. 'It wasn't your fault, son.'

Hearing his father's last words, Jacob spun around and wrapped his arms around his father's core. Although he was sure he and his father were the same height, he felt small in his dad's tight embrace.

'I love you, Dad,' Jacob whispered, refusing to relinquish an embrace he never thought he would get again.

'Welcome home, son,' Paul Brooking whispered while kissing his son's head repeatedly. 'I love you too.'

And then, Alice awoke... Alice had been lying deadly still on the hospital bed for what seemed like years. The room was clinical and open, with nothing inside it that didn't have a purpose. She lay on her side, crunched into a foetal position, with just one white pillow folded beneath her plaited auburn hair.

Chapter 27: The Light and the Lighthouse
Song of the day
"No Surprises" by Radiohead

Jacob couldn't decide on a way forward. This was a pivotal decision, one that had to be made with a clear mind and a calm heart. If he hung out the washing on the east-wing line, it would surely dry better away from the sea mist; but those bloody crows – damn those bloody crows – they always left mess all over that side of the grounds, and they cared little for the brilliant white of his T-shirts. The west wing was getting increasingly hit by ever-more-aggressive waves smashing against the coast. The ocean spray lashed hard against the white stone walls of the lighthouse, like a giant primordial lash, bringing a thunderous clap like shingle thrown onto a tin roof with each giant splash. Jacob was unsure how long he had been living on this gargantuan rock surrounded by a violent sea and a murder of monstrous crows, but he knew he was happy and that this place almost defined him, with its melting pot of beauty and uncontrolled environmental destruction. It was as if someone who knew Jacob intimately had created this place for him. 'The east wing,' he murmured to himself, knowing he was taking a chance. He carried the wicker laundry basket across the lush green of the lighthouse's back yard and over to the wood house, where the washing line sat loosely on the ground.

'KRAAAAAA,' the closest crow called from the large birch tree that the other end of the line would attach to.

'Kraa yourself, you big bag of feathers!' Jacob responded.

As Jacob pegged his clothes on the line, his attention was pulled back to the lighthouse. He swore he could hear his father calling from the kitchen. *Maybe lunch is ready,* he mused while he hurried his pace, eager to see what his dad had created for a well-earned break in play. They had a good system here. Paul Brooking would wash the clothes, while Jacob hung them out; his dad would cook lunch, while Jacob always made dinner; and Paul loved to tend the garden, while his son looked after the welfare of the lighthouse itself – not that they had ever seen a ship to warn. Jacob hadn't yet figured out how this place worked or even if it had a name. But they had made it a home, and they were happy. The larder was somehow always full, and although the weather threatened, it had always been kind.

'I'm coming, Pops,' called Jacob as he pegged up the last shirt. He looked up briefly to warn the crows that any attempt to ruin his work would involve grave consequences, but to his amazement, not a feather could be seen. In fact, he couldn't see a bird in the sky. 'Not even a gull to ruin my washing. Maybe my luck's in.' Jacob smiled, picked up the empty wicker basket and began his stroll back to the lighthouse so as to enjoy another five-star lunch with his best friend.

'Son, I've been calling you,' said Jacob's dad as he put a platter of cured meats and smoked cheeses down on a giant oak chopping board at the centre of a circular table.

'Dad, this looks beautiful,' said Jacob, taking his place in a chair next to a sleeping Peepo. The black Lab had been waiting for them at the window the day they'd arrived, and Jacob had to admit that his heart had lifted immeasurably to see her beautiful shiny wet nose at the window as his father had led them along the beach to what would become their new home.

'Hold on, son, the best is yet to come.' Paul Brooking pulled a loaf of rosemary bread from the Aga. Steam and herb-filled aromas filled the kitchen, and an almost incandescent glow radiated off the bread. Paul laid it down next to a dish of sea-salted butter and smiled.

'Dad, you never cease to amaze me. This all looks bloody lovely, and Mum would be proud if she were here.'

Jacob pulled a slice of ham from the table and slipped it to Peepo, who instantly pricked up her ears as Jacob whispered encouragement to the forever-starving beast.

'You can wash your hands again if you insist on feeding that bloody dog,' said Paul without even turning around.

Jacob laughed. 'What exactly am I going to catch from not washing my hands in this place?'

'What exactly do you think this place is, my boy?'

'Oh, sweet Jesus, Dad, you know I can't answer that. The words always seem to escape me even as I try to speak them, and honestly, Pop, haven't we been through this little dance enough times?' Jacob, although defiant in his reasons, was still a son who did as his father asked, and so he jumped to his feet, sinking his hands into the soapy water Paul had got ready for the plates in advance. 'You know, Dad, I've never cared where this place is, or even what our purpose here may be, but I'm truly glad I'm here with you and Peepo.'

As he went to sit back down, he noticed that Peepo had vanished. Where she had gone in a closed room of this size was a mystery, but Jacob gave it little thought, as, honestly, where could she go?

Jacob and his father ate everything at the table except for a few crusts, which were for the nest of swallows above the barn gate, and a few scraps of meat for Peepo, if and when she ever returned from her mysterious hiding place.

'Let me help you with that,' said Jacob as his dad tirelessly cleared all the plates. He reached across the table to grab the empty glasses, when something happened that shocked him frozen. 'Dad! What's happening?'

Paul looked around to see his son's left hand slowly disintegrate into an ashen vapour trail that left a mist of fireflies dancing out of existence.

The glass remained unmoved by Jacob's efforts to take it, and the fear was spreading through him like the flame that tore away at his arm.

'DAD, I'M SCARED! WHAT IS HAPPENING?'

[219]

Jacob was in full panic mode as the fire spread up his arm and into his shoulder. Each limb disappeared as the flames consumed him, as though he were a sheet of paper. Jacob looked up at his father to see him all but disappear himself.

'Don't be scared, son, you must have known this was coming.'

'What was coming? Dad, what was coming?'

Paul Brooking smiled at his son as he finally vanished. 'I love you, son, but you didn't really think this was real, did you?'

Jacob looked down as the last of his visual self finally vanished into nothing, and a veil of darkness washed over him.

He felt no pain. And he felt no peace. Jacob Brooking, by all accounts, felt nothing.

Summer 2009 St Martin's Hospital, Canterbury

'William,' Alice croaked as she woke with the throat of a woman who hadn't uttered a word in two years.

The man in question stood with his back to Alice on the far side of the room, mid-conversation with one of the nurses, and he didn't even flinch at the frail voice that had escaped her. Alice pulled herself up with great unease, and the nurse drew William's attention to the patient.

'Alice, you're awake,' the doctor said as he hurried eagerly to her bedside.

'William, what's going on? Where am I, and what on earth are you wearing?' asked Alice, gently pulling his stethoscope.

The doctor smiled a toothy grin through his grey beard and shone a pen light into Alice's deep blue eyes. 'So many questions, Miss Petalow, and we can answer them all, but for now please just breathe and let me take a look at you. Two years is a very long time to be in and out of a catatonic state.'

Alice's heart rate increased and her breathing followed suit as the confusion started to overwhelm her. 'WILLIAM, WHAT'S GOING ON?'

The doctor leaned in once more. 'Alice, who exactly do you think I am? You keep calling me William. Is that someone you want me to contact?'

The nurse came to take Alice's pulse. Alice sat shaking as she tried to piece her world back together.

'You're William, my boyfriend,' she said. 'You just told me you loved me whilst on our first weekend away.'

The doctor raised his hand. 'Alice, I'm not William, I'm Dr Williams, and I've been overseeing your stay here at the hospital for the past 23 months.' The doctor pulled up his security pass from the lanyard round his neck and presented it to Alice.

'Consultant J. Williams ... No, NO, I don't understand.' Alice's voice started to fail as her throat fell into an uncontrollable tremble. 'WHAT IS HAPPENING TO ME?'

He's not listening to you, the voice came from nowhere, and Alice barely registered it anyway.

'Alice, we need you to breathe,' said the doctor, while the nurse called for support.

He's forgotten you, he's going to leave you, just like Jacob did, called the voice.

'Jacob,' Alice murmured on hearing the name voiced in her head. She rocked back and forth, struggling to control her breathing like the doctor had asked.

'Do you need Jacob?' the doctor answered. 'We will call him as soon as you settle, he was just here yesterday.'

'WHAT?' Alice stopped hyperventilating. 'But Jacob's dead.'

She hadn't used her legs in two years, and her attempt at making it to the toilet was futile to say the least. Dr Williams tried to catch her, but Alice still took a rather nasty hit to her knee as her legs immediately buckled, like those of a newborn giraffe trying to find its footing, and she hit the ground.

Alice opened her mouth to breathe for what felt like the first time since the doctor had told her the news. But she struggled to draw in anything of sustenance and started to suffocate, despite there being no restriction on her airway.

'Breathe, Alice, you need to calm down.'

'MY DEAD HUSBAND IS APPARENTLY NOW ALIVE AND MY NEW BOYFRIEND, WHO APPARENTLY IS NOT MY BOYFRIEND AT ALL, IS THE DOCTOR TELLING ME ALL THIS,' Alice screeched while gulping huge breaths in between each and every word. She bellowed once more, 'And YOU – YOU, who looks identical to the man who just today, as sunrise touched my eyes and awoke me from dreams, told me he loved me, as he kissed me gently good morning – YOU, of all people, want me, ME, to calm down?'

Alice was overwhelmed and emptied her stomach of whatever protein-rich fluid had been pumped into her these past two years with the sole purpose of keeping her alive. Her world went to darkness once again, and the last of her strength slipped away into nothing. The only remnants of consciousness in her weary and broken form came from a tiny twitch she made every time she heard the voice in her head call out to her.

Alice, come back to us!

Chapter 28: Scar Tissue
Song of the day
"Wasting my Young Years" by London Grammar

Summer 2009
St Martin's Hospital, Canterbury, Kent, UK

Alice hadn't spoken in minutes, but Dr Vivian Phillips didn't have any desire to rush her through this; after all, she wasn't on the clock today. She had been brought in especially. Alice's parents had paid a handsome sum to make sure Alice got all the help she needed from a doctor who knew her personally and had experience with her broken past.

'So, I've been in an induced coma since I cut my throat?' Alice asked.

'Not quite. We pulled you out of it as soon as your stitches healed fully. You were induced because you wouldn't stop trying to tear them out. You nearly bled out on us twice, Alice.' The doctor held back a genuine sadness at the fall of her favourite client and pushed some photos across the desk.

The images showed Alice on the same hospital bed she had woken up on not a day before.

'But these photos show I'm wide awake,' said Alice as she flipped through the pictures, which were dated by month starting a year earlier.

'When you were taken out of the coma, you remained in an unresponsive catatonic state for a further 12 months. We could get nothing from you other than one thing.' The doctor slid one last photograph across the table and placed a painted and finely manicured nail on the image. 'He came to see you every day for the first four months, and then every few weeks after that. He even brought you flowers on your birthday just the other day.'

'Jacob's alive,' Alice whispered.

'Yes, quite alive, although at times over these past few years, I believe he's struggled to believe that's a good thing.'

'Have you kept seeing him – you know, in a professional sense? Is he OK?'

'I believe he's on his way here now. But, Alice, it's been two years. You have to be prepared for a different Jacob to walk through that door. His therapy has been intense, but you would be so very proud of him.'

Alice found a smile for the first time since she had woken. 'But I saw him die – I held him in my arms as he bled out. What do you think that could have meant?'

The doctor smiled. 'Do you think maybe that was your way of forgiving him and letting him go?'

They sat in silence for a moment while Alice soaked in what she was hearing.

'Alice, there is one more thing we need to discuss, if you are up for it? Before we induced you, before the doctors could stop you tearing your stitches out, well, you kept screaming out a name.'

'Thomas,' Alice interrupted, with fear edging into her voice.

'Let's talk about Thomas for a little bit – that's if you're strong enough?'

'Yeah, erm ... I mean, of course.' Alice sighed and looked at the floor. 'To be honest, I'm so very tired of keeping secrets designed to protect other people.' She reached up and scratched at the long-since-healed scar on her neck. Then she raised herself up and gingerly moved over to the en suite, stopping at the mirror to take a look at the horror looking back from beyond the reflection. 'But before we start, can we find a way to shut this bitch up who won't stop screaming in my head?'

Alice's reflection laughed at the audacity of such a pathetic specimen calling her a bitch and smiled a fang-toothed grin as a way of acknowledgement to Alice's true self.

You fucking piece of shit.

Jacob stood tall as his reflection voiced its unwanted opinion from the protection of a broken old mirror crudely stuck onto the men's-room door. A bigger and better mirror surely wouldn't have stretched the budget of the best private hospital in Kent.

Don't ignore me.

'I'm not ignoring you, Ahab,' Jacob replied. 'I thought we were going to try getting along. Remember what Dr Phillips told us to do.'

You cannot reason with me.

'Well, clearly not today, as you are being an intolerable fool, so, yes, maybe I will ignore you.'

She's better off without you.

Jacob straightened his collar. 'Well, on that, old friend, we can at least agree.'

7 April, one year before

'Let me get this straight – you want me to give that bastard a name?' Jacob seemed more interested than normal, and the light in his eyes shone for the first time in months. 'What, pray tell, would giving the bloody thing a name do to help me?'

'Giving it a name, Mr Brooking, will grant you two things – firstly, the ability to differentiate its voice from your own internal thoughts, and, secondly, a better degree of power, if and when you fight back.'

Jacob laughed. 'Fight back? I'm not sure I've ever won a fight against that thing, certainly not one of any consequence.'

Dr Phillips raised a perfectly kept eyebrow at Jacob and peered over her black-rimmed glasses. 'If you have never won a fight with the voice inside your head, then surely you will need all the help you can get.'

She was right, he needed help, as he had hit a bit of a rut of late. The kraken within his mind was nowhere near the threat that it had been in the years before, but it was still there each and every day. He had learned to ignore all but its most abusive barbs, yet at least once a day it would find its mark. That was fine when it was just him he had to worry about, but now there was someone else to consider.

The present

Jacob took a deep breath and placed a firm hand on the bathroom door, both fear and excitement causing his heart rate to dance like the jungle drums in a 1940s King Kong film. Jacob feared he was not the titular ape in this analogy, but rather the petrified young British explorer, out for glory but with no idea what peril lay ahead. 'You've got this, Jay.' Jacob pushed through the door and fell straight into a confident stride as he took the corridor that led to Alice's ward. He had tried to make an effort, with a crisp white shirt paired with a navy tie and matching trousers. He had brought it down a notch, into a more casual look, with an informal sleeve roll that exposed the shipwreck tattoo on the underside of his forearm, a reminder of his time lost at sea aboard the *Summer Breeze* – a reminder of a time lost to himself. He rattled as he walked the halls, with more bangles and beads than a Thai monk. He wanted to impress her, needed to impress her, not because he wanted to win her back, but because deep down he knew that this was all his fault.

'You look like the woman you should be, Miss Alice,' said the ward sister, who had been kind enough to help Alice put some make-up on.

'I look rough and you very well know it, Miss Bonnie, but thank you for trying.'

Alice walked gingerly back to her bed and, with a little help from the ward sister, managed to get herself upright against a couple of large pillows that had lost their volume after one too many Sister Bonnie pat-downs. Bonnie Belmonte was a strong woman of Antiguan descent, and her thick Caribbean accent hadn't left her over a 30-year tenure in the UK.

'You are,' she said, 'what my grandma used to say, a duppy conqueror.'

Alice giggled at the strange phrase. 'And what exactly is a duppy?'

'A duppy, my sweet girl, is a ghost, and you are a ghost conqueror.' Sister Bonnie smiled as she took Alice's hand, her beautiful white teeth separated by a gap in the centre of the top row. 'You have got this, child – on that I promise.'

Alice gave her hand a delicate squeeze. 'Can you tell me about these scars?' She pointed at the tiny marks that ran over her arms and legs.

'Those are from you rolling about the floor like a loon, in a thousand shards of broken mirror. Apparently, when Jacob carried you screaming into the San Diego ER, you were bleeding from so many small cuts that they were lost as to where the actual injury was at first.'

'And what of this big one on my belly? How did that get there? I noticed it when you helped me bathe earlier, but I was unsure if it was just my mind playing tricks on me.'

The sister took a hold of Alice's hand once more and leaned in close. 'My dear child, you really don't remember a thing, do you?'

Alice shook her head as the sister pondered how to answer.

'I think the story of that particular scar is one best told by Mr Brooking,' said Bonnie, 'for I feel I won't do the story any real justice.'

Alice let the sister's hand go and smiled softly. 'I'm sure it can't be any worse than the story that brought me here.' She ran her fingers over the hairline scar on her neck. 'Thank you, Sister.'

'You're very welcome, Miss Alice. Now be strong, for I hear footsteps on my ward floor.'

As Sister Bonnie left Alice to finish the last part of her journey alone, she passed a very nervous-looking Jacob in the doorway and took a moment to place a hand on his forearm, her midnight ebony skin contrasting with his pale colour; he clearly hadn't seen too much sun in the last two years. 'You be kind to her, child. You may have been coming in for one-way conversation these past two years, but today I reckon she might have a little in return.'

Jacob hoped that were true. He nodded and rounded the doorway, apprehension as to what might be said ruining the excitement that had been building every day for the last two years.

And then ... There she was ...

Alice sat on the hospital bed in a white summer frock that fell around her ankles. Her hair was tied back to reveal a slim neckline. She was almost gaunt from a two-year liquid diet that had given her exactly the nourishment she needed to stay healthy and alive but little sustenance. She had certainly lost a dress size or two. But where her body was frail, her sapphire-blue eyes still shone bright with bewitching power, and just like the last time Jacob had seen her sitting upright, they were filled with tears once more. She didn't speak just yet, she couldn't. Instead, she held out her arms and Jacob rushed to fill them with the kind of embrace one can only experience when your love returns from the dead. Both of them held on tightly to what was once lost and refused to let go in fear of reality kicking in, a reality where they were once again apart, and once again alone.

'I thought you were dead,' Alice cried while she peppered his brow and cheeks with kisses.

Jacob brought his hands up to cradle his wife's cheeks and kissed her lips firmly. 'I am not so easily lost to this world, my beautiful Pebble, but I must confess, I am eager to hear about this journey you have endured in its entirety, as it sounds quite the caper indeed.'

'Baby, the nurses said you visited every day. I know it seems crazy, but whenever you were telling me about your day, it seemed to be shaping my dreams. The story in my head was almost mimicking the stories – at least, that's what my nurse has been telling me.'

Jacob smiled and sat next to his wife, taking her hand in his own. 'Had I known that, I might have tried to brainwash you.'

Jacob laughed and Alice punched him in the arm, causing him to hold it in mock pain.

'I'm serious, Jay. The nurses told me your stories. When you started to benefit from your therapy, I saw it happen. When the medication took its toll on you, I saw it happen. And when my mother ...' Alice paused and closed her eyes for a heartbeat to try and find the strength to finish her statement.

'She had a stroke about 12 months ago,' Jacob explained. 'Strangely, it tied in almost to the day with you waking up from the induced coma and falling into that unresponsive state. We nearly lost her, and quite honestly we are lucky to have you both here with us today.'

Alice looked up and took in what Jacob was saying. Every word, no matter the grim nature of the subject, was a pleasure to hear. His absence had been hard, and his presence by her side was a joy she had felt she would never feel again.

'I wonder why I took the news of her falling so ill as a death in my world. What do you think my mind was trying to tell me?'

Jacob took a deep breath before he answered, struggling to find the words. 'I think your mind was confused, for the same month that your mum fell ill, I lost Grandma.'

Alice took her husband in her arms and pulled him close. 'Jay, I'm so sorry, I wasn't there, I didn't even ... What happened?' She shuffled closer and held Jacob's arm tightly.

'She had struggled since losing both my gramps and then my dad. I think she just stopped taking care of herself, and in the end that took its toll. It wasn't your fault, baby, far from it, but maybe the guilt of not being there for me manifested itself through your dreams.' Jacob sighed but looked into Alice's eyes with relief. 'I'm just glad you are back with us, Pebble; we have a lot to talk about.'

'That sounds ominous,' said Alice, yawning. The two years of sleep had taken their toll.

'I'll say no more until John and Angela get here.'

'John and Angela? I'm not sure I've ever heard you call them by name before. It's usually "your mum" and "your dad", and with no small amount of disdain, either.'

Alice was only half joking, although Jacob would have struggled to disagree. He had never bonded with them as Alice would have wanted – not until recently, anyway.

'Pebble, things have changed these past 18 months, and a lot of it has been for the better, but I must confess I have mixed feelings about how this might play out. So, can you do me a favour? I need you to know how much we all love you and how very proud you should be of us all.'

Alice almost couldn't believe what she was hearing. 'Us all? I have to say it's a pleasant surprise to hear you talk about my family like this. I guess I can take solace in the fact that some good has come from all this.'

NO.

NO GOOD COMES FROM THIS.

IT'S NOT REAL.

8 May, one year before

'Ahab? A strange choice even for the most dedicated Herman Melville fan,' said Dr Phillips. 'Tell me, why name it after the captain and not the whale? After all, the whale would be apt, in terms of both scale and design.'

'Because the whale was just trying to go about its business,' said Jacob, 'trying to live its best life. Captain Ahab was the true monster. He was dedicating his whole existence to killing that whale, to sinking that whale and taking its life into the bleak void of the cold ocean floor. This thing inside

[230]

of me is much more like that. It's the evil trying to harm the innocent.'

'Do you believe yourself an innocent party, Jacob?'

'I don't believe I'm guilty of the kind of crime that deserves the punishment I so often receive,' said Jacob defiantly.

'Then I'm glad to say, Mr Brooking, that we are getting somewhere.'

Chapter 29: Ruby Slippers
Song of the day
"The Rip" by Portishead

Summer 2009
St Martin's Hospital, Canterbury, Kent, UK

'Are you ready to talk about her?' said Dr Phillips with an air of caution in her voice.

'Evan? I hope that bitch rots in hell.'

Dr Phillips seemed hurt by Alice's words, a reaction not missed by Alice.

'No, Alice, not Evan, but at least we've established that you're not ready to talk about that part of your life yet. I meant your mother. It must be an amazing feeling to know your mother is alive. How does that feel?'

'Oh ... Honestly, it doesn't feel real that either of them is still here. Jacob or my mum. It's a dream to me, and my mind won't allow it to take root – not until I can see, touch or hear them, I guess.'

'Well, they shall be here soon enough. I hear Jacob was already on his way to see you when he got the call, and your parents are close behind.'

'Jacob and my dad in the same room, and I'm too weak to run away – please, Doc, put me back to sleep.'

Doctor and patient shared an awkward laugh that turned into an even more awkward silence – one that was broken in the most unexpected way.

'You might find this hard to believe, but your father has a new-found respect for Jacob,' said the doctor.

'I'll believe that when I see it,' said Alice.

'Remember these words,' said Dr Phillips, 'if you remember nothing else that I tell you. It's OK that things have changed in your absence. You might even be pleasantly surprised.'

Two hours later

Angela Petalow wrapped her arms tightly around a daughter whom she had thought was lost to another world. Tears of joy and disbelief ran down her cheeks as an overwhelmed Alice held her with equal vigour and love. They refused to break the embrace, and they couldn't find the words to form coherent sentences. 'I love you' was all that could be heard escaping from both sets of lips in between the crying and smattering of long-missed kisses. But the joy and relief they felt was radiating off of them in such abundance that Jacob felt warmth just to be in the presence of such love.

'I never thought I would see you again,' said Alice, kissing her mother squarely on the lips.

'All that matters is that you are here with us now, because we have so longed for this day.' Angela turned and placed a cupped hand on Jacob's face. 'Isn't that right, my favourite son?'

Alice was so overwhelmed with joy that she didn't allow the shock of such an unusually sweet moment between her mother and husband to break into her thought process.

'That's right, Mum, this day has been long overdue,' said Jacob, caressing his mother-in-law's hand in return.

'Oh my god, what has been going on between you lot while I've been away?' said Alice. 'I feel like I've woken up in the twilight zone.'

Angela took her daughter's hands and sat next to her on the edge of the bed, feeling an instant contentment, one that she never thought she would feel again. 'In times of hardship, sometimes the smallest things can bring us all together.'

Alice furrowed her brow. 'What on earth are you talking about? I'm not sure me being asleep for two years would qualify as a "small thing". Actually, speaking of things that are far from small, where's Dad?'

'Well, I guess I would be here.' The deep and brooding voice of her father split a path between Angela and Jacob like he was parting the Red Sea. His huge frame filled the doorway with its unnatural width and height, and his demeanour was stern and unmoving, as always. John Petalow was a man mountain and a colossus, one who had always hated her husband for never being "quite enough" for his Alice, and yet she could see something different in him, something kind and protective. Where once he had been a bull, now he carried the air of a giant stag – majestic and family orientated, despite its strength and indifference towards others outside of the herd. 'I was parking the car, love. I dropped your mother off at the entrance because she couldn't wait to see you.' He took a few strides into the room with his arms still folded and kissed Alice square on the forehead. 'Welcome home, monkey.'

It was unusual to hear so many words from her father, even under such a unique situation, but Alice knew that he was happy to see her back on her feet – well, at least sitting upright.

'And this, my son, I believe to be yours.' John Petalow unravelled what Alice had assumed was a defensive crossed-arm gesture and passed the most beautiful auburn-haired child to Jacob.

This isn't real.

'Jacob, what's going on?' said Alice as her heart rate grew in both speed and aggression.

The silent child smiled at Jacob while holding onto his tie as if for dear life.

'Alice Marie Brooking, I present to you your daughter, Dorothy Gale Brooking.'

LIES LIES LIES LIES

As Jacob turned her in Alice's direction, Dorothy pushed away from the mother she had only ever experienced

[234]

as asleep or in a trance-like state. The flame-haired princess had never known her mum, and all the knowledge she had of her was from the stories her dad would tell her each night. Alice was struggling to figure out what was happening – what had happened – and her confusion threatened to send her back into the false reality she had just come from. Alice reached out tenderly to hold the shrinking child's hand but fell short as a young Dorothy cowered from a touch she had never known, leaving Alice to fall forward and into an abyss she, once again, couldn't have seen coming.

Alice had fallen like this before, after the assault by Thomas many years before, but where on that occasion she had blacked out and woken up on the carpet of her childhood home, this time she hit the ground hard, and the jolt through her body shook her to her bones as she rapidly decelerated to a standstill. A foot of water had broken her fall, enough to stop serious injury, but the air was knocked from her in one huge and forced exhale that left her gasping.

'Alice!'

She could hear William's voice calling her, and yet as she rose to her feet to check her surroundings, only two things embraced her – darkness, and the murky ocean that rose up to her knee.

'Alice! Come back to me.'

William's voice was coming at her from every angle and she felt her equilibrium tested as she took to her feet in the abyss of pure midnight. Alice spun around on a floor so black it possibly didn't exist and looked for the source of the call, but to no avail. Her movements caused ripples in the water, which looked more like oil, and this brought movement to her attention. Things were swimming about her ankles within the dark liquid. Obsidian tentacles whipped about in a frenzy, making it look like the ground beneath her was actually alive. This couldn't be real ... *Could it?* Remembering back to a session with Dr Phillips, Alice clenched her fists tightly and closed her eyes. She focused only on her physical self and released the tension slowly from her fists, before opening her eyes once more.

There sat in front of her was the image from the hospital ward. She was lying on the bed, catatonic and oblivious to her apparent daughter pointing at her motionless body. Alice was watching it play out as if on a screen. She could see her mum rushing around, screaming for nurses to come and help, while her father just placed a reassuring hand on her shoulder. Jacob, with Dorothy held tight in his arms, looked like the father she knew he would be. His eyes were locked on hers, and she could see him mouthing the words, 'You've got this, Pebble, we believe in you.'

'Alice!'

Alice shot round and looked behind, to see herself seemingly unconscious once more, this time on the soft tartan rug of the picnic that William had set up. His hands pressed tightly on her motionless heart, as he knelt by her side. But this was different, because William was looking straight at her, not at the image of her motionless corpse in front of her.

'It's not real, Alice, come back to me.'

'William, I can't move,' said Alice as she met him in conversation for the first time in the surrealness of the abyss.

'Baby, you have to try. It's not real, any of it,' William shouted, trying to stay strong, just in case Alice needed to use his voice as an anchor.

'What's not real, William?'

Then, as though afraid of something he could see behind Alice, he scrambled to his feet, falling backwards as he hurried.

'NO!' he screamed. 'It can't be.'

Alice turned to find the vision of her family replaced by her mirrored demon self.

Hello Alice.

It wore the same white frock as Alice and yet the frock was stained and filthy. This creature of broken skin and missing teeth was grinning, its over-sized fangs the only thing on the apparition that were not rotten with decay. Once again,

Alice was frozen still. The creature, with limbs of unnatural length, stepped forward to grip Alice by her arms. The creature's bony fingers, each ended with black, razor-sharp talons, pierced her flesh as it spoke in its wicked and broken tongue.

IT'S NOT REAL, CHILD.

Alice fell into panic. The stench of the creature's breath was almost overwhelming. Alice clenched her fists and closed her eyes once more. Ignoring the pain in her arm and the hot acrid breath of the oppressor, a feat that wasn't easy as she felt her blood trickle down her wrists, she slowly unclenched her hands and opened her eyes with a bellowing shriek to find her hand holding a tiny ruby shoe, and as she looked up, once more in the real world of the hospital ward, she was faced with a confused Dorothy, a young lady almost amused at the audacity of this new woman in her life, who had stolen her shoe.

'Dorothy,' Alice whispered.

'Dorothy,' Jacob replied reassuringly.

Dorothy said nothing, while pointing at her father with a smile.

Alice watched Dorothy giggle as she reached up to Jacob's face, letting the bristles of his short, well-kept beard tickle her hand. Alice herself tried to hold it together, knowing, without any doubt, where that scar on her belly had come from.

Chapter 30: Between the Infant and the Abyss
Song of the day
"The Soul Searchers" by Paul Weller

Summer 2009
Faversham, Kent, UK

It had been a week since Alice had woken from her nightmare, and yet she felt more out of place in the waking world than she ever had before. She was sure that this was real, but that didn't mean she had wanted it to be so. She sat in the passenger seat of Jacob's Mercedes and watched the beautiful green countryside of Kent zip past at speed. She was unsure how to feel just yet. Everyone kept telling her how happy she should be for having finally woken up, which would have been fine had she had any recollection of being asleep, yet what had actually happened was that the snow globe of her life had been shaken with such vigour that nothing really made sense anymore. She had an 18-month-old child whom she had no recollection of even carrying. She had a husband and a mother back from beyond the grave and a boyfriend who in reality was not her boyfriend and had no idea what the daft young coma victim was talking about. None of it made sense. She had tried to write it all down with Doctor Phillips, and, on paper at least, it all tied in. William, her boyfriend in the dream world, looked like Dr Williams in the real world. She had imagined her mothers death when Jacob had sat by her side one night and spoken of Angela having a minor stroke. It all added up – even the day that Dorothy would have been conceived fell into place. Alice couldn't fathom how she had never noticed a bump of any kind, although she did remember the struggle of getting into her dress on that awful day of mirror shards and Jacob's return. One thing still didn't click, though: why she would imagine Jacob's death and his eventual release from her life.

'Jay, tell me again about the news you gave me this year – you know, when you used to sit by my bedside.'

Jacob took a while to answer. 'Well, I told you about your mum, and about the shop that I saw for sale – the one I thought would make a great studio for you.' Jacob fidgeted with obvious unease as he continued to reel off things that were not of any help to Alice. 'And then I told you that, erm, that I'd met someone.'

Alice felt weak. She was confused and heartbroken at the news that she could never have seen coming, even though there was no reason for it not to have been a possibility.

'Then why are you here, Jacob, if you have met someone else? Or am I missing something? Why don't you help me to connect these dots?' Alice was glad that her supposed daughter was in her father's Range Rover just ahead.

'Because you are my wife, Alice, and despite the fact we broke up – and you cannot deny that we did – it doesn't mean I stopped loving you or even wanting you back.' Jacob sighed deeply and took a moment to find the right line of defence. 'I came back to you that day in San Diego because I wanted to make things right with you. I'd had extensive therapy and had come a million miles from the person who had left you those three months before, but I never planned to find you cutting your own throat open, I never planned for you to go to sleep for two years, and I certainly never planned to meet anyone, even though I had no idea if you would ever wake up.' Jacob tried to take Alice's hand but was quickly rejected. 'Alice, I never thought you were going to wake up, and yet I still came and sat with you each day in the blind hope that you would.'

The Mercedes pulled into the Petalows' driveway. John was carrying a fast-asleep Dorothy into the house.

'I'll get the bags out,' said Jacob. 'Do you need a hand getting to your room, love?'

Alice scowled and reached for the door, but Jacob stopped her with a firm grip on her arm.

'Alice, I've done nothing wrong here.'

Alice sat back once again. 'Then you won't mind telling me everything, will you?'

Everything? Well, this is going to be fun, said Ahab.

Yes, old friend, you might want to stay out of this one, thought Jacob.

Autumn 2008 Faversham, Kent, UK

'Double espresso, Mr Brooking?' said the barista at Barton Millie's Coffee Cup, one of those modern types of coffee house where the staff all had tattoos and suede aprons.

'Yes please, Jessica, and would you be so kind as to run it over to my table with a smoked cheese croissant?'

Jacob handed over a crisp ten-pound note from his money clip and refused the change with a wave of his hand. His morning had been productive. He had worn his best navy suit and tie to try to show the other shareholders at the Gallantry that he was still in charge of the operation despite having to sell 30% of the restaurant to cover Alice's medical bills. He needn't have bothered, as he had methodically picked the shareholders – Canterbury's best offerings of poor little rich kids who just wanted to own a share in a fancy restaurant – so as to ensure they would always feel subservient to him.

He sat at the small table that he frequented most days and laid out his newspaper, pondering for a moment just when exactly he had become so calculated. Still, it seemed to be working for him, as business was on the up: his take from the business seemed to have enjoyed a slight growth, despite his drop in shares and a reduction of time spent in the kitchen. He still wrote the menus and tasted the dishes, and a random fiery tirade at a slack member of staff always kept the crew on their toes, but mostly his days were filled with Dorothy giggling to herself and him marvelling at how such a broken man could create such a happy and perfect thing. Dotty wasn't here today, as he had work to do; she would be sitting in the garden with her gramps. John Petalow had softened since her entry into the world eight months earlier, and the giant of a man would sit and play with her for hours, while Angela would tend to the various wild flowers that filled the Petalows' five-acre garden.

With work out of the way, it was Jacob's time to breathe. Being a single father had come to Jacob with ease; it was the only thing he had found easy in all his years alive. Keeping her happy and safe had given him a focus he had never experienced before. It was all about her, no one else. Dorothy Gale Brooking and her beautiful smile had killed his selfishness in just a few months, and the bond they shared had proved to him that it was possible to love someone so much that it fixes you on every level.

Jacob Brooking had never felt so normal, and it was a good place to be. He would still hear the monster in his thoughts, from time to time – that was normal. As Jessica brought him his coffee and croissant, he noticed her blush, and yet the voice mocked him, tried to bring him low once more.

She thinks you're a loner.

Well, she wouldn't be wrong. Jacob smiled, fully aware that friends were not really his forte.

And old, the voice cackled.

Well, that's just rude. Let's not forget that you are the same age as me, you old bastard.

Jacob had developed a better way of dealing with his inner voice of late. Dr Phillips had told him that if he couldn't win the fight with his inner demon, he should stop fighting it.

'Thank you, Jessica. How's that boyfriend of yours? Still keeping you happy, love?'

'You know how it is, Mr Brooking. Until he pulls his finger out, I'll always be on the lookout for something better.' Jessica turned to hide her blush and gave an obvious wiggle to draw his attention down.

'Really, Jay, you will flirt with anyone, but do you have to tease "the help" with your endless charms?'

Jacob looked up and nearly choked on the first bite of his pastry.

'Oh my god – Evan. I don't know what to say. I ...'

Well, you're fucked.

'Don't panic, Jay, just bloody give me a hug so we can kill this awkwardness.'

Evan opened her arms up to Jacob, which did nothing to ease his fear, but he surprised himself and stood to embrace her all the same.

'Of course. I'm sorry, Evan. How are you?'

'I'm really well, thanks. May I join you?'

Evan motioned at the seat opposite and then pulled herself into the spot. Skinny jeans so tight they were almost painted onto her perfectly curved rear drew Jacob's attention with little effort, despite the crippling fear in his heart.

Evan sighed. 'I must confess, I had kind of hoped you would look worse than you do, Jay.'

Jacob tried to force his grin to look natural, but failed. 'From you I take that as a compliment. Evan, listen, I need to say ...'

Evan cut him off quickly. 'I'm sorry too, but I don't think us bringing up the past is how we enjoy this impromptu coffee, do you?'

Jacob relaxed slightly and drew in his puffed-out chest. 'I am sorry, though, I need you to know that. I'm not that guy anymore.'

Evan reached over the table and placed a reassuring hand on his. 'Jacob Brooking, I'm not made of glass, OK? And if the rumours are to be believed, I hear you have had a harder few years than I.'

She knows.

'I didn't know my news had spread so quickly and was so important to the community in general?'

Evan smiled softly and seemed genuine as she squeezed his hand ever so slightly before releasing it. 'Jay, your wife tried to kill herself and then gave birth to your child whilst in a coma – a coma it seems she might be in for the rest of her life. Do you think that's not gossip-worthy, especially when we share a lot of the same friends still?'

Jacob laughed.

'OK, they may be employees to you,' said Evan, 'but they are friends to me, you big meanie managing director you.'

Evan parted her plump lips to reveal her perfect white teeth and a smile that had always had a power over him, much like her long blonde hair, which today was straightened and fell over her shoulders and past her breasts, almost to her lap.

'You look good, Evan. You always did. Can I get you a coffee whilst we catch up?' Jacob rose, knowing the answer already.

'A flat white please, Jay, and then you can tell me all about it.'

Jacob looked confused. 'All about what?'

Evan leaned forward, rested her elbow on the coffee table and gently cradled her jaw while twirling her hair between her fingers. 'About San Diego, Jacob. About what happened when you left me.'

Summer 2009 Canterbury, Kent, UK

'Jacob, how could you?' Alice felt an overwhelming desire to scream, but the medication was doing its job of keeping her calm, at least on the surface.

'We broke up,' said Jacob. 'I went away for three months, and we haven't spoken a single word to each other in two years. I never thought you would wake up. I thought my life was just me and Dotty, and I bumped into her randomly. Would it make a difference if it was anyone else?'

For once, Jacob didn't sound like he was making excuses. His life hadn't stopped for two years, and he wasn't going to apologise for any choices he had made while struggling on his own.

[243]

'Well, I wonder if my parents would love you so much if they knew?' said Alice, sounding a little spoiled and hurt.

'They already know. I asked your mother's advice before I moved forward. How could I not? They have helped me raise our child, I had to show them that respect.'

Alice turned her gaze from him. 'Respect, Jay? What about respect for me? How about anyone in the world except for her?'

Dorothy let out a cry that immediately brought Jacob over to the mock playpen he had built for her out of cushions stolen from the couch.

'What's up, little boo?' said Jacob as he picked up his terrified daughter from the floor. 'Tell me.'

Dorothy clung to Jacob like he was about to vanish. Jacob went and sat next to Alice and tried to offer Dorothy over, but she wrapped her arms around her dad's body all the tighter.

'She hates me, Jay. That's why she doesn't want anything to do with me.'

'She will come around. This is all new to her. She hadn't heard you talk until last week, and now she's listening to you shout at me.' Jacob knew he had made a mistake with that last comment and so quickly tried to deflate the situation by waving Dorothy's hand at her angry mother.

'Don't you dare use this little club you two have going on to deflect what you have done, Jay. Not her – not Evan.'

Alice's voice was in check, knowing that scaring Dorothy was probably not the best way into her heart, but Jacob knew that he didn't have much choice other than to agree with Alice on this.

'You're right,' he said. 'I should have been more thoughtful. Together or apart, I owed you that, Alice. I was lonely, and knowing you had started dating so quickly after I had left on that godforsaken voyage ... Well, I didn't think.'

Alice looked up at Jacob, confused. 'How do you know I was dating, when you were apparently lost at sea?'

'Because when I held you in my arms, blood pouring from the gaps in the compress I was forcing onto your neck wound, your date turned up to ask why you hadn't showed up to meet him at the Harbour Café. He walked in and attacked me, thinking it was me who had hurt you, but I wouldn't put you down. He eventually guided the paramedics into you from the road.' Jacob's voice trembled as he thought back to that day once more. 'Pebble, you can believe what you want, but I have not sat idle since that day, none of us have, and I'm sorry but I was struggling at the end to do it alone.'

Ten months earlier

'Jacob, hi, it's Evan. I know you have a lot going on, what with the baby and looking after Alice and all. I just wondered if I could lighten the load a little and make you dinner this week. Let you be you for a night. It doesn't have to mean anything.'

Do it, we like Evan.

'Evan, I don't know what to say. That's so kind of you to offer, and certainly it's unexpected. Let me see if I can find a sitter for the night. I'll get back to you soon as.'

You're not even going to try, are you, you're a coward?

'Great,' said Evan. 'I'm excited for you to see the new place, and I expect you to bring the wine – your taste is too expensive for my purse.'

You won't go. I'm not sure you deserve a girl that attractive.

'Too expensive for your purse? Evan, your purse is a £1,500 Prada job. I know that because I bought the bastard thing.'

You don't have the backbone to follow through with this.

'Yeah, but you didn't fill it with money, my darling Jacob. Right, I'll let you get back to whatever you were doing – or whomever, should I say.'

That was an attack, you know it was.

Jacob held up the full diaper that he had been trying to change while speaking to Evan with the phone pressed between his shoulder and ear. 'Trust me when I say this, I would swap whatever it is you are doing with the task I'm handling right now.'

'All the more reason to get back to me with a positive answer, then. Goodbye, Mr Brooking, text me when you get the chance.'

'I'm on it. Give me an hour or two.'

Jacob put the phone down. He could barely hear his own thoughts due to Dorothy screaming at his poor attempt to replace her nappy, and all the chatter the voice in his head was throwing his way.

I'm going to bloody go, he thought, *I need a break.*

What you need and what you deserve are two different things. She will probably slit her throat when you walk through the door, just like Alice di..

JUST LIKE ALICE DID? Is that what you were going to say? Because I'm tired of that broken record. I'm going because I want to go, and nothing you say will stop me. Jacob could hear himself shouting, even though the conversation was in his thoughts.

With that, the creature went silent, and then it smiled a smile that exposed every fanged tooth in its kraken-like beak.

Yes, Jacob, you are going to do exactly what you want to do. All this is on you, it always was.

This time, the creature whispered, and its smile remained long after the sun had set.

Summer 2009

'So, this is it, then?' said Alice, defeated not only by the news, but by Jacob's honest account of it. 'We are not going to work this through and sort our marriage out?'

'I'm not saying anything other than this. You have come back into a world that has kept turning in your absence.

We need to get you fit and healthy, Dorothy needs you to adapt into the mother that I know you are going to be, and you need to find yourself once more. I'll speak with Evan, but you must know that this, all of this, is all about you getting well, not us getting back together.'

Jacob stood up and held Dorothy out so her mother could kiss her brow.

'Goodnight, my angel,' Alice whispered.

Dorothy once again shied away into Jacob's arms.

'Goodbye, Pebble. Call me if you need me for anything.'

Before he could reach the door, Alice said his name.

'Thank you for being honest with me,' she said. 'I don't like what you have told me, in actual fact I hate it, but you never would have been this honest before, so I guess you have changed.'

Jacob smiled, gave a slight nod and pulled the door behind him.

Hours passed and Alice didn't move. *Why her?* was all she could keep asking herself. *Why Evan fucking Laurie?*

BECAUSE IT'S NOT REAL. COME BACK TO US, ALICE. IT'S NEVER BEEN REAL.

The voice took Alice by surprise, for she had made a point of asking her father to remove all the mirrors from the house, and it was so very rare to hear it speak without a reflection. In fact, the only time she had ever heard the voice speak that clearly without a reflection had been at her mother's funeral, in the world that apparently wasn't real ...

Alice snapped, and the tears of confusion that she had shed so many times these past few days returned with a vengeance. 'Where am I?' she sobbed, digging her nails once more into the soft flesh of her thigh.

Chapter 31: The Tell-Tale Heart
Song of the day
"Damn Your Eyes" by Luce Dufault

Autumn 2008
Faversham, Kent, UK

As I take a seat upon this magnificent leather sofa, a sofa of deep stitches and brass finishing, the one that I have admired for so many years, it saddens my heart once more that I didn't have the courage to talk to you about this before, without, that is, having to pay for an hour of your time.

True! I'm negligent, very, very dreadfully negligent. I had been and am always such; I make as little time for you as you do for me, but why will you say that I am in love? The adoration I may have for this man has sharpened my senses, not taken them on flights of fantasy, not dulled them with words that you and I both know have little meaning in this real world, this painfully dreadful world. I know my senses are acute. I know my own mind. I have seen all things in the heaven and in the earth. I heard many things in hell and have come close to living them at times. I KNOW THIS WORLD! How, then, could I be in love? For to be in love, one must not be of this realm.

Take my candour, please, and observe how healthily and how calmly I can tell you the whole story.

It is impossible to say how first the idea entered my brain; but once conceived, it haunted me day and night. I lusted for the man whose affections I had previously won. He had never wanted me the same. But he had never given me insult; even in the days before he left, he had begged forgiveness. For his gold I had no desire, although it certainly had its charms, and he had given it freely. Yet the idea came to me that he was more than just a flight of fancy out of nowhere. I think, in the end, it was his eyes! Yes, it was this! He had the eyes of an avenging angel, a viridian green, with a crystal pupil that refracted light as if not meant to give true reflection of such a wondrous creature. Whenever it fell upon me, my blood ran hot and my pulse rose in both tempo and depth; and so by degrees – very gradually – I made up my mind to take the heart of the man once more, and thus rid myself of the powerless longing forever. Not because I loved him ... Because I didn't want to be so powerless to a man I was getting no return from.

Now this is the point. You fancy me in love. You, a woman of culture and class. A woman of higher education than most can dream of. Women in love know nothing. But you should have seen me. You should have seen how wisely I proceeded – with what caution, with what foresight, with what dissimulation I went to work! Does that sound like the madness of love? He never knew that my new place of work – another restaurant – was opposite his regular coffee shop, a chance that fate had thrown at us both. Fate ... another made-up word for an irrational concept. I was never more taken by the man than during the whole week before I came to you today. And every morning, about midday, I pulled the silk rope of our blinds and opened them – oh so gently! The restaurant was so dark that no light shone out, yet enough was let in for me to see him each day. Oh, you would have laughed to see how unknowingly I had let him into my life! I undid the blind just so much that a single thin ray fell upon my vulture's eye. And this I did for seven long days, every morning at midday, but I found my eye impossible to close; and so it was impossible to do the work; for it was not the man who vexed me, but his power that held me so, unbeknownst to him. And every morning, when the day broke, I went boldly into the window bay and spoke courageously to him, calling him by name in a hearty tone, and inquiring how he had passed the night. Yet I would have to stop when the others came near,

[249]

lest they think me mad. So, you see he would have been a very profound man, indeed, to suspect that every day, just at twelve, I looked in upon him while he sat by the window and drank his elixir of caffeine and dark magic.

Upon the eighth day, just yesterday in fact, I was less than my usually cautious self, a whimsy caused by lack of sleep from an unrelated matter of mind, and in letting in the light, a rare mistake was made. A watch's minute hand moves more quickly than did mine and I lost a quarter of an hour to his gaze. Never before that day had I felt my powers so greatly diminished. I could scarcely contain my feelings of loneliness since the last sight I had of the man, whom you laughably say I must love. To think that there I was, opening the blinds once more, little by little, and he not even to dream of my secret deeds or thoughts. I fairly restrained a chuckle at the idea; and perhaps he saw me, knew I was there; for he moved once more to the table I forever saw him at, as if he knew no other table would provide me with ample view. *He knows*, I told myself, for why else would he always sit there? Now you may think that I drew back, but no. My room was as dark as the cobbled streets were light, and with the veil of darkness, the veil that protected me each and every day, doing the job that I had called on it to do, I watched once more, and so I knew that he could not see the opening of the blinds. I kept quite still and said nothing. For a whole minute that felt akin to an hour I did not move a muscle, and he could not see me. I did not catch acknowledgement in his eyes of green, jade and emerald – yes, emerald. He was still listening to music, an earphone in one ear and one hanging loosely about his neck, just in case a pretty little waitress chose to talk to him. But they could only dream of such a man; just as I have done, night after night, thinking of the man and his lips upon my flesh. And yet you say I am in love. Does my clarity of thought stand for nothing? I care little for your fantasy and the use of words better left in the poetry books of forgotten scholars.

When I had waited a long time – minutes? Hours? Days perhaps? – but very patiently, without seeing him change position, I resolved to open a very, very little crevice in the window itself. So as to maybe breathe a little of the same air that he himself had taken into the very lungs I so desired would breathe their warmth over my shoulder once more. So, I opened it, you cannot imagine how stealthily, until, at length, a bright sunray, like the thread of a spider, shot from out the crevice and fell full upon my vulture's eye. The window was open, it was open wide, and I grew scared as I saw him look in my direction. But I could see nothing to tell me of the crime being caught. The man's face or demeanour remained unbothered, a stroke of luck, as I had directed the ray, as if by instinct, precisely upon the damned spot where I stood watching. He sipped at his elixir and mouthed the words of such a song that I could not imagine. I was fully aware of my actions and of his, and have I not told you that what you mistake for love is but over-acuteness of the senses?

Now, I say, there came to my ears a low, dull, quick sound, such as a watch makes when enveloped in cotton. I knew that sound well, too. It was the beating of my heart. It increased my longing, as the beating of a drum stimulates the soldier into courage.

So I was exposed to him, but even then I kept still. I scarcely breathed. I held the blind motionless. I tried to see how steadily I could maintain the ray upon the form. I understood I was exposed and yet felt thrilled within my own form. Meantime the hellish tattoo of my heart increased. It grew quicker and quicker, and louder and louder, every instant. Mark me well, for I have told you that I am nervous: so, I am. And so I was at the hour of twelve, before our patrons joined us for lunches, drinks, the clamour of false lives and wishes unfulfilled. But amid the dreadful silence of that empty restaurant, so strange a noise as my own heartbeat excited me to near uncontrollable terror. Yet, for some minutes longer I refrained and stood still. The beating grew louder, louder! I thought my heart must burst, and now a new anxiety seized me – the sound would be heard by a customer or member of my crew. The hour had come for me to focus my attention elsewhere! And with a loud yell of frustration, I threw open the front doors and leapt into the cobbled streets, quickly pulling down the awnings to protect our al fresco diners from the very rays that had exposed my eye. Moving quickly and in open secrecy as I kept my back to the man, through fear that he might recognise me once more, in an instant I dragged my menu board to its home upon the floor and pulled the heavy wooden slats into position. I then smiled gaily, to find the deed so far done. But, for many minutes, as I retreated back within the sanctuary of the dark, the heart beat on with a muffled sound. This, however, did not vex me; it would not be heard through my blouse, not by kin nor patron alike. At length it ceased. The feeling dead until tomorrow. I placed my hand upon my heart and held it there many minutes. There was no pulsation that felt abnormal. The rush that the man had pulled upon me had subsided, as it did each day. His emerald eyes would trouble me no more.

If still you think me in love, you will think so no longer when I describe the wise precautions I took for the concealment of my emotions. As the bell sounded upon the hour, there came a holler at the street door. I went down to greet it with a light heart, for what had I now to fear? There entered three handsome men, who introduced themselves, with perfect suavity, as men of the local law firm. They were led to a table with a view of the beautiful town that surrounded them. Their drinks order was taken with jollity and efficiency, for what had I to fear? I bade the gentlemen a good lunch and a good stay.

The men were satisfied. My manner had convinced them. I was singularly at ease. They sat, and they ate in silence before they drank and enjoyed a little hubris, whilst the talk of success and women's hearts won dominated the air about them, and whilst I answered cheerily to any question thrown my way. I was pleasant and open as I always am and have been, for they chatted of familiar things. But, ere long, I felt myself getting pale and wished them gone. My head ached and my heart more so, and I fancied a ringing in my ears; but still they sat and still chatted. The ringing became more distinct. It continued and became more acute. I talked more freely to get rid of the feeling, forgetting my place as host; but it continued and gained definiteness, until, with certainty, I found that I had to make my excuses and return to the safety of the cellar.

My heart once more pounded within my chest and I found myself short of breath. A young server joined me, of young years and fair face, no knowledge of the world yet imparted on her soul. Although not seeking safety like I, she proudly proclaimed, 'Miss Evan, the table by the window, the table of money and of arrogance, they ask for you, Miss Evan, they clamour for your time once more.'

I waved the young cherub away with a gesture of indifference. Why would they not be gone? I paced the floor with heavy strides, as if frustrated by the desires of the men, when it was the desires of one man I wanted and nothing more. Oh God! What could I do? I rallied my thoughts and I took to my task.

'Gentlemen, what shall it be?' I asked with the mime of someone who might actually enjoy that damned profession. But I heard nothing over my own racing heart, as I looked up through the window to see him leave, the man who took my breath from me with nothing but his presence. My heart now throbbed, and I feared all would hear it. It grew louder, louder and louder still! And yet the men chatted pleasantly and smiled as if ignorant to my plight. Was it possible they heard not? Almighty God! No, no! They heard! They knew! They were making a mockery of my torment! This I thought, and this I think. But anything was better than this agony! Anything was more tolerable than this derision! I could bear those hypocritical smiles no longer! I felt that I must scream or die! And now, again! It grows louder, louder, louder, louder!

'Gentlemen, but a moment, please.'

I opened the front door to find the sun, the air and the cobbles of the street, but he was gone, and with that, also the beating of my heart. Only emptiness remained, and the hollow shell of the cold woman you raised took herself aside to devalue the incident as nothing more than tiredness.

So, you may say I am in love, but really, do I sound of such a fantastical mindset? When I remember everything so calculatedly and without whimsical nostalgia, does that really tell you of love, mother?

Chapter 32: Sliding Doors
Song of the day
"Hero" by Regina Spektor

Spring 2010
Faversham, Kent, UK

Look at you. Look at your skin as it catches the few rays of morning light trying to squeeze their way through the curtain break. You are beautiful, in a different way to Alice entirely, but no less so. I can't help but be mesmerised by the ringlets of blonde hair that fall so naturally, and how, even as you sleep in front of me, well, you look like you are posing for a shot. I'm waiting for you to open your eyes, so that I can kiss you without fear of waking you, because every girl who puts up with me must surely deserve more rest than others.

Jacob leaned over despite himself and gently laid his lips on her brow. He whispered *I love you* and slipped out of the bedroom. How had this happened to him? He had been through so much drama in his life – most of it caused by his own poor mindset, of course – that he didn't understand what he had done to deserve two beautiful women in his life, but he did have them, and he was happy.

He entered his kitchen in only his olive-coloured hipster briefs and danced a little as the stone tiles caught his bare feet off guard. He had always regretted not getting the underfloor heating here, as this kitchen floor was so beautiful he doubted it would ever be brought up for another. He methodically poured filtered water into his minimalist glass coffee jar and watched the drops of dark roast slowly fill the pot drip by drip. Jacob had always preferred the pour-over method of coffee-making. Yes, it took three minutes to get a cup, but the depths of flavour were the wake-up that his senses needed to take on the day. He hadn't heard Ahab in his mind for a few days, although he still jumped a little when the toaster broke the quiet perfection of the drip, drip, drip and spat out a slice of his home-baked loaf. He lavished its surface with salted butter and gripped it between his teeth while picking up both drinks.

The sensation of swapping from cold stone to warm carpet sent a tingle up his calves. He nudged the bedroom door open with his bottom as he entered the room backwards, and there he was, only his underwear to cover his shame as he stood, his large thighs constrained by the elastic and his flat stomach rippling with muscles that had only appeared since his dramatic boat diet two years before. With a milky tea in one hand and his drip-poured coffee in his right, he stood, toast in mouth, and marvelled at what lay before him. For as she lay, uncovered by sheet or clothing, a painted nail gently bitten in her mouth and her other hand squeezing the most perfect breasts Jacob had ever seen in life or for that matter on screen or in a magazine, she took Jacob's lust as she had taken his heart.

He placed the hot drinks and the toast on the bedside table, a piece of furniture he had taken from the boat he had been stranded upon. Then he leaned in and placed his lips on hers as he took his place above her, his hands exploring her body from her hips all the way up, until he pinned her arms above her head and entwined their fingers.

Her big eyes sparkled in the morning light as his tongue left her mouth with a gentle pull on her bottom lip.

'I can't believe the first time you say those words, it's when you think I'm asleep, Jay. Really, what is a girl to think?' Evan smiled innocently, which for her was never an easy feat, before leaning in for another kiss. Just before their lips touched, she whispered seductively, 'I love you too, Jay. I think I always have done.'

Look at you. Look at your skin as it catches the few rays of morning light trying to squeeze their way through the curtain break. You are beautiful, in a different way to anything I have ever deemed to fit that word. I can't help but be mesmerised by the colour of your hair, which is both the dark brown of your brooding father's and the autumnal fire of my own, and how even as you sleep in front of me, well, you look like you are a gift from heaven. I'm waiting for you to open your eyes, so that I can hold your little hand without fear of waking you, because every girl who puts up with me and your father surely deserves more rest than others.

Alice leaned over despite herself and gently covered Dorothy with the soft blanket she had kicked off during the night, before slipping out of the bedroom. How had this happened to her? She had been through so much drama in her life – most of it caused by her own poor mindset, of course – that she didn't seem to understand what she had done to deserve to have such a beautiful little woman in her life, but she did have her, and she was happy, she was sure she was, although still confused as to moving forward. Dorothy clung to her dad and could not speak a word to Alice, and, in turn, Alice had found it very hard to bond with her, although she knew it was early days.

Alice entered her parents' kitchen in her university hoodie and a pair of Jacob's old joggers. Her bare feet tingled and warmed as the stone tiles caught them off guard with the under-floor heating her father had fitted a few years back, apparently to help with his gout. He never complained about physical stuff much, so Alice couldn't argue with her father's expensive answer to his pain; it was his money, after all. She poured herself a green tea and threw some Cheerios into a bowl for Dorothy. She hadn't heard her stir just yet but knew it was coming. She may have struggled to bond with Dorothy – she still felt like she was looking after Jacob's child two days a week – but she had the heart of a mother, and taking care of Dorothy certainly wasn't a chore. Lost in her thoughts, she jumped a little when the toaster broke the silence and spat out a slice of Jacob's home-baked loaf. She lavished its surface with margarine and her mother's strawberry jam and gripped it between her teeth while taking her tea and Dorothy's breakfast back to bed.

The sensation of swapping from hard stone to the softness of the carpet in the hall sent a tingle up her calves. She nudged the bedroom door open with her bottom as she entered the room backwards, and ... There he was, with only his underwear to cover his shame as he lay on his side upon Alice's bed, his chiselled body a patchwork of tattoos and his smile half hidden by his grey beard.

Alice dropped her tea, which smashed to the ground, quickly followed by the jam-covered toast.

William sprung to his feet. 'Are you OK? Let me help you.'

Alice looked around the room, noticing it to be the bedroom of the cottage in her dream.

'Dorothy!' she called as she ran out of the room, leaving William picking up the broken mug. Alice panicked. This was home, her make-believe home but her home, so there was no bedroom in which she would find her daughter. She darted from door to door, just to check her sanity wasn't as fractured as she feared, and found nothing. She ran back into the bedroom, where William was soaking up the green tea with a towel. She shrieked at what stood behind him, reflecting in the very mirror in which she had parted ways with Jacob's memory all those years ago. Her hair the red of grease and just as unclean, her flesh broken and unclean, her teeth rotten and broken apart from the pair of long pristine fangs either side of her forked tongue, which were highlighted all the more by the unnaturally large smile that this demonic version of Alice was always wearing.

'Alice, what's wrong?' asked William as she slumped to the floor in front of him, unable to breathe and unable to cry.

Welcome home, child, voiced the demon Alice with the wicked smile of the unclean.

Chapter 33: Johnno was a Local Boy
Song of the day
"Porcelain Gods" by Paul Weller

End of summer 2007
Psychiatric Hospital of San Diego County, California, USA

'What do you mean, she's pregnant?' asked Jacob.

'What I mean, Mr Brooking, is that we have had to put her into an induced coma due to her insistence on taking her own life, and this is more complicated due to the fact she is at least 16 weeks pregnant. You didn't notice your wife's small bump? Have there been any other signs, Mr Brooking?'

The woman tasked with minimising the damage Alice had done to herself just 12 hours before was Doctor Creed, the head of surgery. She was a woman of pure business – make-up free, hair impeccably scraped back. Everything seemed to be measured to perfection. Even the cactus on her desk sat upright at a perfect angle, and this was something that filled Jacob with the confidence he needed to get through the situation.

'No. I mean, I don't know. I've not been around so much the last three months. In fact, as I walked in on her cutting her throat, it was the first time I had seen her in 14 weeks.' Jacob fell into the seat opposite the doctor, completely bemused by the situation. 'Will the baby be OK?'

'The baby seems fine, and her heart rate doesn't appear to be affected at all by her mother's condition. If worst comes to worst and we can't get Alice right, then we can safely deliver like this, but let's hope we don't have to.'

Jacob wasn't listening. '*Her* heart? She's a girl?'

The doctor smiled. 'Yes, Mr Brooking. You are having a daughter.'

Jacob looked up, concerned. 'You seem to suggest she might not wake up. How much of a possibility is that? Please be honest.'

'I don't know any other way to be, Mr Brooking. But right now, nothing is certain. We don't expect anything to happen quickly. She needs to heal, both outside and in. Whatever demon she is trying to fight, we need to help her as best we can, and right now that means leaving her to rest.'

Over the Atlantic

'This is his fault, love, I'm telling you. It's that bastard Jacob, he's caused this.' John was livid. To hear that his Alice was in a critical condition had broken his heart, and John Petalow dealt with heartbreak the only way he knew how – with anger directed at the person he felt was responsible.

'You don't know that it's anything to do with Jacob. The last few times I spoke with Alice she seemed genuinely happy with everything, and I think Jay had a lot to do with that.'

Angela had always been John's voice of reason, but right now that wasn't going well with him.

'He is a drain on that poor girl's happiness, and you know it.' John spoke with the kind of tone that he usually reserved for the people who worked for him; it was rare for his wife to catch this end of the deal. 'Do you remember her as a teen? Always singing, always dancing. Everything she did had an aura of love and happiness. Where has that Alice been the last 15 years?'

'I know you don't like Jacob, I know you're worried about Alice. Do you not think I'm holding back the tears right now? Believe me, I am! But you are not helping, so shut up, remember you are a bloody Petalow, and get some rest.'

John knew better than to reply to this tirade from his wife. Instead, he tried to get comfortable so that he could sleep. The first-class seat was still too small for him; flying any other class wasn't even an option for him, as these were the only seats that fit him, bar the cargo hold. He downed the cheap bourbon that the flight attendant was claiming to be single malt whiskey and closed his eyes. *Bastard Jacob Brooking, ignoring my warning. I'll tear his arms off.* John drifted off with a wry smile, as he knew that was wholly possible for him to achieve. Unfortunately, he slipped into a dream that wasn't such a satisfying image.

He saw friends being killed in front of him. He saw the inside of HMS *Oberon*, the submarine that had been his prison for all those months. He and his very advanced Special Boat Service team had been on that sub in the Falklands during the summer of 1979, long before the war had started, and yet he still saw death.

Jacob Brooking stood there with him. The dead body of his daughter and the rest of C Squadron lay littered around them, mixed with the dead bodies of a dozen other submariners, butchered beyond all reason, with their throats cut or their hearts punctured. Jacob, wearing an Argentine uniform that seemed to fit him as if he'd been born into it, smiled with malicious intent. His hands were covered with blood, and at his feet was Alice, whose neck was broken and bloodied by a clearly one-sided struggle. John's heart started to race. He screamed his daughter's name and lunged at Jacob, but he was easily overpowered by a simple sweep of Jacob's arm, which brought him crashing to his knees.

'She's been mine for long enough now, Viking king. I will do with her as I please.'

In one motion, Jacob brought his hand down on John's exposed neck, meeting no resistance and taking his head clean off. John's decapitated head rolled like a hellish marble drawn from the nightmares of the damned until it came to rest next to the motionless body of his daughter, dead eyes looking back at his own, no speech able to escape his guillotined vocal cords.

As Jacob sat in the first-class waiting lounge, ready for the abuse he was sure to receive, he couldn't help but wonder what would have happened had he not returned to Alice. Was it his proximity to her that had made her do it? Could she sense him returning?

That's madness. I'm thinking like a madman. How could she have known I was coming? I saved her.

Jacob had been trying to convince himself of this for the whole journey to San Diego International, and he was no closer to succeeding after an hour of sitting at the bar, nursing a bourbon.

You're going to be a single father with a brain-dead wife. Good luck explaining that to the Viking, laughed the monstrous voice with a wicked cackle.

This wasn't my fault and you know it; Alice has always had her demons, just like I do.

Her demons didn't exist until she found out about Evan, or before you dragged her away from her family. Or shall we go further back, to when you bought a restaurant behind her back before convincing her to murder her unborn child? Was that not your fault either, Jacob? JACOB???

'WHAT?' shouted Jacob, much to the surprise of the barman, who had been minding his own business.

You know this is all on you.

'But what the hell can I do about it now? I'm here, aren't I? Trying to make things right. What more can I do?' Jacob whispered to himself.

'You can start by bringing the car around to the front,' said a tired voice from behind.

Jacob turned to see Alice's mum standing there with her arms open.

'Hello Angela,' he said, jumping down from the bar stool to accept the hug he didn't realise he had needed. 'Where's John?'

'Getting the luggage sorted. He's ... eager to see you. I guess that would be the way to put it.'

Angela found a false smile to go with this statement, but it did nothing to hide the reality of the situation. John Petalow wanted answers, and he would wring them from Jacob's neck if he had to.

Chapter 34: Nurse Bonnie
Song of the day
"All I Need" by Air

Spring 2010
Canterbury, Kent, UK

Bonnie Belmonte had known the Petalows had money, but never had she expected such a beautiful home in such a rural location. Alice had been inviting her over for brunch every day since her release. They had grown quite close during her stay at the hospital, and there were only so many times Bonnie felt she could delay before Alice took umbrage at the excuses, so here she was. Bonnie knew it wasn't the most professional thing to visit a patient's home, but she had been eager to catch up with the gossip, and Alice had promised cake – and Bonnie Belmonte loved cake.

She pushed open the wrought-iron gate and marvelled at the beautiful garden, which was kept by a particularly green-fingered Angela Petalow. The pinks of lupins and the blues of delphiniums took her eye first, before the vivid red dahlias, which were arranged either side of the large oak door, actually gave her pause for thought and honest appreciation, especially as it was barely into March, a time when most other people's gardens were only just starting to bloom. Bonnie imagined that Angela's garden was like this all year round. *That's some voodoo gardening, I tell you, girl,* Bonnie thought as she knocked on the front door with a double crack of the brass door knocker.

There was no reply, other than the faint sound of Dorothy crying in the distance. Bonnie assumed that Alice was tending to her daughter and would be down in a moment. She rapped against the wood a second time, continuing to look around the wondrous garden. When her third knock went unanswered, curiosity got the better of her, and she started to stroll around the back of Manor Petalow.

'Alice, sweet child, are you to keep me waiting all day?'

At the rear of the house, large French doors overlooked an enormous back garden. Bonnie was about to call one last time, when Dorothy screamed from the window above her. She tried the handle of the back door and let out a sigh of relief when the door sprung open.

'Alice, are you OK, child?' called Bonnie, as she walked through the kitchen and made her way towards the large staircase and the source of the crying. All the doors on the upper floor were closed. She pushed open Dorothy's bedroom door. The child's face was flushed and full of the tears of a young girl too small to escape her bedroom yet old enough to know she had been left alone for longer than was normal.

'Hey, my littlest Brooking, what's wrong, my child?' said Bonnie as she reached down to pick Dorothy up from the ground.

Dorothy's little arms reached up to greet her saviour, her beautiful red hair unbrushed and matted with tears.

'Where's Mumma, my sweetness? Shall we go find her?'

Cradling her tightly, Bonnie took Dorothy out onto the landing. She noticed that one of the doors was in fact ajar, and that what was keeping it ajar was someone's foot. Without hesitation she rushed Dorothy back to her bedroom and sat her down on the bed.

'Dotty, my child, will you sit and play for just a few more minutes whilst I go get Mummy? I promise I'll be right back, and I'll leave the door open, OK?'

Dorothy nodded and crawled over her bed to hide under a mound of fluffy teddies, grabbing a regal-looking hare that sported a waistcoat en route.

Bonnie went back across the landing and entered the room where Alice was lying flat on her back. She knelt beside Alice and checked her pulse. She had seen her like this a thousand times, her eyes wide open and glossy but unresponsive and wider than looked naturally possible. Bonnie rolled her into the recovery position and placed a pillow from the bed under her neck.

'Alice, I know you can hear me, so do yourself a favour, poppet. Wake up before you fall too deeply. Do you really wanna lose another two years? No? I didn't think so. So, wake up.'

Bonnie was instantly back in work mode and her tone was strict and unwavering. She took out her phone, dialled 999 and asked for an ambulance.

'This is Sister Bonnie Belmonte of St Martin's Hospital. I'm with a patient of mine, Alice Petalow. We are just off Perry Lane at Preston Hill, the Petalow Manor, just by the large oak tree. It's set quite far back from the road, but you should find it at, erm, hang on ...' She scrambled through her pockets to find the scrap of paper that she'd written Alice's address on. 'Right, at CT3 1ER. Alice is a mental health patient. She appears to have slipped into a catatonic state. She is breathing with a pulse of 65. I've tried to see if she is responsive to pain, but nothing so far. She doesn't appear to have self-harmed, so I've put her in recovery to continue my assessment.'

'Bonnie,' Alice croaked. She was struggling to pull herself up against the frame of the door. 'Bonnie, I – I slipped back into ... I don't know how long I've been out. Where's Dorothy? Oh fuck, WHERE'S DOROTHY?'

Alice fell back down to her knees as Bonnie reached out to catch her.

'Take it easy, child, Bon Bon has got you.'

Bonnie led Alice to the bed and sat her upright, taking time to check her eyes and her breathing once more. 'Little Dotty is just fine, but I must confess, you have given me a scare. What was the last thing you remember?'

'I remember my alarm going off and I remember making breakfast, then ... then nothing.' Alice looked lost. 'I feel like I've been out for minutes, but you're here and my alarm went off at 7 a.m.'

'Then you have been out for about five hours, and that's OK because no harm was done. Paramedics are on their way – more than likely they will just want to check you over. Let me sort your little monkey out and I'll let them in when they arrive. Where are Dotty's bits?'

Alice looked guilt-ridden as she thought about the neglect of her daughter. 'Everything you need is in the storage cupboard outside her room. What do I tell Jacob when he arrives to get her later?'

Bonnie picked up Alice's chin with her index finger and whispered kindly, 'I'll worry about Mr Brooking, just like I have done for the past two years. Let's worry about you first, though, my sweetness.'

Winter 2009 Knightsbridge, London, UK

'What's the last thing you can remember clearly from San Diego that you know with absolute certainty was a memory of reality and not the false perception that you then started to build for yourself?' asked Dr Phillips without once taking her eyes off Alice, who was stretched out, eyes closed, on the long leather sofa.

'You are asking what you think is a simple question, but in all honesty it may be the hardest thing I've ever had to answer, for what is real in my head has often been what has led me astray. You have to understand that if I didn't see Jacob standing in front of me, breathing in front of me, then I can tell you now as a matter of fact that I saw him die and it was real.' Alice took a deep breath before she continued. 'My memories do not come at me like I was in a dream, for I do not see blurred lines, faint sounds and vacant tastes. I must confess that as crazy as it seems, I see only reality in what I saw, like looking at a photo album – I see every colour clearly, see every face and hear every seagull that would mercilessly fight for the leftover croissant that I swear I can still taste the remnants of.'

'The problem you have is your own imagination. I have sat here with stupid people, people with far too much money who think they have the same problem you have, but they don't have the mind to create the world that your fabulous mind has created. Your world-building is second to none, and that's why you struggle. So instead of looking at what looked like or had the smell of a reality that your mind could easily build, I want you to look at something else.'

'Which is?'

'It's fairly textbook that the things that happened in your false reality were created to solve the issues in your heart. Your mum died because you felt you had let her down. She had been married for decades, put up with all your father's tantrums and mood swings. Didn't you mention he had PTSD from his time in the navy?'

'I did, yes.'

'You felt like you had let her down by not surviving the marriage like she had. Jacob's death was no different. Yes, you were mad at him for what he did to you, but ultimately you just wanted him to be at peace, and you didn't know how to solve his issues without laying him to rest. The art studio had always been a dream of yours. You told me that in session one. So, is it any surprise that you ended up there?'

'And William?'

'The looks of a Greek god, tattoos and a six-pack. He's educated, a millionaire, and he works with endangered animals for a living.'

Alice sat up and opened her eyes. 'It's too perfect.'

'Of course it is. William wouldn't exist in any reality except a false one, or I wouldn't be gay, Alice.'

Alice paused for a moment, slightly taken aback by this revelation. 'So, what do I need to look for?'

'You are looking for what didn't look real. You need to reverse that. Start looking for things that were not part of your script, little moments that surprised you because they were never part of your plan. What do you remember of Jacob that you saw in San Diego, that you never could have seen coming?'

Winter 2006 San Diego, California, USA

Alice had been holding tightly onto Jacob's arm for the duration of the long walk home from the French restaurant in town. The air was warm even in December, but struggling to get out of the British mentality of what winter was all about, she had worn a pink glittery bobble hat and equally vibrant scarf to accessorise her white cashmere sweater and matching jeans. Jacob had taken them out to celebrate her first commission coming in. The fact that she was painting again had given Alice an almost childlike happiness. She would bounce around the house, constantly sketching and screaming out ideas. This was the Alice he had fallen in love with all those years ago, the Alice that he had treated right and the Alice he wanted to spend his life with. They danced through the night to imaginary tunes they were playing through their minds, and the clicks of their heels fell in time with every step. They loved each other. Although those feelings were also false due to the nature of what was to be revealed some months later, the situation was real, and what Jacob was to say next would change Alice's opinion of her husband forever.

'Baby, baby, stop.' He ground to a halt, pulling Alice round to face him.

She smiled. 'Hey you.'

'Baby ...' Jacob hesitated, his words choking him up from inside.

'Jay, what is it? Talk to me.'

'Alice, I'm really sorry ... I've been thinking about everything, everything that brought us here, to this place.'

'San Diego? It was a plane, my love,' said Alice playfully, before noticing tears rolling down his cheeks. 'Jay, you're scaring me. What's wrong?'

'I'm sorry that I made you give up our child. I've regretted it every day since, and I see you walking into that hospital every time I close my eyes.' Jacob trembled, as if voicing his true self made him vulnerable. 'It haunts me in my day and more so in my dreams.'

'You didn't MAKE me do anything. Where has all this come from?'

'We are both aware that had my outlook been different, then we would be pushing a pram right now. It was my broken mind that talked us out of that choice, and I can't take it back, I can't ...'

Jacob was quickly becoming inconsolable. He fell to the floor and wrapped himself around Alice, who crouched down to join him.

'Oh sweetheart,' she said, 'we can't know what would have happened. Whatever has led us here has worked out for a reason. We could have had that child and broken up a month later. Who knows if I can even carry successfully after ...' Alice realised her thoughts had drifted away from her. 'You just don't know. But, baby, I do know this ...'

Jacob responded by gripping Alice a little tighter.

'I know that I love you,' she went on, 'I know that I'm happy, and I know that "where we are" is a beautiful place.'

'You mean San Diego?' asked Jacob with a whimper.

'No, you bellend, I mean us, where WE are, is beautiful!'

Jacob lay there, safe within Alice's warm embrace, while the ocean lapped the shore to their right. Neither of them said a word. Alice occasionally kissed Jacob's brow, and they didn't let go. It felt like home.

Knightsbridge, London, UK

'I hated seeing him upset, but at the same time I don't think I've ever loved him more, or even known him more. That Jacob there was the Jacob I never expected to see.'

[270]

'You had seen him cry before, though, held him as his heart broke?'

'But this was the first time I'd ever heard him tell me honestly why he was hurting. That I think is the most real memory I have from San Diego. I got to see the man I love for the first time, and I got an apology I both didn't expect and didn't know I needed.'

'What are you feeling now, Alice?'

'Like I want to remember more!' said Alice with a renewed fire in her eyes.

Chapter 35: Freudian Slip
Song of the day
"She's Crazy" by JT Coldfire

Spring 2010
Knightsbridge, London, UK

'Say it,' Dr Phillips demanded with force.

'I don't need to say it,' cried Alice. 'We both know what happened.'

'You need to say it, Alice. You give it power by protecting it.'

'I'm not protecting it. I'm not protecting him.'

'Say it, Alice.'

'I can't.'

'Say it!'

Alice was beside herself. 'I ... I can't.'

One hour before

Alice loved her meetings with Dr Vivian Phillips, for she had known her so long that she was almost like family – she certainly felt closer to her than to any of her aunts and uncles. Alice wasn't stupid. She knew that she was paying – or, rather, her father was paying – for the privilege of being listened to. That being said, Alice felt she had a deeper connection than Dr Phillips' other patients would have with the esteemed psychologist. *After all*, Alice thought, *she knows my deepest, darkest secrets.* Her father had spent a fortune on her therapy and had never even met Dr Phillips, so Alice had to make this work.

'Why won't you talk about Thomas?' Dr Phillips asked astutely.

For a slight-framed, middle-aged woman, the good doctor was still the most frighteningly intimidating woman that you could hope to meet. Her £2,000 suit was not only immaculately fitted but pressed and ironed in a way that told Alice that it was done by a man who did it for a living. A lady of class like Vivian Phillips did not iron, press or even hang her own clothes; if Alice was sure of anything in this reality, it was that. But Alice wasn't intimidated by her, even if she knew just by looking at her that Vivian couldn't and wouldn't ever be messed with. The power radiated from her. But Alice knew there was a kind heart behind the professionally curled hair and Parisian styling, and she also knew that the reason Vivian always sat next to her, rather than across the breadth of the giant oak desk, was so that Alice felt like she was having a human conversation.

'Why don't we talk about the mirror once more? I feel like the depth of your issues are coming from there, and while your ability to change the subject is second to none, I think, deep down at your core, you know that this is where our focus should lie. So tell me, why do you think the mirrored reflection takes "your" form?'

Alice sighed. 'As I've mentioned before, it is, at least in my opinion, the reflection of the true character I am.'

'But Alice, you know that you have a kind heart, an intelligent and creative mind, and, let's be fair, most women would die for your figure and that gorgeous mane of auburn hair. So why would a diminished and almost demonic reflection be a personification of your true self?'

'People don't really look at me like that though, do they? I mean, after everything I've done.'

'What exactly do you think that you have done in this world to even make that statement, Alice? List off a few things.'

'Well, I mean Jacob wouldn't have strayed if I'd have been perfect, would he? And I was pretty easily convinced to give up my child.'

[273]

'We have been seeing each other long enough now that you know I'm not buying into any of this. Jacob's misgivings are not your fault. Jacob's decision to push for an abortion based on his own very poor choices was *not* your fault.'

'So, what do you think I see in the mirror? Because we have spoken before on this and normally you do more listening. Today I feel you are pushing me to say something.'

'Is there something you need to say? When you came out of that deep and dreadful sleep, you told me you were tired of protecting people. You know who you were talking about, don't you?'

'Thomas. I was talking ... about Thomas.'

'Are you strong enough to hear my perspective on this? It will be something you don't want to hear.'

Alice nodded. Her hands became agitated, gripping her thighs through the denim of her jeans in the way a passenger might put their foot on an imaginary brake during a reckless driver's journey.

'I think you see yourself in the reflection because you find it easier to blame yourself than to blame Thomas for what he did. I believe the rotting flesh and broken teeth are a sign that you are trying to see through that image of yourself, that you want to blame his behaviour and free your conscience of the self-imposed guilt you currently feel. You know when you look at that monstrous reflection that it may look like you, but it's not you, it's Thomas, haunting you, mocking you. You have to free yourself of that blame.'

Alice looked up to see the doctor looking straight into her eyes as if her whole life was on display. 'But what if I was to blame? I mean ...'

'Alice, you were not to blame. No woman deserves what you went through. Stop protecting him.'

'But I invited him round, when Jacob was working so hard and ...'

'What happened, Alice? Say it,' Dr Phillips demanded with force.

'I don't need to say it,' cried Alice. 'We both know what happened.'

'You need to say it, Alice. You give it power by protecting it.'

'I'm not protecting it. I'm not protecting him.'

'Say it, Alice.'

'I can't.'

'Say it!'

Alice was beside herself. 'I ... I can't.'

'SAY IT!'

'Thomas ...'

'Thomas what?'

'Thomas ...'

What did Thomas do, slut? I don't remember him doing anything

'What did Thomas do?' whispered Dr Phillips.

'Thomas Levit raped me,' Alice said, not realising that she had stopped crying.

Alice wandered about the large office, picking up various trinkets and ornaments from Dr Phillips' many trips around the globe. 'So, you want me to try and picture him, in the mirror, when I feel attacked.'

She was agitated, bordering on angry, and this was exactly what the doctor needed from her.

'In the long run,' said Dr Phillips, 'we need you to stop seeing anything in the mirror except your true reflection. Right now, I want you to start fighting the right battle, and it's not your own reflection you should be fighting, so push for him, when your demon self appears. Call him out, and I believe he will come.'

'Then that's what I will do,' said Alice gratefully. 'Thank you again.' She was standing on Dr Phillips' side of the desk. She picked up a picture in an ornate gold frame. It had a much younger Vivian Phillips atop a camel with another woman sitting behind her, embracing her waist like a koala scared to fall from a tree. 'Where was this taken?'

'Oh my, that would be 1975 I believe, in Cairo. A few years before you were born, Mrs Brooking.'

'It's Ms Petalow again, I'm afraid.' As she replaced the picture and picked up the next, a photo in a much less elaborate frame, Alice caught her breath. 'But before we get on to Jacob, can you answer me this – why do you have a picture of this slut on your desk?'

Alice almost shattered the glass as she pointed at a very young, very innocent Evan Laurie.

'That "slut", Alice, is my daughter. Is this the Evan you have spoken about?'

Alice looked apologetic at the name-calling but stayed resilient in her tone. 'How would you not have picked up on that? It's hardly a common name.'

Vivian took a seat behind her desk and gestured for Alice to move to the sofa. 'I didn't realise because her name is not, and for that matter never has been, Evan. My daughter is Evangeline Phillips. If she has taken to being called Evan, it is clearly to try and upset me. We don't really talk anymore. I saw her once last year, in this very office, and that was it.'

'That would explain why she doesn't share your surname, either.' Alice was angry, but also frustrated that she had no place to direct the anger, with it clearly not being the fault of the doctor that her daughter was the woman she was.

'Tell me, what does she go by now? My daughter of a million masks.'

'Evan Laurie. And, yes, she is the one who stole my husband from me.'

'Evangeline Laurie Phillips – it's her middle name. The name I gave her to remember a love lost many years before. We ... We are not as close as I would like. In fact, quite the opposite.'

'Is she close to her father?'

'Evangeline has never known her father, and maybe my dedication to forging this career is what pushed her away. You might hate her, Alice, but my daughter has been moved from nanny to nanny, from boarding school to university. She is truly loved, but she doesn't know love, not like you do. I won't ever excuse her actions. For many years we fought like cat and mouse as I tried to curb her affections for always getting her own way. But I will say this. When I saw her last year – when she sat in the very chair you are sitting in now – she spoke as a woman who was genuinely in love. It was a side of her I've never seen, and it made me happy.'

Doctor Phillips stood proudly and came around to offer her hand to Alice. 'Unfortunately, I feel this situation now compromises our relationship and concludes our business here. If you need further help, then I have a list of people you can speak to, but honestly ... I think you've got this.'

Chapter 36: The Hand that Rocks
Song of the day
"Sour Times" by Portishead

Spring 2010
Faversham, Kent, UK

Jacob was called into work unexpectedly, and the moment he left, Dorothy started screaming. In the supermarket, she had a full-blown tantrum. Alice tried to control the situation by picking her up, but a distraught Dorothy kicked out aggressively, hurting Alice's chest. When they returned to Jacob's, Alice put her to bed in the hope that she would wear herself out, but young Dorothy showed unflagging commitment to the cause. The headboard cracked against the wall as Dorothy took her frustration out again and again on the frame of her bed. She lay on her back, kicking as if her life depended on it, while her tiny vocal cords provided the shrill noise of an ancient sea monster. How a child who had refused to speak to her since the day they had first met had the audacity to cry and scream at Alice was beyond her comprehension.

'This isn't real,' cried Alice. She gave up trying to calm her down and instead collapsed into the corner of Jacob's bedroom so as to completely shut herself down. She texted him to come home; he read but didn't reply to the message. She was on her own here, and she wasn't coping. All she could hear was the crash of the pine frame and the constant screaming, which was uncomfortably offset by one of Dorothy's toys playing 'Twinkle, Twinkle, Little Star' over and over on repeat.

'Alice, come home to us!'

The voice shouted passionately from everywhere and nowhere all at once. But it wasn't Alice's nightmare self.

'William, William, I can't cope, I don't know what to do.'

Alice cursed herself as she spoke, for she knew that William wasn't real, knew it was her own schizophrenia trying to find an angle into her fragile mind, but now, right now, she needed something; she needed him.

'Alice, I'm here, just follow my voice home.'

'William, I don't know what to do. She won't stop crying.'

'She's not real, none of this is. You have to find a way to see through this illusion of lies and mistruths.'

'I'm trying, baby, but I don't know how to do what you're asking of me. And I'm scared I'm going to do something that I will never be able to undo.'

'My beautiful and sweet Papillon. Remember what Doctor Phillips taught you. Think back to your safety training.'

Alice let out a whimper as she tried to gather the strength to follow through on William's plan. She took to her feet, clenched and balled her fists, drew a deep breath, and closed her eyes.

'That's it ... Follow my voice. And don't open your eyes ... not until you feel me take your hand. Hold your grip tightly, and don't let go ... Now tell me, Papillon ... Can you hear the child crying now?'

'No, William, I don't think I can. Just that infernal nursery rhyme. It seems louder than ever.'

Alice, her eyes still shut and her hands still clenched, felt a calm wash over her.

'Then you are free, my sweet girl ...'

'Open your eyes ...'

'ALICE! WHAT HAVE YOU DONE?'

Jacob's shout came out of nowhere as Alice realised that she had moved, unbeknown to her, straight to Dorothy's bedside.

Before she could see what she had done – she was gripping a pillow so tightly in her hands that blood, caused by her nails digging into her palms, was soaking through the material – Jacob thrust her aside, forcing her to crash heavily against the chest of drawers next to Dorothy's bed.

Dorothy wasn't moving. Jacob picked her up with one hand and ran from the room, dialling on his phone as he moved.

'Ambulance. Take my address first, 175 Hereford Close. It's my daughter, she's not breathing, I've just found her unresponsive.'

Alice slumped to the ground and started to shriek. She screamed and cried until her throat tore and the blood gargled in her mouth, and then she screamed again. She continued until the paramedic found her lying next to the foot of the bed. She didn't respond to the emergency doctor; why would she, when she hadn't even noticed Jacob rip the bloodied pillow from her hands moments before?

'Alice ... I'm going to need you to calm down, or we might have to sedate you. Dorothy, your daughter, she's OK and she's breathing again.' The nurse took Alice by the shoulders and shook her upright. 'Alice, listen to me. She's going to be OK, so you need to calm down.'

'She's going to be OK,' Alice repeated.

'It looks to me like she smothered herself with one of the hundreds of soft toys in her bed. This isn't unheard of, Alice. It's not your fault.'

'She's going to be OK,' Alice repeated.

'Jacob has got into the ambulance with Dorothy and my partner to make sure that everything is tickety-boo. It seems like the little mite is enjoying all the fuss and attention.' The paramedic sat down beside Alice and nudged her gently with her shoulder. 'I'm not going anywhere, Alice, not until I know you're OK. As soon as you're ready, we can make our way to A&E.'

'Thank you,' croaked Alice.

The paramedic, a stern-faced brunette who had clearly hardened over years of service, flashed a small smile at her distraught patient. 'You and your partner did the right thing and called us right away. You saved your little girl by checking on her when you did.'

Guess you know now, spoke her nightmare self.

'It's all real,' cried Alice.

Now I wonder where you are, said Thomas in the dark of her mind.

Chapter 37: Brand New Start
Song of the day
"Roads" by Portishead

Spring 2010
Canterbury, Kent, UK

I'm going away. I know what you're thinking. You think I'm abandoning my responsibilities, you think I'm running away from my problems, but you are wrong, you are all wrong. I have been asleep for two long years, and by all accounts I've been mentally ill for a lot longer than that. But while your worlds kept on moving, mine did not. My real world froze, while I started my own business, met the man of my dreams and lost my two best friends in a fantasy my over-creative mind had drawn up from my deepest fears and highest aspirations. And now ... I'm a mum to a beautiful daughter whom I don't remember carrying. I have no business, and yet I remember building it from scratch ...

Let's not forget Jacob.

And my husband, my soulmate, the man I saw die in my arms, is now in a happy relationship with the woman he cheated on me with, and I cannot process that. I can't fathom why you would do that to me, Jay, I just can't. And yet you seem happier than I've ever seen you before. You, Jacob, Mr Never-happy-with-anything-he-has. Always chasing more, always wanting more. And now ...

Now he's happier without you.

Now you are content for the first time in your life, and with the only woman I've ever hated. Jacob, I need to do this, and you know I'm right. I've found a little retreat on the beach, a place I can paint and read whilst my memories come back, where I can find myself once more. I need this, and I think you know that Dorothy needs that from me too.

Dorothy will grow to resent you, as will your mother.

Mum, don't be upset. We can write every week. And I want to keep you and Dad apprised on my progress. I want to be able to communicate more about some of the things I've been through, and that will only happen if we are all willing to work together.

They will forget you. Remember when you were in a coma? They pretty much adopted Jacob and Evan.

Dad, after all these years I still can't tell if your silence means you are angry or proud of me, so I'm just going to presume that at least you understand.

All he understands is that his happy family was more complete while you were asleep.

And my beautiful little girl ... I can't convey my feelings for you because I don't understand them, but as I look at your auburn ringlets falling around your neck and I look into your eyes, a deeper blue than mine have ever been and circled by a band of emerald that reminds me of your father every time I look at you, I do know that I want to do everything I can to make you happy, make you safe and make you loved.

Her step mum will love her more than you ever could.

Alice took a deep breath, the last comment taking its toll on her heart with the bitter truth than ran through it. She took the door handle in her hand and tried one last time to regain her composure. 'You've got this,' she whispered to herself before she entered the room full of false confidence. Her parents were there, laughing with Jacob as Dorothy waddled between them all, trying to catch a balloon that bounced above her head, her laughter infectious and impossible to ignore.

'Hey, you guys, thank you for coming,' said Alice, drawing everyone but Dorothy's attention. 'We need to talk.

No, that's not right, not at all. What I mean is ... I need to tell you something.'

Old Salty Cottage
Melville Drive
Sandown
I.O.W.
PO22 8SW
14ᵗʰ October

Dearest Dotty

Your father has promised me that he's reading you these, so with that in mind I want him to give you a big fat kiss when you get to the bottom. I want you to know that I miss you terribly and that I'm safe and enjoying the sand between my toes. It is my hope that one day I can bring you back here, so that you can see where I found my way once more. I hope Nanna and Poppa Bear are OK, and that you are looking after your dad. He struggles to even make his bed without a strong woman by his side, so keep on top of him for me, will you?

I look outside and I see the leaves are falling and changing into the colours that match both your hair and your fiery temperament, and it reminds me what a beautiful and amazing thing that I have created in you.

I have sent you some shells I collected from the beach. Ask your dad to put them on your bedroom window for me, so that when you look outside you know that I am thinking of you.

I miss you.

Mum
(Ask Dad to kiss you)

[285]

Summer 2010
The coastal roads of east Kent, UK

Jacob knew it was there and yet couldn't quite focus on the bastard creature that had followed him all these years. The shadow it cast was unnatural in so many ways, like spilt ink over a photograph of the room, and it had always been the same. As Jacob approached his 30th birthday, he had noticed the creature's physical presence less each day, maybe due to his ever-increasing tolerance of its presence. He still hated the creature and was always wary of its place in the day, for it never appeared without reason or purpose, and neither of those things were ever really a positive.

'It's not like you to hide, Ahab. What's so wrong that you have taken to skulking around the shadows looking for carrion to pick at? I thought you were a predator. No? My mistake.'

Jacob mocked the creature slightly but still had an air of caution in his voice. He had played this game for long enough now to know it could change in an instant. Content that the kraken, Ahab, would stay hidden under his bed, he carried on getting dressed, finishing his tie with a half-Windsor knot.

'I'll catch you later, old man,' Jacob whispered, patting the bed on his way out of the bedroom. 'Was a pleasure talking to you.'

He heard only a barely audible grumble in reply.

'Are you ready, ladies?' called Jacob excitedly as he bounced down the stairs.

At the bottom, he was confronted by a vision that just a few years ago he could never have imagined he would see, and it warmed his soul that he knew with complete certainty that this was a reality he had built and not destroyed.

'How do we look, Dad?' said Evan.

She twirled round in a circle, holding in her arms a giggling Dorothy. They were dressed in identical summer dresses of yellow and gold, with their hair tied up and bound by gold ribbon.

'You look ... Well, you look perfect to me. I truly am a lucky man to have you both with me.'

Jacob had organised a day of taking photos at a little spot called Samphire Hoe on the Dover and Folkestone borders. A man-made beach that had been developed using the soil dug out when the Channel Tunnel was built back in the mid-1980s, since 1997 it had been a fantastic tourist spot, especially for those with a keen eye and a good lens.

On the drive down, Dorothy and Evan sang nursery rhymes until the journey got too much for the littlest Brooking, and she fell asleep with her fingers in her mouth and dribble on her chin. Evan then pulled herself a little closer to Jacob, while he navigated the coastal roads with more care than he would have done in his old Benz. He had decided to get something family sized when he had become a father, and the big BMW X5 didn't cling to the road as much as his old coupé when driven at speed, although Evan had commented that since becoming a father, he had slowed down naturally anyway, and she had assured him that was for the better, as it was his whole lifestyle that had slowed down.

'I fucking love you, Jay,' said Evan under her breath, knowing Dorothy could be listening. 'This has felt so different, these last few years ... This "us". You know?'

Jacob gave her thigh a little squeeze. 'I know exactly what you mean, love. Who would have thought openness and honesty would have made me a more lovable man, right?'

Although Jacob was smiling, he knew there was a modicum of truth behind his statement, and clearly Evan knew it too, as she squeezed his hand in return.

'You didn't know you were poorly, babe,' she said, 'although why you kept it from me I'll never understand. But let's be fair, I was no saint either, and I didn't make it easy on you.'

Jacob was waiting for the creature to cut in at any point, but every pause in the conversation brought only silence. 'Easy on me? Honey, I was petrified of you!'

Evan looked at Jacob in disbelief. 'Petrified? But you are so much bigger than me. What could you have feared?'

'Back then I couldn't deal with confrontation as most people do, you know this, but maybe subconsciously I was also scared I was losing you.' Jacob seemed like he was struggling to admit his past feelings, but spoke without prompt. 'Ev, I convinced myself that what we had was nothing so that it was justified in my head, that the affair was acceptable. But I see now that, actually, I was much more myself by your side than I'd ever been with anyone else.'

Evan smiled and pushed her head into Jacob's shoulder. 'Well, if it led us here, to where we are now, then I wouldn't change a thing.'

'Nearly dying on that bloody boat wasn't much fun, but, yeah, I agree.'

The car went into the steep drop of the tunnel that led down to the beachfront, causing everyone's stomachs to flip for a moment. Dorothy's eyes shot open in a wide stare, shocked at the sudden lurching feeling.

'It's OK, poppet,' said Evan, turning to face her at the sound of a whimper, but she had already drifted back off into whatever fairy-tale dream could occupy the mind of a two-and-a-half-year-old girl.

With Dorothy asleep in the car, Evan and Jacob started to unload the picnic basket and camera from the boot of the car, sharing a kiss in between every little task they performed. As Jacob pulled the boot closed, he leaned into Evan and kissed her with such force that she fell against the car, his hands pinning her in place.

'Wow, where did that come from?' said a startled Evan in between more kisses peppered upon her lips by an almost rampant Jacob.

'I just wanted to show you what I thought of you before I showed you this.'

Jacob pulled away, one hand still on Evan's hip. He reached into his back pocket and pulled out a sealed letter with Alice's name on it.

'Baby, I don't understand,' said Evan, recoiling slightly at the sight of Alice's name. 'What's that got to do with me?'

'This is a signed copy of my divorce papers, and if you help me with a task over the coming months, I'd like to post them through Alice's door, because when I propose to you, I'd like to do it as a free man.'

'PROPOSE?' said Evan. 'When you propose?'

Her mouth was agape. She jumped up into his arms, wrapping her legs around him as he spun about, kissing her pink glossy lips.

'Jay, you have completed me. I'll do anything to spend my life with you both.'

As Evan's feet slowly came back down to earth, and Jacob's kisses became deeper and more passionate, he waited for the voice of Ahab to offer its opinion. He waited, and yet ... It never came.

38: The Last Day
Song of the day
"Where I've Been" by Rival Sons

Spring 2011
Sandown, Isle of Wight, UK

'Good morning, Mrs Frodsham,' called Alice as she skipped along the road past the old cottage. 'How are the flowers today?'

Mrs Edna Frodsham had been Alice's neighbour since she had moved here and had never been anything less than hospitable. It was no rare occurrence to see her appear at the back window with a freshly made gypsy tart or Bakewell slice. 'Another week or two before we hit any kind of real bloom, my dear. You make sure you keep warm, pet. It's blowing hard down on the front.'

'I will, Mrs Frodsham, I promise.'

Alice carried on down the road. Her purple bobble hat wasn't really needed, especially as she didn't feel cold today, but it matched her scarf, and she hadn't been able to do much with her hair to stop the wind whipping it up like candyfloss on blustery days like this. She took the cobbled steps down to the seafront, where she had made her home the past five months. Both her fitness and her equilibrium had returned fully after "the long sleep", as she had described it to her local doctor, and with little effort she bounced from stone to stone without catching the crooked and broken edges that had caught her out so many times when she had first arrived. Her Converse trainers sunk into the sand as soon as she reached the bottom, and she instantly regretted not wearing her boots on a day that, although not cold, was far too brisk to go barefoot.

She turned to her right and followed the chalky rock face for 30 minutes before finding the spot she needed, a place where no one else could see her. Her own spot – not one borrowed from Jacob or imagined in her fantasy, just hers. She had come here every day the weather had allowed since her arrival, but today was different, today was special, and she intended to mark the occasion. She took the last few steps towards the final part of her journey. Two large slabs of rock that had fallen from the cliff face many hundreds of years before were her destination. One was curved in the middle and had the look of a fancy chair designed for the aristocracy; the other was more jagged and held anything that Alice wanted to sketch while sitting in her royal chair.

She sat down and took out her sketchbook. She flicked through the pages, seeing numerous drawings she had made of shells and driftwood over the months. Even a crab claw, mottled and dyed by the sun's rays, had found a place in Alice's work. She found the last page completely empty and pulled out a black ballpoint to rectify that.

Dearest Alice

In finishing this book, you have completed the first step of your recovery. You remember once again all that is real and all that is not.
You remember you. Now finish this.

Alice M Petalow

29/4/11

As soon as the date was written, Alice closed the book and took the deepest breath she had ever taken. *This is it, girl. Remember what everyone kept saying. You've got this.* Reaching into her satchel, she took out an aggressive-looking camping knife and removed the safety cover. *You've got this.* She furrowed out a space under the second slab of rock with the blunt edge of the blade, deep enough to fit her leather-bound sketchbook. She forced the sketchbook underneath the large monolith before covering the entrance with loose sand until no trace of it could be seen. *You can do this, Alice,* she reassured herself over and over. She sat back in her cold, hard seat of queens and leaned forward with the knife in her hand. *Last step ... You've got this ...* With a final push, she took the sharp edge of the curved blade and very slowly started to carve her initials into the rock that protected her work. 'Time to go home, Alice,' she said confidently to herself.

Canterbury, one week later

Alice stood with her key in the door. She hesitated, for she knew what was waiting on the other side of it. *You've got this,* she thought to herself as the lock turned with a triple click.

'I'm home, guys. There had better be either a kettle on or a glass of wine poured ready for me.'

There was no response.

'Helloooooooo ... Anyone home?'

She was met with the same lack of response as before.

'Welcome home, Alice,' she said to herself sarcastically, while picking up the post from the floor. Three letters for Dad; one for Dotty, which was clearly a delayed letter that Alice had sent a week before; and one for Mrs Alice Brooking. It had been some time since Alice had referred to herself by her married name, so it made her anxious to consider the contents.

It looks official. It could be anything, Alice mused. *It could be a doctor's appointment. Yes, that must be what it is.*

Alice took a seat on the third step of the stairs – a step that in her youth she had considered her thinking step – and tore open the letter. She read the lines, 'In the family court at Canterbury City, between Alice Marie Brooking and Jacob Paul Brooking ...'

Spring 2012 Faversham, Kent, UK

A year had passed since she had posted back the signed divorce papers, since she'd had anything substantial to do with Jacob, save for Dorothy's birthday party and her infant-school induction. Alice really had no reason to do anything except exchange pleasantries at the midweek handover. She had been polite, more than polite; after all, she got a four-figure cheque through the post each month for her share of the Gallantry. But a kiss on her cheek would be standard, before he would take her hand and tell her she was doing 'really well' – patronising bastard. She wasn't doing well at all, and what right did he have to tell her what he perceived? He certainly had no right to touch her with those dirty and sullied hands, surely thick with the stench of that harlot.

Today it changed. Today she would be honest with him, hear his voice tremble as she released years of built-up angst against his and Evan's false relationship. It had been building.

Her monster still spoke to her every day. Knowing her monster was a representation of Thomas had given it a name, but it hadn't stopped the noise. And she was tired of carrying around her demons. She was tired full stop. Today was the first day of clearing out her closet.

Knock, knock, knock.

He's probably fucking Evan.

KNOCK, KNOCK, KNOCK.

Yeah, knock louder, cause that will stop him.

KNOCK, KNOCK ...

'Alice, what the actual fuck? Use the bloody doorbell, that's what it's for. What on earth is wrong?'

Alice glanced to her right and saw the brass button, but it only took a second to remember why she was banging in the first place, and she quickly turned her attention back to Jacob.

'You're engaged?' said Alice with disgust.

'Erm ... I guess I am. I was going to tell you when I dropped Dotty off tomorrow.'

'Well, you don't have to worry now, do you? I ran into Matt yesterday, and he seemed oblivious as to who he was talking to as he detailed how he had never seen "chef" happier than he had recently.'

'Alice, I'm not sure what you're so unhappy about? We've been separated years.'

And whose choice was that?

'And whose choice was that, Jay? Because it wasn't mine.'

'Alice, stop! I'm not that guy anymore, and do you know what? You are not this girl anymore. So stop and come with me.'

Jacob grabbed his car keys and a second set that she didn't recognise and closed the door behind him.

'I'm not going anywhere with you,' she said.

Jacob opened the passenger door and offered his hand to Alice. 'Just get in the bloody car, love.'

Alice ignored his help and climbed into the car with a slam of the door and a grunt of derision. Jacob looked at the sky and pleaded for a little mercy on his day off, but he knew it wouldn't come.

'Where are we going?' asked Alice. 'Because I can't see what on earth you might think I would care about now.'

Jacob summoned a false smile and took a breath. 'You sound more like your father every day. Just have a bit of faith, will you?'

Alice looked out of the window as the car pulled away, hoping that a tornado would appear, as though they were in an L. Frank Baum novel, and suck them off this plane of existence. This world was just a little too painful for Alice right now, and she felt exposed by its reality.

'I don't get it,' she said. 'I don't get Evan and all her little quirks that seem to make everyone hate her but you. I've never seen you so happy and so bloody composed. You have even left your demons behind, and that's something I just can't explain.'

'Me either, and neither should I have to. I know it makes no sense to you, but honestly I just feel more myself with her, and I can be more myself around her. And you know what? I am happy. Is that so wrong? I mean, I want no different for you, after all.'

Alice scowled but didn't take her eyes off the sky. 'How very magnanimous of you.'

'All that matters now is we try to do what's right by Dorothy, and that's what this is all about.'

Jacob pulled into the tiny parking space behind the row of vintage shops on Whitstable high street and jumped out onto the cobbled streets. 'Well, are you coming?'

'Do I have a choice?' answered Alice.

Good job putting him back in his place, bitch.

'Jacob, what have you done?'

Alice looked up as he pulled away the plastic protection of the brand-new shop sign: 'Le Petit Papillon'.

It wasn't identical to the font in her false reality, but it was close.

'We have built your shop into the old sewing-machine building. It's near identical to the one you built in your dreams.'

'But how did you know?'

'We've been making notes. Me, your mum and dad – actually, everyone you have spoken to about your dream world. I guess we've just figured it out between us.'

'My parents knew about this?'

'Yes. It was my idea. But it was your father who told me I had to do something for you in return ...'

'In return for what?'

'For your share of the restaurant. We valued it at £180,000. This shop has cost slightly more, but this has given you licence to be free once more.'

'The little butterfly,' whispered Alice.

'That's Dorothy, right?'

'Yes ... Of course that's Dorothy. How many other little butterflies do you know? Shall we take a look inside?'

Alice was almost speechless when she saw the interior of the shop. 'Jacob, I don't know what to say.'

'Well, thank your dad more than me. He did more of the painting and woodwork. We were going to do a grand unveiling tomorrow, but since you came knocking at my door ... I didn't really have much of a choice.'

'I am still mad at you,' Alice said without looking him in the eye. 'You can't keep buying your way out of everything.'

'I am not buying anything. This has been bought by your shares in the company,' Jacob said with authority.

'And what if I choose not to take this on? After all, you can't make me give up my shares!'

'No, Alice. No one can make you do anything. Have we ever been able to make you do anything against your will? Christ almighty, Pebble, we couldn't even make you wake up before you were ready!'

'Don't call me that, Jacob. My name is Alice. Now answer the question – what will you do if I don't take it on?'

He sighed. 'Then me and your father will have to share a tear-filled hug and I will have to put the bloody building back on the market.'

Alice's eyes glazed over. She picked up a photo from the counter. The photo was of a black-and-red butterfly on a piece of driftwood – a photo she had taken many years before down at Rye Harbour.

'I love it,' she said. 'I hate you for taking the fire out of my voice today. I hate you for asking that tart to marry you. I hate you for being happier with her than you were with me. But I love this.'

'So we have a deal? If so, the building is yours. I've paid the rates and council tax for a year. All it needs is your touch of magic and those bloody amazing pictures hung on the walls.'

'Thank you, Jay. I do really appreciate what you and my parents have done here.'

'It's my pleasure. Just make sure you invite me to the opening.'

'Of course.' Alice laughed. 'Just don't bring that –'

Jacob cut her off quickly. 'Before you say anything more, I want to say one thing. Her life, although strange and vulgar to you, has not been easy. I love her, and she is wonderful with Dorothy.' He handed the keys of the property over to Alice. 'You might find that you have more in common than you think.'

Chapter 39: I Do
Song of the day
"Save Me from Myself" by Christina Aguilera

Autumn 2012
Tunbridge Wells, Kent, UK

Evan looked in the mirror and saw every negative that had been pointed out by men over the years. Her bust was escaping her dress and her hair was struggling to stay up in the fashion in which she had intended, her blonde locks being of such length that even when they were curled, their weight was constantly trying to bring them down. Her bright red lips were matched by her six-inch heels, while the rest of her look was that of traditional ivory.

'You can do this, Evangeline. He loves you exactly how you are, remember? He knows your past, and you know his.'

'Evan, you look amazing, you old tart,' said Heather as she fell into the room, with a half-empty bottle of prosecco gripped tightly in her hand.

'Hev, if you are pissed on my bloody wedding day, I will never forgive you!'

'I'm not pissed. I just can't walk in these bloody heels you bought me.'

If one was to describe Evan as a flamingo, then Heather was certainly an ostrich. She was larger than Evan in both physical appearance and personality.

'Heather, you look beautiful,' said Evan. 'Now pour me a glass of that, will you? I am shitting myself here.'

Heather poured a tall glass of prosecco and dropped in a fat strawberry from the breakfast basket for good measure.

'There we go, chuck, but I don't; you do. You look amazing. And you know what?'

'What's that, babe?' said Evan while downing the glass of prosecco.

'He fucking loves you, girl. I didn't think so before, but watching him interacting with you these last few years – well, he never takes his eyes off you. Or his hands, for that matter!'

'I know he loves me. I just hope it continues as Dorothy grows older.'

'Aww, it's amazing what being a stepmother has done to you, babe. I never saw it coming.'

'I never saw it coming myself, but she has levelled Jacob out, and she makes me laugh so much. Who would have thought such joy could come from such a tiny package?'

'Have you bloody heard yourself?' Heather beamed.

'I know, I think this is as happy as I have ever been!'

The wedding venue, in the High Rocks forest in Tunbridge Wells, was beautiful in a way that was almost dreamlike. With the evening sun dipping beneath the treeline, a firefly-like swarm of stars had appeared overhead. Jacob stood to attention underneath the arch of wild flowers and looked out at the gathering of friends and family that had come to see them on their special day. He was wearing trousers and a waistcoat in a traditional navy tweed, and a crisp white shirt. A Paul Smith pocket square poked out of his pocket, and his Omega watch was the only other addition to what he hoped was a classic and a lost vintage look. His brother stood with him, wearing identical clothes but hung in a different way. Samuel had always been told, by Jacob no less, that he was the less attractive brother. His style was that of a man who didn't care much for what anyone thought about him. So his shirt was a little less tucked in, and his hair a little less styled. At six feet one inch, Samuel was a touch taller, but they were obviously brothers, and side by side they looked the part.

'Shame Dad didn't get to see you marry the right girl at last,' said Sam, nodding towards their mum, who sat with Dorothy bouncing on her knee.

'Alice was never the wrong girl, mate. I was the wrong guy, though, for sure.'

Samuel put his hand on his brother's back. The violinist started to play, and Samuel leaned in and whispered, 'Damn, son, well done my boy.'

'*It's not so easy loving me,*' sang the female vocalist, who was standing next to the violinist and a man playing an acoustic guitar, whose hair was tied up in a loose bun like a samurai warrior. '*It gets so complicated, all the things you've got to be ...*'

As Evan started to walk down the aisle, all eyes were on her elegant and desirable form, perfectly wrapped in a dress that was short at the front but then trailed off to a small train at the rear.

'*Everything's changing but you're the truth, I'm amazed by all your patience, everything I put you through.*'

Jacob's heart froze. He had been so nervous waiting for Alice, as if he knew deep down they weren't right for each other, yet now he felt completely at ease. Just being himself was enough for Evan and Dorothy. He never had to pretend to be anything more.

'*When I'm about to fall, somehow you're always waiting, with your open arms to catch me ...*'

Evan stood opposite Jacob. He lifted her veil, to reveal her glossed red lips.

'Ladies and gentlemen, friends and family. We are gathered here today to witness the union of love between Jacob and Evangeline. I believe you have prepared your own vows?' said the minister. 'Evangeline, would you like to go first?'

Evan was shaking but was quickly eased by Jacob, who took her hands within his own.

'There was a time, Jacob Brooking, when I knew I loved you, but I never loved us. All that has changed these past few years. That may be down to a certain young lady.' Evan gave a little wink to Dorothy – a wink that was returned by Dorothy blinking both eyes together tightly. 'Or maybe we just grew into one another. But what I am sure of is you are my best friend, and I have never loved two people more than I love both of you.'

Evan looked once more at Dorothy, but she had disappeared from her grandmother's knee and instead was trying to chase a butterfly down the centre of the aisle, drawing a chorus of delight from the crowd. As she returned her gaze to Jacob, Evan saw the face of a man caught off guard by her honest and, for her at least, articulate declaration of love for Dorothy, on top of her love for him.

With tears starting to well in his eyes, Jacob opened his mouth to speak but felt overwhelmed to do so.

'Baby,' said Evan, giving his hands a gentle shake. 'Just remember the hard part's already done.'

'Evan,' Jacob stuttered. 'I thought I wasn't good enough. Not good enough for my family, for my job, and certainly for anybody that dared to love me. I looked at others to complete me. I looked to run away in hope I might find a piece of me I might like. Then Dotty came along and we found our way and I realised something. I was always enough, and I am a good dad, and I work hard. Let me be a good husband to you, the most beautiful and amazing woman I know, and I promise I won't let you down. You have saved me! I love you with all my heart. You have ...'

Jacob paused for a moment, as if waiting for a disapproving voice, as if waiting for the doubt to kick in. It never came, and he finally felt free to say everything that he had always wanted to say.

'You have saved me from myself, and I will show you from today just how much I love you for that.'

Chapter 40: I Move the Stars for No One
Song of the day
"Scars" by Michael Malarkay

Autumn 2012
Whitstable, Kent, UK

'Stop it, Dorothy. Can you not see that Mummy is busy?'

Dorothy didn't care that her mum was busy. She was bored and, like most children of that age and of above-average intelligence, needed to be amused by something that would stop her entertaining herself with something inappropriate every time her mum's back was turned. This particular time, she was playing with her mother's paintbrushes. With Alice being the artist she was, they were not cheap, and so Dorothy's misbehaviour was driving her to distraction.

'Baby, those are Mummy's. You have your own, remember? Over here with your books and toys.'

Alice gestured to the little playpen she had set up in the corner of the studio, an art deco version of an Indian tepee. Dorothy still struggled to communicate with her mum the way she communicated with Jacob. She gave Alice a quick look of derision and threw her mother's brushes on the wooden floor before throwing herself into her corner on her belly. Alice let out a frustrated and muffled scream and pulled Dorothy up by her wrists and onto her bottom. 'Baby, please, just help me out and play here whilst I get some work done.'

She instantly regretted snapping at her daughter, but she was so tired. This wasn't a life she had asked for at all.

The little bell above the door chimed like birdsong, announcing the arrival of customers.

'Please, just do this for me,' Alice pleaded with Dorothy before going to greet her new customers. 'Welcome to Le Petit Papillon,' she said proudly, before realising that she knew her customers. 'Mr and Mrs Fitzherbert – I'm sorry, I didn't recognise you for a moment. Not that I could ever forget you in that wonderful coat, Julianne. I wasn't expecting to see you again so soon.'

Mr Pip Fitzherbert, by far the more pretentious and ruder of the two of them, pushed past Alice and pointed at the Viking Bay piece that Alice had painted as an art student at Canterbury University. 'My wife, in all her wisdom, has convinced me to drive all the way back here – despite nearly being on my own driveway an hour ago – so that we can buy this little oil painting of yours. Why she didn't buy it when we were here I just don't know, but here we are.'

'It's a watercolour, Mr Fitzherbert, but of course, I will wrap it for you now. Julianne, have you decided where you might hang –'

Alice was cut off by the catastrophic crash of what she knew to be her current project falling off its easel and smashing on the hard floor, followed closely by the pitter-patter of Dorothy's tiny feet.

'If you could give me a moment,' said Alice, smiling falsely while backing out of the room. This was how Alice's day had begun, and it was how it was to continue.

Alice wasn't a stroppy person. In fact, her very nature emanated a constant state of happiness, as Alice was the very picture of a woman who danced in the rain and sang loudly, not caring who could witness such an event. But as she tucked Dorothy into bed that night, she felt frustrated by the day gone by. A day wasted. The one sale to the Fitzherberts had been the only highlight; her brush had laid not one stroke on her three current projects. Dorothy was already fast asleep, the journey home having knocked her out so much that her grandfather had carried her straight to bed from the car. Alice was glad to have dinner with her folks, especially with the business just taking off and Jacob on his honeymoon with his new practically perfect wife, as Alice had taken to sarcastically calling her. It wasn't always easy for Alice to find time to food-shop, let alone cook a healthy dinner for the both of them, and her mother's attention to Dorothy gave her time to breathe.

Alice looked at her daughter, exhausted from her day of destruction, and wondered how she could sleep so soundly after spending her entire day being so very pestiferous. 'Where did you come from, baby? You are the only thing I don't remember – carrying, birthing or holding you. I remember nothing and I doubt sometimes you are real. Is that why you hate me? I don't know what you want from me, for you still refuse to talk to me, like I am nothing but a nuisance to you, getting in the way of you and your father's fun.' Alice turned on the night light as she backed slowly out of the room, trying not to wake her daughter from her slumber. She closed the door slowly and rested her head on it. 'I mean, how could I possibly compete with your perfect little family over at the Brooking family home?'

She cursed quietly to herself, before a soothing voice intervened.

'You are a great mum,' said Angela Petalow as she handed her daughter a mug of lemon-and-ginger tea. 'Never forget that.'

'Thanks, Mum, but I'm still fairly sure she hates me. I never asked for this, and it scares me the way she looks at me at times.'

Alice walked into her room and sat on her bed, while her mum loitered in the doorway.

'She doesn't hate you, Alice. She is still getting used to you having her more often, that's all.'

Alice looked up into her mum's eyes and spoke honestly. 'All I remember is hating Evan, and then Dorothy was here.'

'My beautiful Alice, look how far you have come since you left hospital. It's hard to hear, I know, but Jacob is a great dad too, and having seen Evan with him and then also with our Dotty, well ... I can't argue with the fact that they seem

[304]

a good fit. Does that take anything away from you, as a woman, as a mother? No! Of course it doesn't. You will find your way in life. You are the most creative and beautiful of all God's creatures, and you will attract those around you that benefit you on a deeper level. That was never our Jacob. Just be you. Dorothy will come around, believe me, my love.' Angela lowered her shoulders and sighed on behalf of her daughter. 'That little poppet is blessed with love in abundance, just like you are. Your father and I are so extremely proud of you.' Angela walked over and kissed her daughter on her brow. 'Get some rest, my love.'

Alice sipped the last of her tea before sliding down under her fleece-lined quilt and curling into a foetal position, one goose-downed pillow held in her tight embrace. Her heart felt heavy, and the drama had taken its toll on her brain's ability to function properly, so she closed her eyes and tried her best to shut off the noise of the day and the bickering mind voices that followed. Then, as everything slowed to a halt, and her mind gave up the fight, nothing came forward, nothing except the silence of the night.

It couldn't have been ten minutes before a crash woke Alice in a startled panic, causing her to almost fall out of bed in a rush to reach her daughter. Dorothy stood next to the spot where her bookcase used to stand and looked first at her mother and then at the smashed lamp on the floor. The glow from Dorothy's comfort lamp picked out the broken porcelain and glass, like a star system scattered across the carpet. Dorothy jumped back onto her bed and defiantly pointed at Mr Blackberry, her regal hare toy, a favourite gift from her father, which lay next to the shattered lamp.

'What have you done, Dorothy? For God's sake, girl, you need to give me a goddamned break.'

Dorothy didn't cry as a result of her mother's outburst. Instead, she lay on her bed and faced the wall.

'You can turn your back to me all you want, Miss Brooking, but I tell you now that you are going to change your attitude or you can go and live with your bloody father from the minute he returns, and you can stay there until you realise just how easy you had it here.'

Alice picked up every shard of anything that had the potential to hurt her daughter's delicate feet and stood the bookcase up with a rage-fuelled burst of strength. She replaced the books one by one before throwing Mr Blackberry on the bed next to a sulking Dorothy. 'Can I go to sleep now, Your Majesty? Is that OK?'

Dorothy didn't respond and cared little for her mother's sarcasm, leaving Alice to close the door behind her and rest her brow once more on its painted wood.

'I didn't ask for this. Why can't you just leave me alone!' Alice cried with a flushed red face.

As you wish, said the creature in the hallway mirror, which looked like Alice, but sounded like Thomas Levit.

Rain lashed hard against the windowpane, waking Alice up from a dream of beautiful calm. She had been walking through a field of sunflowers, with the sun itself baking down on the ground, as she playfully chased a butterfly while skipping to the song of chirping birds and busy crickets.

WHAT'S WRONG, ALICE? called the creature from the reflection in the window. Its form was barely visible, but somehow the water pounding against it was creating a silhouette. It had been years since Alice had kept a mirror in her bedroom, but somehow her demon self always found a way to show its face and communicate its venom, be it a rainy window or a make-up mirror.

Dorothy, check Dorothy. Alice looked at her phone to assess the time. One o'clock was a good time – if all was well and the creature left her alone, then another six hours' sleep wasn't beyond the realms of possibility. She slid out of bed and onto the cold and uninviting floor while blindly fumbling for her slippers. The rain's beat became more aggressive and overpowered all of Alice's other senses as she staggered blindly in the dark, yawning and stretching all the way to Dorothy's room. She went to open Dorothy's door, but the darkness betrayed her, as it was already wide open. Alice rushed over to Dorothy's bed to make sure all was well. She had felt guilty all night for the falling-out during the day. Whatever was wrong with their relationship, Alice was fairly sure it wasn't the fault of her nearly five-year-old daughter. She pulled the quilt back from the heap of pillows and was hit instantly with the dread she had feared the most.

As you wished, my child.

Alice staggered back. *Dad, she will be with Dad.* Seeking sanctuary with the big bear was something Alice herself had done throughout her childhood, especially during violent storms. She turned to go and check but was stopped abruptly by a lancing pain deep within her foot. The pain was so intense that it brought her tumbling to her knees. Alice muffled her scream between pursed lips. She realised she couldn't take her slipper off to look at the source of the pain, as a shard of glass from the shattered lamp had pierced the bottom of her heel, pinning her plush shoe to her flesh. 'Fuck, fuck, fuck,' Alice cursed quietly while biting down on her lip to avoid waking the whole house up. 'Jesus, Alice, you can do this,' she said. She gripped the glass dagger between her two fingers.

Does it hurt?

Alice looked to her right and saw her demon self in Dorothy's mirrored wardrobe. For once, it wasn't wearing identical clothes. Instead, it wore a white communion dress that looked far too small for someone or something of Alice's size. It was just like ... No, it *was* Dorothy's communion dress.

Does it hurt? the creature repeated. It licked its lips and pressed its filthy blood-stained hands against the mirror's glass front, as if trapped in a transparent cell.

Alice ignored the creature and wrenched the shard out with a suppressed yelp. 'I'm not letting you toy with me, creature.' She pulled herself up and hobbled to the door, leaving a bloody footprint behind her with every step of her right foot.

'Mum, Dad, are you awake?'

Alice didn't wait for a reply. She turned the handle to her parents' bedroom door. On the other side, she found everything she had ever feared. No roof sheltered the decaying corpses of her parents, only a hellish, blood-red sky; no carpet lay beneath her feet, only hard stone and hot volcanic ash. Her parents, flayed and desiccated, were lying on their bed, side by side and hand in hand. Yet as Alice battled herself, convincing herself with every look that none of this could be real, a worse sight caught her eye. The sky filled with rapacious black-winged creatures, too large to be birds. Each one shrieked and clawed for aerial dominance over the blood heaven, a dance that saw blood shed by razor-sharp talons and jagged-edged beaks. When Alice screamed at the horror unfolding in front of her, the harpies' focus turned to her, and in that moment Alice realised that behind the sharp beaks of the nightmare creatures were deformed and black-eyed versions of every girl who had ever bullied her at school. With renewed hunger and wanton desire, the beasts swooped down one by one to devour Alice as they had done her parents.

Alice turned to leave the room, but the door she had entered was gone. In its place was the same barren stone landscape that surrounded her. Black stone and a blood-red sky were her everything now. As she started to run, a quick glance over her shoulder told her that her parents' corpses had disappeared. She ran. She ran until she could feel the bile rising in her throat. Her slippers were torn off by the jagged rock. She kept going, kept on running, until the skin on her feet was shredded. The demonic harpies, easily the size of a Rottweiler and with the harrowed and tortured faces of all of her oppressors, ripped her nightdress from her body and took turns in attempting to tear the flesh from her shoulders and back. As Alice rounded a larger slab of obsidian slate that ran down a slope dangerously steep to a woman running so fast, she ran shoulder-first into the front door of a large detached house that had seemingly come out of nowhere. Alice burst through the red oak door, slamming it behind her and pulling across an archaic iron bolt as a means of defence. She didn't know if these creatures knew how to open a door, but as she slid to the floor to tend her bloodied and blackened feet, she realised she didn't care, because this couldn't be real. It couldn't be ... *Could it?*

Three of the closest harpies slammed into the door with sickening thuds as Alice pushed up onto her haunches and added her weight to it to keep it secure. The creatures shrieked and snapped with fang-filled beaks.

'Where am I?' said Alice as she got herself up to her feet.

You are where you wanted to be, Alice, said her demon self as it entered the room from an arched entrance that led to a kitchen that looked more like a torture chamber.

'You're not real, bitch,' said Alice confidently. 'I'm scared, I'm hurt, but I'm not stupid. You have brought me to your false reality far too many times.'

Do I look like a reflection in your mirror to you this time? I have told you where you are — exactly where you wanted to be. Away from your bastard child ... She will be happier with her "better" parents anyway.

'THAT'S NOT WHAT I WANTED, AND YOU KNOW IT ... WHERE IS SHE?'

Alice took a step towards her dark reflection. Her demon self moved with unnatural form and almost supernatural speed, pinning Alice by the throat as its clawed hand clasped her neck, forcing air and blood to spurt out of her mouth.

I move the stars for no one, Alice, and yet here you are, demanding from me, screaming at me, wanting FROM ME ...

The creature's clawed digits punctured her throat, drawing yet more blood as it brought its face to hers. Its rotten teeth were black and yellow, with pieces of rotting flesh in every crevice. The creature's torn skin was almost translucent, and Alice could have sworn that there were insects writhing underneath the thin layer of flesh used to bind this form together.

What right do you have to ask anything of me? You wanted peace from the child that you deem not your own. I have brought it, and now you see fit to complain about that, as if I should somehow care what you want.

The creature's grip increased, and Alice pulled on its wrists to prevent her imminent choking, but as her attempts only seemed to pull away rotting flesh from its arms, she soon gave up and let the darkness take over.

Not yet, said the creature.

With a snap of its wrist and a turn of its deformed body, it threw Alice across the room, towards the archway, where she smashed hard against the wall. She fought to stay conscious, air flooding her empty lungs.

You will never escape me; you are just a vessel of my omnipotent form.

Alice scrambled into the kitchen on all fours, bloodying her knees as she went. She pulled herself up eventually and glanced through the rear window to see the harpies picking at a corpse at the rear of the house. A creature with the face of Chloe Durby – one of her tormentors from her school days – plucked an eye from the corpse with its jagged beak, swallowing it down as it craned its neck to the sky. Petrified, Alice spun around to face her demon self as it followed her into the kitchen, almost climbing the unit behind her to escape its gaze.

You ungrateful whore.

'You're not real,' screamed Alice. She fumbled for and then gripped a large, rusty, curved knife, which resembled a garden sickle rather than any kitchen blade. Brandishing it above her head like a scorpion, she said once more, 'You're not real.'

Bless you, you pathetic piece of shit. You actually think you can hurt me. I told you before, I will eat your soul and then your precious daughter's after that.

'NO!' screamed Alice, as she brought the blade down towards an on-rushing blur of hatred in physical form, one whose mouth had opened unnaturally wide to expose the venom-toothed fangs among the rotten remains of its normal teeth. Alice brought the blade down in an arc that cleaved the creature's face in two. Its eyes fell apart by a few inches, as if the creature was losing its mask. Even its tongue was split like that of a serpent, yet the creature still smiled as its two tongues whipped about independently.

You can't hurt me, child, but I will embrace your fight, for I relish the pain and the flood of human sensations that come with it.

Its claws sunk into Alice's flesh again. It gripped her tightly by the arms to stop her from launching another attack, and then opened its mouth wide like a boa constrictor, burying its teeth into Alice's shoulder and neck.

Yet Alice didn't move, didn't flinch and didn't make a sound.

Have you given up? See, I knew you wanted it. Why else would you stop fighting me?

Alice smiled, and that smile increased despite the dozen puncture marks across her shoulder and neckline that oozed blood and venom.

'Thomas,' said Alice. 'I can see your face beneath my own.'

The creature withdrew and held its hands up to its falling mask. Thomas Levit was staring back at Alice. His face beneath the monster's was perfect, clean and unbroken.

'You have no power over me, Thomas, and if you ever did – well, not anymore!'

The creature screamed and lunged at her, sinking its teeth into her battered body, but again Alice didn't react.

'You have no power over me,' Alice said proudly, as she closed her eyes and clenched her fists. 'YOU HAVE NO POWER OVER ME!!!'

Alice opened her eyes to find herself sitting upright in her bed. She was drenched in sweat and was fairly sure she had wet herself, but she was safe, and this was real, she could feel it.

'Mummy.' Dorothy was at the door.

'What's wrong, poppet?' said Alice, smiling at her beautiful daughter, the mirror of her younger self.

'Mummy, I had a bad dream,' said a tear-filled Dorothy, holding tightly onto Mr Blackberry.

'Go and get into bed, baby, whilst I quickly go and wash. And then how about I come and snuggle in your bed?'

'OK, Mum.'

With a pitter-patter of her tiny feet, Dorothy ran back to her room.

Alice took a deep breath and stepped into her en suite shower. As the hot water ran over her body, her reflection in the bathroom mirror continued to flicker between her own and that of the man who had raped her. But she couldn't care less, and as she wrapped herself in a towel, she ran her hand over the moisture-covered mirror. Only her face remained.

'I've got you now, you bastard,' she said confidently. 'You have no power over me.'

Chapter 41: Godfather Death
Song of the day
"The Butterfly Collector" by The Jam

Winter 2012
St Martin's Hospital, Kent, UK

'I can't let you stay in there for long,' said Sister Bonnie with absolute authority.

'I know, Bon,' answered Alice with false confidence. 'It's just something I have to do.'

'I get that, my treasure, I really do. Just get from this what you need and then leave it all behind in that room with him. Do you hear me, Miss Alice?'

Alice nodded slowly but in full agreement. She placed her hand on the door and slowly pushed through with a resolute strength she was eager to show through the entirety of the coming conflict, but as she stepped into the room, the wind was taken from her sails almost immediately. Thomas Levit had been a hard man to find. She had visited all his old teammates back at Canterbury RFC – the ones that her father still had connections with, at any rate – but no one had seen him in years. She had hit social media hard in the hope that his name would pop up in certain circles, and yet again, nothing had cropped up. His whereabouts had come, eventually, from a peculiar avenue. She'd gone to see Bonnie, and they'd gone for an overpriced hospital-grade sandwich in the cafeteria. Alice overheard a group of bitching nurses, who were sitting at the next table, talking about him.

She didn't find out why Thomas was at St Martin's until she stood at the end of his bed.

Thomas Nathaniel Levit, diagnosis: Glioblastoma Multiforme Grade IV astrocytoma. Alice didn't understand what this meant. *Treatment: best supportive care. Ward Notes: TLC Two Hourly Turns. No OBS necessary. Nurse to change syringe driver 10/12/12.* One of the nurses told her it was as severe a brain tumour as they had ever seen at Canterbury Oncology.

'No less than you deserve, Thomas.' Alice spoke gently, looking at his frail body and replacing the clipboard. Tubes and wires were coming out of every orifice on his body, some natural, others man-made. A machine designed with the sole purpose of keeping him breathing was sat next to him, permanently humming and clicking, and two drips seemed to be doing their very best to keep the reaper at bay.

Thomas looked up. Alice wasn't sure if he recognised her or not. The hums, whirs and clicks kept the room from being silent, if not awkward, and Alice knew that if death did exist as an entity, then he was most definitely sitting at the head of Thomas Levit's bed.

Alice took her time to soak up the reality of the situation that faced her. She had played this confrontation out in her head so many times with every possible scenario, yet this she had not considered. Thomas was gaunt, far too weak to even raise a murmur to communicate with Alice, and that suited her just fine, or so she thought at first. His sunken eyes looked full of fear – maybe the fear of a man who envisaged his victim getting revenge. Alice wasn't here to kill him, though; she was here to win back her life. She walked around the bed and perched on the edge of his mattress, taking his wrist in her hands to prove, both to Thomas and herself, that she was in control of the situation. Noticing that she could close a very loose loop about his wrist with little effort, she dropped the limp appendage back to the bed with a smile.

'It's been a while,' said Alice. She looked straight into his black-ringed eyes – something she had promised herself she would do. 'I won't beat around the bush. I had to tell you in no uncertain terms that I hate you. I hate you for what you did to me. For not even realising the magnitude of what you did to me, and for the endless suffering you have put me through since that day, just because you needed to give your ego a boost. And then for letting that damage affect my relationship with my daughter.' Alice was unrelenting and focused in her verbal tirade. 'I hate you because as you lie there dying in front of me, you probably see yourself as the victim here.' Alice rose defiantly to her feet and drew herself closer to his almost skeletal face. 'But what I hate the most, Thomas "fucking captain of the rugby team" Levit, is that you are so pathetic right now, so weak, that you cannot even find the strength to come up with some bullshit excuse for your crimes.'

Alice turned her back to him, and her navy-blue dress swung behind her like a cape. The hum and whir of the machines was matched by the click of her heels as she strode away from him. She stopped briefly in the door, without turning about, as she didn't need to face him anymore. 'One last thing before I go. The nurses have told me you have barely any time left and that I am your first visitor in months. So, I hope you enjoy the irony that I might well be the last person you see from outside the hospital walls.' Alice paused to catch both the moment and her breath. 'Goodbye, Thomas. You won't see me again. And believe me when I say that I won't be seeing you either.'

Thomas Levit died 48 hours later, alone in his hospital bed, with only the hums, clicks and whirs of the machines for company. He hadn't recognised the girl that had visited him days before, for she was just one of many people he had surely hurt over the years. She'd had her life turned upside down by this monster of a man, who looked at Alice as just another face. The visit, though, had reminded him of the direction that the reaper would lead him, and Thomas Levit, with little show of the violence he had become renowned for, cried in fear until his heart stopped, the beeps turned to a flat-lined pitch, and the shadow of death took him away.

Chapter 42: To Whom It May Concern
Song of the day
"Big Things Going Down" by Dan Patlansky

Spring 2013
Whitstable, Kent, UK

The task was simple: clear the air and make things right. With the shop thriving in a way her false reality had seemed to predict all too accurately and Dorothy finding a place by her mother's side at last, it had become more apparent that her life was back on track and that actually having her best friend back on board would benefit both her own life and Dorothy's.

He seemed happy now, and it pleased Alice to see him so settled, as it was something she had never seen before. He was great with Dorothy too. In fact, he doted on her so much that Alice couldn't believe his devotion at times. Yes, they could be friends; she was sure of it. In fact, despite his good looks seeming to only get better with age, Alice had found herself not looking at him that way anymore. She pondered for a moment if that was down to Evan's touch. Maybe that was why she could look at his handsome face and appreciate it the way she would a friend's. Jacob just didn't tick those boxes for her anymore. He and Evan looked more suited, anyway. She had seen them out shopping one day at the Ashford outlet in the summer and had resisted announcing her presence, choosing instead to awkwardly stalk them for ten minutes to get the measure of their relationship. They had looked like one of those magazine couples that you love to hate for being a little too perfect. From the safety of a Starbucks window seat, she had watched Jacob roll with laughter as Evan tried to play-fight with him. She had never seen him laugh so loud, never seen him so carefree. In Evan she had noticed a change, too. Since they had worked together at the restaurant, Evan had gone for a more natural look, and it surprised Alice just how stunning she was naturally, and more secure within herself. With true love apparently in her heart, that false confidence had fallen away. Alice doubted she could ever be friends with Evan or even come close to forgiving her, but it was a good thing they were happy, as it made Dotty happy. Dotty adored Evan and her dad, which drove Alice mad with jealousy, even if she was truly grateful for it.

Alice dropped the letter into the postbox and instantly felt a little lighter on her feet. *Maybe this was overdue*, she thought as she climbed onto her vintage push bike, the wicker basket on the front filled with flowers to decorate Le Petit Papillon.

Onwards and upwards, Alice Marie Petalow, onwards and upwards.

Dearest Jacob

Where do I begin to tell my first true love that I am happy for him, and that I want to be free of the restraints that have kept him from being my best friend these past few years, years that to be fair have not been kind to me? I guess I'll start by saying that you can read this freely knowing that this is not an attack. After all, I know how your mind works. I wanted to thank you and Evan (yes, you read that right, feel free to photograph that and send it to my father) for everything you do for our Dorothy. You are a better dad than I ever could have wished for you to be, and our daughter worships the pair of you. Thank you for finding a focus with her that I never knew you possessed.

Which brings me to this ... I don't hate you, Jay. In fact, I don't even hate Evan. Let's be clear on one thing, I am not absolving either of you of the choices you made when we were together. But I do realise now that you had no idea what was going on in my head during the early years of our relationship, and maybe one day when we are old and you are grey, and we are down at Tankerton seafront chatting away like two old hands, sat on a bench because the walk is too much for us, and Evan is long gone from a Botox overdose (joke), well, maybe then I'll tell you what I was going through. But for now, just know that although you were a giant dick, my suicide attempt was nothing to do with you. That being said, you shouldn't have kept your condition from me for so long. It was that lack of communication that ultimately ruined us – that and the simple fact that you shouldn't have married me if you had feelings for anyone else. Let alone the daughter of our therapist (I know, right – you should have seen my face).

I don't want to dig up the past, though, and so I'll say no more and we can move forward. I just felt with the conclusion of my therapy last week – a journey that has taken me over ten years, if you can believe it – maybe it was time we drew a line under our past. I know you struggle to always get to Dotty on time in the week, so I thought we could move things about a little, as I'm now settled in the apartment above the studio. So if you wanted to pick Dotty up direct from me rather than driving into Canterbury, you will save yourself 40 minutes in traffic, and although my coffee isn't as good as my mum's, it will be good to catch up once or twice a week.

We will never be best friends, you and I, and Evan will never share a bottle of wine with me on a summer's night, but I do think we are due some peace in our lives, and honestly I see this as the way forward.

I am incredibly proud of who you have become, Jay. Your father would be too.

Pebble xxx

To my Dearest ~~Alice Pebble~~ Alice

Words cannot explain the gratitude I feel for your kindness, a trait in you that I have never deserved to see. You are right in what you say, communication was never our forte and has never been my strong point at all. When I needed to talk to you I couldn't, and when you needed me to listen, I wasn't there. It was a problem throughout our relationship that I forever felt incapable of being the man that you deserved, and in reading your letter that has once again been proved true, I am reminded once more just how lucky I am to have you in my life in any capacity whatsoever. I am touched by your words and your endless empathy for those who wrong you. And you were right, if I had spoken to you of my demons, of my insecurities, then things would have been different, I am sure. I certainly believe that had I spent more time listening to your pain rather than battling that constant chip on my shoulder, well, maybe I could have lightened your load a little. It took me some time to realise that my biggest failing to you was not as a husband, but as your friend, a friend born all those years before on those Tankerton slopes you speak about so fondly. So, with that said, I am truly sorry, Alice, for not being the friend I should have been.

You are a great mum, a fantastic daughter, and seeing you flourish as a businesswoman is such a wonderful thing that I am filled with pride.

I've spoken to Evan and she's moved by your words. She understands that you will never be friends, but she wants you to know she doesn't see you as an enemy, in fact she never has been.

Thank you for showing me a respect I'm sure I don't deserve.

Thank you for being the influence our daughter needs.

Thank you for being the most colourful and unique pebble on my Plutonian shore.

All my love, Jacob x

Jacob patted the letter, as if to wish it a safe journey, and dropped it into the post box. *Long overdue*, he thought. He had believed Alice to be the answer to all his problems, yet he saw now that he had always been enough on his own. That's how he knew that his love for Evan was real, because he had never needed her; he just felt happier when she was by his side. Alice had enabled his bad behaviour for far too long, and he had repaid her with nothing but misery. He didn't deserve her friendship, but he was extremely glad that he had it.

Chapter 43: Glad Rags
Song of the day
"I Hate Love Songs" by Kelsea Ballerini

Summer 2013
Ramsgate, Kent, UK

Alice wasn't blown away by the idea of tonight. Speed dating had been her best friend Holly's idea; it certainly wasn't something she would have forced on herself. 'We can do it together,' Holly had said. 'We don't do anything anymore. You might as well still be in that bloody coma.'

Alice pulled up at the venue and slipped on her scarlet-red stiletto heels – to drive in them would surely have been a death sentence. She stepped out of the car and onto the cobbles, reset the fall of her strappy white top as it dropped over her curves, and pulled her phone out of her suede clutch bag.

There was a text from Holly:

Alice, I'm not coming. This was all a ruse to get you dating again. So get your ass in there, as I've paid your fee already and I'm tired of you being a loser on your own every night. You're a MILF now, don't forget. Go work that little ass of yours.

The text was frustrating, but not out of the blue. Alice had suspected foul play when her illustrious and bubbly friend had refused the opportunity to get ready together with a few bottles of wine and a shared taxi. *Right, Pebble, you've got this.* She stepped through the hotel doors. With her hair up in a tight auburn bun, she looked the part of the alpha female, even if she didn't feel anywhere near as confident as the image she was projecting.

BZZZZZZZZZ

The buzzer sounded and the first potential knight in shining armour sat down in front of Alice. Already bored by the dull surroundings, she wished she was outside, sketching the seafront.

'I'm Robert, but you can call me "the boy", 'cause my friends think I'm the man. I know, silly right? Although I do have quite a solid investment portfolio – I imagine that's why they gave me the moniker. So, it's OK here ... The Stella seems cheap enough and the fanny is packed in tightly. You know what, though, I think you and me are a notch above the rest. How about we just head off, leave these suckers behind, am I right? No? OK. So what is it you do for a living, Alice, other than day trips to wonderland – you know, because of your name. I reckon you're a secretary, you look like a secretary. I have my own PA. It's like having a wife at work. She makes me coffee and empties my trash bin. Only difference is I don't have to bang her fat ass.'

The fat, balding ginger man in front of Alice didn't stop for breath from the second he sat down, and the sound of the buzzer was a sweet release.

'Hi, Alice. My name's Evan.'

Alice laughed out loud and refused to talk for the duration of the three minutes of allotted time, other than to clarify that she couldn't date a man with the same name as the woman who stole her husband.

'Hello, red,' said the next man, clearly a vegan, his hemp shoes giving it away far too easily. Keith was a miserable man of short stature and clearly stoned. Kieran didn't seem to have a brain cell in his head and fidgeted to such a degree that Alice presumed he had either ADHD or a crack addiction. Gregory wore a pair of old school shoes, along with trousers, a shirt, a tie and a baseball cap, and he smelled of wet dog and cheap lager. The quality didn't pick up for the remainder of the hour, and Alice ticked no boxes to meet any of them again. *You are so much more than this,* Alice told herself as she prepared to leave.

Suddenly, a gentle hand took the loop of her arm and guided her to the door.

'Just keep walking.' The petite girl who had been sitting next to Alice had a thick Tennessee accent. 'The crack addict was ready to make another pass at you.'

They fell into the street giggling, full of the joy that freedom had given them from the dour confines of such a grotty hotel.

'I'm Poppy, and I think you and I deserve a proper drink. That sound good, sugar?'

She looked like a curvy Winona Ryder; Alice was a little jealous of her shape. 'A drink sounds great, but let's move quick before the horde follows us out.'

They joined arms once more and skipped down the back streets until they found a wine bar more suited to the women they were.

'So, you're from Tennessee, but live in Kansas,' said Alice, already on her second glass of wine. Getting a hotel looked ever more likely.

Poppy smiled, running her fingers through her dark, pixie-cut hair. The colour was almost replicated in her hazel eyes, which had a haunting depth.

'That is correct, sugar,' she said, sipping on a botanical gin cocktail that Alice had recommended. 'I still can't believe this isn't a thing in the States.'

'What is it you do for a living?'

'I am, for my sins, an art buyer for a gallery back home. I get to travel all over the world and look at the most beautiful paintings. I majored in fine art at the University of San Francisco and never looked back.' Poppy put her hand on Alice's thigh. 'And you are an artist yourself.'

'What makes you say that?' gasped Alice.

'Because I just spent an hour listening to the most interesting person in the room tell men what she does for a living and then reject the hell out of all their dumb asses, and I can't blame you at all.' Poppy's southern drawl was becoming heavier with each passing drink. 'I mean, I'm gay, and even I could see there were slim pickings on that BBQ.'

'OK, I'm open-minded, I probably could have guessed gay if I hadn't seen you in there with me. So what was that about? Or do you just go to pick up demoralised chicks?' Alice giggled and gave her a nudge of the shoulder.

'Oh, you think that's what I was doing? Because, girl, you looked empowered, not demoralised. I like to people-watch and hear bullshit stories. I won't lie, I'm a bit of a social butterfly, and that seemed the only place to be in this smelly harbour town.'

There was something so refreshing about Poppy's company, and Alice was revelling in it.

'Do you know what we should do now, honey pie?' said Alice in a mock accent that failed to mimic her counterpart with any authenticity.

'Hit me, sugar plum,' Poppy responded in a much more successful cockney accent. 'And don't give me no twaddle.'

Alice downed her wine and offered her hand as she slid out of the booth. 'Let's go dancing.'

'Dancing?'

'Dancing,' reiterated an energetic Alice.

Poppy smiled and took her hand, and they ran through the streets of the small fishing town until they found a place to call their own.

Alice woke up at about 2 a.m. to her phone vibrating across the glass bedside unit. Its sound was like a jackhammer to her head, and it woke her with a fright as she tried to get her bearings in a room she didn't recognise. She fumbled for her phone. Poppy was passed out cold, still fully dressed and holding onto a bottle of water as if it was the only thing that could save her from the upcoming hangover. *Mum? What does she want at this time?* thought Alice while trying to find her equilibrium.

'Mum ... What's wrong?'

Chapter 44: The Kraken and Her
Song of the day
"Grow as we Go" by Ben Platt

Summer 2013
Queen Elizabeth Hospital, Margate, Kent, UK

Evan watched a focused John Petalow stalk the halls of Queen Elizabeth Hospital like a lion caged in a space only twice its size. He was calm enough, yet, like a dormant volcano, it paid to give him some space. She had never been formally introduced to John when she had managed the restaurant floor at the Gallantry. As the owner of the Mile End fish market, John had been sighted often enough, as he ran through fish prices with Matt or Jay over coffee, but Evan had only ever exchanged greetings with him.

Angela had been very welcoming; it had taken Evan completely off guard when Alice's mum had wrapped her arms around her before placing a hand gently on her shoulder and proclaiming that she could see what all the fuss was about. Evan couldn't believe how much Dorothy and Alice looked like her.

Jacob hadn't said much since the news had come in of Dorothy's ruptured appendix. Full dad mode had kicked in and he'd been unnervingly proactive in packing some clothes and toys for her and putting them in the car. But the journey to the hospital had been deathly quiet. Jacob had a need for control that often left him anxious about being a passenger in any capacity; whether in a car or a conversation, he had to be in the driving seat. But he had accepted her offer to drive without a fight and had spent the journey looking up at the stars through the panoramic glass roof of the car.

She drew his hand up to her lips and gave it the slightest squeeze before gently pressing her lips against the back of it.

'I love you,' said Jacob without looking at his attentive wife. 'She's going to be OK, right?'

Evan pulled his gaze around to hers with the deft touch of her painted nails. 'This is a procedure the surgeons have done a thousand times before, and you know what a fighter our little lady is.'

Jacob took heart in Evan's words, before rising to his feet to greet a frantic Alice, who burst through the door like a tempest.

'Jay, what's going on?'

'Appendix is being taken out as we speak. It hasn't burst, but it was beginning to rupture, and this was the only action to prevent a serious problem. The surgeon is the best in Kent by all accounts, and Bonnie has already been on the phone to make sure they are doing everything to the letter.'

Jacob's words were strong and honest, and Alice relaxed enough to start saying hello to everyone, wrapping her arms first around her mum and then her lumbering beast of a father. Evan got a nod of recognition that she returned with a raised hand. Evan had never really liked Alice, but the poor girl hadn't had it easy, and even she had to admit that Alice probably had more reason to dislike her than the other way around.

'I've got to go and stretch my legs, baby.' Jacob bent down and kissed Evan on the top of her head. 'Can you keep an eye on things here?'

'Are you sure you don't need the company?' Evan was a little anxious at the prospect of being left alone with the Petalows.

'No, I'll be OK,' said Jacob, missing the reasoning for Evan asking in the first place. 'I won't be long, I promise.'

He slipped out of the door at the back of the room, opposite the entrance Alice had entered, and fell against the wall on the other side. *What the hell is going on?* he thought as the whole hospital moved as if he was on a ship sailing rough seas.

Jacob pulled himself up the staircase, feeling as though he had been heavily sedated. The hall was spinning. As he pulled himself in front of the top-floor fire escape, it became apparent that his delusion of sea sickness was misinformed. This was no delusion. Jacob pushed through into the open air and was hit by a wave of gigantic proportions. Salt, sand and seaweed hit him like a boxing glove as he was thrown to the deck. *The deck? Where am I? No ... It can't be ...*

Moonlight alone illuminated the deck of the *Summer Breeze*, which was being thrown violently around by a storm all too familiar to him. He knew this place well. The smell of the varnished maple deck and the icy-cold seawater that lashed it with every throw of oceanic anger could not hide the sense of anguish that Jacob felt at being back here. He had nearly died here, painfully and slowly, and the motion of the ship rocking violently sent his trauma-filled heart into relapse.

Jacob stepped back towards the fire escape but paused as he heard a familiar sound approaching from behind. The creature was huge and easily filled the corridor with its mass of wet, leathery tentacles, which, one by one, slapped the floor aggressively as it pulled itself towards Jacob at a speed that belied its size and girth. A giant maw sat at its centre, and it had two obsidian eyes that were the very colour of emptiness.

Did you think that you had escaped me?

The creature's voice was clear in Jacob's head, and yet when the kraken opened its beak to voice the words that Jacob could hear transmitted to him, a high-pitched scream, like nails on a blackboard, cut through his soul.

'YOU ARE NOT REAL; YOU NEVER HAVE BEEN,' Jacob screamed above the noise of the screeching creature, howling wind and thunderous waves.

Then why, pray tell, are you backing away from me as though scared? If I am not a real entity, then surely you could let me close my jaws around you, as I have done so many times before.

'I'm a fool, Ahab, my old friend, but I am no idiot. Do you hear me?' Jacob backed into the brass railing that surrounded the deck. 'What you do to me I know is far from real; it is no more real than any dream within a dream. But I know that what I dream with you tends to have rather bloody and violent repercussions for me on the floor of the hospital hallway or wherever I actually am.' Jacob climbed over the railing and felt the cold, hard lash of the furious ocean on his back.

You won't jump, Jacob! You have never had the heart to escape me. After all, who are you without me? You with your happy little family, with your girls. You will get bored, you always do, and then you will be all alone without me by your side.

Jacob smiled, knowing that he had the strength inside to beat the creature once and for all. No fear shackled him, no power bound him. He was, as he had always been, free to make his own choices.

He let go of the railing just as a barbed tentacle wrapped itself around his forearm. Three loops of viscous black mass looped around his limb like a boa constrictor taking the life of a young deer, and as Jacob resisted the creature's pull, its beak snapping viciously at him, he took a moment to stare into the eyes of his tormentor one last time, so he could truly see his nemesis in this game of real life and false death.

Alice watched Evan get up to follow her beloved husband not two minutes after he had left, bitter that Evan had been sitting here playing happy families with her parents while she was stuck in traffic. *Who does she think she is?* was voiced over and again within the depths of Alice's overthinking mind.

Before she had the calmness and soundness of mind to convince herself to do otherwise, she was on her feet and chasing Evan up the staircase in angry pursuit. *She has no right to be here, none at all. She's not my family or Dorothy's, and we don't need her here.* Alice's lungs burned as she raced to find her. Turning into the hall, she saw Evan go through the fire escape at the end of the ward. A crowd of onlookers were frantically gesturing between them. *First Thomas, then you. You need to be dealt with. You need to hear my voice, all my voices, as I reprimand you for stepping into mine and Jacob's world.* Alice let the air return to her lungs as she recovered her composure. *I'll show you that I am neither meek nor the quiet little butterfly that you believe me to be.* Alice pushed aside the few people blocking the fire escape with a forceful, no-nonsense apology.

Evan had a tight hold of Jacob, who was standing on the wrong side of the security fence that lined the roof of the five-storey hospital. His eyes were vacant, in a place that Alice had seen him visit many times before.

You know this, Alice, he doesn't come back from this for hours, his psychosis is too deep. It always was...

'Evan, baby, where am I?' said Jacob, grabbing the railing with his free hand.

'I've got you, my love. Don't rush. Just slowly step over onto this side.'

Evan stroked his face and never broke eye contact. He trusted her with his life, and she knew what to do in situations like this, for she knew her Jacob. As he stepped over the low fence and fell into her arms, she instantly sunk down to the ground with him and cradled his head against her breast.

'I don't know what happened,' said Jacob as floods of tears erupted from his red eyes.

'Yes, you do.' Evan caressed and kissed his head. 'You were scared for our Dorothy, and you let your demon back in for a moment. And that's OK.'

Evan kissed his brow and then took his hands to help him up.

'It's always OK to be scared, but I've got you, and we have got this. Together,' said Evan, pulling Jacob to his feet with a groan.

'Thank you, my love.' Jacob, with inconsolable tears still running down his face, wrapped his arms around her tightly. 'Together.'

Alice watched them link their fingers into a tight embrace as they headed off the roof.

'Evan, I ... I hope you are both OK,' said Alice, marvelling at the unison between them.

'Thank you, Alice,' said Evan with the smallest of smiles. 'Shall we go get some coffee?'

'Coffee sounds ... Frankly, it sounds great.' Alice let them past and followed closely behind.

You never pulled him round that quickly. I guess it must be love, she thought gladly, but as she witnessed the bond between Jacob and Evan grow, it was only understanding that she gained. She couldn't forgive them. Deep down inside her, in the place where the demon Alice slept, she thought only of hurting them both like she had been hurt.

Chapter 45: The Light Between Us
Song of the day
"Windows are Rolled Down" by Amos Lee

Spring 2014
Reculver, Kent, UK

'You've sold the restaurant?' said Evan as she turned onto the coastal road that led down to the Reculver seafront. 'YOU? You who loves his restaurant?'

Jacob smiled in a way that would have told anyone who looked at him that he was really pleased with himself. 'Sold it.'

'What is going on here, and why the hell am I driving? You never let me drive, and now you're acting more suspicious than a puppy sitting next to a carpet turd.' Despite wanting to know what was going on, Evan was in good cheer. She liked seeing Jacob enjoy his day, even if it was a mischievous game of his, which kept drawing little smiles from his lips.

It felt like the first day of summer. The top was down on Evan's Mazda, and they could feel their skin starting to burn in the heat.

'You are driving because I, good lady, am drunk,' Jacob joked theatrically. 'Well, maybe not drunk, but I've had a few with Matt to say goodbye and all that jazz. And nothing's going on. You really have to stop being so paranoid.' Jacob was giggling to himself like a prepubescent schoolboy now, which only encouraged Evan to press harder.

'OK, smart arse. If you are going to play this game, I guess I'll start playing you at it. So ... how much have you sold the restaurant for?'

Jacob replied as if he was informally reading the price of West Ham United's latest signing in the Saturday paper. 'Two point six million.'

Evan nearly ran into a hedge as the seafront came into view. 'Two point six million *pounds?*'

'I think it's pounds. I mean, I just presumed it would be,' joked Jacob with a pretend hiccup to boot, which drew a slap across his thigh – an action he used as a means to interlock their fingers. 'I love you so much,' he said, kissing the back of her hand. 'I tell you what, park over by this lighthouse and tell me what happened with your visit to your mum's this morning, and then maybe, just maybe, I'll tell you what's going on.'

That morning

Rat-a-tat-tat.

Evan knocked hard on her mother's door. It came across as angry, which wasn't her intention at all. In fact, the opposite might have been closer to the truth. Evan was here to make things right, to make things like they had been before. *Well, not as before,* she thought, because before was rubbish too.

Evan's mother was a curious woman, a woman of pure focus and unbridled drive, ever the psychologist, unable to switch off and just be a mother.

While she wanted to come across as strong and confident, Evan didn't dare use her own key to let herself in. After all these years, there was no guarantee it would work anyway. In actual fact, had her mother's Jaguar not been parked in the driveway, she doubted she would have known if she even still lived here, such was the deterioration of their relationship. The sad irony was that they didn't even live that far apart. Her mother's coastal home in the village of Seasalter was just a quarter of an hour's drive from her and Jacob's house in Faversham. Yet no chance meeting had occurred.

Evan had booked an hour with her mother as a patient at her practice a few years back so that she could try and explain about Jacob, but Vivian had refused to break professional character, and after an hour of listening to her daughter, she had offered professional advice and seen her on her way at the chime of the clock. Getting paid advice was never Evan's intention, and the point of the visit had been lost on her mother. One hour in six years wasn't enough for any child and parent.

The door opened slowly, as Vivian Phillips struggled with the security bolt while holding her phone to her ear. As soon as she saw who had knocked so firmly at her door, she found a way, in a language Evan guessed was German, to end the call.

'Evangeline!' said Vivian in a state of shock. 'I wasn't expecting ...'

'Oh, just shut up, Mother,' said Evan, before wrapping her arms around her tightly. 'I know you don't do affection, but you are going to take this, and then you are going to get the kettle on. OK, Mum?' Evan went to let go but felt resistance.

'Are you sure you wouldn't prefer a glass of Pinot? I've just opened a little French number.'

Evan smiled at the unexpected warm reception and finally looked into her mum's eyes as she was released. 'Not today, Mum. Just a green tea will be fine, or one of those camomile ones that you used to hide at the back of the cupboard. Here, I'll make it.' She followed her mum into the kitchen, hoping that she would remember where everything was.

'No wine and you are offering to make the tea. Do I assume I need to muster some sort of ransom for the safe release of my actual daughter – you know, the one who usually has a more orange complexion and false lashes.'

'It's good to see that time hasn't taken your sense of sarcasm and wit away,' joked Evan as she finished filling the kettle. 'Listen, Mum, we need to clear the air. Will you sit and talk with me?'

'Of course, Evangeline. I would love to.'

'Don't call me that. No one has called me that for well over a decade. Christ, my husband nearly choked when he heard it on our wedding day. He thought we were at the wrong wedding.'

'Your husband?'

Evan proudly lifted her wedding finger. 'Jacob and I were married nearly two years ago in a small ceremony in Tunbridge Wells. Don't tell me you have become so estranged and disconnected from my world that you didn't hear anything? I'm really sorry that you are only now just finding out, but I guess this is why we need to talk.'

'No, Evange ... Evan. It's me who needs to apologise. I gave up hope of you ever forgiving my behaviour as an absentee mother and just accepted our paths to be different. Do I assume this to be the notorious Jacob Brooking?'

'I am officially Evan Laurie Brooking Phillips, and I can't hide the fact that I am both happier and more balanced than I have ever been because of him.'

'I can imagine he will say the same about you. How is he? How is his ...' Vivian hesitated long enough for her daughter to interject.

'His mental health? Don't worry. He tells me everything. You should have seen his face though when he found out who you were in relation to me. I'm not sure any monster that has chased him through his dreams has ever scared him so much, and that's saying something, as I'm sure you know.'

'He's well, then?'

'He's really well. His bipolar really doesn't affect him too much since getting his medication right – well, unless he's stressed, but even that seems rare nowadays.'

'And his psychosis from the BPD?' asked Vivian, straying a little too close to full psychologist mode for Evan's liking.

'He hasn't heard a voice outside of his own in over a year, bar one incident when little Dorothy was poorly, but that was the exception that proves his recovery. It has taken some understanding on my part, but I went to a few classes on dealing with a mental health partner, and actually I find the whole thing quite interesting now. I start at the Open University next year, to do a degree in mental health nursing.'

'I'm not surprised that you have gone down that route at all. You were always so very gifted; I just felt you lacked direction. I'm so happy you have found something you can embrace. So, my beautiful daughter is a step mum. How is little Dorothy?'

'You won't believe this, but she's my best friend. I take her to dance class once a week and we fall asleep in front of a film nearly every Friday night. She is just amazing.'

'I don't know what to say. You turn up here, hardly any make-up on but looking more beautiful than ever before, you are married, a step mum – and by all accounts an amazing one at that ...'

'Is all this a bad thing?'

'Not at all. I just feel like you have done it all without me. It shows what an amazing woman you are, and honestly I take no credit for it.'

Evan took her mum's hand as a show of support. Vivian didn't cry, for it was not becoming of a woman of her stature, but Evan could see she was struggling.

'I didn't ever hate you because you were a bad mother. I hated you because I missed you, you were never there. But that doesn't mean you didn't teach me anything, and I loved you then just like I love you now.' Evan brushed the hair out of her mum's face and looked her square in the eyes. 'I won't forgive you because honestly that would mean looking backwards, and I only want to look forwards. That is something we do together or not at all.'

'Christ almighty, Evan. Now I know you are taking the piss, as that's one of my lines.'

'I did used to listen to you. I missed you so much that I used to break into your office as a kid and listen to your patient tapes, just so I could hear your voice.'

'Oh god, Evangeline Phillips, they were confidential,' said Vivian, laughing. 'So why now? Why do I deserve your presence in my life when I haven't earned it for many a year, if I ever earned it at all?'

'Because I need your help. I'm scared and I need my hand held through a few things.' She took her mum's hand and placed it on her belly. 'I'm pregnant, and as overjoyed as we both are, there are certain things men are useless at. An overexcited Jacob is a wonderful sight to behold, it wouldn't surprise me if he tried to deliver the little mite all on his own, but I need some female calm and composure in planning all this, if you know what I mean?'

'I'm going to be a grandmother,' said Vivian, with tears welling up in her eyes.

'Yes, Mum, you are.' Evan wrapped her arms around Vivian once more. 'We are going to be a family again.'

The lighthouse

'Wow, Ev, that is amazing,' said Jacob, gripping her hand tightly. 'I am so very proud of you. It is an enlightening thing to be able to move into our bright new world with that all left behind. You must be so happy to have your mum back in any capacity.'

'It will take time for us to find our way, of that I have no doubt. At our core, Mother and I are very different people in every respect, and it's been so long that we almost have to rebuild our friendship from scratch.' There was a melancholy in Evan's voice, but Jacob knew that his wife was feeling better for putting that particular demon to rest. 'Now, my deceptive little harlequin, what the hell is going on here? You wanted the rundown of my day in return for this devious plan you are clearly bursting to tell me, and you got it. So pull your fist out of your mouth and bloody tell me the script.'

'I guess now is as good a time as ever.' Jacob smiled. 'So, the lighthouse in front of you – well, I've bought it. It's ours. It belongs to us. It's –'

Evan jumped across the car and mounted Jacob in the passenger seat. 'Are you shitting me, Brooking, are you actually shitting me?'

'It's ours, and we can raise our little family right here. The lighthouse, the attached cottage, the holiday let at the rear and the annex, which I thought you could turn into an office for your studies and then eventually use as a clinic, if things go that way.'

Evan wasn't listening anymore. She was kissing Jacob between every word and, driven by pure passion, unbuttoning his trousers at the same time.

Jacob smiled at the elderly couple walking past. 'Let's get you inside for a look around, shall we, before we alienate the locals on the first day?'

Chapter 46: Parlay and the Mourning Son
Song of the day
"If I Go, I'm Going" by Gregory Alan Isakov

End of summer 2007
Psychiatric Hospital of San Diego County, California, USA

John Petalow gripped Jacob by the throat and pinned him against the wall of the hospital waiting room with such brute force that a calendar on the opposing wall fluttered to the ground.

'She's pregnant?' shouted John, blinded by rage. 'You bully my only child into trying to take her own life and you knock her up for good measure. Why? So she can't escape your narcissism. I should fucking kill you, Brooking.'

The Viking king might have been a huge man, but like most apex predators, knowing that he had no equal often meant he would forget to guard himself, and this was one of those times. Jacob wasn't the beast that his father-in-law was, but he was still a fairly fit young man who had been in enough scrapes in his life to know how to protect himself. You couldn't defend against a man like John Petalow for long, so instead Jacob drove a balled fist upwards, catching John on his chin with a thunderous uppercut that rocked him back a few feet. The Viking king wasn't a man who could be dropped by normal means, and even a punch of real quality wouldn't have come close to hurting him. In the aftermath of the incident, Jacob mused that his knuckles had taken more damage than John's face. However, something changed in John's eyes. A modicum of respect washed over him for just a moment, and he brought his hand up to his jaw and rotated it in a circular motion to check it wasn't damaged. Then he crossed his arms and uttered a single word: 'SPEAK!'

'I didn't bully her into anything. There is more to this than either of us understand, of that I am sure.' Jacob pulled himself straight. 'And, yes, I got my wife pregnant. That is something that can happen between two consenting adults, especially when they are husband and wife.'

'I warned you,' John growled. 'I told you to sort your life out.'

'And I have,' responded Jacob sharply. 'So stop jumping on my back. You may be Alice's father, but you damn sure are not mine.'

'So what do you intend to do here? Are you going to run away, like normal? Bury your head in the sand again?'

'I'll tell you what I'm going to do. When this child comes – which I have been assured can happen safely, whether Alice is awake or not – I will be as good a father as my own, and not a bully and a judgemental arsehole.'

John smiled at hearing Jacob fight back for a change. 'Careful there. Those are some big words you're throwing about, and I'd hate for you to break your other hand on my face.'

'I'm going to do right by her.'

'Her,' muttered the Viking king.

'It seems you are having a granddaughter – or should I say princess to your throne, my liege.' Jacob bowed theatrically as he spoke.

'Enough of that shit. I will only let so much go. Sit down.' John eased his giant frame into a plastic hospital chair and pointed to the one opposite. 'Listen, son, if you do what you say, I will give you my full support, as will my Angela. But I want something in return, and I promise you won't like it.' John leaned forward. 'We want you to leave Alice, and we want her home.' He raised his hand instantly to block the reply he knew was coming. 'Hear me out. She's not happy, we both know that. But when was the last time you were happy? The last time you were not on the run? Alice is not the answer to your problems.'

Jacob sighed. 'I don't think that matters anyway. She found out about Evan and left me about three months ago. I say left me – kicked me out would be more precise. And, as you say, I did all I know how to do. I ran.'

'I guess that explains my friend's missing boat.'

Jacob nodded. 'Some weeks stuck afloat, then some spent getting my head right. I'm not the man you knew before. I'm not even the man Alice knew. But you're right. There is no happy ever after with us.'

'So we have a deal, son.' John offered his hand.

'Yeah, we have a deal. And any help moving forward would be greatly appreciated.'

'I'll talk to Angela as soon as we get back to the hotel.'

'What's wrong?' said Jacob, noticing how defeated John looked. 'Isn't this what you wanted?'

'My daughter in a coma, pregnant, divorcing her cheating husband ... I'm not the monster you think I am. Let me tell you a secret.' He paused for a second. 'I mean what I've said, and I will honour our agreement to help you, but if you tell anyone what I'm about to tell you, I will gut you like a seabass. Not even Alice. OK?'

Jacob nodded, taken aback that his father-in-law, of all people, might tell him something that he wouldn't tell his own daughter.

'I have another child. In 1978 I had a one-night stand with someone I'd met through ... well, it doesn't matter how we met. We never saw one another again – at least, she never saw me. I'd been with Angela for a few months when I saw this lady pushing a new-born baby. I knew it was mine. Don't ask me how I knew – just trust me. It was her baby, and it was mine.

'I was a coward. Instead of talking to her, I slipped away into the shadows in the hope that I never saw her again – a wish that came true. A wish that I have always regretted.'

Jacob couldn't find the words to convey his surprise. This story told of a man that he didn't know. Jacob realised that John hadn't always been so fearless.

[340]

'That's why I respect you in this,' said John, 'and that is why I am the father I am. I failed that child. I won't fail them both.'

'I get that. And thank you. I won't let any of you down in this, I promise.'

John rose quickly and placed a giant hand on Jacob's shoulder. 'I know you won't.'

As John walked away to give the news to his beloved wife, Jacob called out to him.

'John ... I'm sorry that I punched you.'

John Petalow smiled but gave no reply. He didn't need to. He had made ground today with a young man he never thought he could respect for anything, and that was enough.

Autumn 2015

Jacob had been sitting on the tiny gardening stool opposite his father's memorial stone for two hours. The sun was setting, and it was turning colder. Yet he had found it impossible to leave his father's side. He felt comfort here, like he was with an old friend.

'I'm sorry, Dad. I'm sorry I couldn't mourn you when I should have, and I'm sorry I couldn't tell you this before.' Tears rolled down Jacob's cheeks. 'I have missed you so much since you left, and I cannot tell you how I have struggled to live up to the high standards you have set for me as a father, a son and a man. I have made so many mistakes in your absence, and with each one it has become more apparent that I've let you down.'

Jacob put his hand on his father's memorial stone and closed his eyes for a moment, as if to try and communicate his words through a more physical medium.

'I promise you now that I won't let them down like I have done you. I'm going to be better, and I'll make you so proud.' He opened his eyes and sat back down. 'You would be so proud of Sam too. He has these two boys that look the spit of you. Dotty looks like her mum, thank the lord, but she certainly has your spirit, which is enough for me. She would have loved you, Dad, just like we all still do.'

Jacob breathed out, and for the first time on that chilly Saturday afternoon, he felt a little better. He took to his feet, folding up the little stool that had been his perch, and headed back towards the car. He felt sadder than when he'd arrived, but less in turmoil as a result of his one-sided conversation.

'Are you OK, baby?' said Evan as Jacob came towards her.

'I'm good. More than that, actually – I'm truly happy.'

Evan reached for him and kissed him deeply on his cold lips. 'I'm so very proud of you.'

Jacob smiled. 'Proud of me? I'm proud of us, love. Look at how far we have come.' He looked over Evan's shoulder and into the back seat of his BMW. 'How is our little man?'

'Fast asleep at last. If I wake him for a feed when we get home, we might get him to sleep through.'

'I love you, Evan Brooking Phillips. Never change – just as you are is all I've ever wanted.'

'Aww, baby, do we need to look at moving your medication review? I know you have many, but I am not sure I've met this personality,' Evan joked, grabbing him tightly and kissing him passionately before he could form a smart reply.

They put their heads together one last time before a parting kiss saw Jacob head to the driver's seat.

'Let's get home,' said Evan as she slid into the passenger seat next to him.

'Goodbye, Dad, I'll see you soon,' said Jacob. He started the engine. 'He would have loved you, Evan.'

Evan placed her hand on his. 'He would have loved us.'

Chapter 47: My Dorian Gray
Song of the day
"How Was It For You" by Snowy White

Autumn 2015
London, Kent, UK

The oil painting was hanging on the main wall of Blackberries auction house. Alice hadn't moved in over an hour, and the longer she looked at the painting, the more it seemed to look back at her. Alice thought of the philosopher Friedrich Nietzsche, who made the point that you couldn't stare into the abyss without the abyss staring back at you. The strokes of oil, both of light and of dark, certainly held that power over her right now. An almost hypnotic restraint kept her sitting painfully still as the girl within the strokes looked straight into her soul.

'It's an amazing piece,' said the tall man who had appeared out of nowhere and placed a hand on Alice's shoulder. 'But, sweet Jesus, it scares the life out of me.'

Aiden Hewett was the head auctioneer at Blackberries and commanded a great deal of respect within the professional circles that Alice kept.

'How are you, old friend?' asked Alice politely, raising her hand up to touch his.

'I am well, although I would be better if my friends would keep from referring to me as old.' Aiden, who was in his late fifties, had the angled look of an owl, with the slender frame of a marathon runner. His black turtleneck jumper only elongated his look further. 'I didn't know you were here in person; I know you had two pieces on sale today, but –'

'Three. I had three pieces on today. One was under the pseudonym of Angela Marie.'

'This is one of yours? Well, I must say, this is a departure from your usual style, and it has clearly worked for you. Why the change, may I ask?'

'It was my Dorian Gray, and it's a side of me that I didn't want to associate with my other work. My clientele back in Kent are a little on the pompous side.'

'That makes sense from a brand perspective, I guess,' said Aiden, taking a seat next to Alice, 'and explains you using ... your mother's name?'

Alice nodded. 'She doesn't know, but I'm hoping she will take it as a compliment. You said my change in style had clearly worked for me, but I thought you weren't a fan of this particular piece?'

'I most certainly am not. But did you not watch your own auction today? Have you really just sat here, transfixed by the eyes of what looks like a lost version of yourself reflected within a mirror?'

'I'm sorry. You know how I hate watching my own work sell in front of a baying crowd. Did they all sell?'

Aiden reached into the leather satchel by his side and pulled out a piece of yellow paper, passing it to her with a smile. 'Your two normal pieces of work went for a little over your asking price of £2,000. And this monstrosity – well, what does your receipt say?'

'This can't be real?' Alice stared at the receipt, dumbstruck. 'I mean, I think this is my magnum opus, I truly believe that, but still – who would pay £250,000?'

'I believe the buyer was a Miss Palette. Part of an American gallery based out of Topeka in Kansas.'

'You are shitting me?' choked Alice with a chuckle.

'Miss Petalow – we don't use that language here. But, no, I am not "shitting" you.'

The girl in the painting watched them talk for a further half hour before two burly men covered her with a green felt blanket, took her from the wall and placed her securely into a crate. The painting, one made of tears, sweat and toil as well as canvas and oil, was a picture of a girl not unlike Alice. A girl haunted by her reflection, a girl frightened by something that would not leave her shadow, and a girl saddened by a world built on lies and the monster who sold them to her.

Winter 2015 Whitstable, Kent, UK

'Dorothy, it's your holiday,' said Alice, who was doing a fine job of filing her nails in the comfort of her armchair while balancing the phone awkwardly on her shoulder.
'So you get to decide where we go next summer.'

'I know, Mum, but you deserve a holiday too. It's not been a quiet year for you, has it?'

'I love that you are thinking of me, but you are making this choice. You've got a few weeks yet, but it will obviously be cheaper the earlier we book it.'

'OK, keep your knickers on,' said Dorothy. 'I'm on it.'

'Say hello to your grandparents for me, would you? And Dorothy ...'

'Yes, Mumma bear?'

'I love you, poppet.'

'I love you too, Mum. Sleep tight.'

Alice put the phone down and finished her nail maintenance before she got ready for bed. The apartment above her studio wasn't the biggest, but it had an almost regal feel to it. Original oak beams separated each room and Edwardian window frames gave a stunning view of the ocean. Alice loved the ocean dearly, for she slept so much better with its tide gently lapping against the empty oyster shells that littered the bay. Alice felt content within her home, within her life and within her world. It had been a long time coming, and with business getting ever busier, she knew it was only a matter of time before everything else clicked into place.

She washed her teeth in her en suite, her reflection looking back at her. She saw a few more wrinkles than normal and a grey hair or two hiding among her red locks, but she looked good. She looked more like her mum as she approached her forties, but then that was hardly a bad thing, as her mum was the most beautiful woman she knew. She rinsed her mouth out and gave herself a smile in her bathroom mirror before heading to bed. Her phone lit the room up with a jet of synthetic light and a small beep. Alice climbed into bed and reached across to where the phone lay.

How about Kansas? read the text from Dorothy. I hear the locals are friendly?

Alice smiled at the thought of seeing Poppy once more. They spoke daily, but she hadn't had the pleasure of her company since the after-party of her auction in London eight weeks before. The night had ended with a parting kiss that even on her best day Alice could not have explained.

A trip to the States would be great, Alice replied. I'll look into it tomorrow.

A loud knock at her front door woke Alice sharply. *Who the hell is that?* she thought. It was just after 7.30 a.m., although she felt like she had only just gone to bed. She held her throbbing head. The room was spinning. She rubbed her eyes and searched for her sense of reality. She had barely opened her eyes when she realised something wasn't right. Her apartment was fully carpeted, and yet as Alice slid out of bed, she felt only cold hard wood underneath her feet – the same floor that she'd had in her cottage all those years ago in her false reality.

I'm not buying into this. I've been doing this far too long, thought Alice with an inner chuckle. She was far too used to being exposed to the false realities that her broken brain would invent.

'Are you OK, Papillon?'

Alice turned in shock – shock but not fear, as she knew that in this place, there was nothing substantial to fear. William looked back at her. He rubbed his neck with both hands before pulling his chiselled body upright.

'I know you can't be real, but, damn, what a pleasant surprise,' Alice said with thirsty excitement, before she leaned in and kissed him passionately. She knew he wasn't anything other than a fiction created by her cruel brain, but she had missed seeing his face.

William pulled away after two more deep kisses ended with Alice mounting him and pulling at his boxers.

'What on earth has got into you?' said William, both confused and aroused in equal measure. 'This isn't the wake-up call I was expecting.'

'God, you even smell the same. I will say this, my mind really has an eye for detail when it comes to fucking me over, doesn't it?' Alice went back in to finish the job she had started on William before the loud knock at the door hit once again. 'Hold on, baby. They are clearly not going to let us alone. I'll just play the game, I guess. After all, I'm usually brought here for a reason. But you'd better still be here when I return, my handsome but imaginary man.'

Alice rolled off of William's flustered body and, remembering her way through her old imaginary home, made her way to the top of the stairs.

'Oh my,' said Alice. 'This is new.'

She was at least seven months pregnant.

'Wow, I could get used to this,' Alice cooed, rubbing her baby bump. 'It's not real, Pebble. Just enjoy the moment, you daft cow.'

There was another knock on the door.

'Hold your horses. I'm bloody coming. Don't you know I'm carrying a child here?'

Alice struggled to the bottom of the stairs and opened the door.

'Alice – sorry, I know it's early, but I need –'

'It had to be you. My bloody mind couldn't leave me upstairs with William, could it? Please continue, Evan. Honestly, no dream is fit for purpose without you trying to screw me over.'

'I just need to talk to you about something. Can I come in?'

'Please, Your Majesty, come through to the kitchen.' Alice made a regal gesture of welcome. 'Tell me, will Our Royal Highness be joining us, or have you left Jacob alone in bed at home?'

Evan walked through to the kitchen and placed her hands on the sink, almost bracing herself for the conversation ahead. 'I don't even know how to start this without sounding crazy, but I hope you at least understand my intention for coming here and that you see it's not to hurt you.'

Alice had moved to within inches of her without making a sound, and Evan looked down to see a large kitchen knife buried in her abdomen, pushed to the handle. The blood being released was minimal, but as Evan's body went into survival shock, she knew that pulling the knife out would drastically change that.

'Alice, what have you ...?'

Alice drew herself closer and strengthened her grip on the handle. 'Don't you "Alice" me. You know you had this coming, and if this false reality is the only place that I'm free to do it, then so be it.'

That felt good. You know it's not real, so do it again.

'I've needed this psychosis of mine to work for me for a change,' said Alice, twisting the knife, 'and I have to be honest, it feels so good that I'm tempted to do it in the real world.'

Now get back up to William, before you wake up. Alice pushed Evan to the ground and turned about with a swagger, only to find Jacob standing there, pale with horror. He rushed over to Evan and pulled a pile of kitchen towels from the counter.

'WHAT HAVE YOU DONE, ALICE?' he screamed. He drew the knife out of Evan's belly, using the towels to stem the blood loss.

Why do they all rush to her side all the time?

'Come on, Jay, William's upstairs, so let's not waste what little time we have together. She doesn't even exist, a bit like you, really, but if I have to be stuck here, I would rather be upstairs with you.'

'Alice, she is going to die here in my arms if you don't call an ambulance, so CALL A FUCKING AMBULANCE!'

Might as well give up on this. Once again it's turned to shit. My mind clearly hates me. Alice closed her eyes and clenched her fists in an act of frustration.

'Alice,' cried Evan.

Alice opened her eyes and realised she was still in the cottage kitchen. *Focus, Pebble, you've got this.* Again, she closed her eyes and clenched her fists tightly.

'Alice, you're ...'

Epilogue

The creature still existed, but somehow the girl Alice had taken its mask away. It had no form to physically manifest into now, but it still existed as an entity, still watched her and wished for nothing but tragedy to befall her miserable fake life. The creature knew it had to wait, though, knew it didn't have the power to raise its voice right now, so it didn't have a chance of getting her attention, let alone of hurting her. Something would happen to give the creature strength, it always did, as was the very essence of life. For now, the mirrored demon self of Alice Petalow would be patient, a trait that it didn't normally possess.

It climbed into a selection of bad memories – one of Thomas, one of a murdered child and one of a cheating husband – and it closed its eyes to accept the sleep of the wicked, the sleep that it needed, and it wondered if it would dream like the girl Alice would dream.

The creature closed its metaphorical mind's eye and hoped that it would dream. But as it drifted off, onto a plane of existence outside of hate and jealousy, there was nothing.

In the waking world, Alice looked down at the carnage in front of her that wouldn't disappear.

The End

Follow PW Stephens

Twitter @AuthorPStephens

YouTube PW Stephens

Instagram the_broken_pebbles

Tumblr PW Stephens

WordPress pwstephens.wordpress.com